IN THE DARK,
HE IS AT HOME.
IN TIME,
HE WILL
KILL AGAIN...

A woman out of time

"*What* do you think you're playing at here? You could have been killed, or worse. No woman of breeding should be out alone on any street, but *here*—"

Then a frown puckered his forehead, and Sara knew, suddenly, that he didn't know how to place her. For any respectable woman of his time, even knowing about the slums would be a degradation.

"Look," Robb said, more gently. "Are you down on your luck? Because if you are—"

"You'll do what?" she asked, irritated by his sense of entitlement.

Again, that scald at his cheeks . . .

She looked at him pointedly, and raised her eyebrows.

"Very well," he said. Then withdrew a card from his pocket and gave it to her. "My card . . . If you should need any assistance, in the future—"

A shadow eclipsed them both from the side of the nearby alleyway: David, coming up quietly beside them.

"The future is a damned long way from here," David said grimly.

JACK KNIFE

Virginia Baker

J

JOVE BOOKS, NEW YORK

THE BERKLEY PUBLISHING GROUP
Published by the Penguin Group
Penguin Group (USA) Inc.
375 Hudson Street, New York, New York 10014, USA
Penguin Group (Canada), 90 Eglinton Avenue East, Suite 700, Toronto, Ontario M4P 2Y3, Canada
(a division of Pearson Penguin Canada Inc.)
Penguin Books Ltd., 80 Strand, London WC2R 0RL, England
Penguin Group Ireland, 25 St. Stephen's Green, Dublin 2, Ireland (a division of Penguin Books Ltd.)
Penguin Group (Australia), 250 Camberwell Road, Camberwell, Victoria 3124, Australia
(a division of Pearson Australia Group Pty. Ltd.)
Penguin Books India Pvt. Ltd., 11 Community Centre, Panchsheel Park, New Delhi—110 017, India
Penguin Group (NZ), 67 Apollo Drive, Mairangi Bay, Auckland 1310, New Zealand
(a division of Pearson New Zealand Ltd.)
Penguin Books (South Africa) (Pty.) Ltd., 24 Sturdee Avenue, Rosebank, Johannesburg 2196,
South Africa

Penguin Books Ltd., Registered Offices: 80 Strand, London WC2R 0RL, England

This is a work of fiction. Names, characters, places, and incidents either are the product of the author's imagination or are used fictitiously, and any resemblance to actual persons, living or dead, business establishments, events, or locales is entirely coincidental. The publisher does not have any control over and does not assume any responsibility for author or third-party websites or their content.

JACK KNIFE

A Jove Book / published by arrangement with the author

PRINTING HISTORY
Jove mass-market edition / February 2007

Copyright © 2007 by Virginia Baker.
Cover design by Erika Fusari.
Text design by Laura K. Corless.

ISBN: 978-0-515-14252-5

JOVE®
Jove Books are published by The Berkley Publishing Group,
a division of Penguin Group (USA) Inc.,
375 Hudson Street, New York, New York 10014.
JOVE is a registered trademark of Penguin Group (USA) Inc.
The "J" design is a trademark belonging to Penguin Group (USA) Inc.

PRINTED IN THE UNITED STATES OF AMERICA

10 9 8 7 6 5 4 3 2 1

*This book is dedicated to
the best weird sisters a girl could have—
Lyn, Cara, and especially Jani Sue,
who knows me better than anyone
and still has the grace to gift me with her fellowship.*

*To the fabulous efforts and support of my agent,
Marlene Stringer, of the Bova Agency,
and my editor at Penguin, Jessica Wade.*

*Most of all, to my very own Sara,
eight years old, who inspires me with her smile
and the wonder in her eyes.*

And to my father. Daddy, I miss you.

PROLOGUE

I

The knife in its cradle of leather slept just under his heart, warm and dreaming: deep needs; the sweetest nightmares.

Overhead, the sky was clear. Filaments of snow covered the tilting eaves: Quick gusts of it floated to the ground, a visitation of ghosts that swirled along the filthy cobblestone street. On the corner, children in rags shivered and sang of Christ, each clear note fluting the alleys, ribboning through the sodden fog: That sweet, unearthly melody.

He loved the fog. It dampened the ugliness of the place. Vast warrens of brick. The high slum stink of piss and cabbage and beer. Gaslight stuttering, coal smoke stinging his eyes. But the fog, it made the women beautiful. Angels' wings swirling around their bodies. The cotton-ball glow of the gaslight, and their faces, always smiling.

Those begging, whining smiles.

There was always a woman.

Like this one, slinking around the mouth of the alley. She would be naked beneath her grubby dress, stinking of other men but so easy, so ready for him.

Knowing the gleam in his eyes as he watched her.

Oh but not knowing.

He returned her smile with his own and wondered where he would put her body when he had finished with her, filled with the music of angels singing, with the heat of his seed and the cold blade and the frost of the sickled Christmas moon flying silent overhead.

II

March 29, 1888 * Inspector Jonas Robb
* Prosper Alley, Westminster * 7:35 AM

They never found the knife. They found the blood—so little of it, but enough: one sliver, like a necklace laid along the woman's bruised throat.

Prosper Alley sat in a cranny of mews along the river. Inspector Jonas Robb heard men and women banter as factory shifts from the lumberyards and glass manufacturers passed one another in the street outside the alley. Ferries from the river bellowed low notes of greeting, and the smell of the Thames (salt and the low pong of rotting fish) was a presence unto itself.

"No one seen nothin'," PC Tompson told him. "Cut her throat to the bone. Can't find no one as hated her enough to do that." Tompson hesitated, shifting his weight. "Yer don't think it's like—I mean, them two whores in Whitechapel . . . the last one were just yesterday."

Robb looked again at the body. Her throat was cut, but there were no other wounds, no mutilation. Whitechapel was miles away, the worst of London's slums; but even Westminster had its poor quarters, like this alley, just off the Charing Cross thoroughfares. Now it had its dead whores, as well.

"There are no mutilations," he said quietly. "But when the mortuary van comes, tell the coroner we need to know whether her killer was right-handed or left."

Tompson nodded, sickened by the thought.

Alone with the body, Robb knelt on one knee and took off his hat. Her eyes were still open. Cold rainwater dripping from the roof had pooled in them, magnifying color and expression to a startling clarity: a drowning woman looking up out of the water.

Robb closed her eyelids gently. Her lashes were long and brushed against his fingers, still soft, and Robb felt disgust roll through his belly with a heavy sense of loss.

III

"My dear. I simply cannot believe you've come here." Emma. He had not seen her for months. "Really," Osborne said. "This is unconscionable."

"Is it?" she asked. "I don' fink I know that word. And I'm not sure I know you anymore, neither."

He waved his hand, dismissive. "We all move on. I left you money, plenty of it."

"It's not the money," she said, quiet and still.

"What, then?" Sir Jay Osborne asked. Pricked by her stillness. Venomously ironic. "Don't tell me—you've lost your character."

"I've lost a man," she said. "A man what loved me. Needed me, more like. And he don't need me now."

He was silent for a good while. "No," he said. "I don't need you now."

She smiled. It crackled her face, crazing the surface. "Don'tcha?" she asked, bitter and fierce. "Not even to tell the world who you are, or were? How I found yer mewlin' in that alley four years ago? What would yer toff friends think o' that, Jay? Or that yer name, Osborne, idn't nothing but a word on a street sign?"

Farley, his assistant, looked solemnly at The Jay, the woman's execution already signed in his eyes.

Osborne shook his head. "My dear, who would believe you?" he said quietly, gently even. "Certainly my friends in Whitehall and Mayfair would never connect me with such a wretch."

Emma looked uncertain. High society was strange to her, as out of reach as the moon. "They'd care that you weren't quality," she said.

He closed his eyes against the crimson snap roaring in his head. His fingers tingled with it. He shoved his hands into his pockets and turned his back on her, faced the desk where all the paraphernalia of his new life gleamed. "Get out," he husked.

Silence from her, behind him. Then, tentative, "Jay—"

"Get out," he roared, and swept the desk clear of everything on it, all its tokens of civilization and humanity. Pens and inkpots clattered to the floor. He ignored the sound, clutching the sides of the desk until his knuckles were white.

He heard her leave, the rustle of her skirts with the stink of the gutter still in the folds; the warm, familiar smell of her body hovering like a ghost, then gone.

Farley shut the door after her.

"Arrange it," The Jay said quietly.

Farley nodded, eyes somber, and never said a word.

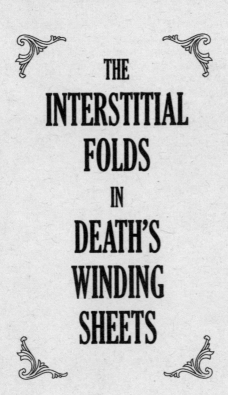

THE INTERSTITIAL FOLDS IN DEATH'S WINDING SHEETS

book one

CHAPTER 1

June 5

June 5, 2007 * Sara Grant
* Washington, D.C. * 12:15 AM

She was running for her life.

In the dark, in an alley she had never seen before. Gaslight stuttered incoherent shadows against filthy brick walls that wept, water dripping from canted rooflines down the faces of the buildings she ran between. Her heels struck the cobbles under her feet, adamant *tocks* that rang between the walls. The stone was hard, pitiless—rutted, with a crazed cant from ages of ill use, cemented into the road centuries ago.

She knew about centuries. They were bodies of time, oceans of time, and she was swimming in one of them, going against the tide down a back street in a past that had lived and died before she'd been born. Every door seemed to yawn and accuse: *You don't belong, you don't belong, you don't belong here—*

The gaslight flickered crazily to reveal, ahead of her: a dead end. She hit the wall with her hands and whirled to meet her attacker, straining to see through the shifting light and billows of fog—

—to glimpse only shapes, the outline of a man: A featureless golem cut out of ice, its form gray, both darker and brighter than the fog. It looked at her, with its eyeless face, and the jolt of that glance struck her hard—a frigid seawater shock of fear. Drowning in it; gasping: choking on the salt and that heart-stopping jolt of cold—

She woke into yet another darkness, immediately familiar: her room. Not quite awake—half in, half out of worlds—she couldn't be sure what had thrown her from sleep: the jarring buzz of the phone or the touch of that glacial eye on her skin.

Still cold with that saltwater dread, she reached for the phone. Adrenaline burred her voice: She asked *"Who are you?"* and had no idea where the question came from—or who would answer.

Her father, on the other end: Fear in his voice, fear that echoed the dream's freezing water, chilling her once again. "Sara, you must come to the site. There's been an accident. The Portal. *Avery*—"

"Is this line secure?" she asked, cold spiking her belly.

She threw on a coat. Caught her reflection in the mirror, her face a pale apparition. For one startling heartbeat, she seemed to be under water: brown eyes wild, dark hair floating around her shoulders. Looking beyond, she was almost surprised to see a modern room behind her.

She drove to the site without thinking, barely seeing the road. Hearing only the horror in her father's voice and the last words he had said ("Sara, *hurry*") before he'd cried out in pain—terrible pain—and dropped the phone.

June 5, 1884 · Ostrog · Dartmore Court, Whitechapel · 9:15 PM

They called him "doctor" and let him patch the small wounds they'd trust to a Russian Jew and that was all. Sometimes they paid. He lived with others like him—the poorest émigrés from the mother country, most of them begging and stealing like him, to stay alive.

The sign above him said DARTMORE COURT. Coming through its arch, he was immediately enveloped in its womblike space, a forgotten yard squeezed between brick buildings. Cuddling into that darkness, Ostrog curled his fingers around a rum jug's cork and set about making his throat a rocky riverbed to the liquid's fiery course.

Soon, he was warm with it. Sound was hushed and colors ran along the edges of his vision, muted rainbows smeared on warped glass. Skirts of the women passing by were nothing more than parrot feathers. And the sky—

Was buzzing around him, not a sound in his ears but in the air, a terrible pitch, the fury of angels on the other side of the world. Something was growing there, in the dark. Not a light he could see but felt in his bones. And that murderous, monstrous whine piercing his ears.

"Oh, God!" Ostrog screamed, but couldn't hear the words. The hair on his head lifted around his face. Trash swam in a current of air and he strained beyond it to see—

Light. The reflection of water in an underground cave. And inside, the shape of a man, convulsing; arms outstretched, muscles straining. A smell like lightning smarting Ostrog's nose.

In a wink, it vanished. All but the man, who was made whole out of nothing, standing in the courtyard. For one stretched second, he tottered against the air and Ostrog saw him clearly, a rail-thin starveling with a staring, raving face.

But a god in his eyes.

He howled, bowling Ostrog over, smashing the jug. Rum vapor blossomed a sharp and sugary smell, the sudden, bright breath of angels. Ostrog's head met the wall with a sick thud and a flash of pain.

Silence settled. The sound of the street beyond Ostrog was muffled and hushed, like cotton in his ears. He lay with his cheek against the cool stone and never even knew he was weeping.

June 5, 2007 * Sara
* Coral Mountain Facility * 12:56 AM

The nightmare she'd come out of was nothing to what she stepped into at the bunker. Marines led her directly to the Portal, where a cacophony of small disasters shrilled like burning islands around her. Lights on the main panels flashed fiercely; the stink of burning wire and the Klaxon screaming.

At the center sat the pale eye of their storm: the Portal itself, calm, serene. An incandescent cylinder of energy, no broader at its base than a child's plastic pool. Watery ghosts of light swam with the energy patterns moving inside.

Out of the flickering cacophony, Lyn Bouley, the Project's engineer, took her arm and steered her under a gantry of stairs. He was shouting at her over the noise: "You've got to go now, Sara. Bradford is ready to pull the plug. If you're going to go at all, you've got to go now."

"What are you saying? Where's my father? My God, has the Portal been damaged?"

"No. We've isolated the problem. It's okay. I've set your vitals from the tests we did last month. But Sara, listen, Bradford is seriously twitchy."

Sara looked out at the gantry. General Bradford, their military liaison, stood at the Portal. Another man stood beside him. Black Ops. Had to be. He wore no uniform, but it steamed on his skin: Grim determination, as if there had sprung an instant enmity between his blood and the Portal's serenely floating energy.

In the background, someone shut off a hissing steam line and the noise skittered down to the mindless shriek of the Klaxon. Sara held up a hand. "Stop. Just—What's happened?"

Bouley set his mouth, grim. "Jonathan Avery passed through the Portal early this morning. *Wait*, Sara. There's more. He got Joan Reed to do it for him. At the last minute, Joan . . . jumped into the Portal with him."

Sara turned away. Cold, freezing. Suddenly numb. Noticing, for the first time, the darkness at the base of the Portal. No body there, not anymore. But still, that darkness. Her mind produced dozens of quick images: Impromptu nightmares, none of which she wanted to see. She had to walk, and prowled the metal ramp, arms around herself, tracking blindly for her father.

Next to her, pacing her, was the man she'd seen with Bradford. He was young—mid-twenties; her age. Black-Irish good looks, but a severity she could see in every line of his body. Only extreme military discipline formed that kind of physical power. His eyes, the burnished blue of gunmetal, watched her carefully. He took her arm, his voice low and calm. "I'm David—Captain Elliot. You're looking for a body. There wasn't one. Not after a few minutes. She disappeared."

"And Avery?" Sara asked.

"No sign. It's possible he made it, they tell me."

She shivered under his hand, obscurely grateful for its warmth, for the simple grace of human touch. Then she noticed his fingers on her wrist. He was reading her pulse. "I'm fine," she said, pulling away. "Where's my father?"

"You haven't heard?" Elliot asked.

Bouley joined them. "Jesus, Sara," he said miserably.

She grabbed the engineer's arm. "What?"

"He's in the clinic," Bouley told her. "His heart. It's just an incident, Sara. A small one. He'll be all right."

Her vision blurred oddly, not tears but disorientation. As if the world had gone slowly into spin cycle and left her standing, still as a spindle, at the heart of its rotation.

Bouley towed her slowly away from Captain Elliot, under

the stairs again, and she let him. It was warm there, and she couldn't see the lights of the lab doing their slow, circular dance. Somewhere, outside her suddenly small world, someone cut the Klaxon. It wound down with a wail and Sara shuddered.

"Your father's going to be okay," Bouley said. "But Sara, you know what it would do to him, to have the Project shut down." His eyes were watchful, weighted. Telling her just how serious it could get. "You have to go. Go get Avery and bring him back. Bradford doesn't realize how important that is. He thinks he can shut off the machine and that fixes everything. You and I both know what Avery could do if he's not stopped."

"They're not going to stop him?" Her skin was numb, out of context with the reality she knew as chaos spun around her in small, decelerating orbits. "But—this could all disappear. *We* could all—"

"Bradford doesn't want to hear it. So you have to go. But you only have this one chance, now, while he's not expecting it."

"You've set my vitals?" she asked.

"Matched to Avery's coordinates. Don't look so surprised. This place went ape. It wasn't hard to load in all the confusion."

"And you've *seen* my father?" she asked. Her eyes wandering around the lab, looking for him even when she knew he wasn't there. "You *know* he's okay?"

Bouley grabbed her head in his hands and locked his eyes with hers. "Sara, *stop*. Listen. Your father is stable. For now. But one minor attack of angina is nothing compared to our world not existing, and with Avery running around in the past, you know just how easily that could happen—"

"All right," she said—stony, fierce. "I need to go. I'll go."

Bouley put a hand on her back. "I knew you would," he was saying. Handing her something—a bag. Her fingers, cold and stiff, barely caught the handle and then gripped it, a lifeline of leather as the engineer pushed her along the gantry.

Her father.

"Don't tell him where I've gone," she said to Bouley. "Don't tell him a thing until I get back."

Bouley nodded, his head stuttering in the air of the still-flashing warning lights. "I know, Sara. I know. But go, *now*, for God's sake—just get into the Portal—"

She had time to think *Daddy, where are you?* when her feet stepped up onto the dais and it hit her—a searing slam of light and energy as Bouley ran to the control panel and hit the button, freezing her there in a howling crucible to watch as all hell broke loose in the lab beyond her.

"Shut it off!" Bradford was screaming. "Shut it down, now!"

Bradford—and Elliot, who was younger, faster—were running toward her. Bradford stopped at the console and pushed Bouley aside, his hands hovering over controls he didn't understand, didn't dare touch.

And Captain Elliot dived for the Portal.

Jesus, Sara thought. *Just like Joan; he'll be just like—*

But one of the Marines in the lab dove at Elliot, knocking him off course.

The last thing Sara saw was his hand, reaching out, skimming the shimmering veil beyond her.

And then there was nothing.

June 5, 1884 * Jonathan Avery * Beggars Alley, Whitechapel * 9:42 PM

He bowled everyone out of his way. Looking for something, some light not seen. Gouged and scratched from thrashing into being in this place, which is a horror like birth, and the blood like a caul. He will not think of that birth, though the steam of it is still on his skin: the pain of that wrenching, stabbing delivery parsing his mind to mirrored fragments, shattering with the bone-grinding whine of his coming and the unseen wind that howls through his head and will not be still. So out of his mind he does not notice the growing weakness of his body until it collapses into shadows, against the cold of brick and wet cobbles and he weeps, a hitching, hiccupping drone of terror.

June 5, 1884 * Emma Smith * Beggars Alley * 11:59 PM

In the darkling shadows between midnight and morning, she hurried past the alley. A low moan caught at her—the keening of a wounded creature; an eerie, wrenching sound, bewilderment in every thin exhalation.

Cautious, she peered into the alley and saw a man, thin as a scarecrow, hunched and crying on the street. Then he looked up at her, and her breath caught. Eyes like a fallen god's, brilliant with tears and madness and something else: an intelligence lost but so intense, it pulled her soul right through his and she knew, no doubts at all, that he was hers to take care of, to bring back to that breathtaking surety of self she saw adrift in those eyes. She touched his arm, gently.

"Call me Emma," she told him. He looked at her, comprehending her name and the need for names. Amazed by his own grasp of it: clinging to that recognition. "What do I call you?" she asked. "You look a bit ragged, luv. Like a scarecrow."

"No, not a crow," he rasped. His voice was a soft scrape against stone, but the words—so beautiful. A faery king or a gentleman's speech. And a depth that thrilled through her bones: "A jay. Call me Jay."

"Jay who, then?"

He looked around, eyes unfocused. A street sign caught his glance. *Osborn Street.* "Osborne," he said. "Jay Osborne."

Emma looked at the street sign, then back at the man, smiling crookedly. "All right, luv, if you say so. Come on, then."

She gave him his pack. Heavy, it was, and no buttons. A smile of silvery metal ran along the top. He looked at it as if he'd never seen it before, like it hadn't been hanging off his back when she'd found him. He fumbled with the metal tab. Then his fingers caught and dragged the tab along the top of the pack. It opened like a wide-mouthed fish, tiny metal teeth along its jaws.

Peeking out of the top pack was a silver box, shiny as a mirror. Warily, he pulled it out. Slots in the front and back. A hinge at the side. God only knew. "What is it, luv?" she asked, though he stared at it more stupidly than she.

"I don't know," he said, but in his eyes, a sort of wonder was building: the possibility of worlds pivoting on the thing's shiny surface. And the reflection of his own face staring, in wonderment, back at him.

June 5, 2007
* David Elliot * 1:13 AM

Sitting on a chair in the chaotic light-and-steam show of the lab, Bradford was telling him, "Get her. Bring her back. Her and Avery both."

The engineer was shaking his head. Muttering something

about resetting the machine and looked genuinely surprised when Bradford took out a pistol and pointed it between his eyes. The engineer shut up, stopped breathing almost entirely. Then slowly—eyes like a kid's, wide and hurt—shook his head again.

"I'm not afraid to use this," Bradford told him.

"It's true," Bouley said. "It takes at least three hours to reset the machine." Bradford cocked the trigger. "It's true!" Almost crying now. "I'm telling the truth. *Look* at it, for God's sake!"

The Portal was quiet, its energy banked to a murmur.

"I think he may be right, sir," David Elliot told Bradford. He looked over the control panel and understood none of it, but even he could see the null/voids registered on the readouts. "But it doesn't matter, does it? We know where they went. We know the *when* they went to." He nodded calmly to Bradford's pistol. "We have the time."

Bradford stowed the weapon. "Good," he murmured. "Get this thing ready, then, Mr. Bouley. In three hours, we launch again."

June 5, 2007
* David * 4:26 AM

He noted the shiver along his skin as he approached the Portal, a quiet crawl that stirred the hair along his arms and then deepened as he came within inches of touching it.

The faintest tremor of his own trepidation added to the vibration. It really did look like a small tub of Jamaican sea, still reflecting the light of the sun overhead and the pale, smooth sand underneath. And that was just strange enough, in this gray, metal room, to raise the hair along his neck.

"Ready to go?" Bouley asked, approaching him. Wary now, and watched: Two Marines with sidearms shadowed the engineer. Bouley handed Elliot an old-fashioned duffle. Scuffed dark leather, it was heavy, and tall enough to sit level at his breastbone.

"As ready as I have to be," David said. "What's in the bag?"

"Survival," Bouley told him. "Money, clothes, papers. Everything you'll need, including a MED Kit."

Elliot's eyebrows rose. "Isn't that illegal? Taking a full MED Kit to a world that hasn't even seen aspirin yet?"

Bouley grunted. "You can't afford the fictional conceit. You won't survive without it. If Avery didn't take one with him, dysentery will get him before you do."

"Uh-huh. And you sent Ms. Grant without a kit of her own?"

"There wasn't time. I found her a purifier and some antibiotics. Clothes and a few guineas from the museum collection upstairs. That's all."

His glare was hard and bruised with resentment—for the guns, for taking control of the Portal. For what it might mean to Sara Grant.

"I'll find her," David said quietly.

Bouley barked a dismal laugh. "Chances are, you'll land right on top of her. *And* Avery. But if that doesn't happen, you'll need to be prepared."

"How prepared?"

"For anything," Bouley said, his face tight. "The rest is just—contingencies."

"Contingencies. Uh-huh." David picked up the small aluminum briefcase at his feet. Slipping the latch, he opened it silently. Inside, the elegant lines of a custom-made P38 Ghost sat like a shadow against a gray foam cutout. From the front of the case, David pulled out six boxes of ammunition and a box of sedation darts. He stowed the boxes snugly into the pockets of the leather duffle and slipped the Ghost into his waistband. He added his own field kit to the stash: a heavy nylon bag filled with gear. Then a knife—sleek and wickedly serrated. That, he slipped into his boot. "And there's all the protection I need," he said. "Rubbers, the Victorians have."

Bouley looked at him, small and sick. "Sara won't like the Victorians," he said nonsensically, and moved to his controls.

The Portal was fully powered now, its penetrating energy slipping past David's skin, reaching out for bone. This close, the power of it rippled his clothes and hair.

In that growing light, there was the past. But the past, he knew, was dead and buried, and walking into it would be like walking into a grave.

Bradford, standing behind Bouley and the controls, said, "It's time, son. Bring them back—both of them."

David nodded. He turned to face the placid blue pool.

Not knowing if it went anywhere at all. Not knowing if

Bradford would wait for him to come back, if it did. But knowing, no doubts at all, that the ghosts of a hundred years waited
silently beyond.

David closed his eyes and stepped inside.

CHAPTER 2

00:00:00

Sara

She held her breath in this place where breath was meaningless, lungs striving to expand, release, to find air where there was none. No color, no sound. Just a void that reduced her awareness to a pinpoint of wavering light.

Realizing: She had no idea where she was going.

Coming out of it like falling through a corn chute in an old silo—that sensation of descent and then standing, without impact, on her feet.

David

There was no light or darkness. This was the space where the world would be, before the hand of God moved over it and made it good.

His need for air squeezed the walls around his heart, that wrenching, collapsing weight as his lungs filled slowly with the hot, thick water of an ancient, boiling sea—

—dying—

—had to be—

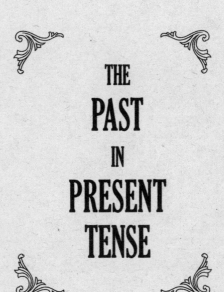

THE
PAST
IN
PRESENT
TENSE

book two

CHAPTER 3

September 5, 1888

Robb · Huntingdon Street Men's Club, London · 5:46 AM

A discreet knock woke him instantly. Robb rose stealthily out of bed and opened the door. The night manager of the club stood frowning outside.

"Really, sir, I do hate to disturb you like this. Are you sure you want me to wake you? I could have simply told Mr. Tompson to try you again in the morning."

"Perfectly sure," Robb murmured. "It's all right, Mason. Where's Tompson?"

"In the entry, sir."

Robb went to the entry immediately, wrapped in a silk robe. Tompson's eyes were wide and seemed bruised, as though he'd seen something that had hurt.

"What is it?" Robb asked.

"Another one, sir. On our patch," Tompson said. "Just another whore and I wouldn'a bothered ye, except—"

Stunned, Robb said, "But—it's been months since the girl in Prosper Alley. Are you sure it's the same?"

"Aye, sir. Throat cut. Just like the other. Only this time, he cut her up a bit." He looked sick, recalling it. "Should I tell anyone else, sir?"

"No," Robb said. "Not yet. I'll call for the coroner and come as soon as I'm dressed. Give Mason here the address. Then go back right away and secure the scene."

"Right, sir," Tompson said miserably.

Robb ran up the thickly carpeted stairs, the sound of his own heart beating so loudly in his head that it hurt.

Robb
* Bingham Street * 6:26 AM

He wondered who she had been. He'd seen his cousins' dolls thrown like this, tossed on the floor when the girls were tired of playing with them. Arms sprawled. One leg bent under the other.

He knelt at her side, and took off his hat.

A scuff mark against the wall caught his attention. Beneath it, the crescent of a finely cut boot heel was cast in mud, slowly drying underneath the eaves. Any other shoe prints the rain hadn't already erased were made by wide boots, crudely crafted. But this one: it was clear, and above it was a smudge of polish on the wall. The mark of a gentleman. Boots like his own, but no wear marks had dulled the edge of that heel yet.

Robb pulled out his notebook and began to sketch, re-creating the scuff and the scene around it in detail.

"Got anything?" a voice above him asked. Robb looked up and then stood, putting his sketch away smoothly. Tom Bulling, one of the hacks from the Central News Agency, stood over the body.

"You know if I did, I couldn't tell you," Robb said mildly. "Did you see anything?"

Bulling laughed. "Not me. She was a whore. Dangerous profession, you ask me. Dying all the time, and who cares? But with that mess in Whitechapel, well—the Boss, he's full of new ideas, he is. Man like me has to have initiative, just to keep up with Sir Jay Osborne."

Robb nodded. He had heard of Sir Jay. New ideas, many new connections. "Strange thing to report in a newspaper," Robb murmured. "Doesn't appear to be connected with Whitechapel at all. Not something you'd think the public would want to know. Are you going to write about this, then?"

Robb used the kind of irritation that expressed ultimate disdain from his class. Hated using it, especially when Bulling knew there was an "Honourable" in front of his name.

Sardonic, Bulling tipped his hat to Robb without making any promises and left him to wonder just what the man would write about the death of a woman desperate enough to sell herself for food.

Robb took off his own good wool coat and covered the

woman's mud-stained face with it before heading off to find a cab that would take him down to Westminster station.

"Hey," PC Tompson called out to him, "that coat must ha' cost a quid or two."

Robb only smiled and wandered past King's Ferry Road to Bridge Steps Way, where cabs waited for passengers.

Tompson shook his head. "He's an odd one," he told the younger constables around him.

"Bloody toff," one said.

"Stuff that," Tompson said, sharpish. "He's a good man."

They watched Robb walk away. Watched him, coatless, tip his hat to a group of ragged women at the corner that even a blind man could not mistake for ladies.

"But odd," Tompson admitted.

Robb
* Whitechapel Coroner's Office * 9:14 AM

"I don't know what I'm asking, really," he said, and hesitated. He was an inspector, but from the Westminster precinct, not Whitechapel. Aware that the Whitechapel coroner, John Perridore, owed him nothing.

"I don't know much about what's happened in Whitechapel," Robb said quietly. "Never thought I'd have to. But with these killings in Westminster—I need to know."

The coroner grimaced. "Aye. Right," he sighed. "What do you need to know, then?"

"How these women died, the specifics of their wounds."

"Well, first," Perridore mused, "there was the Tabram woman."

"Wait," Robb said. "What about Fairy Fay? Annie Millwood and the others?"

The coroner made a face. "Read those in the *Times*, did you? The only thing those women had in common was public hysteria and bad newspaper reportage. Before the *Times* said so, certainly no one in our business thought to connect them—too far apart, didn't fit any pattern. Well, wasn't a pattern to fit, then, was there? They were killed in different places, their deaths spread out over more than a year. Four women—one a month between December and April. Smith was the last one of that run—just when our own people decided to pursue the connection, the killing stopped."

"And started again with Martha Tabram?" Robb asked.

"Who knows?" the coroner replied, prosaic. "Tabram was killed early August, and Nichols late the same month. Could be it's starting again. Could be something completely different." He wrinkled his nose. "Mass murder makes a good story, but there's no medical proof they're connected, if that's what you're asking."

Robb nodded. "What about these latest, then—Tabram and Nichols?"

"Tabram was stabbed to death—thirty-nine stab wounds in all. Hit the lungs, liver, spleen, and stomach. One deep thrust to the heart, cutting through the chestbone—had to be made by a very rare knife, though, because the other cuts weren't near as deep."

"Had she been strangled?"

"No. Died of her wounds."

Robb recoiled. "My God," he said, sick at the thought. Knowing his own precinct was far more sheltered. Though the coroner nodded, agreeing with him, he could see in his eyes a sad amusement at Robb's innocence.

"Then, with Nichols," the older man said, "we saw the same sort of thing—multiple stab wounds. Focused on the abdomen. Her throat was cut, ear to ear, right down to the vertebrae. Severed the major blood vessels on both sides of her neck."

"Anything else?" Robb asked.

The coroner frowned, silent and assessing. "What are you looking for?" he asked.

Robb shrugged, struggling with his unease, which was vague, near to formless, but would not let him go. "I'm not even sure." He held out his hand, and the coroner shook it warmly. "Thank you. You've been very helpful."

"You're welcome, for what it's worth," Perridore told him. "If I come across anything pertinent, I'll send it to you, just in case, if you'll give me an address."

Robb almost took out one of his cards, but thought better of it. He didn't want his social rank to come between them. "Just send it to Westminster Station, in care of my name," he said.

He tipped his hat and left, letting his mind glide along a dozen paths, fishing for ideas, random thoughts that might connect to form answers. Nothing came.

His unease, which had grown since closing the dead woman's eyes, continued to eat at the peace within him.

Robb
* Westminster Station * 9:56 AM

Robb came to Pershing's office, opening the door to warm paneled wood and the heavy cherry desk. Superintendent Pershing didn't bother to smile, and neither man addressed the other. Pershing was a gentleman, a son of minor gentry, with pretensions. Robb was the second son of an earl, with no need for pretensions and no use for them. Hostility crackled between the men every time they met.

"There's been another one—a woman murdered on Bingham Street," Robb said. "A prostitute. Her throat cut."

"And?" Pershing asked.

"This is the second one in our area," Robb pointed out.

"Seven months apart," Pershing said, dismissive.

"Five months and seven days," Robb said. He hesitated. "I've been to the Whitechapel coroner's office. There have been five women murdered there the same way, two in just the last month. Now we have the same problem."

"We do *not* have the same problem," Pershing said, suddenly forceful. "It's a completely different thing, and I will thank you to never suggest any correlation between them again."

Stunned speechless, Robb simply stood and stared. It took a moment, but he saw it there, in the belligerence of Pershing's gaze and the tightness of his mouth. Of course. Whitechapel command was under intense scrutiny—names in the press now, every movement reported in detail.

"You're afraid," Robb said. The words dropped like stones in a pond before he could recall them.

"And you're out of line," Pershing told him, suddenly fierce. "And hardly the man to talk to me about fear."

Robb narrowed his eyes. "What, sir, do you mean exactly?" Precise, each word freighted with challenge. Not so long ago, his ancestors had begun duels with a question put just that way.

"You know damned well what I mean. An earl's son, poncing about in the streets as a common inspector—it's thoroughly insulting to your honored father."

"Ah." Robb smiled grimly. "Told you that himself, did he?"

"He didn't have to." Pershing was incensed now—knowing Robb's father was far beyond his social ambitions. "I have sons of my own. Certainly I hope better things of them than a low-paid pitiful rank that no decent member of society would even let through the front door. You're so damned intent on earning this job. You didn't *have* to earn it—that's the point. Leadership is yours for the taking; it's part of who you are. You could have been commissioner. Instead you insist on being in the streets, for God's sake, and for what? To learn the trade—of detective, of all things."

"You'd be surprised," Robb said evenly, "at how much there is to learn."

Pershing sneered. "And I'm sure you could tell me. *You*. Graduate of Eton, Oxford—a colonel in the Hussars, for God's sake. All gone to *this*." He waved his hand at Robb, indicating his clothing, which was plainer than any gentleman would have worn.

"This," Robb said coldly, "is what keeps me from being garroted in the streets by starving children who could sell one of my better shirts and eat a whole year on what they'd get for it. *This* is a damned sight more honorable than ordering good men to their deaths because one has purchased his commission cheap and hasn't got the experience to fulfill his command better than the men he sends out to die. I do my job. I *know* my job. And believe me, sir, that is more than enough for me."

Pershing shook his head. Robb hesitated, but the echo of rain pooled in a dead woman's eyes goaded him. "I could take this to the commissioner," he said quietly.

Pershing barked a laugh. "You could. But he'd want to hear it even less than I do." He waved Robb away with a weary hand. "Get back to your streets, Inspector. Do your job your way. But I will hear no more about connecting any death in our area with the Whitechapel murders."

"And when I find the next dead woman with her throat cut, what then?"

"If she's had her throat cut *and* been stabbed a dozen times, *then* you come to me," Pershing said, his patience exaggerated.

Robb clicked his heels together, bowing with equally exaggerated formality, knowing the elegance with which he did it was something Pershing could only dream of attaining, and only partially despising himself for the small, savage pleasure it gave him to see that fact register on Pershing's flushed and inelegant face.

But outside Pershing's closed door, Robb prayed the bloody ring around this second woman's neck had been the consequence of a singular fury, a sudden drunken impulse and nothing more. Anything, God help them, other than what he thought it really was.

CHAPTER 4

∽⭒⭒⭒∾
September 6, 1888
∽⭒⭒⭒∾

Bulling
⋆ Offices of the Central News Agency ⋆ 2:36 PM

From his desk, Bulling could see into Sir Jay Osborne's office. Watched as Sir Jay himself stuck his head out of his door and yelled, "Bulling!" and went back into his office, flexing his fists.

"Oh Jesus," Bulling whispered. Stood up, straightened his coat. With shaking legs, he went up the stairs and stood at Osborne's desk.

Sir Jay was bent over the desk, still standing, arms planted wide over the surface. Reading the morning issue of the *Westminster Local*. Or not reading it. His eyes did not scan the page, but focused intently on a point through and beyond the smudgy gray paper.

Finally he raised his head to look at Bulling. His eyes were cold, and once again, Bulling felt his pulse beat somewhere around his ankles.

"I see a squib here on page fifteen," Sir Jay said mildly, "about a whore who was killed yesterday on Bingham Street. You can imagine my surprise. I don't recall sending you out to cover that story." He paused, looking over Bulling's sweating face. His words were so pointed, they were almost delicate. "So why did you? Write that story?" he asked softly.

"I, uh—" Bulling licked his lips. "A copper there, an inspector, told me not to write it up, sir."

"And you called attention to us by writing it anyway?" Sir Jay looked at Bulling, incredulous. Then, suddenly, he swept everything on his desk to the floor. *"Idiot!"*

Oh Lord, it was a rant. Hardly nobody survived a rant. Bulling, almost breathless, locked his knees against falling and ignored the detritus of Sir Jay's desk scattered around his feet, though some of it was heavy and hurt, and ink raddled his trousers halfway to the knee. Suicidal now—if he was sacked, he'd nothing to lose—Bulling said, "I didn't think you'd want rozzers tellin' us what to write."

Sir Jay, poised to let his anger fly, paused and looked more closely at Bulling. "Indeed not," he said. A small smile touched his lips; it curled ironically once and was gone, like the tip of a hat when one gentleman passes another. "They actually assigned an inspector to this?"

Bulling nodded. "He was a toff, too. I knew toffs were our audience, see. But then I thought, you know, what kind of toff works as a cop?"

"A *toff*," Osborne said, working the words like candy. "Working as an inspector. How delightful. What was his name?"

"Robb. Jonas Robb. The Honourable. Father's an earl, I think. Works out of Westminster Station."

"If he's an inspector, he's hardly quality, no matter what his father's title is," Sir Jay told Bulling, softening. "And he's certainly not the kind of man I'm influencing here. I have a specific agenda for our papers. Next time you write a story, make sure it's one I tell you to write." Sir Jay raised his eyebrows. His green eyes, almost crystalline, took on a cruel humor. "Unless you'd rather go back to working on street corners shouting rhyming doggerel for a living."

"No. No, sir," Bulling said, his face grim with the memory of cold and wind, and sleet that cut bloodlessly to the bone.

Sir Jay smiled. "All right then. Get to work, my boy."

Bulling blinked twice and retreated slowly, uncertain as to where his feet were or how well they would hold him up; they were that numb, bumping against the strewn flotsam of Sir Jay's inkpots and pens on the floor. As he closed the door, he heard soft but vicious laughter within the office, and knew that he'd sold something precious, meeting the devil at a crossroads he had not even known he'd ventured along.

CHAPTER 5

September 7, 1888

Sara
* Dartmore Court * 2:52 AM

She slammed from the netherworld into darkness and the reek of dank air around her. Gaslight stuttered and shivered in a filthy casement overhead. The cobbles were hard under her sneakers, and broken objects scattered shadows along the dark courtyard—wooden wagons, barrels, leather bridles rotting in the damp.

She heard voices, but they seemed distant—as if the courtyard itself were miles removed from the press of people, from light and life as she knew it.

"My *Christ*," she whispered. Clenched her jaw to keep her teeth from chattering. Bent to the bag at her feet and had to close her hands into fists to stop their shaking.

Inside the bag she found a plain cotton dress with long skirts and an apron, and lace-up leather ankle boots. All of it was thin and patched. Even the cotton linens had buttons, no zippers— just a frayed cord tie.

Oh God, she thought. *Good God, where am I?*

Jack
* Dartmore Court * 2:53 AM

At the back of the courtyard, far back, he watched out of the silence of deep shadows. A woman. She had fallen into the courtyard out of nowhere.

So beautifully muscled, her body. So out of place. When she stripped away the outsized nightshirt, he could barely breathe for watching it. Long legs silvered by moonlight, skin golden along the flat curve of her belly and her breasts. His hands ached to hold them, palms itching for their weight.

Sara * 2:54 AM

The voices on the other side of the courtyard came to Sara more clearly now. Shouts and laughter, fighting and singing, heaving and a vicious, guttural swearing.

Her knees shook as she changed her clothes. Keenly aware of how close dozens of drunken men were to her position, she shimmied into the thin skirts of the dress, plunging her arms quickly into the sleeves. The darkness was a sporadic shelter under the sickled moon; clouds slipped over its face, a dance of veils that revealed her every time its lunar smile fell on the courtyard.

Buttoning the halves of the top, she found they wouldn't quite close all the way.

The sense of being watched was heavy on her skin, the air's damp moisture like small, sodden kisses. Quickly she stowed her own clothes in the bag and rummaged through it. She found what they had sent her with and knew it wasn't enough: a bottle of Keflex-S, a water purifier, a handheld electronic encyclopedia, a bag of coins.

She didn't count the money—knew that pathetic handful wouldn't last long. Instead, she held the largest coin up to the moonlight. She squinted, but couldn't make out the imprint, which might have told her where she was and maybe when. Saw the brief glimmer of a woman's profile, hair piled high on her head, but no details. She pocketed the coin.

And heard the scrape of a shoe nearby.

Sara froze, crouched over the bag. Along the dim alley that was the courtyard's throat came a man and woman, strangers to one another; the man impatient, the woman drunk: pulling up her skirts and bending over a barrel. Her breasts hung heavy against the low neck of her dress, pillowing rhythmically as the man moved behind her.

Sara gasped. The woman looked up, saw her—and laughed, pitiless, for the both of them: two women bent over their respective burdens, so much of their bodies bared to the hazy moonlight.

Jack * 2:55 AM

He stopped, stood very still. Watched the temporary coupling in the courtyard, the roughness of it stoking an agony of need within him. The other woman, in the darkness (so near—he could reach out, he could touch), was stripping out of the shirt-waist, and she—

She fumbled with a ridiculous oversized shirt, throwing it over her head and breasts; buttoning the shirtwaist over it.

Oh no, please, don't cover them, no—

She didn't listen: stepped farther into the shadows, not even knowing he was there.

Frustration arrowed through him but he kept it silent, sucking in desire. Watching the others, grunting in the darkness.

But thinking of her.

David
* Dartmore Court * 2:56 AM

. . . and then he was out of it, and it was like being born—squeezed and pummeled into awareness. Breathing. Air against his face, in his hair. Seeing again. The shape of bricks in the wall. One vivid globe of smoking light. The shadows of a narrow space that opened out to a courtyard between buildings.

He saw the bag before he saw her, sitting on the cobbled floor of the courtyard. At the far end of the court, near the opening, a woman was sprawled over a barrel, her buttocks exposed to the man behind her.

David's hand moved instinctively to the gun in his waistband.

A slam of light, heavier than the flash-bang of the Portal, exploded at the back of his skull. He knew he was still alive when the silver curtain in front of his eyes played movies for him in scarlet and the searing-cold white of pain.

And he knew. Sara Grant was not in front of him.

She was behind him.

Jack * 2:57 AM

His teeth ached with the fury of it. She'd *hit* him. The big man who had come out of nowhere: hit him with a fist-thick plank. From *behind*—

Dear God! The lightning-sharp arrow of hate and desire that tore through his loins. Reeling with the thought of it: a *woman*, hitting a man like that. He waited for the big man to hit her back, but he didn't. Just stood in her way, and would not let her pass.

They could not be strangers. They were arguing, their words like nothing he had ever heard. So he stayed in the shadows of the courtyard, loins quivering and watery, and listened.

David * 2:58 AM

He heard the plank hit the ground as she darted out of the shadows. His scope of vision was viciously narrow, eyes focusing only by force, scalp screaming, head ringing from ear to ear. He managed to stand in her way—a wall of muscle and anger—and hoped it was all he would have to do for at least one solid minute before he had to move.

Her muscles tensed. She would hit him again—this time with her hands or feet. He knew it by the way she stood, and the determination on her face.

Wearily, he pulled the Ghost out of his waistband.

"You shit," he said, without heat or even much surprise. With one hand, he tested the bloody knot at the back of his head—and held the gun perfectly steady with the other.

She looked at him, very still. "I'm not going back. You can't make me. You don't know the science behind it, how to use the Portal—"

Very still himself, lethally quiet, David said, "I know enough. I know that when the light comes, you have to go."

"But you don't know how to make it come," she pointed out. "And if you don't know that, you can't take me back. Or Avery. If you don't know how this works, you can't get home—ever."

David thought about it. Made a show of stowing his gun. Of not paying attention to her. "Ever's a long time," he said. "I don't think they gave me enough money for quite that long, though they did give me a goddamned pile of it just before I left. And unless you want to end up with your butt over a barrel like that poor bitch over there, you may need me just as much as I need you."

She looked at him, looked past him to the entry where the whore had done her business. Without warning, he went for her—closing in, wrapping her up like a spider in a web with the big knife just under her throat. She stilled instantly in his grip.

"Good girl," David murmured.

"I could beat you senseless for that," Sara whispered.

"You could. If I were shit-faced drunk and tied in chains."

She told him, viciously, "I'm trained at combat-level martial arts."

He laughed softly. "With those nails?"

She said nothing, but he could feel her analyzing the hold he held her in, scoping for weaknesses; moving her muscles to probe where and how she could move against him. *Good girl*, he thought again. This time, he didn't say it. Instead, he asked, "Have you killed anyone yet?"

That stopped her. "No, of course not."

"I have," he said. A quiet fact, almost simple.

She raised her eyes to his: sharp, assessing—searching for the truth of him as surely as she had searched for a way out of his grip. He gave her the one truth he knew she could believe.

"They told me to bring you back. They didn't say I had to bring you back alive. We're going home now. And you're going to tell me how to get there."

She hesitated, then nodded. Took in a deep and shaking breath. To talk, he thought; to tell him what he needed to know.

Instead, she screamed—a full-throated detonation of sound he felt as much as heard; a deliberate weapon, her mouth wide and hard, her eyes daring him to shut her up, to cover her mouth. To let go with just one hand, so she could move.

An old man stuck his head out of a window above them. And outside the courtyard, the sounds of human congress fell silent. Then a group of angry men began to fill the tight concourse of the alley, spilling out into the courtyard. All of them were armed and pitifully dangerous: switchblades and rakes and scythes.

David swore, released Sara Grant, and stowed his knife.

"Wassit out 'ere?" Shouted one of the men, a butcher, by the look of his leather apron.

"Yer all right, missy?" the old man asked from his window. "Not seen Jack, now, 'ave yer?"

Shaken, Sara looked at her rescuers—at their weapons—and aimed a surprisingly raw Cockney accent at the angry men. "Naaaaw, we was just havin' a bit o' fun, like."

But she slid away from David as she spoke—out of reach of his hands.

Most of the men filtered back out of the courtyard, shaking their heads, disgusted. The butcher, still angry, shook his cleaver at her. "You shouldn't ought to go scarin' folk these days, yellin' like that. Who knows when yer'll need help, and yer'll scream yer bloody head orf and nobody'll come. Bloody whore."

The butcher gave them an evil look and turned to exit the courtyard. Sara, close to the archway, glanced back at David.

"You shouldn't have covered for me," he told her.

She smiled, a grim little moue sharpened by a hint of mockery. "I don't need any of these men to hang for your murder," she said softly. "That might change time."

Then she slipped through the archway, disappearing into morning's flotsam of humanity filling the open thoroughfare outside.

Sara
* Crossingham's Common Lodgings, Whitechapel * 7:46 AM

The reeking exhalation of open sewers heated by sunlight brought her awake, a stench that pooled like strong oil at the back of her throat. A sheen of gray light spilled into the room from the window, the glass thin and watery.

Sara put her hand on the doorknob, and hesitated. A heartbeat of anticipation swept through her, so strong her stomach ached with it. Then she opened the door onto another world. Dark brick buildings and cobbled streets; Cockney accents strong as salt; the grainy sky lowering clouds dark with soot; the thinning fog losing its foothold on the street as morning warmed its way into afternoon.

London.

She breathed in slowly. A shiver kindled in her blood, spreading to a firestorm in her bones. This was no sepia daguerreotype. This was alive, the colors of humanity brilliant under the gray skies. She took slow, careful steps down the wooden stairs to the street, as if the air itself would somehow crumple and warp when she touched it. Or the buildings would declare, as they had in her dream, *You don't belong, you don't belong here—*

Careful to stay out of the way, she stood on the curb and

stared, delighted by each detail. Carters hauling slatted crates into wooden wagons. Women shucking peas into dirty aprons. Men lounging on the curbs, laughing and playing cards. One old man sat at his windowsill, toothless, an aging sentry watching the street. Litter filled the gutters. Paper skittered like ground-borne birds, gray and white, and she realized that color press would take years to develop yet.

Her back crackled against dry paper and she turned to find a parchment leaflet tacked to the post behind her:

POLICE NOTICE.
TO THE OCCUPIER.
ON THE MORNING OF AUGUST 31, A WOMAN WAS MURDERED IN OR NEAR WHITECHAPEL, SUPPOSED BY SOME ONE RESIDING IN THE IMMEDIATE NEIGHBORHOOD. SHOULD YOU KNOW OF ANY PERSON TO WHOM SUSPICION IS ATTACHED, YOU ARE EARNESTLY REQUESTED TO COMMUNICATE AT ONCE WITH THE NEAREST POLICE STATION.
METROPOLITAN POLICE OFFICE

The notice was cracked and dry, streaked with rainwater. Surreal: She brushed it with her fingertips. The paper crackled. The nape of her neck tingled with the feel of it on her fingers.

Slowly, Sara turned to the placard on her own building and read, with a shock of recognition, CROSSINGHAM'S COMMON LODGINGS.

A scream shattered the dreamlike quality of the place. Not a laughing shriek or a cry of pain, but wailing: the keen of a harbinger, a woman coming down the street. Sara turned her head and could feel the tendons creak in the slow motion of rising adrenaline.

The woman cawed to the people who clustered quickly around her, "Gor 'elp us, he's come again. Down 'anbury Street. Another woman, all cut up. Oh Gor, oh Gor."

Sara read the notice again. Goose bumps bloomed on her arms and her body knew before she did. Logic told her this notice could announce a random murder, one of the many casual killings that happened so often here. It didn't have to be anything more than that.

But if that was so, why did her skin shiver and dance on her arms?

Hysteria sparked and shimmered, palpable as the day's coming heat. Sara knew these people saw death all the time. Why would one dead woman cause such furor among them?

Remembered the belligerent little man in the window asking her, "Not seen Jack, now, 'ave yer?"

The goose bumps broke out again—rising up, fine and hard, on her scalp. It couldn't be. And yet it spread through her, a silent, certain thrill: To be at the center of that investigation. What a study it would make. To see the body of a victim. To watch the police work. To witness the reactions of the people in the slums.

To watch journalists take the story of a common serial killer and turn it into incendiary politics: Jack the Ripper.

She took a step, then stopped. The hysteria crept to the surface of her own skin in a cold and sudden sweat. She looked up at the window of her room, hugging her arms, holding herself against the shiver that had blossomed in her blood and jittered there, thrilling and hot.

Inside, there were only walls and windows. While outside—

—was Captain Elliot. He was out there, looking for her. He would find her, if she wasn't careful. But outside . . .

More people were gathering, their fear galvanizing, spreading from face to face. That fear was electric, explosive: disturbance distilling to discord in the growing heat of the day. The emotions so real—an unsettling antenna that quivered and swayed under the pressure of its own current.

She left without looking back, breathless, and jittery, joining the growing procession of men and women hurrying past, on toward Hanbury Street.

Robb
* Hanbury Street, Whitechapel * 8:16 AM

Robb made his way through the crowd surrounding the building, chilled by the depth of anger he passed through. It was like moving through aspic. Fear and fury warped every face.

That morning, Perridore had sent him word: There had been another killing. This time, he had to see it for himself.

He passed by 29 Hanbury Street to where the body lay, in the small, grassy yard. Around the yard, people watched like crows, standing in windowed stalls, sitting on the fence, on the roof overhead. Some had even filtered into the yard, where dung balls sat like thick toadstools on the dirt-packed ground.

As he passed through, one young woman glanced at him keenly. He noticed the intellect behind that quick flash in her eyes—studying him briefly, then turning back to the yard, stunned by the violence of the murder but taking in every detail.

He followed her eyes as she examined not the body on the grass but every other point he would have examined himself: egress and entry to the yard, the clapboard fences around it that were high but easy to scale. Then she scanned the crowd for an on-looker who was not shocked at all, and watched the Whitechapel crew do their work.

As if she were taking notes in her mind, photographs with her eyes.

Frowning, Robb mingled with the Whitechapel boys, polite and unobtrusive. This was not his place and they knew it. When an opening around the body came up, he quietly made his own examinations and concentrated, fiercely, on keeping his break-fast where it belonged. This woman had been dead when this was done to her, he told himself grimly, and hoped it was true—hoped that was the reason for so little blood; that she hadn't been killed somewhere else, alive and in agony, and dumped here after.

"See anything we haven't?"

Robb looked up and was surprised to see Detective Inspector Abberline himself. Robb shook his head, aware he was on deli-cate ground, just being here. "No sir," he said quietly. "I'm only here to make sure I don't have the same sort of thing on my patch."

Abberline's face sharpened. "Think you might?"

"I don't know," Robb told him honestly. "I had one six months ago. Throat cut. Not stabbed, though. Then another three days ago. This time, her breasts were scored. But—"

"But you're not prepared to say it's the same man," Abberline said, and smiled grimly. "Can't say as I blame you. Wish I didn't have to say it myself, but after this, I don't think we'll have the luxury."

Abberline moved on to speak with his sergeants. Robb stepped back, taking fresher air—air that smelt of dung and un-washed bodies, but not that hideously sweet copper-penny stench of blood. The woman he'd noticed earlier had moved along the ring of bobbies to stand just behind him. He realized she had spoken to him, and turned.

"May I see her?" she asked again.

He turned to look at her and had the breath swept from his lungs: eyes tilted up to look into his; her gaze direct—assessing him, disturbingly frank.

She was as exotic as a lily in a field of dandelions.

Robb frowned, and looked back at the body. His own gut still ached from that first examination. He turned again and asked her, "Why would you want to see this?" And then, more gently, "Did you know her?" The woman hesitated, then nodded. Reluctantly, he motioned to the guards to let her through, and said to her, "My name is Robb. Inspector Robb."

"I'm Sara," she said, and said nothing else. A curious shiver guarded her words, and he found it impossible not to notice her as a woman—the surprisingly fresh scent of her, the warmth and health of her skin—and that disturbed him. He led her to the body, suddenly wishing, fiercely, that he could shield her from its horror.

To his surprise, she looked not at the dead woman's face but at the horrific wounds. Counting, almost clinically, the number of times the killer had cut his victim.

"Look, are you quite sure you knew her?" Robb asked, unnerved. The woman, Sara, looked up at him, startled.

"Said I did, dint I?" she said, sharpish, and Robb relaxed. The accent was pure East End. But she looked at the victim's face as if reminded of her task, staring intently. The victim had been a large woman. Her red hair was frizzed with curl, the face long and broad.

"I think I know," she said slowly, which Robb had expected. But then she said something so out of the blue, he answered before he could think not to. "What's the date?"

"The eighth," he said immediately. "September." Then looked at her as if she were mad. She didn't look mad. Instead, she seemed oddly composed, concentrating not on him or the ridiculous fact of her questions but on some internal calendar.

"The year?" she asked, frowning.

Robb cleared his throat. "Eighteen eighty-eight," he said, each word precise. And waited, wondering what she would say next. The intelligence in her face, that whole demeanor of absorbed detachment—in her own way, she was as riveting as the scene itself. He saw her thinking, searching her memory—as if she hadn't so much known the victim as known *of* her.

"Annie Chapman," she finally said.

"Are you sure? How well did you know Miss Chapman?"

"Missus," she corrected. "An' I didn't really know 'er, ta speak of. Seen 'er abaht."

Robb nodded, took out his notebook. "And where exactly do you live, miss?"

The look she gave him then was that of a duchess, affronted at his impudence. The full force of her personality hit him like a sudden wave. It should have been funny—she was an unfortunate, for God's sake. It wasn't. He cleared his throat. "In case the other investigators need to ask you any questions. And your last name, if you don't mind."

"None of your business," she said sharply. The high Cockney had vanished.

" 'Look, I need your name and address. We can't take your testimony into account if—"

The flare of those keen eyes should have warned him. In an instant, she was beyond him, and past the bobbies who laughed appreciatively at the flash of her legs.

Swearing, Robb pelted after her—and was blocked, immediately, by the swarm of bodies gathered outside the yard.

The crowd had jelled to a hot pudding of frightened women and angry men. One old crone planted herself in front of him. She was rigid with anger and fear—transmitting it, like a disease, to everyone around her.

"*Four*," she cried at him. "*Four* rozzer stations in the neighbor'ood. Always stickin' their noses in the bizness of honest folk. But come ta this, they dint see nuffink."

Confusion and violence licked through the packed bodies. Ignoring them, ignoring the press of their slow-boiling rage, Robb scanned the crowd even as he was pushed around by it. Looking for the girl named Sara, and catching sight of the whiteness of her collar and cuffs.

Quickly, Robb moved up behind her and took her firmly by the elbow.

She rounded on him, furious. God, she was fast. If she hadn't been boxed in by the crowd, she would have run. He cleared his throat. "You need to give me your name," he said.

"Why should I?" she demanded. She'd dropped the Cockney,

her language clear and concise, and yet he could not identify the accent.

"Your actions this morning were damned strange," he said. "You must admit—"

"To nothin'," she said sharply. The patchy Cockney accent returned and Robb realized, finally, that she didn't do it half so well as a native. If he'd been listening closely, he would have known: She wasn't from here at all. "Look," she said and sighed, impatient with him. "There's a man after me. It may go bad, he finds me, see? I idn't puttin' my doss abaht fer the world ta know."

Robb hesitated. Something was wrong; he knew that but could not place it. The strength of her stare was unnerving. "I think you'd best come with me, miss," he said.

Amazingly, she laughed—a throaty thing, filled with the certainty of her own will. The sound was foreign, almost alien, in the mouth of a woman. According to all his sensibilities, it should have repulsed him. Instead, it thrilled him, and made him want—amazingly—to laugh with her.

"Oh no," she said, shaking her head, dropping the act altogether. "You aren't the first man to say that today, and I didn't go with him, either."

Robb blushed. "I meant nothing untowards, miss."

"And I meant what I said," she told him pointedly.

They stared at each other for long seconds. She was unflinching, utterly unapologetic. He was shocked by that insubordination—and helpless in the face of it, without resorting to physical force.

"This is ridiculous," he finally said—quietly, firmly.

She said nothing in response. Just stood there and raised an eyebrow.

"Damn it," Robb whispered, and took her by the arm.

In response, she turned to the press of bodies and suddenly cried, "Rozzer! Filthy rozzer! Come ter take me in. Help! Oh *Gor*, help!"

With those words, the pushing, pulsing bodies around him were transformed. The crowd became a wall of faces, surrounding him in a tightening circle. The ugliness of it, so sudden and fierce, took his breath away.

"Yere, whoo'r you?" a woman yelled.

And then a volley of outrage erupted from the crowd, men and women shouting epithets, throwing questions like punches:

"Where yer takin' 'er?" "Whatchoo doin' w'our women?"
"Yere, there, bloody toff. You. Take yer hands off 'n that girl."
"Filthy rozzer—can't do nuffink about these murders, but yer'll
take the women right off 'n our streets!"

Hands pushed him—testing him. Robb tightened his hand
on the woman's arm. But instead of running, she looked at the
crowd and was as surprised by their reaction as he was himself. A colossal fisherman with a filthy beard barreled up to
them, yelling. Robb pulled the woman (*Sara, her name is
Sara*) firmly behind him, just as the fisherman pulled back his
fist.

And then a single voice arrowed through the building uproar.
The fisherman stopped. They all stopped at the sound of that
voice, at just one word:

"Hey."

Robb turned. A man stood in the middle of the street.
Dressed in a burlap jacket dyed an outrageous shade of yellow-
gold, he didn't look like much. But Robb knew the weight of his
influence as the crowd pulled away from him, leaving an area of
clear space a good twenty paces round.

The man smiled when he saw Robb, a slow grin that grew
malignant as it spread. He said: "Filthy rozzer, takin' our
women. The Jay wouldn't like that, now would 'e? Got better
uses for them women than a rozzer'd have."

The crowd tittered—nervous, high-strung laughter. And
Robb realized they didn't trust this man any more than he did,
but they were in thrall to him, like it or not.

Six large men seeped out of the crowd. They, too, wore yellow jackets.

The lead man said, "Not to be allowed, then, is it? Takin' a
fine thing like that outta here for hisself."

The crowd roared a negative. Robb saw that weapons had
appeared. Scythes and axes, even brooms.

The Yellow Jacket stopped ten feet from Robb and Sara,
hands on his hips. "Don't wanna know about our dead, do ya,
cop? Gorram toff. You dint see it, it dint happen." Hate spasmed
the man's face, twisting it viciously, and he roared, *"Well it
happened."*

The crowd, behind him, stood silent. Their eyes were bruised
and accusing, faces wounded by their abandonment.

"An' it keeps on happenin'," the man said, quiet words that fell hard in the silence.

Soundless frictions of rage, whispers of it, forked along the ground. A pressure built in the air, like a coming storm, and the man said, almost casually, "Cut 'im up, boys."

The woman, Sara, stepped out from behind Robb and said to the men, "Stop, please. He didn't *do* anything to me."

But it wasn't about her anymore, Robb knew: It was about the woman lying dead in Hanbury Street.

Slowly, the Yellow Jackets advanced. Flashes of steel as they unsheathed skinny knives and fat, squat shivs.

This time Robb moved Sara Grant behind him with a degree of force that surprised them both. He gave her a glance that told her to stay where she was and turned to face the oncoming gang—ten paces away now. As they approached, the crowd closed around them, like curtains on every side.

A numbness, like anesthesia, floated through Robb's body as he realized: He couldn't protect her. He stood wary, as ready as possible. Every nerve in his muscles acutely aware of the knives in their hands and the fact that not one man in the crowd was going to step up to help.

Then cries went up along the street—screams and the sound of scuffling. The crowd shifted, breaking the wall of faces into startled individuals. Slowly, starting from the back, men and women began to notice what was happening beyond them, and to run.

The Yellow Jackets hesitated. In the brief gaps of the growing stampede they could glimpse an unforgivable trespass: On the other end of the long road, men in blue uniforms were taking women away. Dragging them when they would not come. Hitting them with truncheons if they struggled. Constables of the Metropolitan Police Force, pulling these women from their homes.

Even Robb gasped at the sight of it.

The screaming, the fracas in the street: its pitch changed, the sound of a crowd boiling into a mob.

Drawn by the uproar, the inspectors and constables of Whitechapel Station emerged from the yard like a hive of shaken hornets. Fueled by frustration, already incensed by the latest murder and their own impotence, they waded into the street.

Bobbies from the murder scene formed a thin blue line, trying to round up the running crowd. The constables at the other end of the street—the ones rounding up women—had no idea of what they were moving toward. Two separate fronts of police herded this bawling, brawling swarm toward its inevitable center point without realizing—

—if they met—

"Oh, God," Robb said, fiercely but softly. He turned back to Sara, saying, "You'd better go."

But she had disappeared. Robb swore, a recital as futile as canned prayer, and made his way into the edge of the oncoming fray.

Sara
⋆ Hanbury Street ⋆ 8:35 AM

Sara hid behind a brick wall in the middle of the long street and watched as a full-scale riot came to life around her. To her left, at 29 Hanbury Street, a ragged row of blue-coated bobbies and constables struggled to keep a mob of men from overturning the coroner's wagon. She saw one of the inspectors go down, clubbed as he fell. Two others fired their pistols into the air, scattering the violence around them instantly. It reformed just as quickly, like running pools of mercury.

To her right, more constables were fighting to hold their own ragged flank. A Black Maria rocked as bodies bumped past. And still men in uniform were dragging women toward it. The women swore, kicked, and cried—as if this kind of thing had never happened, never could.

And Sara knew: It hadn't happened. Not once. Not ever.

Avery.

He'd changed things. Already.

"God *damn* him," Sara whispered.

In front of her, one young woman tried to run past a burly, sweating constable. He caught her easily, holding her hard by the arm. The girl began to wail and shook her head wretchedly.

That simple gesture hit Sara hard. This woman was not history. She was alive, a victim of changes to her time. *Avery's* changes.

"I *can't* go wiv you," the girl sobbed. "I idn't no whore. I got babes at home what needs me."

"Come on, girl, make it easy on yerself," the constable told her, and grabbed her around the waist. The girl screamed, kicked out at him, and the constable drew his truncheon, raising it in the air.

Out of the swarming crowd, Inspector Robb appeared and took the constable's arm before he could bring down the heavy wooden baton. "There's no need for force," he said firmly. His coat had been torn, his cravat come loose. Dust smudged the front of his shirt and his hair was rumpled, dipping into his eyes.

"Who'er you?" the constable asked, his face flushed.

"Inspector Robb," he said smartly. "And you are?"

The constable's face softened, but only a little. "Bosley, sir. But Inspector, she won't come lightly, like. An' you know what the *Times* said about cleanin' up the streets. Sir Jay, he's right appalled by prozzies right here on the streets in the middle of the day!"

He was still holding hard to the girl's arm, twisting it to keep her still.

"Prostitutes have always been on the streets in the middle of the day," Robb said. "Most likely they always will be. Let the poor thing go."

"We got our orders!"

"Whose orders?"

"Commissioner Warren hisself."

Robb swore under his breath. "Yes. All right. And you're carrying them out. But without violence."

"But Sir Jay—"

"—is not your superior," Robb finished for him sharply.

Bosley paused. "'E'll ear abaht this. Tell 'im mysef, Inspector. Don't think I bloody won't."

"Yes," Robb said, a fierce delight darkening his face. "You can write a letter to the editor."

Bosley still hadn't let go of the girl's arm. She had started to quiver with the effort of holding herself at such an awkward angle, her arm and neck cramping. People pushing to get around them jostled her to the point of tears. The two men, locked in their battle of wills, had not noticed.

Sara knew then she had to change this. Had to reinstate this woman's reality, if she could. She stepped out from her cover and asked, "Why're yer taking her? She already said she weren't no dolly."

Robb glanced up at her sharply, frowning. But Bosley looked Sara up and down—noting her curves, and the clear, healthy blush of her skin. "Careful, luv," Bosley said, panting with the exertion of holding the crying girl. "Don't wanna get caught up in this, do yer?"

Sara promptly adjusted her accent to mirror Robb's—cultured and precise, cuttingly cold. "Are you sure you're doing this to clear the streets? Or are you just handling young girls in the street for free?"

Bosley, dumbfounded, swore and let go of the girl. He looked at Sara hard. She could see he was confused and that he didn't like it: She spoke with the crisp authority of a lady, but she didn't look like a lady of any kind, nor was she in a place any lady would be.

Sara didn't miss the sharpening in Robb's eyes. He, too, had noticed the change in her. "Go on, Bosley," he said quietly. "I'll take care of this one. Sara, wasn't it?" Robb asked, watching Bosley slink heavily across the street.

He turned from Sara before she could answer and smiled at the still-sobbing girl, who stood now in front of him, cradling her left arm. She looked down when he addressed her, her manner suggesting a woman who had been in service once. "Go on," Robb told her quietly. "Before any of the others see you."

He pressed a shining coin into her hand—half a crown.

She looked at him, at the half crown in her palm, for a rabbit's heartbeat. Then she backed up, wide eyes fixed on his face, clutching the coin and her skirts as if he might change his mind, and turned and ran down the maze of vendors in the square.

Sara watched her go, watched until the shadows of the buildings swallowed her up. She realized then that Robb was not watching the girl. He was watching *her*. She turned, looked up to meet his eyes, which were a fine, honeyed hazel, very clear. Filled with keen interest and the gravity of his pursuit, the force of which he focused, now, on her.

"I'd best be going," Sara murmured, stepping back.

Robb looked out over the milling street, where shrieking, swearing women were hauled into the black wagon, and nodded. For every step back she took, he took a matching step forward. "I should say," he said. "And yet, you still have so many questions to answer."

"You know I won't answer anything," she told him, half-breathless. Remembering the Yellow Jackets, and how she had triggered them against this man. God, he might have been killed.

"To start with," Robb said (and she realized he was quietly livid), "what do you think you're playing at here? Don't you realize? You could have been killed, or worse. No woman of breeding should be out alone on any street, but *here*—" He looked down, clenching his jaw; a quick tic shivered there and was gone. He looked back up at her, eyes stern. "To whom do I speak about this?" he asked soberly. Then a frown puckered his forehead, and Sara knew, suddenly, that he didn't know how to place her. "Look," he said, more gently. "Are you down on your luck? Because if you are—"

"You'll do what?" she asked.

Again, that scald at his cheeks—more anger than embarrassment, this time. "Ladies have no defenses here. A woman born to these streets at least knows how to live here. I could help you get an honorable position."

He stood watching her, waiting for her answer—severity warring with concern in his eyes. He was tall for his time, a full handspan taller than she was, and she topped five-seven. Though she knew he could afford a finer coat, refinement defined him regardless of the clothes he wore. The fine lines of his body spoke of power and grace. But his face—there she saw strong lines that became almost beautiful at his eyes and mouth.

"It's kind of you," she said, "but I don't need your help."

"Very well, then." He withdrew a card from his pocket and gave it to her. Oddly, he clipped his heels together and bowed slightly, a movement as thoughtlessly graceful as a small ballet. "My card," he said. "If you should need any assistance, in the future—"

A shadow eclipsed them from the side of the nearby alleyway. Sara turned to see David Elliot coming up quietly beside them.

"The future is a damned long way from here," David said grimly.

Immediately on edge, Robb stepped in front of Sara, blocking the other man's approach. This time, she didn't stop him. Instead, she said, "David."

Robb looked back at her. "You *know* this man?"

"Damned right she knows me," David said dangerously.

"The one I didn't want to run into," Sara admitted.

A sharp displeasure clouded Robb's eyes, followed quickly by a dark, prickly curiosity. "We haven't met," he told David, rigidly formal. But Sara noticed that, even so, he did not introduce himself, nor offer his hand.

"No," David said, equally reserved. "Just got here myself."

"American?" Robb asked.

"Knocked around a few places."

"Ah."

They closed the space between with each word.

Sara put a firm hand between them. "It's all right, Inspector. I may have avoided the man's company, but you can trust his intentions where my honor is concerned."

Layers of antagonism sizzled in the space between the men until Robb seemed to realize that he had no claim on her, and this man just might. Confusion wavered his resolve. Robb stepped back, glancing at the ebbing riot around them.

"If you trust this man," he told her, "you should allow him to escort you home."

Sara barked a quick, bitter laugh. "He would enjoy that, I'm sure." She kept a wary watch on David, whose eyes glittered dangerously.

"I see," Robb said, looking between them. Hesitant, still clearly conflicted, he tipped his hat. Again, that slight bow. Imbued with elegance, it was a power in itself: that hint of another world. "Good day to you both, then," he said.

And then, just a few steps away, he turned and in spite of David's presence said to Sara, "Remember my card. London can be difficult. If you need anything, you will not hesitate, will you?"

A crash and the splinter of wood signaled the death of the coroner's van. It landed on its side, and a shout of victory went up on this side of the crowd.

"You should both get off the streets," Robb said. "Out of the slums would be better."

Then he left them, carefully making his way through the brawl towards a knot of inspectors taking back the overturned van, fighting fiercely with rough men who grabbed at the body inside.

David's hand closed on her arm.

"Don't—" Sara said.

"Let's get off the street," he said.

A drunken man pinwheeled by them, brushing her shoulder as he went down. David steered them to a nearby porch, above the conflict. Sara watched as Robb strode into the melee, shouting orders at the constables to use the upended coroner's van as cover. Then his broad shoulders disappeared behind the thick wall of the roiling crowd.

Sara
* Porch of Bell's Dry Goods,
Whitechapel * 11:42 AM

They stayed on the balcony as the wave of violence spread through the streets, overtook it, then ebbed like a tide going out to sea. It was almost noon, hot in the full sun.

But the real heat came from David. Eyes on the slowly dispersing crowd, he had not forgotten his orders to take her home. His deadly calm steamed beside her, the still buzz of a live wire. She expected, at any moment, that he would simply bundle her off to the Portal. In this melee, no one would even notice.

Instead, he turned to her and said, "Avery wasn't there last night. So where was he?"

Sara looked out over the street, where the violence was slowly petering out. Relieved, she said, "More important—what has he *done* here?"

"Tell me."

Sara swept her hand around her. "This didn't happen."

"It *is* happening."

"It is," she said. "But it *didn't*. Not anywhere in recorded history. It may be happening, Captain—but it wasn't supposed to."

"How can you be sure?"

"Bloody Sunday. Take that as a litmus. It happened almost a year ago. Only one man died and it's history. But this—this isn't recorded in the historical register, and it's bigger than Bloody Sunday. A lot of people died here today." A trickle of sweat beaded down Sara's neck and ran along the collarbone.

"And yet, it's not recorded. I've never heard of this happening."

In the street below, a bobby caught sight of them. His uniform was torn and covered with dust. He pointed his stick at them, wary and still furious over the violence of the day and the disruption it meant to his world. "Y'ere, now, what you doin' up there?" He shouted. "Get inside, like decent folk is."

David waved at the bobby, nodding. Then he took Sara by the elbow and carefully guided her through a maze of back stairs. His size and killing experience—an unseen shimmer of well-harnessed violence—ghosted them past patches of men still spoiling for a fight, winding through unknown territories back to her flat at Crossingham's door.

Robb
* Westminster Station * 4:33 PM

He burst through the door of Pershing's office, interrupting Pershing with an assistant commissioner—a man Robb knew well from his father's circle, General Ardus Brazelton. Robb stopped just through the door, flushed and disheveled, filthy with dust and blood, his clothing torn.

Both Pershing and Brazelton stared at him, amazed as much by his battered appearance as his sudden entry. They rose from their seats.

"Good God, Jonas, what's happened?" Brazelton asked.

Robb brushed aside the question, too angry to placate anyone. "Whitechapel?" he asked Brazelton, ignoring Pershing altogether. "Warren ordered a cleanup of prostitutes there?"

Brazelton frowned. "Not to my knowledge."

"Somebody did," Robb said. "They came just as Abberline was trying to clean up after this morning's murder—another prostitute, gutted like the last. The crowd there was already boiling when a full complement of bobbies began rounding up women at the other end of the street."

"Certainly something must be done about prostitution, Inspector Robb," Pershing began.

"In front of their homes?" Robb exploded. "With their husbands and children looking on? Not even stopping to discern between whores and honest women just coming home from the factories?" He tried to calm himself, and succeeded, precariously. "We come in on one end of the street to 'clean it up' while on the other end, one of their neighbors lies dead because we could do nothing to catch the madman who's killing them. And what, Mr. Pershing, do you think happened when those two fronts met?"

"My God," Brazelton breathed. "A riot."

Robb nodded. "Not unlike Bloody Sunday," he told them. "No doubt you'll read about it in the papers tomorrow morning."

"I'll speak to Warren," Brazelton said. "Do we need more men out there?"

"I've already sent them," Robb said, grim. "It's been contained. But dozens of the men from Whitechapel Station have been injured, including Abberline. Detective Sergeant Leach is dead. God knows how many others."

Brazelton looked sick. "Damned good thing you were there," he told Robb. Then he frowned. "You *are* assigned here at Westminster, aren't you?"

"Yes, but—"

"I've loaned Inspector Robb to Whitechapel," Pershing said smoothly, shooting a warning glance at Robb, his eyes bright as a crow's. "He has such excellent experience on the street. They can use every good man we have."

Brazelton looked doubtful. "If you feel you must, Pershing, though I doubt his father will thank you for it." Then he turned to Robb, to Pershing's bitter annoyance. "I'll speak to Warren myself. I can't imagine him being unwise enough to deploy a troop to the slums at all at a time like this, much less to arrest a few unfortunate women."

He nodded a quick good-bye to both Robb and Pershing. With his leaving, Pershing's office grew cold around the two remaining men, neither of whom looked at the other.

"Whitechapel?" Robb finally said, his voice dry and husked with the emotion of the day. Like high tide, it had run a fierce course through his blood; now it ran out again, leaving him depleted but oddly clean inside.

Pershing said nothing. Robb looked at him, at the bright hostility in the man's eyes, and Pershing said, "You can go there now."

"I'm being reassigned?" Robb asked. To his surprise, a surge of hope ran quickly through his blood.

Catching it, Pershing said, "No." Then, words clipped, he said, "Consider yourself on loan. For the duration."

Robb glanced around the darkly paneled room as if for the last time, feeling a weight slide away from him he had not even known he carried.

Sara
* Crossingham's Common Lodgings * 6:22 PM

Saturday evening, and nothing moved. Police patrols walked the empty streets. The cobbles echoed their footsteps heavily, a warning to those who heard them to stay inside.

David, watching at the window, asked, "So how much of today was your fault?"

Sara hesitated, then said, "I don't know. I engaged Inspector Robb in conversation and shouldn't have. He became suspicious. When he pressured me for answers, the crowd around us got ugly."

David stared at her, blue eyes stony. "You started a riot."

"That is not a given," she said, stung. "It would have taken more than my few minutes at the scene to catalyze such a distinct upheaval to the record. This would have happened whether I'd been there or not. It was Avery's influence. He's changed something here. He may not even be aware of it, of how his actions might have prompted a change—"

"Like your few minutes, you mean?"

She met the cold judgment in his eyes. "I didn't do this," she said.

"It wasn't Avery I saw there, smack in the middle of a riot that wasn't supposed to happen. It was you."

"Well, I *am* here to study history," she reminded him, seething.

"But not to *make* it."

"No, but as long as I'm here—David, you have no idea how important a study like that could be, to observe an event not as history but as a present, living reality."

"And the damage you do, 'observing' the way you did today? What about that?"

"Negligible," she snapped. "All I know about this morning is that no police force in England has ever conducted a mass roundup of prostitutes in the slums. Especially not at a time like this, with Jack the Ripper preying on those same women."

Slow words conveyed worlds of contempt: "Jack the Ripper started a riot?"

"In a way, yes," Sara said. She stood, fighting the agitation, the shiver of it just under her skin. "Captain Elliot, let me paint you a picture here, so you can be clear about what's happening. England is at a precarious place in history. Europe has been rocked by revolution. Riots like this one have toppled governments in countries that are already struggling."

She came to the window, looking through it to the empty streets. "Except in England," she said, "with its extraordinary cultural concepts of honor, and loyalty to the crown."

She turned to him, leveling her gaze with his. "But because of these murders—because all the powers of the government couldn't stop this one man—that loyalty broke down." She nodded toward the west, where Buck House stood but could not be seen from these streets. "From this point on, England will never again have a Queen with a capital *Q*. The monarchy that emerges from this will be purely small print: An icon to be treasured, even coddled, but never a power in the world again. If Avery has done anything to tilt that balance, England as we know it could be destroyed. And given British influence in world history, that one change could be a disaster to the timeline."

"These murders weakened the English government that much?" David asked, watching her.

"These murders nearly brought the whole thing down. If there'd been more than the official five they ended with, even just a few more, historians say the slums could have exploded. Revolution, civil war—who knows how bad it could have been."

He leaned back against the shabby wall. A slow, bitter smile quirked at his lips. "And you started a riot."

"How could *I* have changed anything?" she cried.

"Jesus, Sara—we're changing things just by being here. By renting this room when someone else might have had it. By bumping into someone, making him late for something that becomes important down the line."

"Chaos theory," she scorned. "You're an amateur, thinking of time like a river, as if you could throw a stone into the water and change its course immediately."

"That's the theory," David said.

"It's one theory. There are others."

"What's *your* theory?" David asked, quietly pointed.

"More like dominoes. Kick over a long string of dominoes and what happens? It starts at one end and then moves along the line toward the other end. In our case, Avery being here in 1888 is the first domino in the line. If he makes a change that kicks that domino over, that single change then has to ripple through every single *individual* domino *all* the way down the line until that ripple effect gets through its very long course to 2007."

"And that's different *how*?" David asked. "From the stone in the river that changes the flow of water as it hits?"

"The difference is, the stone impacts the flow of water immediately. The first domino impacts only the second domino, which then strikes only the third—on and on, down the line. Each domino has to act on the next. With a structure as complex as time, you're talking millions of little dominoes falling, and not all of them impact the main line. Some veer off and end in their own little events that aren't even connected to one another. So Avery could make a change here and it might take days or weeks or years for that to ripple through to our time. Which means we might be able to stop that change from getting any farther than this year, by figuring out what he's done and resetting the line."

"And do you know how fast the dominoes fall, Sara?" David asked. "Days or weeks or months isn't exactly precision mathematics. What exactly is the rate of change here?"

Reluctantly, she shook her head. "I don't know."

David closed his eyes briefly. He didn't move, but she could feel the tremor of it hit him, and the sour fear-sweat that blossomed as he took in the implications. He said, "So unless we can get ahead of the dominoes Avery has already kicked over, our future is screwed. And we don't even know how fast it will happen."

"At last you see the problem. That's why this isn't just about finding Avery anymore, David. It has to be about fixing whatever he's done. Until we do that, we can't even try to go through the Portal, because we won't know how the dominoes have fallen or how fast or—"

He walked toward her slowly, until he was close enough to touch without moving. "You can quit with the dominoes now, and maybe tell me why, if you're so damned sure of your theories, your friends would send us here knowing there'd be a damned good chance we'd never come back."

He didn't wait for an answer. Instead, he slammed the big leather duffle Bouley had given him onto the table and unlatched it with quick, efficient tugs. They both looked inside. Piles of bills threatened to overflow—pound notes. Thousands of notes in each bundle; hundreds of bundles in the bag.

"Je-*sus*," David hissed. "I knew it. Damn it. They don't expect us back."

Sara dug through the layers of money, finding fine cloth and shoes underneath—much better stuff than what they were wearing.

"Good planning," she said, insisting in the face of his doubt. "If we had to follow Avery outside the landing zone, we might need to follow him anywhere."

"They knew, Sara. *Knew*."

"Maybe so, but not because they were planning to leave us here. That would be ridiculous." She was dismissive, stubborn. Still, she rummaged through the duffle, picking up a thick leather wallet from on top of the banded bills.

Her fingers shook minutely when she saw it, the smallest shiver. She clutched the wallet hard, but made herself look inside. There, she found standard-issue birth certificates for the time. Letters of introduction on cream vellum written in the spidery tracery of a quill pen. Statements of citizenship.

David, standing over her, said quietly, "Denial is a nice place to visit, Sara, but they don't let you live there."

"Contingencies," she whispered. "Standard Operating Procedure—SOP. It means nothing."

She threw the leather purse back into the duffle.

A draft outside whined through the window. It prickled the skin on her arms, skittering her words—so soft, she barely heard them herself. "It all depends on Avery. On what he's done here. On what we can undo."

Minutes passed. She looked away, but knew he was still watching her—a heft of judgment like waiting stones. The silence was broken, finally, by the long intake of his breath: reserving action; resetting the game board to factor in new parameters.

She looked up to see him scanning their papers, reading, taking in their new identities. Seeing what he had to work with. Surprisingly, he began to laugh, a soft sloughing like dry leaves tossed along a breeze.

"Bastards," he said. "They thought of every damned thing we'd need." He showed her a marriage certificate, with her name, and his.

Sara bristled. "No. No way. *Not* a husband. I won't act the wife for anyone—not for you or anybody else."

"Not even to save the world?" he chided. Then noticed how tightly she held her arms against her breasts.

He tipped the corner of the certificate into the candle's flame. The paper caught, and he let it burn to within an inch of his fingers before he dropped it into the empty chamber pot.

"All right," he said. "How about a brother?"

CHAPTER 6

September 9, 1888

David
⋆ Ryder Poor House, London ⋆ 7:10 AM

But no matter how the rules of the game had been redrawn, his priority remained. He had to find Avery.

Stepping inside the third poorhouse he'd found, David blinked to see through murk, the flying dust and low light coming from a few lit candles.

They were already working. Kids no more than six picking flax, sorting wool. Men and women dismantling old clothes and resewing them into shabby new garments. One woman finished nursing an infant and passed the child to a matron, then went to work, sitting on a hard chair, with the others. She looked like she'd given birth just days ago and was still sore with it.

"May I help you?"

David turned. The man in front of him was short and thin, the hardness of the realities around him stamping the edges of his face, where compassion was buried deep but not quite forgotten.

"I'm looking for my uncle," David told him. Showed him a photo of Avery that Bouley had given him before coming, a color PR headshot modified to somber sepia matte with Avery in an ascot. "He hasn't come home, and we're all a bit worried."

"Not familiar, I'm afraid," the proprietor said, clearly noting David's frayed clothing and comparing its quality to that of the man in the photograph, who was so obviously rich.

"How many other poorhouses are there?" David asked. "He didn't have any money—at least, we don't think he did—when he disappeared."

The man grunted. "There are only two left in London. This

one and Haymarket House. Sir Jay has seen to that. Put the lid down smartly on Poorhouse Acts with that newspaper of his."

"Social reformer?" David asked.

"God. Or you'd think he was. He owns the news. But yes, a reformer of sorts. Though compassion like his does more damage than good. The poorhouses needed shutting down, yes, but not like this—"

"So where do the others go?" David asked. "When there's no room here?"

The man's eyes glittered with a bitter truth. "The streets, of course. Where they die, of exposure, disease, starvation." He raised his hand, swept it over the dim room. "But really, where else *would* they go?"

Robb
* Montcliffe Townhouse * 9:56 AM

"Jonas, when *are* you giving up this ridiculous police posting?" Matthew asked.

They were in the conservatory. Scattered players sat at various points on the chessboard. Indoors, the humid warmth of the deep-rooted trees was a fresh scent.

"I don't plan to give it up," Robb said, standing between Matthew, his father, and the board. Thinking that, perhaps, he should not have taken the day off. Ah, but he'd had a whole hour with William, just the two of them.

Now, William dozed in the sunlight beyond them. So frail. Could a grown man weigh so little and still live? William's face was a parchment mask; his hair, cropped unfashionably short, showed the sharp edges of his skull and the skin stretched too tight over it. His oldest brother. Heir to the family's fortunes. It was clear he would never live to inherit. And this was the greatest pain Robb knew.

"Do sit down," his father murmured. "You needn't hover."

Robb dragged a small garden chair up to the table, turned it around, and sat on it backward. His father glanced at Robb's inelegant stance once, quickly, then went back to his game.

"Having too much fun to leave yet?" Matthew asked idly. Robb's younger brother, Matthew was dressed for hunting and smelled of leather and grass. It was a good smell—familiar and warm.

Robb paused. "If you could call it that."

"What *do* you call it?" his father asked. "Chasing scoundrels in the streets. In the slums, I ask you. Even this horrific creature cutting women's throats."

"Really?" Matthew asked, turning to Robb and looking at him keenly.

Robb shrugged, chafing under the attention. "It's nothing," he said, hating himself even as he said it. To each woman, her life had been all she'd had.

"What do you mean, *nothing*?" his father protested. "It's all over the newspapers. Another woman murdered just two days ago and they have no—what do you call them? Clues? Jonas himself is working the case," he said to Matthew, nodding toward Jonas.

Robb said warily, "I've only just been assigned to Whitechapel. We're not even sure there's much of a case to be had. There are many murders in the slums. Some of the dead are women. I have investigated such deaths in my own precinct, but haven't seen any connection between them."

"It's in the newspapers," his father said, indignant—as if that made the facts more real than Robb's experience.

"You shouldn't believe everything you read in the newspapers," Robb said. "They often print whatever they want you to believe, regardless of the truth."

"Of course they do!" his father fumed. "But this new fellow, Sir Jay Osborne. He's rebuilding the entire system. Making the press credible. A gentleman, he is—"

"Is he?" Robb asked.

"That's true, you know," Matthew pointed out. "It's said he's a gentleman but nobody knows quite how."

"I'm not entirely sure myself," his father said, "but he's close to the royal family. Got to be at least a—well, I don't know, really. But a gentleman all the same. Makes it all right."

"Does it?" Robb asked. "He's everywhere, and it's all so sudden. I actually had a constable challenge my authority in the streets over him, the day of the riot. I keep hearing his name come up—"

"Man of the hour," his father murmured, unfazed.

"Another fascinating social climber," Matthew said, putting his father's queen in check. "But what about these murders? Now that's interesting."

"Women in the slums!" his father said. "Prostitutes. Haven't you heard? Six of them. Seven if you count the one reported by the *Westminster Local*. The disgrace of it—"

"But where's the mystery?" Matthew asked. "You'd think whores would get killed all the time."

"They do," Robb said slowly. "And I don't know why Sir Jay is making such an issue of it, especially in Whitechapel."

"Bound to be more, they say," his father said doggedly, driving home some dire point he'd picked up in the *Times*.

"Why do you think so?" Robb asked.

"Because," his father said, sweeping his hand above the board. "Sir Jay believes there will be. More murders, more embarrassment heaped on the government. Got to wonder how much more poor old Salisbury can take before he breaks." He leaned back, pinning Robb with his most pointed stare. "Really, Jonas, if you'd just read the newspapers instead of criticizing them—"

"Jonas is right, Father," Matthew said. "It's not as if prostitutes have never been murdered before. I'd wager the *Times* is blowing it entirely out of proportion—probably to sell more newspapers. Not much doff in good news, right, old boy?"

"But Sir Jay is a gentleman," his father insisted.

"Really, Father, so is Jonas," Matthew said, unimpressed. "And since I don't know this Jay fellow, I'd be more likely to believe in blood."

His father harrumphed, but looked to Robb nonetheless. "Do you really think so, Jonas?"

Robb detested having his father come around to his way of thinking only when Matthew insisted on it. But Sir Jay's theories were dangerous enough on the street. Robb didn't want his father parroting them through society as well.

"These are the slums," he said carefully. "Anyone could get his throat cut there."

"Don't I know it," Matthew said, suddenly grinning. "Been slumming there a few times myself. Always have to take care."

"These women *can't* take care," Robb said—the sting of it surprising. "They live there. Work there. They don't have a coach-and-four to take them home when they're done."

"Be an interesting woman that did," Matthew mused. Robb thought instantly of Sara Grant and was glad neither man noticed the immediate flush of warmth in his face. "Met a woman like that," Matthew said, "I wouldn't have to spend so much time with my fellows, now would I?"

He and his father laughed, and Robb's heart sank. He knew a private joke when he saw one. He had always known his brother's preferences, but saw for the first time why his parents' marriage had always been such a cold, forbidding place. And why his father would never force Matthew to marry or produce sons.

A tremor of fear shook Robb around the heart. The threat to them both, should society find out—

God, how lonely it had to be. Robb suddenly put a hand out to touch both of them, then stood and quietly left the room.

CHAPTER 7

September 12, 1888

David
* Crossingham's Common Lodgings * 6:22 PM

David traced the raised oval bump on his wrist, the shape of the transponder implanted under his skin. "What are these for?" he asked. He turned to Sara, holding up his wrist. "It's not like the folks back home can track us across time."

"No," Sara said, and smiled tiredly. She sat on the hard floor, her crossed legs cradling the PDA. Studying again.

How she could stand the stink of the place was beyond him. An open sewer at the back of the building emptied directly into the drinking water that fed the pipes in their flat. They'd learned fast to put the mucky liquid into a tub, to let it sit for several days while the sediments drifted to the bottom. Only then did they skim the fluid off the top and filter it in the purifiers. Even with ultraviolet treatment and activated carbon, he still didn't like to drink it.

He lowered his shirt cuff over his wrist again, covering the place where his transponder pulsed with its own slow heartbeat. "So what *does* it do? What does all of this do? How does it *work?*"

Sara raised an eyebrow. "Are you worried because you haven't found Avery yet?"

"The more you look, the more you see changes," David said quietly. "I've been over half this city, Sara. I haven't found him yet. So if I'm here, I want to know how things work."

She leaned against the bed, sighing. "Your transponder activates the Portal," she said. "It also tells the Portal where to take you. The Portal itself doesn't move. Once it comes to a given place in time, it remains there until we pull it out from the other side. To go home, we have to get back to where the Portal has landed. In our case, that's the courtyard."

"That will be true for Avery as well?" David asked.

She nodded. "When we find him, we'll have to get him there."

David sat at the table, stretching his legs. He'd covered forty miles in the last two days. "What's the rest?" he asked. "How do our transponders interact with the lab from here?"

"They don't. The transponders are programmed at the facility prior to launch. The interface for doing that is small but effective. It's the calculations that need the supercomputers. Those are complex. The rest," she said, "is simple."

"Millions of dominoes don't sound all that simple," he said, looking out the window—watching something outside. "Tell me what was supposed to happen with the Project, before Avery hijacked the Portal."

"What do you know?" she asked. Spreading her hands as if to say, *give me a starting point*. Didn't like talking about it, then.

"I know you were selected to go on the first launch," he told her. "I know Avery was not happy with that choice. He wanted to be first, so he made that happen. I know he didn't expect his launch to go balls-up because the lackey he got to push the button for him decided to go too. I know she died and he went somewhere. That's pretty much all I know." He tilted his head and shrugged. "I couldn't help but get the idea that what Avery had in mind for the Project was not in line with what you or your colleagues were planning. So tell me, Sara. What was your job going to be, on that first trip back in time?"

She considered him for long moment—surprised, no doubt, that he had seen so much in so short a time. Then she nodded, looking away from his eyes. "I was supposed to plant a buoy," she admitted. "Make a small change, something the scientists at the Project could track through history. Then come back. That's all."

"A small change," he said, and shook his head. "Jesus."

"Small changes couldn't possibly impact history," she said, immediately defensive. "There are too many variables involved between one point and the next for any one small change to leave a mark. David, we're not talking temporal disasters here. We're talking tiny ripples, like a small cluster of dominoes that's not connected to anything else."

"Dominoes again," he murmured. "And how do you decide what's connected?"

"I don't know. But you have to start somewhere—"

"Do you? Because I have to tell you, Sara, I don't see any point to this that justifies the risk."

"The point is to know what really happened in history," she said, angry now. "So we can learn from it. It's called science."

"People don't learn from history—they just repeat it. That's called human nature. And knowing what I do about the dumb things people do, letting guys like Avery anywhere near a power trip like the Portal is a bad idea."

Sara said nothing. Her face was tight; she was angry, he knew. But she couldn't argue the point.

"Why would he do that?" he asked. "Avery, I mean. Risk changing time to a point where he might knock over his own world at the other end, maybe annihilate the fact of his own existence in the process?"

Sara let out a long-held breath; to David, it sounded like a small white flag—surrender. And disgust. Not for him, but for Avery. "He never held to our primary goals for the Project. And no, he didn't believe our theory about time."

"Maybe he was right," David said. "At least about the theory. Nobel Prize–winning physicist, you have to wonder if he knows something you don't."

"Maybe," Sara said. "Or maybe an ego like his just can't imagine not existing."

"Anyone who's been on that ride through the Portal can imagine not existing," David said.

The weight of that experience settled between them, along with the silence of so many unknowns. "Then that's all the more reason to find him, isn't it?" Sara asked grimly.

CHAPTER 8

Sara
* Whitechapel * 7:42 PM

She wandered farther from their door at Crossingham's every day, observing the slums and its people. The level of industry surprised her. Two large soup kitchens fed whoever stood in line. Three orphanages sheltered more than a thousand children. One big stone edifice with a sign said OSBORNE CHARITY HOSPITAL, EST. 1887. She realized she knew the place. It should have been the London Royal Hospital.

At St. Katherine Docks, sailing ships were being built, barques and clippers. Stacks of new planks exhaled the breath of cut wood and paint, a fresh counternote to the fishy stink of the Thames running slowly just beyond the dockyard. And on Thomas More Street, along East Smithfield, dozens of new businesses sat along the sidewalks. The paint on their signage hadn't yet been chipped or worn by the elements: Wilson's Tannery, Fiddymont Ale Distributors, Shipmaster's Bank, Lyon's Rope and Hemp, Puckeridge Tea Packing Company.

When she inquired within, she found that each new place had been established between 1885 and 1888. But when she asked about the owners, she was told, at varying levels of color, to shut her mouth and move on.

"It wouldn't be a man named Avery, would it?" she asked at the tannery.

"Who?" the crone at the door asked. Clearly, she had never heard the name.

The Shipmaster's Bank had little to boast of as a financial center. The one-room office openly displayed stacks of money, and inside, rough men counted the bills and did the sorting. They looked up as she entered, surprised. Civility sat like a thin plastic film over their faces, masking an almost feral cunning underneath the skin.

The man in charge approached her. Like the others, his clothes were rough fare, and dark—something more like a burglar would wear than a businessman.

"Never heard of any Avery," he told her. He smiled slowly, openly appreciating her curves. "But yer wanter watch out, pretty thing like you. Askin' questions 'round yere." He shook his head. "It's a dangerous hobby."

"Dangerous?" Sara asked.

His brutal intelligence was home to a viciousness she'd never encountered: casual, as matter of fact as a viper's stare. "Might disappear, see? Girl who asked too many questions." He narrowed his eyes, the light in them predatory, almost playful, and traced a finger along her shoulder.

Sara smiled, took his hand almost tenderly. Then she twisted his middle finger back until he was breathless and halfway to his knees.

"Thanks," she said, meeting his surprise coolly. "I'll be sure to take your advice to heart."

The man stood when she let go, looking at her as if she'd pulled an outrageous magic trick. Amazingly, he and the other men in the place laughed.

"Good fer you, girl," the manager said. He nodded his dismissal, and Sara knew it was only the razor's edge of his amusement that kept him from killing her.

She left the Shipmaster's Bank without turning her back.

Later, she checked her PDA and found no record of any of these companies. Nor the Charity Hospital, or the foundries, the soup kitchens.

Twilight purpled the sky, a sheet of deepening indigo over the water lapping along the docks. Sara looked out over the new ships, listening to the saws working their way through lumber, and the sharp rap of hammers. The sun was nothing more than a memory on the horizon and still, they kept working.

"What are you doing here, Jon?" she whispered. And knew there was only one place she could go to find out, and it wasn't in the slums.

CHAPTER 9

September 14, 1888

Sara
* London Public Library * 10:02 AM

When she asked for newspapers, the librarian—a small man with round spectacles—almost dropped the books he held.

"Really, miss. Women are not permitted to read newspapers," he sputtered.

"Is it illegal?" Sara asked mildly.

"Of course not. One wouldn't think it would have to be. Women of quality simply know better. Of course, if there's a ladies' periodical you would like to see—"

"No," Sara said, "I would like you to bring me the *Times*, the *Post*, the *Observer*, the *Weekly Dispatch*, *Punch*, and the *Pall Mall Gazette* for September ninth, eighteen eighty-four."

"But, *why*?"

She took a long breath and told him, "I am making a study of social trending in London for a specific year. For that, nothing serves but the daily record of a newspaper."

"Social trending?" the librarian asked blankly.

"The progress of short- and long-term movement in a specific set of time-series data after other components have been accounted for," Sara said.

The little librarian peered at her keenly over his glasses. "Oh my dear girl," he said, aghast. "Are you ill?"

David
* Fordingham Asylum * 10:28 AM

"You've seen them all, sir. I'm afraid, if your uncle is not here or at the hospitals, he must certainly be deceased."

Even in the administrator's office, the screaming was a constant presence. Muffled by wood and carpet, it was an underlying note, like the persistent buzz of a mosquito.

"You must have records," David said. He met the man's irritated stare and did not blink.

The administrator sighed, eyes flicking over David's threadbare clothing. On great sufferance, he went to a bank of wooden filing cabinets and pulled the A's. Then he stood aside to show David just how impossible a task he was asking.

It was a deep drawer. Inside, hundreds of paper files stood at attention, each a representation of humanity lost in the dank halls of this place.

David waited.

After a long moment, the administrator frowned and began looking through the files, flipping through angrily. He stopped long enough to sigh and say, "This may take some time, sir."

Sara
⋆ London Public Library ⋆ 10:56 AM

In the reading room, Sara sat surrounded by piles of newspapers. The librarian's concession to propriety was, in typical Victorian fashion, to erase the sin by hiding it. He had bundled her into this tiny room before anyone could see her reading scandalously inappropriate materials.

"Really, miss," he fussed, "this is beyond acceptable. Ladies do not read newspapers."

"Just wait until you get the Internet," Sara murmured.

His eyes widened and Sara saw the hurt in them, not just offense but honest distress. She almost softened, almost smiled, and then realized: he actually thought she was mentally unbalanced.

"Go on," she whispered. "I'll be fine by myself."

David
⋆ St. Luke's Hospital ⋆ 11:56 AM

David waited outside the wardroom for the matron, a thin woman with a quiet but rigid dignity. The cold-stone decay around them was overlaid by the stinging scent of vinegar.

"Your uncle then, is he?" she asked, scowling. "If you don't mind me saying so, I don't recall anyone as tall as you coming through these wards. Bear any family resemblance?"

"He's a few inches shorter than I am, green eyes, dark hair. An inventor. We think his accident may have been electrical."

The matron's eyebrows rose. "I've not seen such wounds in all my time. But you may look, of course."

In the ward room, rows of narrow cots lined the sweating walls. Those who were conscious watched silently as he passed, their eyes overwhelmed by shock, pain dwarfing the souls within each ravaged body. With nothing to mitigate fevers or the agonies of postsurgical wounds, everything hurt—a touch of breeze on the skin, movement, even the impact of sound would explode through blood and muscle.

He saw no IVs, no tubes, no machines; no anesthetics or painkillers. Just gray sheets stained with drying blood, sweat, and waste.

This was the tenth hospital he'd come to. None of them bore any resemblance to any medical facility in his experience, not even makeshift field operations. Shocked, he thanked God and Lyn Bouley for the MED Kit. Knowing that if Avery had been injured in his entry and had come without a kit, there was little hope he had survived.

Still, David stopped at each bed, comparing wasted faces with his picture.

"You didn't find him, I see," the matron said. "Do you know how bad he might have been?"

"No, we've had no word. But he could have come here at any time—and may have lost his memory in the accident."

"Have you tried the morgue?" she asked gently.

David nodded. "At every hospital. Can you direct me here?"

Sara
* London Public Library * 12:02 PM

She began with September 10, 1884. Four years ago. Establishing a statistical baseline. All six papers were laid out on the table. Each gave a differing point of view on events, but they all told the same basic story. Gladstone was prime minister. Britain was expanding into Africa. The 1884 Reform Act had just become law, extending voting rights to males owning or renting property. And, to the outrage of the kingdom, the Australians had beaten the English at cricket, 2 to 3.

Sara opened her PDA. Inside its intelligence-bred memory chips, she had at her command every existing publication in the world, from the Middle Ages to the latest update of the Library of Congress. She said to the PDA, "Show the *Pall Mall Gazette*, September ninth, eighteen eighty-four."

The PDA shivered and within moments, she saw the *Gazette* appear in the air in front of her, a life-size representation of the actual paper, suspended as a hologram above the PDA's screen.

She read each article, comparing the actual copy, in this time, with the digital representation from her own.

They mirrored one another word for word.

Sara stood, went out to the reference desk. Inside the cool, vast space, more of the tables were taken as scholars engaged in study. Most of the women were gone. Sara glanced at the clock and realized it was tea time, prime social visiting hours for ladies. She passed the quiet readers as silently as she could. The rustle of her taffeta skirts on the floor made more noise than the hushed turning of pages, and the young men looked up, eyes widening as she went by.

At the desk, she told the librarian, "I'll need the editions for eighteen eighty-five, same date."

"Miss, this is folly. Please, go home."

At one of the desks, an older man noticed her presence at the reference desk. Saw the edition of *Punch* in her hand. He made an audible noise of disgust, collected his briefcase and strode righteously out of the library.

The librarian drew himself up, rigid with virtue. "You see? You are upsetting the patrons. Really, miss. I do not want to call in the authorities."

Sara leaned across the counter to murmur in his ear. He leaned close in return, accommodation an instinct. To the world around them, it would look innocent, even charming: a lady asking a favor; requesting an embarrassing item—a more liberal women's daily, perhaps.

Instead, Sara said softly, "Little man, you and I would both be a great deal happier if you would just do as I tell you. Now go get my papers."

David
* St. Luke's Hospital Morgue * 12:10 PM

The room was wet with dripping cold and stank of oil and human gases. David checked on every dead man in the chill room
but did not find Avery among them. He came out to find the matron waiting.

"Not there, then?" she asked, and sniffed, wiping her nose
with a damp handkerchief. "You seem a good man. I hate to suggest this, but have you tried the madhouses? The workhouses?
The local establishments for the destitute? A man who didn't
know himself could not survive long. If he's not in hospital, he
might have been taken to one of those."

But everywhere, the result was the same: no Avery. As if he
had never arrived. David thought it was possible, despite
Sara's certainty that Avery was here, and was working his influence. The disruption of Joan Reed jumping into the Portal
might have thrown the machine off so much that the man
might never have materialized on this end. And if that were
so, what was left of Jonathan Avery could now be spread so
thin across time and space that even ghosts had more temporal
mass.

"Jesus," David whispered.

Sara
* London Public Library * 1:46 PM

September 10, 1885. The Berlin Conference was still carving
up Africa for European consumption. The 1885 Redistribution
Act gave voting rights to male agricultural laborers. Robert
Gascoyne-Cecil, third Marquess of Salisbury, was prime minister and facing criticism in Parliament: Police reports indicated a
rise in organized crime in the East End. Conservatives saw no
need to address it. Liberals disagreed.

Again, she compared the papers, article by article. Counting
each article to make sure she hadn't skipped over anything:
Forty-two, forty-three—

She paused on forty-four. Rechecked the number on the digital version: Forty-three. But in the actual paper, *Punch*, there
were forty-four articles.

Sara searched, comparing each article again carefully, quickly.

And found, on the tenth page, a squib about the rise of gangs in the East End:

ORGANIZED GANGS
GOING THE GOVERNMENT ONE BETTER

MEET THE EAST END'S NEW PMS, GUV'NOR!

"IT IS A NEW FORM OF GOVERNMENT," raged *Punch*. "ELECTED NOT BY THE LORD OR BY PARLIAMENT, BUT BY THEIR PEERS. JOBS HAVE APPEARED OUT OF NOWHERE. NEIGHBORHOODS ARE SAFER. WHY? ASK THESE PRIME MINISTERS OF THE PAVEMENT IN THE MEANEST SLUMS OF LONDON. NO POWDERED WIGS HERE: THESE BLOKES WEAR YELLOW BURLAP JACKETS."

"Bingo," Sara whispered. She shut off the PDA and opened the door.

The librarian stood at its threshold already, five neat papers in his arms. He said nothing, just gave her the papers and shut the door.

She heard it as she turned, and dropped the papers, where they slid, whispering, to the floor: The click of the key being turned on the other side of the door, the tumblers of the lock engaging.

David
* General City Morgue * 1:48 PM

David bit back the bile at the base of his throat, coming out of his sixth morgue, where bodies were stored on top of ice blocks that melted incessantly in the heat of the day. The air was only relatively fresh outside. The afternoon sun cooked the middens where refuse was piled like small mountains on the street, heaps of offal from butchered animals and the day's chamber pots.

A wagon rumbled past him, wooden wheels grinding slowly over the stone road. In the cart bed, a body not yet consigned to ice put off odors that scorched his gut.

Without warning, his system rebelled. He ran to the nearby alley, knowing already, without a doubt, that the man in the cart was not Avery—not any more than the dozens of other dead men had been, their bodies cold and blue, resting on beds of relentlessly melting ice.

Sara
* London Public Library * 1:49 PM

"Open this door," she said, knowing he could hear her beyond the frosted glass insert.

"I cannot," the librarian said, voice quivering. "You are clearly unbalanced. A doctor has been summoned. Just sit quietly, miss, I beg you."

"Oh for heaven's sake—"

She looked around the small room. A number of books, not yet catalogued, were stacked on the windowsill. She took one in hand and rapped the corner of its binding hard against the door's glass insert. It exploded outward.

Ignoring the alarmed cries from the librarian and his patrons, Sara reached out, turned the key in its lock, and opened the door.

"I'll be leaving now," she said calmly, brushing glass off her dress.

The librarian blinked. "You—you won't come back, will you?"

The silence on the floor of the London Public Library, she was certain, had never been as profound as it was at this moment. Then, she heard the slap of hands meeting dryly. One man began to clap, applauding her exit. It was, she recognized, a drumming out. He was literally clapping her out of the library.

Others joined him. The force of the sound intensified.

Fury and alarm sizzled along the edges of Sara's nerves as the clapping men closed ranks behind her. They might as well have been shamans, shaking totem rattles at her back: furiously reasserting their dominance with a faith and a righteousness that would surely make her vanish.

Head high, cheeks hot, Sara sailed out of the library on that wave of vehement applause.

Sara
* Crossingham's Common Lodgings * 11:52 PM

In the murky dark of their room, Sara lay on the wooden cot, chafed by the hay-stuffed mattress and the cotton chemise. She was still seething; adrenaline was a sea that had overflowed its boundaries and moved heavily, still, in her blood.

As it began to recede, sound (real sound, not just that echoing memory) became tinny, as if she were hearing through a seashell. She heard the men rambling along the streets outside, the harsh laughter of the whores and the hopeless wail of hungry infants who knew they would not be fed. And listened for David, who slept across the threshold, on top of a few thin blankets.

He was there, but silent.

Sara burrowed deeper into the straw mattress. Remembering the intimations of violence at the library: The faces of outraged male virtue, and a forcefulness behind their authority that stopped just short of laying hands on her.

When she finally dozed, that buzz of violence followed her. She woke up thinking, *That dark stain in front of the Portal. It had been Joan.*

Opening her eyes to murky darkness, the glow of the gas lamps outside. Knowing Avery had been planning his illegal jump for months.

Jonathan Avery.

The man who had said, in a moment of unguarded exuberance, "What's the point of *going* if we're not going to *change* things?"

That man. *Here.*

The air in the flat at Crossingham's didn't move. Sweat gathered at her throat and ran a lazy path down to her breasts. "David?" she whispered.

"Yeah?"

"We have to find him."

Silence. Men roaring in the streets with laughter, the night crickets of the East End. Then David said, "You really think he made it here?"

Sara frowned. Sat up. "I know he did. The changes here—"

"Not everything that happened here is recorded on your PDA. Isn't that the point of time travel? To find out what we're missing?"

"Not changes like this," she whispered. Then, "You think his launch was aborted?"

"I don't know. I couldn't find him. Not hide nor hair."

He rose from the floor, a crouch and stretch. Then he moved

stealthily to the window. "But I think somebody may have found me."

"Who?" Sara asked. She rose from the bed.

David nodded out the window. Slowly, Sara approached it, peering past the thin, watery glass. In the streets, three men with yellow jackets sat at various points around the building. One whittled a block of wood with his big knife. Another read a shabby newspaper. And one simply waited, leaning against a post and watching the street.

"Tomorrow," David said, "first thing, we put that money in the bank."

CHAPTER 10

September 17, 1888

David
* Bank of London * 9:33 AM

The interior of the bank was cool, air whispering along the marbled floors. David approached a desk. The man behind it smiled, then saw the scuffed and dusty duffle David carried. His smile disappeared. "May I help you, sir?" he asked, clearly inferring that he could not.

"I'd like to open an account," David said. He was dressed in the middling finery Bouley had sent with him, but still—he couldn't disguise the battered ugliness of the duffle he held.

The man behind the desk all but laughed outright. "Really, sir, I have no idea who you are—"

"He's all right, Pinder."

David looked around. "Inspector Robb," he noted.

"Mr. Robb, the Honourable," Pinder corrected. The smile he had for Robb was warm and large. "You know this gentleman?"

"Yes," Robb said, smiling wryly. "I can vouch for him."

"Excellent," Pinder told David. "How much would you like to deposit into the account?"

"All of it." David hoisted the heavy duffle onto the desk and unlatched it. Pinder stared, open-mouthed. The light of beautiful avarice kindled in his eyes and he smiled hugely. "Keep the bag," David said.

"Oh, yes sir."

Sara
✦ Outside the Bank of London ✦ 9:45 AM

The news cart across the street bore the stamp of the Central News Agency, selling both the *Times* and a garish broadside called *The Comix*. Sara wandered over to the stall, picked up the *Comix* and scanned it idly. According to its masthead, it had been established in 1887. It was a graphic novel, of sorts. It had few printed words, but illustrations portraying the news were splashed over the thin paper in lurid reds and black. On the cover, Commissioner Warren was drawn with blood on his hands, and Prime Minister Salisbury as little more than a sinister shadow. The police, depicted obliquely behind them, were doing nothing: just standing, two men with their hands behind their backs.

At the core of her belly, foreboding dropped another cold degree.

Seeing her, the newsagent snarled, "Get along now, luv. Yer puttin' me custom off."

"How much for both?" Sara asked.

He looked at her, narrowing his eyes. "Why ye want the *Times*? Gettin' the papers for the boot boy, are ye?"

"No, I'm gettin' 'em for meself," Sara snapped. "And ye'll sell 'em to me, too, yer know what's good fer yer."

"Jaysus, woman. A penny apiece."

Osborne
✦ Bank of London ✦ 9:56 AM

A grandly arching window offered a clear view of the street just off the private antechamber, a room reserved for the bank's most treasured customers. One man sat waiting in a comfortable chair at this window.

He was not typically a patient man, but the view outside the window was worth watching: A young woman stood on the street below him. So beautiful; unusual. So very alive.

In her hands she held one of his newspapers. The *Times*, of all things. And—was she was actually reading the pages?

Sara * 10:06 AM

She flipped the *Comix* into the trash and unfolded the *Times*. And stopped suddenly. Breathless.

Opening the *Times* was like opening a door onto the twenty-first century. The layout was modern. The type was large, with breathable gutter spaces between the columns. No process color, but black-and-white photographs were strategically positioned across the page.

She could have bought this paper at the Starbucks two blocks down from her townhouse.

The banner-style headline flew like a flag across the front page:

RIPPER STRIKES AGAIN

How many more will it take?

How they had gotten the mortuary photograph of Annie Chapman's slack face, Sara didn't like to think.

Robb
* Bank of London * 10:22 AM

After introducing Sara's American to Pinder, Robb retreated to a quiet vantage point in the lobby and watched the American take piles of pound notes from the leather bag.

Where in heaven's name had it all come from? A child of the rich, Robb knew no one carried their fortunes in a bag. And even if the man were the cowboy Robb suspected he was, he would have had to have robbed a thousand banks—

Sara * 10:35 AM

Stepping back into the shadows of the bank, she took the quilted reticule out of her pocket. Leaving the PDA concealed within it, she held it close to her mouth and began, softly, to speak. "Cross-check newspaper listing, *The Comix*, spelled with an *x*."

The PDA hummed within its calico bed. On its brilliant blue screen, the words *No listing* appeared.

"Cross-check publisher, the *Times*."

The name appeared on the screen: George Harworth.

Sara frowned. Thumbed through the *Times* to the second page, where the masthead was listed. Went straight to the top to see who was listed as the publisher.

"Shut down," Sara whispered.

The PDA went silent, its bright screen vanishing.

Osborne * 10:36 AM

He watched her come out of the shadows, moving toward the stairs. He almost laughed. It was preposterous. They wouldn't let her in. She approached the doorman, who kindly refused her entrance, of course. She insisted, pointing to the bank's lobby. The doorman shook his head, becoming irritated as she persisted.

Gods, the look of frustration on her face. Delightful. Stirring in him—what?—

"Sir Jay?"

He turned reluctantly.

The manager smiled, handing over a sealed sheaf of papers. He noticed the altercation at the door outside and said, frowning, "Good heavens, whatever is Henry doing with that unfortunate woman?"

Sir Jay Osborne smiled. "Don't worry Henry over it. I'll take care of that one."

The bank manager, though dubious, knew better than to interfere in the affairs of the rich. "If you say so, sir," he said, and left the room.

"I do say so," Osborne murmured. "When and where and how."

David * 10:44 AM

David signed whatever Pinder gave him. When Pinder handed him nothing more, he assumed he was done and stood up to leave when he suddenly sighted his quarry.

A tremor raced through his muscles once and then was silenced to a still and predatory readiness as David tracked his target, heartbeat pinging like sonar in his temples.

Across the lobby, nearing the entrance, was Jonathan Avery.

Robb * 10:46 AM

The American stood. Something had caught his eye and suddenly, he was making his way across the lobby. Moving quickly. Moving like nothing Robb had ever seen in a man. Robb had seen a panther in Nairobi move like that once, hunting its prey to the ground, and the prey not even aware of the cat's most deadly intentions.

Carefully, as silently as he could, Robb followed.

David * 10:46 AM

Quickly David crossed the lobby, keeping Avery in sight.

The doorman inside the heavy double doors, inlaid with their mosaic of glass, smiled at Avery and opened the door for him. David caught a quick glimpse of Sara outside and saw her turn away from the bank, standing on the sidewalk just as Avery skipped lightly down the stairs.

David quickened his pace, reaching for the door. If Avery recognized her—

But Avery only brushed past Sara, his hand passing within inches of her hair, raised as if to touch and then redirecting smoothly to adjust his silk hat.

The outer door closed behind him and just as David moved to open it, a hand clutched his arm. David brushed it off: Sara was out there; so was Avery. He was not going to stop for anyone.

Then the hand closed around his arm more firmly, swinging him around.

Robb * 10:47 AM

Robb took a half step back when the American snapped his head about to identify what hindered him. The intensity in his face was a sudden scald. Definitely the panther, disrupted from his hunt. But hunting whom?

"Care to have luncheon with me?" Robb asked quietly.

The American glanced through the window of the closed front doors. Whatever he had tracked, it was no longer in sight—but wasn't far. "I don't really have the time," he said.

"Of course you have the time. And the club is always a better alternative than gaol."

"Am I being arrested?"

"Not at all. For now, I just have a few friendly questions."

"Save them for later."

Robb smiled, letting it be a wolfish, thoughtful thing. "I'd like to keep it unofficial, for the lady's sake, but if you insist that I take you in—" The American hesitated; frustration steamed from his skin. "I trust my club would suit you better?" Robb murmured.

Whatever quarry had so riveted him was too far gone to pursue. Now, Robb had the American's full attention—and wasn't sure he liked it. The notice the man focused on Robb was a harsh thing, almost feral. He was a true predator, giving up one chase for another.

"No, the club will do fine," the American said. Quiet, and yet he stood with a savage sort of readiness, a dangerous stillness that spoke of the knowledge of violence and its uses.

"Good," Robb murmured. He walked down the steps to the front sidewalk, not looking back to see if the American followed.

Sara * 10:48 AM

Across the street, Sara hugged the *Times* and waited for David to come out of the bank. She saw him with Robb, watched them approach the corner of the bank. Where they were going—why they were going there together—she had no idea.

"Turn around, David," she whispered.

Robb
* Huntingdon Street Men's Club * 10:56 AM

The American sat down heavily. All pretense to attention, to that startling readiness, was gone. He slouched in his chair like a sullen child, bored and fractious in his good suit. "What do you want, Robb?" he asked.

Infuriated by that rudeness, Robb snapped, "Your name. Identification, if you have any."

The American just looked at him. "You might have asked for my name *before* you vouched for me," he pointed out, and drew a flat purse out of his pocket. He proffered a letter of introduction from Archduke Wilhelm in Switzerland—a distant cousin of the queen. The name on his papers was David Elliot Grant.

Robb sat back. "And your, ah. The woman. Your—"

"Sister."

God help him, he couldn't help it. Relief glimmered in his gut, but did not mitigate his anger. "Sister?" he asked grimly. "Am I to see her dressed like the queen any time soon?"

A flicker of humor passed over the other man's face. He had seen the relief in Robb's eyes and now a terrible sort of amusement came into his own. And with it, oddly, a small lessening of the tension between them. "Why are you following me? You didn't just happen to be at the bank."

"No," Robb admitted. "I saw you coming out of the Gentlemen's Boarding House. I couldn't help but notice the change in your, ah, apparel." He leaned closer—quiet, intense. "What are the two of you doing?"

Grant raised his eyebrows, and Robb caught the whiff of hesitation, as if he were gauging what he could and could not say. "We're looking for someone," David finally said. "An uncle of ours went missing last week. We understand he was heading for the slums just before he disappeared. No offense, but we thought it would be better to look for him ourselves."

"The matter is delicate, then. Give me his name. I'll help you search, and I'll keep it quiet."

It was as much challenge as offer, but David only nodded. He took a photograph out of his pocket and slid it over to Robb.

"His name is Jonathan Avery. He's forty-six but looks younger. Tall—six feet, two inches. Wiry build. Dark hair, green eyes."

Robb studied the face, noting the large eyes and the formidable intelligence behind them. "And you thought you saw him in the bank?"

"Possibly."

"And yet you didn't call out to him," Robb pointed out.

David hesitated. "He may not be himself. May not know himself."

"An amnesiac? Poor devil." Robb handed the photograph back to David. "Are you so sure he won't be aware of himself?"

"No, not entirely. We know he was involved in an accident. What that accident did to him, we don't know. But it may have been traumatic."

"He didn't look traumatized," Robb murmured.

"No, he didn't," David admitted. "And that may not have been him. I only caught a glance."

"Sorry, old boy. What kind of accident was it?"

Again, that hesitation. "He was experimenting with electricity. We couldn't get a clear description of what had happened. The woman with him at the time survived the accident but died shortly after, and wasn't able to tell us much."

"Electricity?" Robb raised his eyebrows. "You come from the oddest people."

"You have no idea," David said.

Robb watched the irony twist in the other man's eyes, and asked, "Why the slums?"

David shrugged. "Something the woman said, before she died. They were both getting ready to leave for London when it happened. He was heading to Whitechapel. We don't know why."

Robb nodded slowly. "I understand the need to look for yourself. But for your sister to be there, that's something else. That is entirely unacceptable. Especially with this killer in the slums—"

He paused as Mason brought port in two bell glasses. Studied the street outside, taking in the sounds muffled beyond the glass, and the almost-silent ticking of the grandfather clock behind them. Then he drank the sweet, golden liquid in his glass quickly, all of it, making a face as it burned in his throat.

"Your sister," he said, hoarse. "Get her out of there, before she gets hurt." He winced against the fumes of liquor in his words and stared at David with implacable eyes. "This 'Jack' won't distinguish between her and any other woman living in the slums. And neither of you knows what might come looking for you while you're looking for your uncle."

David
* Outside the Bank of London * 11:42 AM

He saw her near the newsagent's cart, leaning against the hard concrete of a balustrade. "Got any news for me, miss?"

Sara whirled and with wide, wild eyes, blurted, "David! I know where to find Avery."

"So do I," he told her.

She stared up at him, stunned. "How?"

"Saw him. While I was depositing the money. He came out before I did. I would have followed him, but your friend Robb insisted that I explain a few things."

"Avery. He was that close?"

"He brushed right by you. If you didn't see him, how did you know where to find him?"

She handed him the morning issue of the *Times*, open at the masthead. And there he was, Jonathan Avery—face stiff over a starched white collar, staring at the camera as if he possessed the biggest secret in the world, and it was a darkly funny joke.

"It's him," Sara said. "He's here. He's been here long enough to acquire the *Times*, three years ago. Three *years*."

David threw the paper into the trash. "*Shit*. No wonder we couldn't find the bastard. He wasn't sick *or* injured. He's just damned rich and fragging time."

The afternoon sun spread like gunmetal on the street. Sara looked away, blinded by that iron sheen. Then she lifted her head and met his eyes. "We could be looking at a catastrophic time shift."

Around them, men strode along the sidewalks, faces heavily occupied by vitally individual thoughts. Groups of women sat in rolling carriages, chatting. Street vendors hawked papers, kidney pies, and peppermint tea. Their world was not a stage; their fears and anxieties were not minor fictions. All of them, rich or poor, were by themselves a world within a world.

"Shit," David whispered.

Sara
* Dartmore Court * 10:28 PM

"You think this thing is still here?" David asked.

The courtyard was wide, a dark sea of uneven cobbles littered with empty barrels and old wagonry. Mud gritted under their shoes and the harsh circle of the lantern in her hand threw juddering shadows along the bumpy floor, crazing the dim illumination of the veiled moon above them.

"It's here," Sara murmured. "You just have to keep going."

Her voice, so close in the darkness, filled the illusion of zero space and still seemed somehow small.

Osborne
* Element Alley * 10:28 PM

They were easy to follow, she and the man. They stood out in a way he could not define, even to himself: the way they walked, how they held themselves. All the way from the bank, he had watched them.

Then they came to the courtyard. He knew the place—locus of his nightmares. But the woman: She was a dream of beauty in this place (which was filth, a stain on the earth), and she was so close—

Sara * 10:32 PM

She touched the wall on the side of the courtyard. The brick was rough under her fingers. "It's here," she murmured. "Just a few more steps."

Behind her, a sudden, piercing stream of light flooded the cobbles, a tunnel of clarity in the murky dark. Sara looked back. David held a slimline flashlight by his ear. He took the lantern from her hand and set it on the ground.

"I don't see it," he said.

She touched his wrist. "Doesn't it hurt?"

He looked down, at his wrist and then at her. It *did* hurt—an itchy ache in the muscle surrounding the implanted transponder.

"Turn off the light," she said.

He did, and darkness closed in. The courtyard's void seemed to grow as their eyes adjusted to the dark, the sense of hollow space around them.

"There," she whispered.

And it *was* there: the faintest shimmer in the murk, a brief mirage of faint blue froth. Its consistency intensified as each of them took hesitant steps forward. The closer they came, the more solid it grew until they stood just an arm's span from the brilliantly glowing shape of the Portal.

He handed her an envelope, and she read what he had written:

> *Poss. have found Avery. If/then: he's been here 3 yrs +*
> *prominent position. We can re-acquire, but must neutral-*
> *ize impact on this end.*

Her heart rolled with the word *neutralize*. She thought a moment, then added, *Give us time*.

"I don't know if this will work," she told him. "It's not a conduit for communication."

"It's a gate. It's made for things to go through it," he said. Without warning, he pulled the hideous knife from his boot and dug the tip of it into his wrist. Blood welled up, dripping from his wrist, but he dug in and tweezed, then pulled the knife back to show her his transponder, lying on the flat of the shaft. The size of a thin cough drop, its green eye blinked lazily on the mirrorlike steel.

"Jesus, you *are* a jarhead," she said, grimacing.

"I like to think of myself as multifaceted."

Sara paused. "What if it doesn't come back? If the message goes through but they don't send your transponder back?"

"They'd send it back," David said. "They don't want us here any longer than we have to be."

"But what if they don't?"

"Then *you'll* send it to me when *you* get back. Could we stop talking about this and just do it?"

"That's your lifeline home," she told him, nodding grimly at the gleaming transponder. "Without it, you'd be stuck here—"

"I know," he said. "But we don't really have a choice."

She saw the determination in his face, harsh in the pale blue light of the Portal. That he would kill or die for the mission, she knew. But that he would risk internment in time—this seemed beyond death, a risk no soldier had been asked to make before this.

In the white-knuckle strength with which he held the transponder, she knew he was aware of that potential sacrifice and would still do it; knew he was right about the need to do it. She dropped the clean transponder into the envelope, sealed it, and gave it to him.

He'd brought his MED Kit. He set it on an upturned barrel and opened the lid. It was stocked, she saw, for everything short of major surgery and viral epidemic. Scalpels glittered in a foam bed, smaller than their full-sized cousins but just as sharp.

"Let me do that," she said, brisk and broaching no refusal. She broke open a vial of anesthetic and squirted the liquid into the wound. David hissed.

"I didn't need that," he said.

"I did," she told him. She broke open a suture kit, prodding the ends of the cut where he had dug out the transponder. She stapled the edges together quickly, then bandaged and neatly taped it.

When she finished, he didn't thank her—just stood and tossed the envelope into the Portal's light.

Sara closed her eyes against the inevitable flash.

There wasn't one. Nothing. No percussive detonation of light. No winking out quietly. It simply sat there: a placid shimmer in the darkness, almost angelic.

The letter sat on the cobbles. It had simply dropped to the ground, as though the energy of the Portal weren't even there.

It hadn't moved a century. Hadn't, in fact, moved an inch.

Osborne * 10:51 PM

Going together to that place: There was only one reason a man went there with a woman. The woman *he* wanted. Explosive tracery of heat in his loins. Jealous and fierce—so fiery, it made him sick.

The man was bigger, yes, but: He had his own gun, his own knife. He had surprise—

He had the shadows.

Sara * 10:53 PM

"I saw you put the transponder in the envelope," David said, coming up behind her. "Why didn't it work?"

Sara put her hand through the Portal and picked up the envelope. She opened it, slid the transponder into his palm. "He has a key," she said, grim and shivering in the serene blue light. "He's locked us out."

"He can *do* that?"

The Portal's light glowed in Sara's skirts. She faded back against the wall. As she moved away, the glimmer grew fainter—the Portal diminishing to an outline, flickering like St. Elmo's fire. When she stepped near it, it thrummed and shimmied and was fully blue again.

"It still works," she said. "The Portal as a conduit remains active, triggered by the proximity to our transponders. If it were broken, it wouldn't show up at all."

"He knew we'd come after him," David guessed.

"Planned for it," she said, nodding. "And if he planned for this, what else has he planned?"

"He wouldn't have to plan anything else," David said, apprehension raw on his face. "This is enough. This finishes us before we've even started."

He shook his transponder in his hand, then pulled his arm back to toss it into the shadows of the courtyard.

Sara grabbed him, her face severe. "Don't. David, don't ever throw this transponder away. Never be without it, not ever."

He opened his hand, showing her the slowly blinking lozenge. "What good is it now?" he asked.

She took the transponder from his palm and tucked it firmly into the small, tight pocket at the top of his vest. "That's hope," she said. "The Portal isn't gone. It's just locked. And you can bet the man who locked it wouldn't come here without a key."

"Jesus," David whispered. "I hate this place—"

"I know," she said, and touched his arm. "But we're not going to be here forever."

Then, she heard it—the sound of grit, the scrape of a shoe.

Sara turned. Saw a figure at the courtyard's entrance, a sketch of a man—tall, with the fluttering outline of a cape. He didn't move, but stared, instead, at the pale, hazy shape of the Portal.

"Someone—" she said.

But David was already moving, pulling her away from the delicate shimmer of the Portal and into the shadows. Once again, the iridescent blue danced out of sight, a specter shape lingering only briefly on the eye before it winked and went out.

The man at the entry stared deep, and Sara wondered if Avery ever wandered the slums, feeling the call of the Portal in his own skin as he passed this narrow place.

The moon sailed into the clouds and the silhouette at the entry disappeared.

Osborne • 10:57 PM

In the dark, he slid to the back of the courtyard. Here, in this place of his birth, the only origins of himself he knew, she conjured phantoms: that pale ghost, sketching threat and bright intention.

And then it went out, a slow and mocking wink. Taunting him. Frustration, fury: *To be so close*. To reach out and touch.

Indecision whined through him, a hungry dog. He wanted the woman. This woman, no other. But that sapphire ghost, with its restless, hungry mouth. That light echoed in his dreams.

Fear eclipsed his desire. Whimpering with it, he clung to the shadows in the courtyard and ran for the only way out.

Sara * 11:01 PM

She shivered next to David, listening for the sound of footsteps. His breath of warning was so soft, she barely heard it:

"He's here," David breathed.

Without the Portal's light, the courtyard was hollow and seemed vast.

David closed his hand over her arm, warning her: be still. The ache in her wrist was maddening, insistent. The moonlight guttered out—eclipsed by a shape larger than its dim light, or a cape, fluttering by.

Osborne * 11:02 PM

The gods betrayed him—that demon light exploding into brilliance as he passed.

Sara * 11:02 PM

A blocky shadow ran for the arched entryway. It passed the place where the Portal slept and the night went nova. Sudden light screamed his presence: Jonathan Avery. Morphing from shadow to man, cape billowing as he dashed, sobbing, for the entry.

"Jon, stop!" Sara cried.

David caught him, twisted him into a writhing bundle. Avery was not trained to any form of combat, but he was panicked, wild: berserker eyes, vicious snapping teeth, tearing the bandage from David's wrist—

David swore, pushed Avery away from the wound. Avery went for him again. David kicked and hit home, his foot landing hard in Avery's chest. Avery staggered, tripped.

And fell into the Portal.

One scream and he was gone.

That agonizing cry echoed off the walls. It faded to nothing but darkness, a dank evening murk hovering around them.

Sara took in one breath, two. And then, shaking, whispered, "Oh God. My dear God."

Sara
* Ten Bells Pub, Whitechapel * 11:52 PM

"Where do you think he is?" she asked.

Shock was settling in, the tea in her hands cold and bitter. They sat in a corner of the Ten Bells. At the blue-tiled entry hall, half a dozen women stood, working up the courage to venture out onto the streets.

David turned the thick ale mug in front of him in circles, neat quarters like the stations of a clock. The mug itself was empty. "Closed conduit," he said, "going nowhere."

"No," she insisted. "He would have gone back. Standard protocol. The transponders are all set to go back. Unless you program them differently, it's an automatic coding."

David stopped turning the mug. "Then why are you asking?"

"I guess," she said, shivering, "because *back* may not be where we left it."

He looked up from the mug, his eyes hard. She saw in them that echo of light: explosive, percussive light, and Avery screaming. "Doesn't make much difference where he went," he told her. "Our job still stands. We find out what he's changed, and make it right."

He leaned close. The blue of his eyes had leached to something bleak, and an underlying darkness that was fear.

"But this just became a one-way trip for you and me. Because wherever Avery went, he took the key to the Portal with him."

CHAPTER 11

Robb
* Prussian Café* 10:20 AM

"Uncle Leopold," he said, standing as the dapper old man approached.

Robb had often asked the fates why he hadn't been born into this man's large family, a robust brood of cousins who traveled often, married happily, and always had small children tucked cozily in the nooks of their rambling country homes. Robb embraced him, burying his heart once again in the soft comforts of Leo's gray wool coat and the sinewy shoulder underneath.

"Good to see you again, Jonas," the old man said. He sat next to Robb, at ease under the iron bluster of the sky. "You're looking well. Tell me—do you feel as good as you look?"

Robb laughed. His uncle caught all the undertones in his face; always had. "Difficult case," he admitted.

"The Whitechapel murders?" his uncle said shrewdly. "Don't look so surprised. What kind of advisor would I be if I didn't keep up with the gossip? Nasty thing, those killings. Give you nightmares, I don't doubt. And your father?" he asked, switching gears with a typical lack of boundaries. "Has he been pressuring you to hoist the family flag of late?"

Robb smiled. Thought of Sara Grant—that brief meeting, the echoes of characters on her face: Like ripples over the surface of a pond, the deeper parts unknown. A mystery. The color of her eyes, the sudden, unexpected expression of his soul. Knowing that what had sprung up between them should have been unseemly, and yet wasn't. It sat in his blood as if it had always been there—constant and inevitable and only looking for its own recognition. He had met her once, but had wanted her—had looked for her—his entire life.

"Ah—is she pretty?" Leo asked.

Robb despised the scald of heat on his face. "No," he said neatly. "She is not pretty. She is glorious."

"And proper? Of good family, of course?"

When Robb hesitated, his uncle frowned. "Much as I'd like you to be in love with the woman you marry, an improper woman is a burden to any man—especially the heir to an earl. And you will have to assume that role some day, my boy. When the time comes, you will need a woman at your side who can see you through it."

The sadness in his uncle's face kept the anger, the frustration of his situation at bay. The specter of a title being thrust upon him left him breathless as the trap of it closed in. He wanted none of it—neither William's inevitable death or being a lord; wanted only the graceful simplicity of his own life. And knew, with a bitterness that surprised him, that neither God nor reality gave a damn about what he wanted.

"I wouldn't say she was improper, uncle," he said slowly. "Not scandalous so much as . . . well, different. Unusual. No—extraordinary."

"You don't know her well, do you?" his uncle asked, his eyes shrewd but not without sympathy.

"Know her? I've met her once. And why I keep thinking of her, *missing* her— It doesn't make sense."

"It never does," Leo said gently, smiling his pleasure. He laid his hand over Robb's. "Her Majesty will be happy to hear of it. And now she won't be so inclined to find a bride for you."

Robb started. "She'd do that?"

"Been known to," Leo mused, his hooded eyes ancient with all they'd seen. "She likes to see everyone as happily ensconced in matrimony as she was herself. Doesn't like to think that lightning doesn't strike for everyone. Now if I could just keep the prince out of trouble—that would be something. Scandal fits that boy like a hand-sewn glove. He's as stupid as he is lazy."

"Uncle!"

"Well it's true. Gotten himself involved with this Jay Osborne. Badgered his mother into giving the man a knighthood. Now he's agitating to get him a spot in Parliament. On the Liberal side, of all things. Honestly. Can you imagine it? A newspaperman in Parliament?"

Robb listened carefully, then said, "That riot in Whitechapel. I was there."

"Good God, Jonas," Leo said, shaken.

"The thing is, one of the bobbies there seemed to think Osborne's editorial opinion was more important to him than orders from Commissioner Warren."

His uncle nodded. "A powerful man, Sir Jay Osborne. Made himself an icon. Voice of the people. And he has so many voices, everyone thinks he's talking to them. Which gives him as much influence over lords as he has in the slums."

"Is he dangerous?" Robb asked.

"Oh, all powerful men are dangerous, my boy," his uncle said, and smiled. But Robb saw the troubled inward-turning of his thoughts.

"Do you think this Osborne is using the prince?" he asked.

"Who *isn't* using the prince?" Leo pointed out, incensed again. "All he requires of any man is entertainment, and there are too many happy to provide it. They all have a purpose—from politics to trade, and there goes Prince Albert, oblivious and not giving a damn, as long as he's having a good time."

Robb listened to the sadness that crept into his uncle's words and felt a portion of the infinite weight of responsibility the old man bore every day, as an advisor to the queen.

"Been sick, you see," his uncle was saying. "His health is failing. Not as strong as his mother—never was. And now there's this damned newspaperman, pulling his strings. God knows what he has on the boy to make him dance the way he does." Leo stared out over the striations of green planted along the street; Robb didn't think his uncle even saw the trees. "Whatever it is," Leo murmured, "it's enough. A man to watch, Osborne is. A man to watch closely indeed."

CHAPTER 12

September 19, 1888

Sara
* Dartmore Court * 9:13 PM

Sara stood in front of the Portal, its shivering energy an archetype of want and need: the doorway home. She touched it. The veils of current parted for her, but did not take her in. Whatever key Osborne had possessed, only it could unlock the dampeners. And Osborne was no longer with them.

Sara moved away from the glow of the Portal and taught herself to breathe again in slow, desperate steps. Closed her eyes and leaned against the clammy bricks, pulling in the fetid air.

"You okay, luv?"

Sara opened her eyes. She hadn't even heard the girl come in. Shaken, she said, "Yeh, fine. Needed a minute."

The girl quirked a smile, sat down on a barrel, and lit up a smoke. Sara thought, absurdly, *It will be decades before a woman can do that safely in public.*

"Know whatcha mean," the girl said. "Name's Lottie. Yer new here, aincha?"

Sara sat next to her. Shook her head at the offered cigarette. "Yeh. This place—" she said, and shivered.

Lottie read her easily, her own face stamped with hard-won wisdoms. "Nothin' like it, Whitechapel. Whole world the toffs know nothin' abaht. But tha's the good news, luv. If they don't know, they can't stop us."

Sara stilled. "Stop us?"

The girl laughed. "From livin'. Workin'. Have'n a bit of our own." She fell silent, brooding. "Dyin' too, I suppose. Even the Jackets ain't bin able ta stop that."

"Those men with yellow jackets," Sara said. "Who are they?"

"Law and gub'ment round yere. Do a good job, fer the most part. Got more jobs now than ever, see? Got in-dus-try. Not nearly so many men now what can't feed their kiddies. Run shelters, too—even the horspital fer them as need it."

"But they can't stop the Ripper?"

The girl guffawed, a bitter, shrewd burst of humor. "*G'on.* Women bin dyin' yere longer than anyone knowed or cared abaht. More'n the cops could even guess. Jack's just a boogeyman." She stood, crushed the butt of her smoke under her shoe. "You shouldn't be yere by yerself, place like this. Bin plenty'a bodies found right yere. Strangled, mostly. Beaten, raped. Men get mean when the drink's on 'em."

Sara looked around the courtyard. "How many women?"

Lottie shrugged. "Yere? I dunno. Least eight, I heard, this year."

"The police—"

"They don't know none of it. Weren't for The Jay sayin' it in the *Comix*, nobody'd a'knowed at all."

"All those deaths? They're reported in the *Comix*?"

Lottie cocked her head. The feathers on her cap shivered, too ragged to catch the breeze. "Good point. Not even 'e tells it straight. Lots abaht the Ripper. Jack this, Jack that. But nothin' abaht anyfink else. Wonder why." She stood, shook out her skirts, primped her hair.

"Who's The Jay?" Sara asked.

Lottie laughed. "Gawd, if yer don't know that, I indt gonna be the one ter tell yer. Jesus, *Who's The Jay?*" she repeated, and shook her head, sardonic. "Come on, ducks. Yer too pretty ter be found dead yere. Get back ta' that fine man yer got in yer flat. Stick w' that one, yer'll be safe enough."

Sara turned, noting the shrewd light in Lottie's eyes, the ironic smile. "You know where I live?"

Lottie chuffed. "These days, deary, a girl's gotta know everyfink."

CHAPTER 13

September 20, 1888

David
* Crossingham's Common Lodgings * 10:47 PM

"You did what?" Sara asked.

"Found out where Osborne lived," he told her. "Paid off his servants. Chaos reigns: Osborne is missing and now a bunch of servants are gone, too. The majordomo is crapping kitties and ready to take anyone. I arranged to interview for the job."

"You have no idea how to be a servant."

"I don't need to know. I just need a chance to look around his house before they realize he's not coming home and close the place down. Don't worry, they won't see me. They never do. I'm trained to it, Sara. If there are clues to who and what Avery has been in this time, most will be there."

"Why go now? They won't talk to you this late at night."

"To watch the house. Reconnoiter. Know their routines before I go in. Will you be okay here, by yourself?"

Sara nodded. "As long as I don't go near the London Public Library or the St. Katherine Docks, I seem to be fine," she said. Then, more serious, "I'll nose around here. There's a big discrepancy between what the police or the papers know and what seems to be going on down here. I'll see what people will tell me."

He nodded. Threw her a bag of money, a thick bundle of coins with a solid feel in her hands. "Keep in touch," he said.

Jack
* Midgling Alley * 10:52 PM

The girl looked down at the coin he had given her. It shone in her palm, a bright circle of gold. Too much, they both knew it.

She was lovely. So young still, fresh from the country: a milkmaid's peach skin and wide blue eyes. Was he her first?

Slowly she pulled up her skirts, not looking at him.

He helped, running his hands along her thighs, as she lifted the thin cotton higher. Oh, she *was* new at this: She still wore her linen. An experienced whore wore nothing under her skirts.

He undid the drawstring slowly, widening the waist until the thin cotton fluttered to the ground, puddling around her ankles with a sigh. Her skin gleamed in the murky light, mother-of-pearl, shivered with the dimpling of goose bumps.

"Cold?" he asked softly.

She clutched the gold coin. Tears now, flowing faster with each lace he undid at her bodice.

"There's more where that came from," he told her, freeing her breasts: lush as new apples; pale worlds within his hands. "You could come with me."

"I can't," she stammered. "Please, stop. I can't do this."

His hand stuttered, cold against the sweet curve of one breast. "Why can't you?" he asked. An undertone of steel crept into the words, silvery and hushed.

She saw in his eyes what her refusal would cost. Her face crumpled, smooth cheeks distorting to a sob. Like wadding up a beautiful picture.

"I thought as much," he whispered.

He brought out the knife without even thinking to strangle her first, or surprise her from behind. Seeing the sudden flash and gleam of it over his head, the girl began to scream.

David
* Park Street, by Midgling Alley * 11:04 PM

David felt it before he heard it: the sudden intake of breath, tension in the throat. Fear, sudden horror. Then the scream, so close he whirled without thinking and slipped into the darkness of the alley to his right.

He kept to the walls, feeling his way quickly. The scream, cut off, ground to guttural choking, a desperate fight for air. Just up ahead, a man held a woman against the wall by the throat—a rich bastard with a top hat and cane.

David stiffened his right hand to a scythe and spiked it hard at the man's wrist. Fabric tore. The man wheezed and dropped back. David heard a faint *ting* of metal on the cobbles, and the bastard fled, leaving David with the impression of strength, and madness, and no clear view of his face.

David let him go, watched until he reached the mouth of the alley and ran out into the street. Listened as the swift steps faded. The he turned to the girl, asking, "Are you all right?"

She held the edges of her bodice together with both hands. Nodded, but couldn't look him in the eyes. The shame on her face burned the air between them. David opened his bag and took out a wad of cash. He held them out to her and her eyes went wide.

"I don't want anything for it," he said bluntly.

He didn't blame her for not believing. She was a beautiful girl, not yet used to degradation. Her own small cotton purse lay on the ground. David stuffed the cash into it and placed it back onto the cold cobbles of the alley floor.

"It's enough for a new start. For something better," he said. "You're not cut out for this."

He stepped away, leaning against the far wall.

She watched him for a dozen heartbeats, then slowly slid down her side of the wall until she reached the purse. Snatched it up, wary, as if she expected him to pounce. But he kept to his side of the alley, unmoving, and his eyes did not judge the shame in her.

"Thanks," she said, her voice husky. It hurt her to talk, hurt to breathe, he could tell. He nodded and she sidled away, looked at him once and then sprinted from the entrance with surprising grace and speed, leaving her cotton linens puddled in the alley behind her.

David bent to shoulder his bag. He saw a small bit of gold glimmering on the alley floor, and picked it up.

A cuff link. Oblong. Artfully crude, faintly Etruscan, the gold mellowed to an ancient burnish. The object in the center, pressed into it like a wax seal, was ridged around the edges—etched with the indelible image of an arched gateway. That image resonated, in a wry sort of way, with the Portal.

David put the cufflink in his pocket: a talisman, speaking hope—even though he knew, with all the bitter veracity of experience, there was none.

CHAPTER 14

September 21, 1888

David
* Osborne House * 8:32 AM

He faced Osborne's majordomo stiffly at attention. The major-domo assessed David as he would an animal, walking around him twice. And then, amazingly, he smiled with sheer predatory joy.

"Get George," he told a small girl nearby. She jumped to do it. "Aren't you a fine specimen," the majordomo whispered.

David held his eyes on a midpoint to nowhere, his body still, a taut line of muscle and intensity that belied all humanity while the majordomo quickly inspected him for familiarity or insubordination or even intelligence behind his uniformly regimented stance.

"Very nice," the majordomo said.

The door opened behind David. He heard a surprised whistle and turned to see a young man, eyes wide, brows comically raised. They could have been twins. The youth, George, broke out in a splendid grin. "Jaysus, will you look at this? It's me double, come out o' the faery hills to haunt me."

"That's enough," the majordomo said. George snapped to attention next to David. The majordomo put stiff caps on both their heads. Once again, he took their measure, his smile broadening. Seeing that they had the same broad shoulders, that their hats were almost level, and their eyes were a kindred shade of blue. That each had dark hair and bronzed skin—the same Black Irish good looks.

"Very nice," the majordomo said. "You can start today, both of you. Coachmen. George, congratulations on the promotion. Eddie will take your place as boot boy. You may inform him. Show our new man the ropes, would you?"

Outside, in the clean air, David said to George, "What was all that about?"

George laughed, a lilt like music in his voice. "Toffs," he said. "Always like a matched set o' coachmen. Almost as good as a fine pair o' horses. They like brothers, if they can find 'em. But you and me: look at us, boyo. We're a cut above all that. Practically twins."

"Yeah, practically," David said, noting the formidable intelligence behind the mirth in the young man's face.

Nearing the stables, a clatter on the cobbles scattered the quiet of the morning. George pulled David off the drive and into the grass just in time. A black carriage drove by, the wind of its passing swaying the bushes. David watched as it turned in the driveway and stopped, rocking like a small galleon on its high wheels.

"Boss must be home," George said. The neutrality in his voice gave David an instant portrait of Osborne as a master.

He didn't want to tell George how short-lived his promotion would be; that Osborne wouldn't be coming home.

The driver of the carriage jumped down off his perch and opened the gilded door, unfolding a built-in set of metal steps.

Into the sweet morning light. Out of the dark mouth of the carriage interior. He stepped down the metal stairs, and for that startled moment, David forgot to breathe.

Dr. Jonathan Avery, aka Sir Jay Osborne.

Cape over his arm. Bareheaded, hair rumpled. Sour-faced and frowning. Eyes vicious, a perfect storm behind them. He stalked into the house without a word.

"Holy shit," David breathed.

"Been out for days," George agreed. "Probably slumming. Dumb bastard. Looks like he's been through hell, don't he?"

CHAPTER 15

~~·~~

September 22, 1888

~~·~~

Sara
* Crossingham's Common Lodgings * 9:22 AM

Avery—*alive!*

She wore a wool shawl around her shoulders and still shivered, intermittent upheavals that gusted the core of her for long seconds. The letter in her hand, from David, quivered each time the shaking claimed her.

The air in the one-room flat was chill, rain drilling its dull tattoo on the street, on the roof over her head. But it wasn't the inclement weather outside that made her so cold. It was the knowledge of what Avery had done. That he had planned this thing so thoroughly. He'd thought to program his transponder to return him here, instead of home.

And that's what made the shivers come, starting at her gut and spreading out to shake her shoulders. Wondering—

What else had he thought of?

CHAPTER 16

September 23, 1888

～✕✦✕～

David
* Montcliffe Townhouse * 10:42 AM

David jumped down from the back of the carriage and opened the side door. His employer, Sir Jay Osborne, stepped out without giving him a glance and seemed not a bit worse for wear for having tumbled through the Portal six nights ago.

A riding party was coming in—horses and the sharp smell of leather. Osborne, smiling, asked, "Good riding, my lord?"

The man at the head of the party laughed, jerked his thumb behind him. "Not a decent conversation between us. Pitiful. Join us next time, will you, Osborne?"

"Gladly, my lord," Sir Jay said. He glanced at the other men in the party. "And these are your sons?"

"Two of them—Matthew, Jonas."

The men on horseback behind their father each nodded to Osborne. David noticed that one of them looked closely at Sir Jay, and he damned himself for ever having shown the photo of Avery.

Jonas Robb. Inspector. His focus was intent on Osborne: thinking, remembering. Eyes widening.

Robb
* Montcliffe Townhouse * 10:56 AM

"You're an inspector?" Osborne asked him. "How fascinating. The people you must meet."

Robb nodded gravely, thinking of the photograph David had shown him. "I do meet a very odd few."

"Really? Who are your latest?"

Robb smiled crookedly. "Just lately? A brother and sister of means, living in Whitechapel."

"*Living* there?" Osborne asked, scandalized but also delighted with the story.

Robb nodded. "Amazing, isn't it? Told me they were looking for their uncle, who had apparently gone missing." He watched Sir Jay carefully. "No one you'd know?"

"Good God no," Osborne said, laughing.

"Chap had a terrible accident—experiment involving electricity, it seems. May not even know himself anymore."

Osborne raised an eyebrow and straightened in his chair. Behind the eyes, Robb caught a stutter, as if some inner lantern had blinked its outrage once and then winked out, extinguished by the force of its own fury.

Osborne, smiling, seemed entirely unaware of it. He leaned forward. "Actually, I was sure that one of my reporters had mentioned meeting you—a Mr. Bulling. He wrote a story about a death in Westminster. You tried to talk him out of it. Perhaps it's just me, but still—there's something about the police dictating the direction of the news that's so disturbing."

Ah. Bulling. "That was ages ago," Robb murmured.

"Shame on you, Jonas," Matthew said mildly, lounging with the dogs by the fire. "Interfering with the news."

Sir Jay smiled. "A trifling matter to most people, I know. But I can be a bit possessive of these things, you see."

"A woman's death?" Robb asked softly. "How could anyone possess such a thing?"

Osborne veiled his eyes. "I meant the news, of course."

Robb leaned forward. "My uncle," he said, "advises the queen. Tells me you're a man to watch."

"How kind of him," Osborne said, uncertain.

"So, in fact, does a bobby I met on the street during the Whitechapel riot. Seems to think your opinions are just somewhere north of the word of God."

Osborne laughed. "Not so persuasive as that, surely. We do have a presence among the lower classes," he admitted. "A flagship paper for that audience, mostly illustrated. Keeps them abreast of current events."

"Seems effective, then," Robb murmured.

Osborne shook his head. "All too easy," he said, deprecating, "to influence the poor."

"Is it?" Robb asked, watching keenly.

Osborne's buoyancy stuttered under Robb's scrutiny. Lord Montcliffe rose from his chair, clapping Osborne on the back. "Don't let him gull you, Sir Jay," he said. "Not every son rises to his father's expectations. Good God, look what he does for a living."

Robb * 11:20 AM

Robb stood under the loggia between the kitchen and the stables, still smarting, angry that his father's cuts could still go so deep—that he would let them.

Across the courtyard, Osborne's coachmen lounged outside the stables, talking. They could have been twins, the men almost as well matched as the glossy black horses decked in their traces. Osborne would stay for dinner, Robb was sure. And was just as sure that he himself would not.

"Parker," he called. "Get my mount ready, would you?"

"Leaving so soon, sir?" Parker asked.

"Afraid I must," he told the man, who had taught him to ride without saddle and reins when he was six years old.

Parker nodded, shouted orders to the stable boys. In the courtyard, Osborne's driver was climbing atop his box. "Where is Sir Jay off to?" Robb asked.

Parker paused in his arrangements. "Appointment with Lady Hamblin. Wealthy widow," he said, waggling eyebrows. "Taking your father with him, I hear."

"Ah, scraping an introduction," Robb said, nodding. He watched as Osborne's coachmen readied the horses, then jumped gracefully onto the back of the carriage. The driver snapped the whip just above the horses' backs and the carriage heaved into sudden motion.

On the way out of the courtyard, one of the coachmen turned and looked back at him. And he recognized—

It was David Grant.

Robb
* Lady Hamblin's Stables * 11:48 AM

At Lady Hamblin's, Robb parked his mount outside the stables himself. He brushed off offers of service and found David

Grant in the courtyard, sitting with a slightly younger man. Grant did not seem surprised to see him. The other man stood, but Grant did not.

"Can I help you, sir?"

"Your name?" Robb asked.

"George, sir. George O'Connessey."

George glanced back at David, who still lounged at the wall. That glance could have seared meat, and Robb read it easily: *What are you doing? Get on your feet!*

But David only smiled.

"Found your uncle, then, have you?" Robb asked acidly. "Plan to get him help in his delicate condition? Take him home soon?" He took a step closer to David. "What are you really doing here?"

David shrugged. "Working," he said, and pushed away from the wall. In the coachman's uniform, the impression of animal grace was just that much stronger.

"Who *are* you?" Robb asked quietly.

Just as level, David said, "No one you need to worry about."

"As long as I don't get in your way?"

David inclined his head, and Robb chuffed a bitter laugh.

Stiff beside David, George's eyes were wide and wary. Robb hated seeing that look. "It's all right, George," he said. "I'm not angry with you. But *you*," he said, and pointed at David, "You, I'm going to watch."

David
* Lady Hamblin's Stables * 12:10 PM

"You're not gonna queer me chances on this job, are ye, bucko?" George's eyes were dark, too intelligent to be flinty but hard with concern.

"No, George. I promise. I won't queer it for you."

"Shake on it," George said.

David gave him his hand. Frowning, he asked, "What did you tell him your name was?"

"O'Connessey," George said. "George Conor O'Connessey."

Dazed, David shook on George's hand, the dry strength of it unreal against his own palm. Worlds meeting worlds.

George O'Connessey. A face on a cracked black-and-white

picture, bleary and smudged. Old stories. A shadow who had died nearly seventy years before David's own birth.

His great-great-grandfather.

David had just shaken hands with him.

CHAPTER 17

❧❀❧
September 25, 1888
❧❀❧

Sara
* Central News Agency Morgue * 4:10 PM

It was a big room, much bigger than she'd expected. Inside, she found vast rows of cabinet shelves, burnished oak and cherry. Each one was labeled with the name of the paper inside. *Punch. Westminster Weekly. The Gazette. The Times. The Post. Sunday Times. Birkshire News. Birmingham Post. Bucks Herald. The Police Gazette. Daily Mirror. The Daily Telegraph. The Evening Mail. The Guardian. London Daily. London Observer. Manchester Times. The Observer.*

Her PDA listed fifty thousand newspapers and periodicals for England, 1800–1900. Most were small, serving local or specialty audiences. But the majors—they were all here. *Here*, in the morgue of the Central News Agency.

Sara looked at the masthead on each title's most recent publication. The names of the editors were all different, the offices scattered all over London. But the listing for publisher was always the same: The Central News Agency, owned by Sir Jay Osborne.

He had acquired all the major media sources of the time. Every one.

"What is he *doing*?"

In this vast vault of a room, her voice echoed the dread of her question, but returned to her, mocking, without an answer.

CHAPTER 18

~~❦~~

September 27, 1888

~~❦~~

Robb
* Whitechapel Station * 11:52 AM

Robb stood at the outer edges of a huddle of inspectors and detectives and listened as Abberline read the letter, dispassionately noting mistakes in spelling as he went:

"*'Dear Boss, I keep on hearing the police have caught me but they wont* (no apostrophe there) *fix me just yet. I have laughed when the* (not 'they,' you'll note) *look so clever and talk about being on the right track. That joke about Leather Apron gave me real fits. I am down on whores and I shant* (no apostrophe, again) *quit ripping them till I do get buckled. Grand work the last job was. I gave the lady no time to squeal. How can they catch me now.* (A period, you see—not a question at all.) *I love my work and want to start again. You will soon hear of me with my funny little games.'*" Abberline grimaced, loath to read the rest. "*'I saved some of the proper red stuff in a ginger beer bottle over the last job to write with but it went thick like glue and I cant* (no apostrophe) *use it. Red ink is fit enough I hope ha, ha. The next job I do I shall clip the ladys* (one lady, no possessive) *ears off and send to the police officers just for jolly, wouldn't you.* (Doesn't seem a question, does it?) *Keep this letter back till I do a bit more work, then give it out straight. My knife's so nice and sharp I want to get to work right away if I get a chance. Good luck.'*

"He signs it, '*yours truly, Jack the Ripper*,' but he can't quite shut up just yet. He goes on to say, '*Dont* (no apostrophe) *mind me giving the trade name. PS, Wasn't* (with an apostrophe, this time—he does know how to use them) *good enough to post this before I got all the red ink off my hands, curse it. No luck yet. They say I'm a doctor now. Ha ha.'"*

"A hoax?" Robb asked.

Abberline smiled. "What makes you think so?"

Robb shrugged. "Because he sent it to us, I suppose. Why not just send this to the press? They would certainly publish it, and that would give him the notoriety such a man might want."

"Throw us off," Abberline said, and nodded. "Keep us busy looking in all the wrong directions. Could be the killer, or it could just be some idiot with nothing better to do and no closer claim to fame than this kind of interference."

"Tha's wicked," Pauly Johns said, indignant. They all looked at the younger man for a long silent moment.

Abberline nodded. "Yes, it is. Which is why we're not going to breathe a word of it to anyone. If it is this bugger, I'll not give him the satisfaction of crowing his deeds to the public."

"And if it isn't him?" Thicke asked.

"Then it's a sick bastard taking advantage," Abberline said. "We keep it to ourselves, regardless." He took the letter back and folded it up, slid it safely into a drawer in his desk.

CHAPTER 19

September 28, 1888

Sara
* Osborne House * 9:52 AM

She kept a low profile at the back steps until David stepped out of the stables and drew her into the shadows of Osborne's big black carriage.

"So he came back," David said. "How did that happen?"

"Round-trip settings back to the facility are standard, but not mandatory. He reprogrammed his chip to suspend him in stasis until it was safe to return here. Long enough, no one waiting at the Portal would suspect. Days, maybe."

"Days. Jesus. No wonder he looked like hell."

"But he has the Portal key. Has it with him, somewhere. If it's here—"

"I'm already looking in the house. If it's there, I'll find it. But that's only half the problem, Sara. We still have no idea what he's done here."

"I do, maybe. I don't have any context for this, but it scares me."

David looked around the courtyard, knowing Harris, the majordomo, would be watching for him. "Go on."

"Avery, as Osborne, has bought up all the major press vehicles in London. He's created a monopoly. I'd bet nobody is even aware that he controls the news as thoroughly as he does. Editorial is always under a different name. The offices are in different buildings. But if you read the fine print, you realize— he owns everything."

"So Osborne needs to control the press to accomplish whatever he's doing here."

Sara nodded. "It ties together, I'm sure. But I'm just as sure the slums are part of it. There are so many new companies— companies not listed in my PDA. Some are legitimate and should be registered in public recorded, but they're not. Others are fronts. I don't expect them to be recorded, but the dates they came into being are all centered on the point when Osborne started buying up newspapers. They'd be perfect for laundering money. Then there are the Yellow Jackets. They're no ordinary gang. They're organized, part of the industry that's so new to the place. They're damned close to supplanting the government on the street. Like a lot of things in London, they didn't exist four years ago. And they're connected with one powerful leader. I don't have proof, but I'm sure that man is Osborne."

"Osborne's running the slums *and* influencing the establishment?" David swore softly. "Two trains, each heading toward the other, both driven by the same man."

Sara nodded. "A man who can plan when and where they collide."

"And you're right in the middle of it—in the slums, where Osborne still has a presence. He runs into you there, he has the advantage, Sara."

She hesitated, and took a step away from Osborne's carriage. Its mahogany sides were almost black, hints of red hidden in the wood. "You think he would? Find me there?"

David looked at the big black carriage. "When he goes out in this thing, he stays out all night. Won't take anyone but his dog-boy, Farley, and I don't think Farley would say anything to anyone about what Osborne does when he's in it. I've only been here a week, and so far, he's been out in it twice. So yes, now that you've brought it up, I think it's a possibility."

"He'll be killing again. Tomorrow night," Sara murmured. "The Ripper, I mean."

"Jesus," David said. He glanced between her and the imposing red brick house. "Don't do it, Sara. This is not the time or place to study history. Lock the doors. Stay inside."

Sara said nothing. She stared at the red glints in Osborne's carriage, thinking, *If this isn't the time or place, what is?*

He touched her chin, holding her focus with unwavering eyes: grim with the knowledge of violent death, starkened in its context to her. "You watch your back," he said. "I don't want to read your name on Jack's victims list when I'm in high school a hundred years from now."

Bulling
* Offices of the Central News Agency * 3:52 PM

A fine sheen of sweat broke out on Bulling's chest, just under the sternum. "You asked for me, sir?" he murmured, standing at attention in front of Osborne's glossy desk.

Osborne looked up and smiled, but an undercurrent seethed under the pleasantry on his face, a murderous, but almost casual, agitation. Bulling had never seen it before, not even during one of the Boss's famous rages.

"Ah, Mr. Bulling," Osborne said. "Met your inspector last Sunday. Charming fellow. Interesting family. Interesting work. Meets the most interesting people." The skull under his skin, in the gleaming lamplight, burned like a death mask. He blinked. "You still have the postcard?"

Bulling cringed. "Yes. To send October first, sir, as you ordered."

"Ah, but will the rozzers publish it this time, do you think? They did nothing with the last one. Imagine, not sharing what they know with the press." Osborne leaned back in his chair. "And did you make any promises?"

"Yes, sir—about the ears, as you said."

The smile on Osborne's face stretched wide and hot. Bulling looked away from it. "Anything else?" Osborne asked softly.

Bulling nodded, staring down at the plush carpet, the vibrant crimson and turquoise strands woven in Turkey by hand. For his life, Bulling could not look at that smile again. "Yes," he whispered. "I gave them the name again, sir."

Dry laughter from the other side of the desk. Bulling shivered. "Yes, that's right," Osborne murmured. "All good killers must have a name. Makes better theater, knowing what to call our nightmares. And did you use the blood?"

"No, sir," Bulling croaked, stomach rolling. "Couldn't. It clotted. Used painter's ground, from the *Comix* art studio. Looks like the real thing."

The leather of Osborne's chair creaked. Bulling snapped his eyes up, tracking The Jay's movements. But Osborne only walked to the window, silent over the thick carpet, where he stood looking down over the city. He took a fat cigar from his pocket and cut the tip cleanly off. Farley stepped up to light it.

"Nice touch, Tom," Osborne said, and nodded. "Very nice touch."

He pulled deep on the cigar and blew the smoke out in one smooth stream. Backing toward the door, Bulling thought of Moloch: the smoldering fire of the cigar, smoke in Osborne's smiling mouth and the reflection of orange sunset in his eyes.

Sara
* Ten Bells Pub * 9:45 PM

She watched the women, sitting together. They were old friends, according to history. Liz Stride, tall and willowy, engulfed in sadness. Catherine Eddowes was small, almost fragile. And Mary Kelly—early twenties, fresh-faced and in full possession of the best of her years.

Tonight, Sara had a unique opportunity to talk to these women before their deaths. Her heart skipped heavily in her chest, tattooing a sudden, irregular rhythm. A sick, hollow pit opened in her stomach.

Elizabeth Stride. Catherine Eddowes. Mary Kelly.

She approached them quietly. "Buy yer a drink?" she asked.

They all looked up at her, Mary Kelly narrowing her eyes: She was a beauty herself, a rose among daisies, and knew it. She bristled, but Eddowes patted her arm. "C'mon, Mary, yer gonna turn down a free drink? She don't look like no competition fer yer job. She'd be out on the streets, else."

"I don't do the streets," Mary retorted sharply. Her accent, pure Irish, had the hint of her solid middle-class upbringing behind it. She shrugged. "Well, not unless I have to."

Sara sat, slowly, into the realm of ghosts. Kelly and Eddowes were poring over a paper—the gory *Comix*.

"Gossips say yer kin read all sorts of fancy," Stride said. She pulled a letter out of her pocket. "Kin yer read this fer me?"

Sara nodded, took the letter, noting the name on it: Elizabeth Gustafsdotter Stride. The reality of the paper and the name hit Sara harder, at first, than the warmth of the woman sitting next to her. Liz Stride. Sara looked at the woman's face, searching her eyes without thinking. Sensing a long-standing sadness, a force of solitude—pain, like a low-grade fever, living in her limbs.

Stride frowned. "Is it very bad news?"

The woman would die early Sunday, Sara knew. She handed back the letter, her hand shaking. She told Stride, "It says your request for recompense for the *Princess Alice* has been denied again. There's no record of a man named Stride among the dead."

Eddowes snorted. "That old thing? Bin ten years, Liz. Yer'll get nothin' from it. Leave it go."

Stride folded the letter, quiet, and the sense of heaviness about her increased. More sadness, more bad news. It was true, then: Stride had survived the *Princess Alice* disaster, the worst in British history prior to the *Titanic*. When the *Alice* sank, Stride claimed she'd lost her husband and her two children.

Ten years ago, and she was still mourning. Sara recognized the almost doll-like stiffness about her—wrapped in the fragile protection of grief. And knew: For Stride, the *Alice* felt like yesterday, and always would. If anything, her grief compacted with every day she woke up to find it true again. Sara knew that kind of grief. It was small, yes: the way a dark star was small, with its crushing weight.

She put a hand on Stride's arm. Under her fingers, the cloth of the woman's coat was warm with the low, secreted heat of the living. Stride's eyes fluttered. She turned slowly to Sara and smiled, already halfway absent from her life.

The drinks came and the women sipped at the warm, heavy ale that was almost a meal for them. Impulsively, Sara ordered some bread and cheese, paying for it, when it came, with the smallest coins she could find in her purse. Then she brought a copy of the *Times* out from her thin coat.

"Oooo, that's me man's paper," Kelly said. She took the *Times* from Sara and scanned it. "Always thought I'd be a good reporter. Too bad they don't let women do that sort of thing."

"Got better uses for us, now, ain't they?" Eddowes said.

"Can't read all of this, mind," Kelly said. "What's that word?" she asked, pointing it out to Stride, who just stared, quiet and pensive, into her ale. Kelly showed it to Eddowes.

"Hell if I know," Eddowes told her. She looked to Sara. "Wot's it say?"

"*Egregious,*" Sara told them. She hadn't bothered to regain her Cockney with them, and none of them seemed to notice or care. Again, that sense of standing outside herself, of being alive among the dead, overcame her.

"Huh? Wot's that mean?" Eddowes asked.

"Outrageous," Sara murmured.

"My friend on the paper—read me one of his articles," Kelly demanded. "It's not like I can't read but I can't read what he writes. Too damned many words like *egr-e-gious*."

"What's your friend's name?"

"Wot's it to you?" Eddowes snapped.

"Reporters put their names on their articles," Sara answered, finding her lips numb. "It's called a byline."

Mary barked a laugh. "A *byline*, eh? Don't you know a few things. Tom Bulling—that's 'is name."

Sara paged through the paper, found several articles by Tom Bulling and read them. When she was finished, she said, "There seem to be a lot more women killed in the slums than what they print in the *Times*. Why?"

Eddowes shrugged. "They don't know about it, mebbe," she said, rousing herself. "Don't care, more like. Now there's a way to get yer rent, Mary. Tell yer man some of the gossip yere-abouts. Some of the things yer hear—"

"Nah," Kelly said, scornful. "They ain't gonna pay for what they already know. Tom says the Boss tells 'em what they can and can't write. Frosts Tom that much sometimes. The Boss calls it 'editorial direction.' My sorry arse. In't nothing but one man tellin' us what he wants us to hear. The Boss ain't no better than the rozzers or the lords, you ask me, no matter how he jumps hisself up—"

"Hush, Mary Kelly," Eddowes said sharply. "The Jackets hear ye talkin' like that, they'll hide yer proper."

"Why would the Yellow Jackets care what Sir Jay Osborne prints in his paper?" Sara asked.

Eddowes frowned, shot Mary a warning look. Kelly shut up, but didn't like it—arms crossed, frowning; a sullen child with a willful heart. Suddenly she laughed, all the clouds dispersing and the sunny smile back again. "Maybe if the Jackets *shagged* me proper, I wouldn't need ter work off that twenty-three p I owes me landlord outside."

They all laughed at that, a ribald, desperate release of fear and worries. Sara handed the paper back to Mary. She was a young woman, still; jaded, but not hard yet, and beautiful—her wide blue eyes fey and wise at once.

"I'm Sara Grant," Sara said to Mary, holding out her hand without thinking.

"Cor, aren't you fancy, duchess," Mary said, still laughing. "I'm Mary Kelly. Pleased to meet yer."

That pit again—opening up and swallowing her whole: Sara took Kelly's hand and shivers broke out over the skin of her arms, awe simmering just over her breastbone. "You too," she whispered.

"You all right, love?" Kelly asked.

Feeling the warmth in Kelly's hand, the minute movements within the flesh that spoke of blood and life, the echo of the heartbeat under her skin.

Sara said, "No, I'm all right," her throat tight as she let go of Kelly's hand.

Knowing that Mary Kelly, so alive tonight, would be dead in November, not two months from now. That she would be killed by the same man who would murder the dour Eddowes and the grieving Stride late tomorrow night or early the next morning. That the two women would die just hours apart. That the killer would be interrupted with Stride but not with Eddowes, who would bear the brunt of the night's work, her face slashed with a calculated ferocity, her uterus torn from between her legs.

Terrible, yes. But not as bad as Mary Kelly, who, in the Ripper's fury, would be so viciously mutilated that neither her friends nor her lovers would be able to identify her.

CHAPTER 20

September 29–30, 1888

Sara
* Crossingham's Common Lodgings * 7:00 PM

The day's warmth lowered as night dropped and dread sank to a cold ball in her belly. Outside, the flare of gas lamps being lit warmed the shadows, glowing in the fog. Outside . . .

Sara shivered, a heavy, rolling thing.

Outside, if women died a death she had no knowledge of, that was one thing. But *this*—

To know, and do nothing.

She was a scientist, trained and indoctrinated in the gospel of noninterference. She believed in it wholeheartedly, could see the logic, the potential for disaster in doing anything else. And though she could justify herself in every scientific and moral term she could muster, the truth was deeper, and simpler.

She sat alone in the dim, bare room, growing colder as night came on and the day's wan heat dissipated like the last exhalation of an unseen heart. Knowing.

—*and just watching*—

Could she do that?

David
* Osborne House * 9:15 PM

Every time Avery left his house for public purposes, David rode on the back of his caleche and opened the man's door when he got where he was going. But there were other nights when he left his driver and his coachmen at home.

For the third time in less than two weeks, David watched the carriage sail out into the dark. "This happen often?" he asked the driver.

The old man scowled and nodded, chewing his pipe in the cooling air of the courtyard. "Aye. Takes ma rig out least twice a month, sometimes more, with that Farley. Don't like that sod much, I don't. Hard on the horses' mouths, see?" He shifted on the stone bench uncomfortably. "It's not like I couldna take the master where he needs to go, yer know. Not like I don't know a gentleman's got needs."

Mary Kelly
* Ten Bells Pub * 9:45 PM

Mary Kelly was down on her money, had a ha'penny in her pocket and little else. Knew she'd have to go out, and soon. She would have to settle: Go down with rough and dirty types who didn't pay enough to make the feel of them inside her and the spunk on her legs worth the effort. God, it was a far cry from middle-class Limerick. And further still from the salons of Paris.

Across from her in the pub, a rat of a man drank his ale and watched. She knew when his eyes were on her—her skin crawled each time. Well, he had finally found her: Hercule, the *placeur* who had gone to such expense to get her to France as a registered prostitute. He'd threatened then to cut her throat if she ran away. She'd gone anyway, and why not? His promise of setting her up as a courtesan in Paris was nothing like the truth: a grim room on the Rue de Royale, shared with another girl even as they worked.

Well, she wouldn't go out there alone, that was sure. Beside her, Kate Eddowes nattered on, an animated sparrow with the drink on her. "C'mon," Kelly said, standing. She sniffled, more stoic than she felt. In her stomach, the ale churned like a black lake in a squall. She pulled Eddowes away, and Liz Stride followed quietly after.

On richer nights, Kelly's favorite trick was to rob the drunks and then run back into the pub, exchanging shawls with other women to confuse her pursuers. She knew the ruse would work on that half-drunk Frenchman. But it wasn't a shawl she had tonight. In the street, she dragged Eddowes under a shadowed eave and told her, "You know we got to work tonight. I lose my room, won't none of us have a place to stay."

Eddowes shivered. "Who wants ter work on a night like

this?" In two days, it would be October. Ground mist edged along the cobblestones.

"Who ever *wants* ta work?" Kelly scorned.

Eddowes shrugged. "There's better times, or were," she said, holding her arms and looking around them. They both knew what she meant: It was the perfect night for conjuring a boogey.

"There, girl," Kelly said, and put an arm around her. "We'll all stay close. Here." She took off her bonnet—the fancy one, with feathers and everything. She'd worn it for weeks, not letting it off her head. Now she gave it to Eddowes.

"Yer not," Eddowes said, but her eyes were keen. She loved fine things, Kate did.

"Go on, take it," Kelly said. "Wear it for good luck."

Eddowes took the hat gently. She turned it all the way around twice, then slowly raised it to her head, big grin on her small bony face. Kelly helped her tie it, not in front but in the back, like a proper French lady.

Eddowes peered into a barrel full of rainwater, smiling at the face she saw reflected there. That image shimmered and danced; in the gaslight, it looked more red than the actual pale white of Eddowes's skin. Kelly shivered.

"Go on now, get to work," she told Eddowes viciously. "Before I change me mind about that hat."

Eddowes laughed like a young girl, well used to Kelly's change in moods, and walked out onto the street with her back straighter than Kelly had seen it in years. Eddowes caught the arm of a passing carter and smiled at him. The carter, surprised, smiled back and let her lead him, laughing, into a nearby alley.

At the door of the pub, the mousy little man who'd watched Kelly for hours now turned. His eyes followed the bouncing feathers of the bonnet on Kate Eddowes's head. The Frenchman slunk quietly from the pub door to a wall by the alley, waiting for his quarry to finish.

Kelly smiled. He had words for the woman in that bonnet, he did. Wouldn't he be surprised, just?

Sara
* Commerce Street * 10:20 PM

Eddowes and Stride had less than three hours to live.

Snatches of music from the pubs and halls fell like eddies of snow through the streets, filled with people and smoke, laughter and the heavy tang of ale.

She wore men's pants. David's old shirt, and a broad-brimmed hat. She was just tall enough to pass for male. Scanning the street, Sara quickly spotted Stride, standing still and silent in the street, sadness like a fog around her.

Ten years ago, Stride had cheated a spectacular death when she had been employed on the saloon steamer *Princess Alice*. On September 3, 1878, traveling along the Thames, the *Princess* had collided with a large screw steamer, the *Bywell Castle*. Seven hundred people had died. Stride, clinging to a funnel, had watched her husband hold their two children against the rising water—and disappear, swallowed up under the filthy tributary of the Thames.

After ten years, that unspeakable hurt still clung to Stride, distinct and unshakable—a sweet and terrible grief.

To live through that. To die like this.

Sara felt sick, knowing she could do nothing to stop it.

She followed Stride, keeping her distance. Things were moving very quickly now.

Liz Stride
* Berner Street * 10:45 PM

Liz Stride wandered down Berner Street, past the Jewish Socialist Education Club. She'd thought of being a socialist once, but her man wouldn't allow it. Oh, but he was gone now. That heavy pang—it was sleet on the soul, thinking of them.

A stranger called to her from across the street. She ignored him, her throat sore with the press of tears. It came upon her, like this, always. Jesu, what would he have thought, her working like this again?

She was tired to her soul, but smiled when the man approached her. He was dressed well, and young. She slipped her hand quietly into the crook of his arm and followed him into the pub.

Bricklayer's Arms Pub * 10:58 PM

J Best and John Gardner were drunk. Not staggering drunk—not yet—but working at it earnestly. The last pub had thrown them out, but Best knew where to go: the Bricklayer's Arms. A rumble of thunder overhead made them hurry, laughing.

"Don't trip, now," Best said to Gardner. "Yer holdin' both of us up." It began to rain, a hard, driving volley that stung where it landed. "Jesus! I'm gorra drown!" Best shouted. He and Gardner ran for it.

Just inside the door, a man and woman stood, looking out into the rain. The man had his hand on the woman's breast.

"Bloody toff," Best yelled at the man. "Yer own women not enough fer ye, are they? Got to come down yere and take ours too?"

Thunder echoed in the distance—Big Ben tolling eleven. The man grabbed the woman's hand. They ran out into the rain.

"Bloody toff," Best said again. He threw up on Gardner's shoes and stood, staring down at the mess sadly. "Now there's a waste of good beer."

40 Berner Street · 11:30 PM

The Jewish Socialist Education Club let out. More than a hundred men and a few women streamed into the streets, laughing or carrying their arguments past the walls of the turbulent establishment.

Next door, at number forty-four, Matthew Packer wiped his face with a tattered handkerchief. The last of the sudden rain had died down, leaving him sodden and cold, but the fruit in his cart glistened with fat droplets of water under the simmering gaslight. Custom was good. Even the socialists had to eat, between arguments. Fruit was precious. Few of the students had money to buy, but someone always did. Like the toff approaching him now, whore on his arm.

"Evenin', sir," Packer said. "Buy some grapes or apples for the lady?"

The toff dipped into his pockets. "Choose what you'd like, my dear," he said. The woman selected a small bunch of grapes and some cachous to sweeten her breath, and the man paid, smiling.

Inside the Socialist Club, some thirty men still remained. Russian voices, mostly. Their deep, boisterous singing hung over the street as much as the heavy clouds overhead. The damp air stretched with a slow, somnolent energy.

The breeze freshened, and Packer wondered, briefly, if it would rain again.

64 Berner Street · 11:45 PM

William Marshall, laborer, stood outside the door of his lodging. His muscles hurt in the damp, but the freshening air made up for the pain. Across from him, at number sixty-three, a man and a woman stood talking. Well, didn't they always?

Snatches of what she said came to Marshall, like an opera sung on the street, the story sad, even tragic:

"I don't want to do this. I lost my husband on the *Princess Alice*—"

The toff said, "My dear, that was ten years ago."

"Not for me," Stride told him, her voice low. "For me, it's every day. I see their faces. My babies crying. The water—"

The toff laughed. "You'd say anything but your prayers," he scoffed. Smiling as he said it, as if a twist of the lips could forgive his glib humor.

"No, it's true," the woman said, protesting not the truth but the pain of it, that verity bringing goose bumps on Marshall's skin.

The man shook his head, still smiling.

Ah, he only wants a good time with yer, lass, Marshall thought. *Save yer sad tales for a man who cares.*

Then the man bent to kiss the woman, and Marshall went back into his rooms, closing the door against the rising cold.

Sara
· Dutfield Yard, off Berner Street · 12:20 AM

Stride had had three customers since Sara began her vigil—two, men of the slums; one, well-dressed but young. In the deeper shadows of Dutfield Yard, where Stride's body would be found, Sara waited.

If it happened at all, it would be soon. The next fifteen minutes would tell her everything she needed to know.

40 Berner Street · 12:30 AM

Israel Schwartz had stayed late to argue the merits of Zionism with Chaim Mindel at the Socialist Education Club. Mindel would, God willing, be sailing for Palestine in just two weeks' time.

Schwartz wished he could go. To taste the golden air of

Jerusalem, to see the sun come up over the Temple—he could die a happy man, having seen such a thing.

The drizzled air of London, grimed with soot, was not the heated sweetness he imagined over Zion. He hated the dark streets, shivering in the strange light of gas lamps; hated walking them alone. He hurried through them now.

At the side of the Socialist Education Club was a gate; beyond that, a passage running into Dutfield Yard. Schwartz saw a woman standing just within the gate. A big man, his clothing rough, took her hand, trying to pull her into the streets.

The woman said, "No, not tonight. I'm tired. So tired."

The man threw the woman onto the footway. She cried out— a hopeless thing, lying in the mud, her skirts ruched up around her knees. Crying.

Schwartz crossed to the other side of the street. There, another man was lighting his pipe. The pipe man looked up when the woman cried out, and he turned to snarl, at Schwartz, *"Lipsky."*

Schwartz shuddered. A man who would use an insult like that to a Jew would think nothing of beating one to death.

He quickened his pace, thinking of home. The man with the pipe followed after him, and Israel Schwartz, to his shame, ran down the street to the railway arch, where he hid in the shadows until he could be sure he was once again alone on the streets.

Sara
* Dutfield Yard * 12:45 AM

It was time.

Sara came as close as she dared. Hidden behind a corner of the yard, she could hear and see: Elizabeth Stride in the alley at the mouth of the yard. She was not alone. A man shambled down the alley beside her, his arms around her, a halting, clumsy waltz of paid-for passion.

Stride was saying, "I don't want to." Her skirts and back were covered in mud. She was crying.

"Well, I wan' it, if yer don't," the man said. He pinned Stride against the wall and hiked her skirts up. Stride, raising her face to the water dripping from the roof, didn't fight but only braced herself as he spread her legs and, grunting, fitted himself into her.

Sara turned away and shivered against the wall. The Ripper was a carter. A *carter*—

The bricks against her back were cold, dripping rain. Droplets glittered, tears on the face of the stone, on Sara's cheeks as she looked up and around her. The walls of the yard were too high to scale. And the exit was blocked by the grunting, heaving man who held Elizabeth Stride against her will and who would pay for the use of her body by cutting her throat.

Sara could go nowhere until this was finished. Steeling herself, wiping her eyes to clear them, she moved around the corner and forced herself to identify this man whom history would call Jack the Ripper.

He was not what she expected: Tall, and running to fat. More clumsy than cunning. Not so much hateful as ham-fisted. But he did have a knife. The hilt of it sat in his belt.

He finished with Stride. Her skirts fell like curtains over her legs as he pushed away from her, did himself up.

Sara closed her eyes, expecting a scream at any time. It didn't come. Instead, she heard Liz Stride crying, and the wet, hard sound of a slap.

"Wot the 'ell yer cryin' abaht, woman?" the carter asked. "Ain't yer never been took by no man? I'll pay yer, for God's sake."

Liz, hands over her face, fell slowly to her knees, weeping. "Please," she said to the man, spreading her hands in hopeless supplication.

He held a coin out to her. Crying too hard to speak, Stride ignored the coin and reached, instead, to touch the hilt of the man's knife. The carter stared at her, uncomprehending.

Liz bent her head back, stretching her neck. It glimmered, pale and wet, in the darkness of the alley.

"Yer can't mean it," the carter said, horrified.

"Please," Stride wept, closing her eyes. She held her arms out, as if preparing to jump off of a terrible precipice—the prow of a ghost ship only she could see.

The carter drew the knife out of his belt. It glinted in the hint of moonlight that began to clear the clouds.

Liz, kneeling in front of him, waiting. The carter, staring at the knife, at her, mesmerized.

Liz took his knife hand in both of hers, and slowly drew the blade to her throat. Dove against the sharp edge. The carter stumbled with her weight and the knife bit deep. Blood spurted against the wall, against Stride's hand and face.

A cry of pain and frustration came from Liz. She was wounded, perhaps mortally, but suffering. Her eyes, stretched wide, caught the carter's gaze and would not let him go. She clutched his apron, imploring, dragging him down.

A corkscrew of helpless anguish wound through Sara's guts. Then the carter took Stride by the head and cut across the snag in her neck to the other side of her ear. Stride fell, limp, into the mud on the ground. With a mewling cry, the carter ran out of the alley and into the night.

Above them, the storm moved on. The clouds etched a chiaroscuro of spectral shapes and moonlight as it cleared.

Catherine Eddowes
* Bishopsgate Station * 12:55 AM

"You go home now, missus," PC Hutt told Catherine Eddowes.

Since early evening, she had slept safely and deep in a cell at the Bishopsgate Station. "What time is it?" she asked Hutt, scratching her head under the black bonnet.

"Too late fer you ter get anything to drink," Hutt told her.

"I shall get a damn fine hiding when I get home," she mumbled.

"And serve you right, you had no right to get drunk," he told her. She passed him wearily. Hutt pushed open the swinging door of the station. "This way, missus. Please pull it to."

"All right, all right," Eddowes told him, grumping.

Hutt said, in passing, "Good night, old cock."

"Good night, my arse," she grumbled, pulling her shawl close.

Outside, she headed toward Aldgate High Street, where she'd been found earlier that night, huddled and drunk on the street. Another drink was what she needed, not sleep. If she could chat someone up, she might get it.

The bonnet on her head was rumpled. She threaded her way toward Aldgate, using the entrance to Duke Street, at the bottom of which lay Mitre Square.

Sara
* Duke Street * 1:00 AM

Sara had to get a ride to catch up to Catherine Eddowes. From Dutfield Yard to Mitre Square, it took ten minutes in a cab and would have been impossible on foot. Only hysteria could have convinced anyone that Jack had struck in both places, with so little with time and so much distance to cover. And Sara knew, certainly, that the carter was not Jack.

The way Stride had fallen on his knife, and the horror in the carter's eyes—he had not been the Ripper.

Whoever the Ripper was, he would strike tonight. He had not been interrupted with Stride, as everyone assumed. He had never been near Liz Stride. But he would be there with Eddowes.

And Sara had to be there, again, to know who he was.

The cabby refused to go into the little warren of streets closing in on Mitre Square. He let her out at Whitechapel Road, a broad thoroughfare running through the slums. Knowing Eddowes's route to Mitre Square, Sara backtracked to Duke Street and saw Eddowes in moments, walking alone—a ghost in a night of shadows.

She had to stay close. There was no record of exactly when Eddowes would be killed, or where—only that she had been found in Mitre Square.

Sarah watched as Eddowes stumbled along Houndsditch, muttering to herself. No one approached her. From Houndsditch, Sara knew, it was only a matter of minutes. Duke Street was on their left, and at the end of Duke Street, Church Passage pooled into Mitre Square.

But Eddowes passed Duke Street and went on to Aldgate, a wide thoroughfare bleeding off the Whitechapel Road. It was busy, even this late. Pubs and other establishments lined the street. Women screamed laughter while the men, equally drunk, clung to their shoulders to keep from falling. A few men brayed lewd suggestions at Eddowes as she passed. She retorted carelessly back at them, but didn't stop.

Sara watched as Eddowes went into the pub, and leaned against the door of a dressmaker, sighing. This was hopeless. Eddowes wouldn't be out for hours, once she started drinking.

And yet, her body would be found in Mitre Square at one forty-five AM—just twenty minutes from now. How it happened, Sara didn't know.

The pub door opened explosively. Eddowes pinwheeled through the open door and onto the street. A good deal of laughter punctuated her falling.

ʼ "Don' come back 'til yer got the doff," the publican shouted, red in the face and angry.

The door swung behind him as he went back into the pub. The sound of it carried over the noise of the street, a hard, stuttering clap. Eddowes rolled onto her butt and looked around, stunned by the fall, and bewildered. She began to weep, the quiet bawling of a child, disappointed in everything but the constant affirmation of her own insignificance.

Then, at the end of the street, Sara's eyes caught the sudden flutter of a cape. She leaned against the dressmaker's door, hugging the shadows there.

A tall man approached Eddowes, holding his hand out to her. Hesitant, Eddowes took it. The man pulled her up. Sara saw a flash of teeth as he smiled, but not his face. Under the wide brim of the silk hat, this man could be anyone.

He tucked Eddowes's arm in his.

Sara followed them out into the street, watching the top hat move like an ocean liner in a sea of tattered ships and muddy waters—tiredly riotous men and women making their way from one pub to another. Soon, it began its winding way into the smaller alleys.

This, she knew, had to be the man who murdered Eddowes. Keeping her eyes on the alley, Sara moved swiftly through the crowd. Closing now—

Intent on her pursuit, she didn't see the group of young men move in front of her. She collided head-on, lights spangling behind her eyes as she was thrown against the gutter.

Catherine Eddowes
⋆ Church Passage ⋆ 1:20 AM

In an alley with the gentleman, Catherine Eddowes vowed she would do this once and never do it again. John would never forgive her if he knew, but Jesu God, she needed a drink. Her head walloped with every blink of light from the moon.

She turned against the wall in the dark, hiking up her skirts. The toff put a hand on hers. "Not yet," he said.

Something stirred in the alley with them and Eddowes almost screamed. The toff laughed gently. "No need to be afraid. It's just my protégé. Please, Francis, come into the light. Let the lady take a look at you."

The man who glided into the light wore a brocade coat almost as gaudy as a working woman's skirts, with naval braid on the cuffs and gold epaulettes.

"Both of you?" Eddowes asked.

The toff nodded, smiling sympathetically. "I'm afraid so."

"I don't do this," Eddowes said suddenly. "I'll take yer on, but I'm no whore, to do two at once."

"I know, my dear," the toff said. He reached under her chin and slowly tugged on the sash that held her bonnet in place.

"It's just that I'm so tired," she said, the fire going out of her. "I need a drink. I need it bad—"

"Of course," the toff said, and held her tenderly. "Oh yes, my friend and I, we can take care of you," he whispered.

The man beside them touched her hair. The bonnet tumbled to the ground, and Eddowes shivered as his quickening breath anointed her bare head.

Sara
* Aldsgate Thoroughfare * 1:30 AM

Swearing and laughter. Sara lay on the ground. A group of young men surrounded her—not the rough custom of the slums, but four rich young toughs bullish in their quickening maturity and full of their own power. The largest filled the air with ugly curses, brushing off his hat, which had fallen when Sara had collided with him.

"Damned idiot," the boy said savagely.

Slowly, carefully, Sara got up from the ground. The youth grunted, shoving her shoulder. Sara shuffled back but held her ground and they began to move around her, encouraging each other to be the first.

"Go on, Freddy—clock the git."

The big one (Freddy, apparently) moved out of the ring and into it, confronting her. He took another swipe at her, not a shove but a proper Oxford boxing blow. Sara countered it easily, brushing aside the drive. Freddy swung again, with more force and less accuracy. Sara sidestepped, letting the thrust of his swing carry him over her boot—a simple twist, and the boy was headed for the ground.

On the way down, he grabbed for her head. Her hat went flying. Her ponytail fell down her back.

The boys, stunned silent, simply stood and stared. Freddy gaped at her. Then a slow fury spread across his face—the understanding that he had been bested by a woman, in front of his friends.

He got up fast and charged her, the other boys suddenly hooting and screaming for his victory. She punched Freddy as he came, a hard thrust to the solar plexus. He fell to his knees, gasping, made a sound of fury and lunged for her again. This time, she kicked his face. He went down for good.

The other boys roared to his defense. Each tried to grab her at the same time and failed, their uncoordinated effort doing little more than allowing her to move like flotsam on an eddy of water, constantly dancing just of their reach.

They went for her clothes. Because she was a woman. For that, she beat them senseless—a whirlwind of air and movement, leveraging every opportunity.

Grabbed from behind, she used the arms restraining her as an anchor, launching her feet into the oncoming rush of boys and bowling them over. Then she dropped and let the momentum of her weight carry her attacker over her back. He lost his grip, and she whipped back and spun, sweeping his legs out from under him. Straightening, she met the rush of the boy who'd gotten up from her first defense and felt the air crack as his fist struck just above her cheek. She fell back with the force of it and used the blow's momentum to spin and bring her own leg up, fast and hard, into his face. He went down with a thud while someone grabbed the hank of her hair and yanked it hard. Again, she slid along the line of his attack, going with the force of it. Grabbed his head and swung her knee up. Heard the unmistakable crack of bone and prayed she hadn't killed the whelp but only hurt him hard enough to make him stop.

With all four of them on the ground—two puking and spitting blood—Sara ran to the alley she had seen Eddowes enter.

Kate wasn't there. The alley was empty.

But under Sara's feet, blood pooled in the darkness, and the sweet, coppery stench of it made the world roll slowly beneath her.

Staggering out of the alley, she hurried back along Aldgate to Houndsditch, feeling the variations of wall against her hands as she made her way, half blind, along the firefly-flicker of a blood trail guiding her through the winding alley down to Mitre Square—

Sara
* Mitre Square * 1:40 AM

—To the silence of it: the ghost of a sudden breeze passing over her arms.

She stood above the body of Catherine Eddowes—dumped in the square, still cooling; amazed horror on her face.

Sara forced herself to think analytically, to take in every detail she could see in the thick, dim light. Eddowes's small face had been severely hacked, her nose and lips shredded, her left cheek gouged, the teeth caved in. The cut throat was a ring of exposed flesh, deep enough to see bone. Her abdomen was flayed and spread—like Chapman, the entire cavity opened and emptied.

Sara searched the area but realized, quickly, that both the uterus and left kidney had been taken.

Livid purple bruises circled Eddowes's throat. Her skirt was ruched up past her knees, the fishy stink of semen fluttering up, delicate as herring. Her eyes stared at a point just over Sara's head and Sara recoiled from the realization that whoever had killed her had watched—had slashed her throat and let her bleed.

Sash of the black bonnet clutched in her hands. A small tin at her feet. A full pound note fluttering under her heels.

Sara's stomach rolled. She clenched down on it hard.

The man in the cape. It had to be. Who else could afford to leave a whole pound at a dead woman's feet? But what had stopped him at the Aldgate? What had made him bring his kill to Mitre Square?

And Sara realized: the only interruption he could have had was the sudden altercation that had passed between her and the boys.

The rabbit hole had swallowed her up and she hadn't even felt it happen.

David
* Osborne House * 4:28 AM

Carefully, David opened the door into the silence of a sleeper's world—an alien place, for those awake; eerie and empty of life.

He searched Avery's room again, the fourth time since he'd been here. Exploring the closet, the dressers. Moving slowly, the focused beam of his penlight stabbing the darkness.

He found nothing, and moved, then, through the house: a wraith of shadow—unseen, unheard—to Avery's office.

At the desk, he went through Avery's papers. Useless. Letters from politicians. Financial reports of the household. The same as always, except: David saw a glint of metal in the corner of drawer. He pulled it out. The jingle of metal told him it wasn't what he was looking for; these weren't the key to the Portal, just keys to a safe.

A safe.

Carefully, David stood, searching for it. He found it hidden, as he expected he might, under a façade—an end table by the fireplace chair. Carefully, he looked inside. He saw jewels, certificates, deeds.

And, at the back, a white nylon rucksack he knew did not belong in this time.

"Bingo," David whispered.

"I thought a lot of things o' you, but not that you'd be a thief."

David whirled to see George sitting in Osborne's chair at the desk. He hadn't even heard him enter the room. God, but the family business came naturally, didn't it just?

"I'm not stealing," David said quietly. "I'm taking something back where it belongs. He has no business having it."

"That's what me ma always said about me pa's money when she took it out of his pockets at home," George said. Oddly, there was little rancor in his voice. "He was always drunk when she did this, mind. And I suppose I should be grateful, because if she hadn't, we bairns woulda starved." He stepped out from behind the desk. "Yer queerin' me chances here, aren't ye?"

"No one will associate you with this," David said, holding the bag.

George shook his head. "Not that. We're a team, and we're only good to them as long as we stay that way. Now that you have that, I don't think yer long for this place."

"No, I'm not. But if it's a job you want, you can come with me. I didn't need the money, and I can do more for you than Osborne will."

"I wondered how you knew an earl's son well enough to

tweak his nose." George nodded to the windows. "It's gettin' light outside, boyo. If you're gonna take that, you'd best leave before Harris wakes up—"

The clatter of hooves interrupted him. *"Jaysus,"* George hissed. "It's Osborne."

David shut the safe and grabbed pack. "Will he know our faces?"

"Hell no. They never look at our faces, lad."

"Good," David said, and led George to the servants' door. They slipped out under the remaining shadows and into the boxwood.

Osborne stepped out of the carriage. He stood in the patchy light as if absorbing the shadows. Then, as Farley put the horses away, Osborne walked slowly to the house, contemplative, sated. The proud cant of his shoulders radiated the deepest satisfaction. He picked a late fall rose, buried his face in its flesh and breathed deep. With his thumb, he popped the head off the stem. Then he then took the stairs up to the house lightly, cape swinging, and went inside.

"Creepy little shit," David whispered.

The moment Osborne was out of sight, David took hold of George's arm and pulled him away, through the shallowing shadows and into the gray tips of morning reaching along the main street.

CHAPTER 21

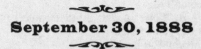

September 30, 1888

Sara
* Crossingham's Common Lodgings * 2:46 AM

She hadn't waited in the alley for the sun to come up, and would not stay alone in Mitre Square with a dead woman at her feet. She'd slipped beyond it just before one forty-five AM, keeping to the shadows, and been well away when she'd heard PC Watkins crying out the words she knew he would: "For God's sake, mate, come out and assist me. Another woman has been cut to pieces."

Despondent, Sara had trudged slowly back to her room and locked the door. She sat in the darkness on the hard bed and then slowly, silently wept.

Sara * 6:48 AM

The morning woke her as it always did, with noise in the streets and the thin gasp of sunlight filtering through the casements. She sat up from where she'd fallen asleep, curled on the bed and stiff, still in David's shirt. His scent lingered, surprisingly comforting.

She dressed and went to Mitre Square. He was there, as she knew he would be. Robb, sketching the scene, puzzling over the horror of it. She watched him touch the dead woman's hand once, briefly, then turn away from the mess of her abdomen, the anger in his face a devastating thing, profound and unsettling.

Sara stayed in the crowd, waiting for Robb to feel the weight of her gaze, for his eyes to seek hers out. His head lifted as if scenting her, then he turned and caught her eye. His eyes widened, and the sudden fury she saw in them had nothing to do with the Ripper.

"What in God's name happened to you?" he asked, striding

over. His hands clutched her shoulders but his touch was soft—a delicate, tentative reverence in his fingers. He touched her face, turning her cheek. The bruise there was an ugly purple thing; smaller bruises ran along the rest of her body, marks she was glad Robb couldn't see.

She shrugged. "I met up with a little trouble."

"I'm glad you came to me—"

"That's not why I'm here."

He drew back. "Indeed. Then why *are* you here?" His jaw ticked, a small spasm of irritation and confusion. "And why is your brother working for Jay Osborne as a coachman?"

Sara looked around the square. People noticed her talking to a rozzer. The mortuary van made its slow procession into the square. Beyond them, bobbies readied the body for transport.

"Come with me," she told Robb. "There's nothing more you're going to learn here."

"You know something?" he asked. "Why am I not surprised?"

She stopped his sarcasm with her eyes, looking up and not hiding the horror she had been through during the night. She turned to make her way out toward Church Passage, not watching to see if he followed. She knew he did.

Mary Kelly
* Church Passage * 7:35 AM

Kelly shifted in the crowd, looking toward the body, trying to get a glimpse. Death was an awful thing, but describing it was worth a drink at the pub, if you had details. Information was a commodity, Tom was always telling her.

"Hey, Marie," she said, joining some women she knew. "Anyone we know?"

"Jesus, dint yer hear?" Marie asked. "It's Kate. Kate Eddowes. And Long Liz just blocks up from 'ere. Throats cut. But Kate's the worse fer it—all hacked up, she were."

Kelly sat down on a barrel in the street. "Jesus," she whispered. "Both of them." She looked up at Marie, her own voice chafing in her throat. "Kate have anything on her?"

"Wot yer mean?"

"Gave her my hat—she liked it so."

Marie gave her a look of pity, one that said she should have known better. "Too bad, ducks. It's lost now."

"You mean, she didn't have it when she was found?" Kelly asked. She clenched her fists so hard on her knees that her fingernails dug into the flesh of her palms.

"Oh she 'ad it all right," Marie said. "Clutched in 'er hand, it were, when she died."

Kelly cried out, a short, sharp gasp of horror, covering her mouth. Above her hands, her eyes were wide and blind with fear.

Marie patted Kelly's arm. "There, luv. Coulda bin any of us. Wasn't yer hat wot did it. T'were the Ripper, sure ta be."

But Kelly hadn't heard the last. She had slid, boneless, to the ground.

"Make room, make room fer 'er," Marie said as she stooped over Kelly, fanning her with a shawl. "Fainted dead away, poor dab. Can't imagine why."

Lottie
* Church Passage * 7:52 AM

Lottie Hanaman stood in the crowd with a handful of men around her. Each one of them wore yellow jackets.

She turned to their leader, John Mallory. "Two, John. In one night."

"The Jay'll take care of it," Mallory said. But his face was heavy with the knowledge that, so far, nothing had stopped the killings yet.

"Then why hasn't he said? All these murders, and he's only reported half a dozen in them fancy papers a'his. Wha's 'e pullin' yere?"

"Shut yer yap," Mallory told her. "He takes care of everyfink else, don't he? Yer got a job 'causa him, don'tcha?"

"I got a job," she snapped bitterly. "Flat on my back, ten hours a day. Come morning, I can't even feel ter pee, I'm that damned numb. If The Jay's done so much fer us, how is it the women 'ere is still whorin' to make a livin,' John? And 'ow come he's not caught Jack any better than the rozzers 'ave?"

"Shut up, woman," Mallory growled.

She didn't. Took his arm and wouldn't let go. "Who's gonna be next? Me? Yer sister? Yer mum?"

Heads didn't even turn when he slapped her. Shaking his head, disgusted, Mallory nodded to his crew and moved along the street with them in tow.

"Would yer even read abaht it if 'n it *were* me?" Lottie murmured, alone now, holding her reddening cheek.

Sara
＊ Church Passage ＊ 8:10 AM

"She died in the square," Sara said, leading Robb through Duke Street to Church Passage. "But she was attacked here. You can see the blood. Then they brought her to Mitre Square to do the rest." She stopped at the entrance of the passage, letting Robb move past her and then ahead. Heard the sharp, sick intake of his breath. Her voice was hollow. "You've found it, then."

"Yes," Robb said quietly. "I found it."

The full light of midmorning gave the passageway enough light to make it out. Blood on the wall, on the ground, puddling in the mud—a filthy, curdling clay of earth and hemorrhage.

"They bled her like a pig," Sara whispered.

Robb turned, consternation warring with curiosity and concern. "You *saw* this?"

Sara hesitated. She should not be telling him. Wouldn't be. Except, to get his cooperation, knew she had to give him something. For what she had to know about the other murders, she judged it worth the risk.

"I saw them," she said, "go into the alley. I would have followed, but I was stopped."

"You would have followed? Woman, are you insane? He butchered her. You do realize he could have killed you just as easily, don't you?"

"I don't go into alleys with strange men," she said pointedly. "I'm not a whore."

"Then what were you doing here after midnight? In fact, what are you doing in the slums at all? What's your brother doing, shadowing the one of the most powerful men in the city and claiming he's a missing uncle who's lost his mind?" He was relentless now, firing questions with the full strength of his frustration. The mystery of who she and her brother were was no longer the slightest bit appealing—not this close to the horror of these murders. "And what the hell happened to your face?" he finished, furious.

Sara said nothing. She simply stood with her arms around herself, intent on the alley floor.

"Sara—"

"It's not just one man," she said abruptly. She pointed to the ground, where the mud left castlike prints on the cobbles. Most of these footprints were smeared from the struggle, but a few were clear enough to make distinct patterns, in three different sizes. "See? There were two men here."

Robb stared at her, long seconds that might have weighed heavily on anyone else. When she ignored him—studying only the scene around them—he took out his notebook and began to sketch. First, Kate Eddowes's hop-picking boots, worn and bulky but much smaller than the others. Then the clear outlines of good shoes, cobbled only once—a large man, with large feet. And the clear lines of a fine evening boot, the edges sharp and distinct.

"They were both big men," Sara said. "At least one of them was tall. She died looking at him."

"What makes you think that?" Robb asked, startled.

"When I found her, in the square, her eyes were wide open—focused on a distinct spot. It didn't seem like an accident. She had only just died, you know. If you followed the trajectory of her gaze, if she had looked at her killer while she died, it indicates the spot where a man six foot two or better would have stood."

"Sara, she was already dead by then. She bled out here. Then she was dumped in the square, before—before—"

"They started cutting her? I don't think so. There was blood in the square. Not much, but she did bleed. From her face, from the abdominal wound. She was alive when they did that."

"But they had cut her throat—"

Sara nodded. "Reports from Dr. Guillotin indicate that some of the machine's victims blinked for up to five minutes after their heads were severed. Is getting your throat cut so different?"

"My God," Robb whispered. Sara hunkered, scanning the blood-soaked mud. He bent down with her. "What are you looking for?"

"I don't know, but if I find it, I'll tell you."

"That's good of you," he said—holding to irony in the wake of horror.

"You have no idea," Sara said soberly.

They both looked for a long time, but no remnants, beyond the footprints and the blood, remained. Still squatting, Robb said quietly, "What are you really doing in the slums? Where do you come from?"

Sara stood. "Maryland," she said.

"Looking for your uncle?"

She smiled. "Found him, I think."

"Not where you expected him to be."

"No."

"You had no idea, had you?" Robb asked, wonder in his face.

She shook her head. "I wish I could explain, but I can't."

A dissatisfied sensitivity stretched uncomfortably between them. The Grants' strangeness was nothing Robb could pin down, and that was not illegal in any sense. And yet—

"Will you please leave the slums now?" he asked.

"No," she murmured. "Not yet."

"David's found your uncle—there's no need for you to *be* here anymore."

Sara indicated the puddle of blood in the alley before them. "I'm more concerned with this. There's something happening here—something terrible."

"That much is obvious," Robb said, angry.

But Sara shook her head. "You don't know the half of it. This killer—I have to find him."

"No!" Robb stood quickly. This time, he did shake her— took her by the shoulders and shook her sharply once. "That's *not* your job. It's mine, if it's anyone's."

She looked at his hands on her shoulders mildly, then up at him and shook her head. "You can't do this without me. There are things I know that you can't find anywhere else—"

"*How* do you know?"

"—and there are things you have access to that I need, to resolve this."

"Sara, there are things about these murders no lady needs to know, or should."

Her face took on a sobriety he had never seen in any woman. "Show me," she said.

Robb
* Westminster Station
Records Office * 9:15 AM

He took her first to Westminster, using the excuse that she was a witness, hinting that he was working in concert with the Home Office. Avoiding Pershing.

Tompson brought him the files. "Good to see yer again, sir," he said. But he looked twice at Sara, uncertain.

"He's struck again," Robb told Tompson. "She might have seen something, witnessed this last murder."

"Another murder, sir?" Tompson asked, horrified.

Robb paused. "Yes. Down in Mitre Square, and another woman dead in Dutfield Yard. No doubt this morning's paper will have all the news of it."

"Two in one night," Tompson said, grieving. "The man's a monster. When yer blokes goin' to catch 'im?"

Robb put his hand on Tompson's shoulder. "We're doing all we can, believe me. But I need to go through the files. If we find anything here like we've found there—"

Tompson nodded, but his eyes were large with the implications of it. "If yer sure, sir," he whispered, and left them alone.

Robb closed the door. "Before we begin," he said, sitting down, "tell me. How do you know what you know?"

She shook her head. "I can't tell you that. Not yet. Please, Robb—trust me."

He took a breath—a deep one; it seemed to reach beyond his lungs and well into his stomach. And yet he was a man well used to secrets and the need for them, from his own time in the Hussars, and from the knowledge he had of his uncle's work.

"You and your brother," he said. "You ask a lot of a man."

"What I know you can verify yourself. It's nothing that isn't recorded somewhere."

"Then what value is it, if it's something I already know?"

"I didn't say you knew it. That's the problem. Robb, look at what just happened with Tompson. He didn't know about Mitre Square. You had to tell him. And he will know, later—but only because he'll read about it in the newspapers."

"So?" Robb asked, and spread his hands.

"So what about other murders? What about the files from other stations? Think about it. Each precinct keeps its own records. How often do they share information? You know of women who have been killed in this area. Did Abberline know about them, before you told him?"

Robb shook his head. It had been his own initiative that had brought him to Abberline, not the other way around. He had not heard of anyone at Whitechapel asking other precincts about women who might have been killed the same way. Their focus was on their own turf, and there, they had their hands full.

Sara touched his arm. "Robb, how many other women have been killed that we don't even know about yet? How many precincts *are* there in London?"

Robb closed his eyes. A trapdoor had opened up under him, the thought so ugly and yet so obvious—

"Thirty-five," he whispered.

She took the file from his hands and scanned it while he watched, reading quickly. When she closed the file again, she was pale but re-energized. "Can you get the murder books from the other stations? Files like these?"

"From thirty-five stations? No. I haven't got that kind of authority. But I know someone who might."

"Who?" she asked.

He smiled, still brittle. "An earl's son does have connections. Especially when his uncle is the primary advisor to the queen, and her cousin as well."

Sara
* Crossingham's Common Lodgings * 6:46 PM

She walked alone to her flat. It was not late, but twilight had long set in; shadows pooled on the ground, converging into evening. Still standing in the street, she looked up and saw: a dim light flickering in her room. She crept up the stairs.

Before she reached the top, the door opened. David came out onto the landing.

"Where the *hell* have you been?" he demanded. He looked closely at her, then touched her cheek, moving the livid bruises into the gaslight's dim circle. "Jack?" he asked, dubious.

She winced, shook her head. "Toughs. I took care of them."

"I just bet."

He handed her a rucksack. She looked up at David, met his eyes.

"We have a problem," he said.

CHAPTER 22

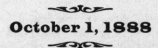

October 1, 1888

Robb
* Offices of the Central News Agency * 5:46 PM

Early evening. Robb and Abberline sat in Sir Jay's plush office. Osborne, sitting opposite them at his desk, gave an excellent impression of a good man distressed by events but determined to make the best of them. He had glanced just once at Robb when they'd first arrived.

"We received it not an hour ago," he told Abberline. "I called you immediately, of course."

"Saucy Jacky," Abberline snorted.

"It seems to be real," Osborne said smoothly. "As if it were sent just after the murders. He mentions both killings."

Abberline nodded, tucked the postcard in his pocket. "Thank you for assisting our investigation, Sir Jay. If you don't mind, I'll ask you not to put this in your newspapers."

"I wish I could accommodate you, Mr. Abberline, but the evening edition has already run, and we've published the full text of the postcard on the front page. I do apologize if this was an error on my part." Osborne stood, dismissing them.

Abberline nodded to Osborne and led the way out. But on the steps of the publishing house, with the racket of the printers shut behind them, he turned explosively to Robb. "What sort of idiot *is* the man?" Abberline demanded. "To print something like that for everyone on the streets to read?"

"Is it that inflammatory?" Robb asked.

Abberline, in answer, passed the postcard to Robb.

"I was not codding dear old Boss when I gave you the tip, you'll hear about Saucy Jacky's work tomorrow double

*event this time number one squealed a bit couldn't finish
straight off. Ha not the time to get the ears for police.
Thanks for keeping last letter back till I got to work again.
Jack the Ripper"*

The postmark was dated October first.

"It doesn't have to be genuine," Robb said. "Any fool could
have read about the two victims in the early papers, then posted
this letter for delivery this afternoon."

"And the ear? We never released that information to the
press."

"Osborne sends his reporters to each site," Robb said. "Any
one of them could have seen the body. I would ignore this one,
sir, and the last. They give us nothing to follow up. If it is Jack,
they're diversions, nothing more."

Abberline nodded, led Robb into a nook at the end of the
building. "Most of them, I'd say you're right. But take a look at
this one. Desk sergeant found it on his blotter this morning. A
different tone altogether."

He handed Robb a grimy note with stains on it, oily and
brown. Robb didn't like to touch it.

*"Beware I shall be at work on the 1st and 2nd inst, in the
Minories at 12 midnight and I give the authorities a good
chance but there is never a policeman near when I am at
work. Yours, Jack the Ripper."*

Robb looked up at Abberline. "We have to be there," he said
quietly.

Abberline nodded. "There's not a chance in hell the bastard
will show up, but if he does, he's finally ours."

The taste of it, so unlikely and yet the only hope they had,
was almost sweet.

"Finally," Robb said, like a prayer, breathing deep and holding it close for as long as he dared.

CHAPTER 23

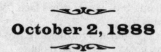

October 2, 1888

Osborne
* Osborne House * 9:33 PM

His rucksack was gone. Osborne scanned the walls of his library safe as if he would find the bag just by looking twice. Ridiculous, he knew—but that abrupt sense of vulnerability, at once vast and constricting, overwhelmed all rational thought. He must have left it in his room.

No, you only ever opened it here.

A stillness centered in his gut. The safe was not locked, but neither was it empty. Stacks of bills were still there, boxes of jewels, deeds to properties. Only the bag, the white bag with all the magical tools he hadn't even begun to understand. That was gone.

Osborne slammed the door of the safe shut. What was lost was irretrievable. That bag. It was more than just fantastic toys. It was a part of him, the key to a past he knew how to use no more than the many devices within it.

"Harris! We've been robbed!"

He pulled on the bell-cord, shouting as he did it, knowing Harris could not hear him. But the jangling—a barrage of frantic ringing—brought Harris at a run nonetheless.

"What is it, sir?" he asked, breathless.

"We've been robbed," Osborne repeated. "Who has been here while I've been gone? Have there been any signs of a break-in?"

Harris, shocked, shook his head. "We have received no one into this room, sir. And none of the windows or doors in the house have been forced. I unlock the doors every morning, and they were all secure."

"The windows?"

"The windows are sound, sir. I check them myself every night and every morning. There is nothing amiss—"

Osborne whirled, pointed at the safe. "Then who got into that? How was it done? Check the servants—" He stopped. A terrible understanding broke on Harris's face. "What?" Osborne demanded. "What is it?"

"Our two new coachmen went missing two days ago. They left without giving notice. Just walked out."

"And you have no idea where they've gone?"

"No. No sir, I don't."

Osborne stood very still. A quiver began in his belly, began there and spread through his limbs, a flash fire along his nerves. "Get out!" he screamed. "Leave me! Leave me alone!"

Whimpering frustration ground in his jaws: Coachmen. *Fools*. They'd throw the whole lot in the river before they even knew what they had.

A rime of frost blossomed in his bowels, growing sharp along the bottom of his belly. He looked again into the safe.

They hadn't taken the money. Or the jewels. Or the deeds.

But they had taken the bag. As if they knew, even more than he did, what the things in it were for.

Osborne looked around the room again, expecting—what? Ghosts? Men materializing out of thin air? Ridiculous.

And yet he knew, with a sudden, staggering fear, that he was not alone in London. Someone from his past had found him. Someone who knew him—more than he knew himself.

"Farley!" he snarled, throwing open the door to the library. As expected, Farley was already there, waiting.

Osborne put on his coat and hat and something else that Farley, alone, could see. That other part of him; the one that swallowed him up and took him God knew where. He was afraid of it, but the darkness threatening inside was worse—that threat of memories pressing. .

"Bring the carriage," he growled.

CHAPTER 24

October 2–3, 1888

Robb
* The Minories * 11:56 PM

It was late, almost midnight. Soon enough, Robb thought, it would be October third and yet another chance to catch the Whitechapel murderer would be gone.

Blowing on his hands, feet leaden with cold, he leaned against a dripping brick wall within the shadows of an alley off the Minories. Chandler and Helston, as shoddily dressed as he was, shivered across the square, trying to look busy or so down on their luck they had nowhere else to go.

This was the second night they'd watched the place. Last night had been the greatest disappointment. They'd hoped the letter's timing had indicated the previous midnight, the demarcation between the end of the first day and the start of the second.

Nothing had happened. Not a damned thing. They had left their places before noon on the second, sore in body and mind, to eat and sleep and try again tonight.

Filthy rainwater from an earlier downpour still dripped from the caves above, hitting the battered leather of Robb's hat with metronomic regularity. He huddled into himself, drawing the thin coat around his shoulders as if trying to get a bit of sleep against the wall. His muscles ached, feverish, from spending the previous night out, and he wondered what men did who lived here, when they hadn't the money to find a place to lay their heads after a day's work—days he knew were twelve to fifteen hours long. The misery of it was overwhelming.

The tolling of Big Ben, miles away, were small detonations in his muscles. He counted, uselessly, knowing the time all too well. Twelve bells. Midnight.

Still they waited. The air took on a hollow cast and was hard to breathe: the heavy weight of hope; the silence of the night.

The single hollow boom from Ben. Twelve-thirty. Robb stood as still as he could, ticking the minutes off in aching exhaustion.

Another rumble of the clock, dull thunder miles off. One o'clock.

Frustration gave way to disappointment, anticipation bleeding out of them, and the air was colder now than ever.

Finally, the last bell. One-thirty. The birth of a new day solidified the failure of the night. Robb glanced at his colleagues and saw the same weary despair echoed in their faces.

Helston walked quickly to Robb's alley. "This is crazy, guv. 'e ain't showin' up 'ere, an' that's a fact."

Robb nodded, the acceptance bitter. "You're probably right. Go home. Get some rest. Tomorrow—"

A wavering shout, almost a scream, sheared his words.

"Tha's down Leman way," Helston said, ashen.

"Whitechapel Station?" Robb asked, horrified.

They broke into a run, joined by Johns and Chandler. Ducking down two alleys and pelting up Commercial Road, they followed the sounds of a bobby's mindlessly shrilling whistle.

The man was still blowing it when they got to him—eyes wild, hectic spots of red standing out on deathly cheeks. Helston dragged the whistle from his mouth.

"What is it? What you seen?" Helston cried.

The bobby, incoherent, sobbed and pointed to a pile of refuse down the street. His hands, his body, shook fiercely. "There," he panted, gasping. "Oh God, there."

Robb ran to the pile of refuse, eyes straining against the darkness. Catching sight of what he thought was the gleaming alabaster of broken statuary before he realized—

His mind would not take it in. Refused. He looked closer, and immediately and forever wished to God he hadn't.

She had no head, no legs. Just the torso—sheared at the lower ribs and the neck. The spine stuck out like severed cane, knobby at the end, trailing blood and gristle. The cavity of her abdomen was scooped hollow, the womb torn from its anchor of flesh.

Between the neck and ribs, one arm tapered to a hand that was young and showed no signs of labor. Firm flesh on her back and ribs. Small breasts, beautifully shaped.

Robb staggered away from it, closing his eyes. He leaned his cheek against the cold stone wall beside him and let it chill the stinging heat of shock and the rising nausea that followed.

Dizzy, he let the rush of it pass and did not try to fight it. He expected it to come up—the horror, hot in his belly and his throat—and didn't even care. But it ebbed without discharge, releasing him to the cold reality of the wet wall beneath his cheek and the full horror of the thing that lay behind him.

Robb
* Montcliffe Townhouse * 3:42 AM

He lay with that same cheek against the thick pillow of his bed at his father's townhouse, shock and instinct taking him home. For once, he accepted Jasper's help without complaint, sliding gratefully between the cold sheets of his bed while the sleepy maid started a fire in the grate. Soon enough, it was roaring, dispelling the cold in the room but not the ice knotting his bones.

For a long time, Jasper said nothing. Robb was aware of the older man watching over him and didn't care. Jasper had been there for him since he was six years old, and it was a comfort, that watching. For once, Robb sank into all the privileges of his station with a mindless, abandoned gratitude and was simply and senselessly thankful for Jasper's quiet presence.

"Would you like some hot milk, sir?" Jasper asked.

Robb shook his head, not opening his eyes. At this moment, it felt as if he would never want to open them again.

"You've had a shock, sir."

Robb answered the distress he heard in Jasper's voice, not the words themselves. "Yes," whispered, admitting the worst.

But it was all he could say. How could he convey the horror he had seen, thrown on the trash heap as if it had not been flesh and blood, a woman breathing, alive only hours before?

He must have dozed. Two nights of surveillance had to claim him. He didn't want to sleep—didn't want to see—

But in his dream, it had a head, thick dark hair spilling over the smooth breasts like a garment of silk. There was no blood, and Robb, feeling an ancient horror in his bones, bent down to raise the curtain of hair from her face—

"Sara!"

He woke bellowing her name—bawling it—though only a choked remnant escaped his throat.

Jasper, sitting by the bed, started up. "What is it, sir?"

Robb shook his head, ribs aching, throat tight, the images of the dream still echoing in his flesh.

Now, if he closed his eyes again, he knew what he would see. *Who.*

He sat up, leaning against the headboard, still shaking but wide-eyed and once again sick to his stomach, breathing the fast, shallow gasps of those in shock.

He knew Jasper watched him, ready and wary, but could not communicate his need or even know what it was. Jasper moved to cover him with the thick down comforter but Robb waved him away, breathless, wordless, feverish—unable to tolerate even the touch of cloth on his sweat-soaked skin.

After long and long, his breathing began to deepen. Some of the blood came back to his face, and with it, echoes of the night and his dream and that helpless, overwhelming grief.

Jasper sat down beside the bed again. "Would you like me to sit with you, sir?" he asked.

To his amazement, Robb burst into tears and did not have the strength left to be ashamed. He was a child again, with no father to turn to but this one. He held out his hand and Jasper took it, smoothing his hair while he wept.

Robb • 10:32 AM

He slept late, still weak from the storm of his dreams.

Jasper brought him breakfast: warm tapioca and slowly melting cream, a dish of strawberries and mild tea, some toast. Robb tasted, certain he could not eat, but the mild flavors and sugar immediately woke his appetite. He ate it hungrily.

"I believe this is yours, sir," Jasper said, handing Robb a letter. Robb took it, nothing that the script was unlike any he had seen, neat but not flowery:

Robb, you will be pleased to know we have moved to a new neighborhood, one I believe you'll appreciate far more than our last. We've been here for just a few days.

We will let you know when we are ready to receive. David
& I look forward to seeing you. —Sara Grant

He folded the letter with shaking hands.

"Thank God," he whispered, noticing the sun rising in the casement for the first time. "Thank God."

POLITE
SOCIETY

book three

CHAPTER 25

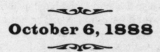

October 6, 1888

Sara
* Grant Townhouse * 10:32 AM

"Have you figured it out yet?" David asked.

Sara turned the object in her hands. It was a silvery walletlike thing, hinged like a book with flat, mirrored screens inside and minute filaments underneath. No power button she could find. "No. I've been at it for days and still don't know what it is. But all these other things—David, if Avery *is* in full possession of his faculties and knew what to do with what's in that pack, the changes he could have made to this time . . . We couldn't even begin to measure them. Or reverse them. He may have put something unstoppable into motion."

David shrugged. The elegant lines of his new coat magnified the tension of the gesture. "Maybe. But we don't know that yet, do we?"

She picked up the pack. Much of what it carried, they had in their own kit—medicines, syringes, scalpels, staples, splints, and tapes. A PDA like her own. A small digital camcorder.

But the other things that were more disturbing. Four two-way radio earbuds. A bulk of ammunition and two guns—the smooth, blunt shadow of a Glock and the feral silhouette of an Uzi.

"What about money?" David asked. "There wasn't room for any in the pack. Unless he brought another with him, for currency. Which means we have no idea how much he came with or how much latitude it would give him here."

Sara smiled bitterly. "He's always known what wealth could buy him. And you've seen the slums. If he hadn't come with money, he wouldn't have gotten one foot out of the place. So he must have brought it with him, and in large amounts."

She frowned.

"What?" David asked.

"Maybe nothing. It's just that there's not that much vintage currency floating around in our time. The Project would have known if anyone else had purchased large quantities of dated currency, and they would have told you. The amounts Avery would have needed to bring here would have thrown up flags."

She tapped a restless finger against the silver case. Its purpose, its importance, she didn't know. The tapping petered out slowly.

"Oh God," Sara said. She opened the sides of the case, holding it like a book. "It's a counterfeiter."

"Not likely," David said. "The DEA raids counterfeit ops all the time. The copiers they use are the size of compact cars."

"They didn't have the luxury of Jon Avery's genius. He created a lot of little toys for us to use on the Project. Look at those coils. And here: a nuclear power source, like my PDA. That would give him a solid ten years of operation."

She put it down. Taking a fiver from David, she slotted it into the machine's narrow mouth. Like a coin changer, it sipped the bill up into its guts. There was a whir of sound, soft as a whisper, and a sudden glow around the edges. In seconds, it stopped.

The bill popped out the other side. Sara held it up. All the coils and ciphers were intact. The ink superimposed on the original still showed a portrait of Victoria, but in a different pose. It was all in a different color, and the amount read not 5 but 100.

"The secret to Osborne's rise to riches," David said, grim. "How much could he make with this?"

"Millions." She opened the device, showing the glassy twin surfaces and the mirrors and minute apparatus behind them. "There's no ink. It's lasered onto the paper. He could make these bills indefinitely. I keep reading that the value of their money is weakening. No wonder. He's flooded the market with fake bills, with no gold to back them."

"And this other stuff?" David asked. "Guns, antibiotics, surveillance. If he's put any of this into use—"

"But he *hasn't*. Even the guns haven't been touched, and it's pretty obvious what they're for. The camcorder, the intelligence equipment—nothing. He hasn't even opened the MED Kit. It's like he didn't know what any of this was."

"Sara, even serious amnesiacs don't lose hard-wired skills. If he doesn't know how to pick up a gun, he's had some real damage we don't know about."

"Well, maybe *you* wouldn't forget to pick up a gun," she said. But she could see that of the items in the pack, most had not been handled.

"If there was serious mnemonic damage," David said, "it would explain a loss of even skill-based memories. He wouldn't have known how to use much of this. Might not even know you."

"He followed us to the Portal," she said. "He wouldn't have done that if he hadn't remembered me."

"He didn't say your name. Didn't even try to approach you. If he had remembered you, he would have done that. Would have wondered what the hell you were doing here and wouldn't have been quiet about it, either. He didn't remember, not directly, but something drew him to you just the same. And I think you know what that something was." David hunkered down next to her chair. "How well did he know you, Sara? Before?"

She shifted, restless. Heat bloomed in her face, a stinging path that juddered along her skin. Without realizing it, she brought her legs closer together, until her knees touched. The truth was private, intensely so. But if it was something they could use—

"He wanted me," she confessed, and shrugged, painfully stiff. "It sounds silly, but little things— He was always there. Touching, standing too close. Watching. I could always tell where he was in a room by that feeling of his eyes on me. But I can't imagine he'd remember that, when he doesn't even remember himself."

David had slowly straightened, eyes narrowing, as she described Avery's behavior. Judgment sat in his eyes, a darkening horizon that had settled to a fixed bearing, an unforgiving latitude in the geography of his mind. On the map of his moral compass, Sara saw, Avery was now an outlaw.

"Memory is a strange animal," David murmured. "A change in context can make strangers of people we'd otherwise never forget. Even if he didn't recognize you outright, the attraction that drove his obsession—and yes, I would call it that—could have influenced his interest, even if he didn't know why. If he saw you at the bank, that's all he'd need to draw him."

"Into the slums?" she scoffed. "A gentleman, like the one he's become?"

"A fixation like that is a force of nature," David said. "It could easily overwhelm common sense. But there's an upside to that. If we could use it, if we could force him to remember you—"

Sara paused, curling her fingers around the counterfeiter, which was warm now with her own heat. "It's a dangerous thing, forcing memory on an amnesiac. If he remembers too suddenly, the shift could drive him mad."

"It's obvious there are things Avery doesn't know. But there's one thing we'd better hope he still remembers—how to unlock the Portal. I've searched his house. Whatever the key is, he knows enough to keep it close." David stood. "What if he remembers just enough to use that key again, and leaves us stranded here?" he asked quietly.

They looked at each other, knowing—there was only one way to be sure. Dread filled her belly, a sudden storm of apprehension and a loathing so intense she was sick with it. Like a ghost of skin, she recalled the feel of Avery's fingers, touching lightly—her arm, her neck or shoulder; never obvious, but always lingering a heartbeat too long.

The thought of what she had to do left her breathless, feeling strangely naked. "We have to see him," Sara whispered.

David nodded. "We have to put you right under his nose, and see what happens."

CHAPTER 26

October 9, 1888

Robb
* Grant Townhouse * 10:52 AM

The conservatory was lush with greenery and color. Massive callas and stargazer lilies dotted the jungled profusion of broad-leafed banana trees. Hip-high elephant ears spread their vast leaves in luxuriant circles around the trunks of dwarf trees, and golden-tasseled prairie grass drooped gently. The air was fragrant with the sweet undertone of ginger and the clean, cool scent of water running into the stone pool.

Sara sat in a deep wicker chair. She wore a simple white day dress, frothed in heavy ivory lace. Her feet were bare and her hair was down. She wore no corset or the many required petticoats. She looked ready for bed, but was fully dressed. Robb didn't know whether to be embarrassed or not. But Sara only smiled.

"It's good to see you again," she told him.

"You as well. Thank you for your letter. And your invitation."

He could not help the pleasure of seeing her again; of seeing who she really was: a peer, on footing with his station. The pleasure of it almost overwhelmed him.

"Are you still pursuing your, ah, uncle?"

"More than ever," she replied, but did not elaborate.

"Where's David?" he asked, aware that he was alone with her. And that as much as he wanted to be alone with her, it was not done; in the moist heat of the conservatory, lush with life, he did not dare it.

"David is upstairs," she told him. "Dressing for the club."

Robb raised his eyebrows. "Which club?"

"Osborne's," Sara said, meeting his eyes meaningfully. "I'm sure he would appreciate an introduction."

"Ah. The Huntingdon. My club as well, you know," Robb said.

"I do know," she said quietly.

David came into the conservatory, dressed in dark gray wool suited to the weather, beautifully cut. Strangely, the elegance described, rather than hid, the lines of muscle in his shoulders. He moved through the foliage, quiet and dangerous, even when he didn't have to be. Absurdly, Robb thought of William Blake: *Tyger, tyger, burning bright* . . .

"We have a favor to ask," David said.

Robb nodded. "I thought you might. And I'm pleased to help with any introductions you might require. I just thank God you're back in society."

"I don't think you understand," Sara said. She was clearly ill at ease. "We need your help—"

"Getting close to Osborne," David finished.

Robb watched them both, eyes darkening. Felt the joy of being there slowly evaporating.

"I won't use you," Sara told him. Her voice so low, it was almost a whisper; her resolve a thrill in his blood.

David would, he knew. With no concessions to politeness, David chafed beside them with no patience for social graces. Their home was beautiful, just a few houses down from his uncle Mersey, who was a lord. But the luxury of his surroundings, the clothes on his back—none of it tempered David.

His quarry was outside, not here.

Robb cleared his throat. "If you're determined to meet him—Osborne—I could help."

"Robb, are you sure?" Sara asked. Her eyes were wide; in this light, luminous.

But David said, "What's made you so eager to help?"

"I've finally met the man," Robb admitted.

"Don't like him?" David asked.

"Can't stand him," Robb confessed, and knew it was true. Sir Jay Osborne filled Robb with a loathing he did not understand, borne of the instincts he had honed on the streets—warnings he could not ignore.

"Robb, what's happened?" Sara asked.

Robb shrugged, not quite an apology. "He's become a friend of my father's. Put himself quite deliberately into that seat, first scraping an acquaintance and then insinuating himself into our circle."

"What could your father offer Osborne?" Sara asked. "Other than the social connection, and he already has so many."

"A man like Osborne can never have enough connections," Robb said, thoughtful. "But the timing is odd. He's had years to make the acquaintance, but did so only after I had a run-in with him."

The look in her eyes—alarm, and a certain fear. "You never said—"

Robb smiled at her. "It was nothing. I tried to bully one of his reporters out of writing a story. One of the deaths in Westminster. He visited my father shortly thereafter."

"To get to you," Sara said.

"You think he'd care that much?"

"I think he'd gut you where you stood," David said.

He was lost in this, he knew. He had no idea what they were doing. Osborne was a scion of society. And yes, he *was* an uncomfortable mystery. But then, so were they.

"You're right," Robb said slowly. "I don't know why he's scraped the connection, and I don't like the coincidence." He looked shrewdly between Sara and David. "On the other hand, I don't know why you two are so keen on pursuing him, either. The only thing I *do* know is, if I'm a part of this, I can keep an eye on all of you." David narrowed his eyes. Robb had the distinct impression that he would have to be very crafty indeed to keep up with David when he didn't want to be kept up with. "My father is holding several fetes this month," Robb went on carefully. "A ball this Friday night. And a country house gathering the next weekend. I could invite you to both."

A look of unease passed over David's face, as if he were trying to envision himself in either setting and not succeeding; surrounded by glittering jewels, seas of lace and silk; leather riding boots and red wool jackets and people who would know his station the moment he walked into the room and said *how-do*. If David Grant was who he said he was, a fete or two should not pose a problem. And if he was not, he would be found out—mercilessly.

"Osborne will be there," Robb reminded him. "First at the ball, then over the weekend. A very intimate setting it is, too. An excellent place to watch someone you're curious about."

Knowing just how tempting that bait would be, Robb folded his arms and leaned back against the deep wicker chair. The sunlight, striking the windows above them, seemed bright with irony.

"Bastard," David chuffed.

"Of course we'll come," Sara said. "We would be glad to, wouldn't we, David?"

"Great," David said. "Yeah."

"This," Robb said, with great satisfaction, "should be very interesting indeed."

CHAPTER 27

October 12, 1888

Robb
* Montcliffe Townhouse * 9:32 PM

Fresh flowers gilding the entries, and the dining room over-flowed with delicacies, topped with ice-carved statuary and rose trees from the conservatory bursting with bloom.

Had it been his money, Robb thought, he would have used it for better things—opened a small school for teaching orphans or outfitted a hospital in the slums. He thought, *You are a socialist at heart—admit it. Or, at best, a communard.*

But not tonight. Tonight, a small worm of pride struggled in his heart, an eagerness he was at odds with, a suspense of anticipation so strong it was an ache.

Sara
* Montcliffe Townhouse * 9:46 PM

Robb, smiling, stepped down the long staircase to receive her personally. "I'm glad you could come," he said formally, though his smile was not formal at all. He hesitated only the briefest moment. "Mother, Father, may I introduce Miss Sara Grant?"

His mother pinpointed Sara in her sights intently. She was a countess, and new acquaintances did not enter into her circle without warrant. But this was the woman her unmarried son had invited, and so she smiled at Sara, eyes warming as she took in the distinction of her dress, its elegance and the fineness of its cut and cloth; the size and taste of her jewels, which held too much depth and fire for paste.

His father took Sara's hand, clearly appreciating more than

the stylish simplicity of her gown. "A pleasure, my dear. Tell me, where is your family from?"

Which was the polite way of asking who "her people" were. Sara smiled. "We have recently spent time abroad, traveling. Mostly at the home of a distant relative, Archduke Wilhelm of Bern. But our family home is in the Hamptons, of course."

"Of course," Robb's father murmured with a catbird smile. American heiresses, with more money than lineage, had their own cachet among titled Victorians.

"American?" Robb's mother said. A small, discreet smile crept to her lips.

"Yes, Mother, they are permitted in country these days," Robb said smoothly—painfully aware of their presumption. He cleared his throat. "And this is Miss Grant's brother, David."

David stepped up to meet Robb's parents. He hesitated only the slightest moment, then bowed to His Lordship and bent charmingly over the lady's hand. He smiled, but was not overly forward, and the gravity with which he carried himself broadcast his intent as a man of serious bearing and means.

Sara was amazed by the transformation. So was Robb. His eyes, so sharp, took it in thoughtfully.

His father took David's hand and shook it warmly, in the American tradition. "Your family is in shipping, then?" His Lordship asked David. "Or politics, perhaps?"

"Exploration," David told him. "Funding scientific research and expansion. New technologies. Historical education. With some varied military interests, of course."

Lady Montcliffe smiled even more broadly, and His Lordship rocked on his toes and gripped David's elbow warmly. "Excellent. Love a good adventure myself," he said. "Africa's an exciting place right now, full of possibilities. You'll have to visit again, tell me more about the explorations you've undertaken."

David smiled, nodding. "I would enjoy that, sir."

Robb turned from watching the interchange between David and his father, smiled and had no idea of the bitterness behind it. Turning to Sara, he held out his arm. "Allow me?"

He led her to the ballroom. Suffused with sudden joy, the feel of her in his arms. They swept into the current of dancers like a thistle borne on the waves of a slow-moving stream.

Sara* 10:15 PM

He entered the room fashionably late, and the crowd seemed to waver, a communal hesitation that acknowledged his growing importance. Jonathan Avery. Known as Sir Jay Osborne in this place and time, he greeted his hosts in the world he had commandeered as if he belonged to it more than they did. He turned to the ballroom to accept the sudden excitement of his arrival with the smallest bow; stood and allowed those assembled to admire him even as he dismissed their notice entirely.

She could see him absorb the power of it, converting it to something else—something electric and even dazzling.

His gaze, sweeping them all, stopped suddenly. He stared at Sara. His face, his entire demeanor, changed when he saw her. In an instant, the urbane gentility transformed to the sudden heat of a predator. It was intense and fiercely focused: A blistering act of domination.

But was it recognition?

Sara raised her chin.

The world outside her body was slow and suddenly sharp. His eyes did not waver. And yet, for all the oxidation of hunger in his stare, she sensed no remembrance, no memory of her in context to himself.

What did he know? Was she like the tools in his pack—a ghost in the broken machine of his memory?

Sara looked to David, saw him put down his glass and cross the floor. Robb, sensing a change in David's bearing, followed, watching carefully.

Osborne got to her first. Wordlessly, he took her hand, bent over it, brought it to his lips.

She said nothing; just watched—distant, analytical—for his reactions. Something in his eyes blazed: evasive memory, a fascination made combustible by the backwash of a recollection even he could not comprehend.

"Sir Jay," Robb said, doubtful and cool. Seeing that silent eruption between them, and Osborne's feverish appetite. He took Sara's hand from Osborne's. "How kind of you to join us."

Osborne smiled, stepping back. He made a great show of it, drinking in the sight of Sara—putting his hands behind his back as if admiring a painting in a gallery. "I wouldn't miss it," he said, smiling. The civility of his countenance did little to disguise the ferocity behind it. He turned briskly on David.

"And you are—?"

David said nothing. He met Osborne's challenge quietly with his eyes and the unwavering fact of his presence at Sara's side. *Had Osborne ever even seen his face*, she wondered, *when David had been a servant at this man's house?*

"Sara's brother, David Grant," Robb told Osborne.

The predatory fire in Osborne's eyes flared and banked quickly. Sara knew why: if David was her brother, he was the key to her—an ally Osborne would need.

"It's good to finally meet you," David said quietly. And then, feeling her stiff and shivering beside him, he drew them away from Sir Jay with a nod. "If you'll excuse us."

"Of course," Osborne murmured. He nodded, gallantly turning to an older woman and her husband waiting nearby. But never, they noticed (as everyone did), taking his eyes from the young Miss Grant for long.

Sara · 10:32 PM

She did not want to speak to him. A great black hole had opened up, surprising her with its force. Images of Joan, distorted and dying. Joan, who let him make love to her and made promises even she herself knew he'd never keep. Sara didn't doubt—not for a moment—that Avery's chief attraction to the woman had been her access to the Portal. Maybe Joan had known it, too. If she had, she'd chosen not to look too closely at what Jon Avery had offered her. She had risked everything to open the Portal for him—her freedom, certainly. But as a woman, Sara knew the more frightening thing Joan faced was losing him. And at that last crucial moment, Joan had decided that this was the risk she could not take. She could not live without even his sad rendering of love, and rather than lose him, she had jumped into the Portal with him.

But the Portal had been set for only one traveler.

Sara closed her eyes. Knowing there would have been no outward mutation of Joan's body. But inside, the rhythms of the organs would have been altered, electrical stimuli—synapses and heartbeats and even the electrical fields within each cell—would have been catastrophically imbalanced as the body struggled to reconcile a differential in time, space, and mass that it could not possibly adjust to by itself.

Did he remember any of it? Had he given any thought to what had happened to his lover? Would he care if he did?

Sara's throat ached with that unexpected anger. And while his eyes tracked her from every corner of the room, and she avoided his touch as she always had. She smiled and did not show the dislike that had turned, in that singular flash point between them, to solid loathing.

But there were only so many dances, she discovered, she could have with an earl's son. Passed around the ballroom like a party favor, she found herself swept, suddenly, into the arms of an unexpected partner: Avery.

He held her in a dancer's embrace and the unyielding persona of Sir Jay Osborne. He studied her for more than a minute as he swayed her, sensuously slow, along the floor. Saying nothing, absorbing her as if she were a scent, strong and heady.

Finally he murmured, "I seem to know you."

"I don't think so," Sara said carefully, aware of the rigid stiffness of her back, where his fingers rested light along her spine. "My brother and I have spent most of our lives abroad."

"You seem to know me," he said, inclining his head.

"You've made quite a name for yourself in this place."

They had danced to the edge of the galaxy of dancers, the open doors of the terrazzo close enough to cool the sweat on her body and spread the chill of it along her breasts.

Sir Jay smiled. "Yes, I have. Are you sure I don't know you? So familiar—"

He reached for her and Sara stepped back. He followed, undeterred, perhaps even charmed by her modesty.

The foyer, full of people, seemed the safest place. Sara backed into it, slowly, watching his eyes grow bright with their own wolfish humor; as if they were playing by the rules of a well-accepted game, and both knew it.

Late guests came through the foyer, surprised to be greeted by Sir Jay. They glanced, inquiring, at Sara—seeing them together, as a couple. Osborne smiled with his own arcane mischief. "Miss Sara Grant," he told the newcomers brightly, not correcting their assumptions. "We were just on our way to the conservatory. Do join us."

Face hot, Sara allowed Osborne to lead her into the conservatory. Typical of every one she had seen, it was lush with foliage, dark and damp—as close to an allegory of sex as the Victorians, unaware, allowed into their homes. She struck up conversation with the latecomers, but they knew better than to get in Osborne's way. The discreet understanding between the gentlemen put increasing space between them, until finally she and Osborne were alone in a warm thicket of spreading banana leaves.

"Who are you?" Osborne breathed. He stepped close. "I know you. That neck—"

His hands were hot at her waist, and the weight of a large ring bit into her hip.

Surprised, she looked down. The ring was muted gold. Not shiny, almost coarse. Etruscan style, with the elongated horseshoe shape.

The Portal. Her breath caught.

"You like it?" Osborne murmured, bringing it into the light.

"It's—lovely," Sara said.

The large façade stood out over the band by more than half an inch: a face too thick for simple gold behind it. A fine line ran along the sides.

"It's like a locket, is it?" she asked, touching the metal.

"It is," he said, smiling, growing close. "But I've never been able to open it. It's a mystery. You see?"

He took the ring off his finger. Eyes gleaming, he slid it slowly onto hers. It took every effort not to move away from him, from that heat in his body, so close to hers. She concentrated on the ring. Examined the seam for its release, but couldn't find one. Closed her fist and felt an odd throb in her palm—an almost living warmth.

Osborne breathed a knowing smile. "You see? A mystery. Like you." His hand raised to her face.

She heard Robb's voice. "Sara?"

"Robb!" She called his name sharply, and couldn't keep the relief of seeing him out of her voice.

"Sir Jay," Robb said evenly, joining them in the little copse of trees. With him in the circle, the small, artificial grove seemed larger, the air suddenly clean. "You've been entertaining my special guest. How kind."

"My pleasure," Osborne told him, his eyes bold.

Robb's jealousy, like burning fireflies, ricocheted in the

small space, stinging her skin. "Still writing about death?" he asked, chillingly polite.

"Oh yes," Osborne said, turning all of his predatory energy to Robb; in some odd way, it made his consuming interest in Sara more obvious, an unseen tether at her wrist that he held, firmly, within the confines of his maddening, deliberate smile.

"And do you think we'll see any more of it?" Robb asked, quiet and deliberate.

Osborne laughed, his delight completely at odds with the subject. "Of course, Inspector. A man like Jack does not stop. Very little, in fact, gets in his way."

His eyes gleamed at Sara, an unspoken promise behind them.

"You sound as if you admire him," Robb said softly.

Osborne smiled and lowered his eyes, not the least bit put out by Robb's suggestion. "Not at all," he murmured, deprecating.

Then he flicked his gaze up, his glance thin as a razor, sharpened by the mocking gleam of laughter. His words were a lie, and Osborne took acutely amused delight in them. He nodded at Sara, his gaze lingering over her. "My ring?" he asked softly.

Reluctantly, with Robb watching, Sara handed Osborne his ring.

Osborne kissed it reverently, as if the gold were a surrogate for her skin. Ignoring Robb's frown, the sharpness in his eyes, Osborne slipped the ring back on his finger, and winked.

"Good night, my dear," he said, saluting her with his maddening smile as he left: a languid visitor at havoc's door, always welcome.

When he was gone, Robb turned to her, furious. "What the hell was that all about? I could have wrung his neck for you, called him out—"

"A duel?" Sara asked, incredulous. She sobered quickly. He would have done it—put his life at risk for her honor.

"Who is he, Sara? Really. Not your uncle, certainly. Then who? And why were you here—with him, like this?"

This last question, almost a cry, revealed the anguish behind his questions. He was unable to reconcile why she had been alone with Osborne, in this place—his hands on her, his ring on her finger.

"I needed—" A lump rose in her throat, made it impossible to continue.

Robb stared, then whispered, "What could you possibly need from a man like Osborne?"

To her horror, she broke out in a rash of sudden heat—burning her face, her throat. "I needed to know what he knows," she said abruptly. Robb lowered his head, listening gravely; her voice was a husk of spent frustration. "Obviously, he's not the man we thought we'd find."

Robb straightened. "No, he isn't," he said, quiet, but relentless. "He's not the man David described to me at all. He's not ill. And he certainly knows all too well who he is."

Sara shook her head. "No, he doesn't. Not the way I know him. Not who I know him *as*. That makes him dangerous, Jonas."

Robb blinked. "How could he not know who he is and still be what he has become in society?"

She smiled at him, rueful. "I don't know, but he's obviously managed."

"He's not really your uncle, is he?" His eyes asked, painfully, *What are you into here?*

"No. Robb, how did Avery—Osborne—come into society?"

"Avery," Robb said softly. It was the name David had given him weeks before. "Thin air," he said, narrowing his eyes at the discrepancy between the names and setting it aside, for now. "But then, so did you. Are you sure you're telling me everything?"

"I'm sure I'm not," she said, drawing irony like a gauze between them. "But a lady does not divulge everything about herself on her first outing with a gentleman."

"This is serious, Sara," Robb said, suddenly forceful, taking her arm. Startled, she looked up and saw he was not so much angry as alarmed, and unaware of how his hand tightened as his anxiety swelled with her silence. "He seems to know you," he said. "And you know him—under another name."

"Am I speaking to The Honourable Jonas Robb or to Inspector Detective Robb?" she asked coolly, looking pointedly at her arm.

Robb noticed the force of his grip and immediately let her go. "I'm sorry," he said. Contrite, but ironic. "The two are always the same. You know that." He took her hand, his fingers determinedly gentle. "Who *is* he, Sara? I have to know."

In his eyes—in the warmth transmitted from his flesh to hers—she knew it was not just Robb the inspector asking.

"A scientist," she told him.

"A scientist? *Osborne?*"

"I know it's hard to believe, but yes. A scientist. Brilliant. Arrogant. Reckless. There really was an accident. He lost his memory. That didn't stop him. He has become Sir Jay—a man who has put himself in places of influence that could be disastrous to your government."

Stunned, Robb leaned away from the implication of her words.

"What are you saying?" he asked.

"I don't know," Sara said. She realized he had taken her too literally, taken the potential for Avery's changes to topple his world as a specific political threat. "I'm not saying anything."

"Treason is saying something," Robb said heatedly.

"Yes, but we have no details. It's all ambiguous—sketches and shadows, nothing provable. We don't really even know what he's doing or how. That's what we're trying to find out."

"And all these discrepancies?" Robb asked. "Between what David has told me of your search and the truth of it? It's been two years since Osborne came into society. David said you'd been searching for days, that this accident occurred only weeks ago. The difference is obvious, and unacceptable. Explain it."

She shook her head, smiling sadly. Under the reflected light of glass walls, the bruise on her cheek was spangled. "If I do that," she sighed, "I'll have to tell you everything, and I can't."

"Why?" It was little more than a whisper, but held all the force of his confusion.

"Robb, you told me you have an uncle. Your favorite. That he works for his government." She raised her eyes to his. "So you understand the need for secrecy."

"You—you mean you're agents? For the Americans?"

She was surprised but said nothing; let his assumption hang between them, neither affirming nor denying it.

He looked at her seriously, compelling an intimacy between them. This was the crux of it. She and David had asked an overwhelming trust from him, and given so little of their own truth in return. He had skirted it, flirted with it, let it go on a whim and the good graces of her smile. But that could not hold, she knew. Not with what she was saying.

He told her, carefully, "I can't wait much longer for an explanation. I'm an inspector, Sara. Charged with protecting the citizens of this city and beyond that, a royal, for whom the protection of this country is my highest calling. As Robb the man, I trust you with my life. But Robb the inspector has no such luxuries. I have done a great deal for you and your brother. Bringing you into society, getting you close to Osborne. I have done this under the assumption that you were trustworthy from the start. My instinct—my desire—is to trust you, both you and David. But as a protector of the crown—"

"I know," she whispered.

She reached across the space between them to take his hand. He clutched her fingers, brought them to his lips and rubbed the silky skin of her palm against his cheek.

She felt the tender flesh of his lips under her fingers, and sighed. He lifted his head, and she saw in his eyes an understanding of her so piercing, so perceptive, she had to look away.

"I need some air," she said. Stifling under a strange guilt: by the need to use him like this; by the transferred assumptions of this world and her place in it. By the light in the fine hazel of his eyes, which seemed, in the misty glow of the conservatory, to be suddenly more home to her than her own.

A breeze from the terrazzo's open doors reached into the heady warmth of the conservatory. Straightening her chin, she strode out onto the terrace, where moonlight filtered through the mid-October clouds and shone sporadic light on patterned stone.

Robb followed. She heard his shoes scuff behind her. Closed her eyes and lifted her face to the shifting light of the stars.

He stood beside her. She could feel his vibrancy and shook with the way it transmitted across the space between their bodies, minute shivers that thickened her blood and made it slow and painful in her veins.

Sara waited for him to say something, anything; to ask, again, *Who are you?*

Instead, he said, "Marry me."

His voice was quietly severe: with intent and the desolation it exposed in him. Sara caught her breath, and said nothing.

Shaking, she excused herself and returned to the crowded, glittering room filled with men and women, laughing, sparring, dancing—pawns and marionettes alone against the backdrop of the warm, glowing light.

CHAPTER 28

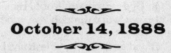

October 14, 1888

Sara
⋆ Grant Townhouse ⋆ 6:25 AM

"Avery. He didn't know me."

They were sitting on the terrazzo outside their big house. The stone was cold, still dewy at dawn. Neither of them had slept.

"He didn't even remember you from the night in the courtyard. And that's evidence of more damage than we thought."

She nodded. "It's possible his personality has fractured to multiples, each one unknown to the other. Makes him more dangerous than ever."

"But we do know where he is," David said. "And I do have sodium pentathol." He shrugged when she looked at him. "Standard Black Ops truth serum."

"Won't work. He can't tell you what the primary personality doesn't know. Use it and you'll just make his psychosis worse."

"We can't wait for him to remember," David said quietly. "Every day we're here, the problem just gets bigger."

"I know," she whispered. Out on the broad lawn, a white peacock paced his way along the grass—a pale shadow in the dim light; his slow, halting walk so like a wedding march.

"I had the key," she whispered.

David turned to her sharply. "Had?"

"It's his ring. I had it in my hand, but he asked me to give it back."

"And you just handed it to him?"

"Robb was there."

"Is there a reason we care that much about what the inspector thinks, Sara? Without that key—"

"We need him," she said tightly. "We can't touch history

ourselves. Any changes we make, we leave behind our fingerprints. We have to work through people—influence, guide, orchestrate."

"Like Robb?"

She sighed. "Oh God, especially Robb. He's our connection here. Everyone else we work through, we have to go through him to get there."

"He's a man," David said quietly. "Flesh and blood and warm to the touch. A man who's trusted us more than he should have already. That wasn't for me, it was for you. He deserves better."

She swallowed hard and stared blindly at the grass. "He's a man who deserves his world to unfold as it should. If he knew what we were trying to do, he'd do the same himself."

"And Avery?" David asked. "If he knew what we were trying to do?"

On the lawn, the stately cock pecked at a hen, scattering the small flock before him.

"Avery can't ever know," Sara said, her eyes sober. "He's a human bomb, one we have to dismantle. If he goes off before we're ready, he'll take us all out with him."

CHAPTER 29

Robb
* Whitehall * 2:43 PM

"Uncle, I have a favor to ask."

Robb sat in his uncle's study, a richly paneled place, warm with its crackling fire.

Leo raised his eyebrows. "At last, he asks a favor. What is the world coming to?" Robb didn't smile, and Leo's attempt to pry him out of his gloom faded into the warmth of the paneling. "You know I will help you in any way I can. What has happened, Jonas?"

Robb hesitated. Now that it came to saying it, he wasn't sure how to get it out. "I have made some friends," he began.

"One of whom is a lady, I've heard," his uncle said. His eyes were wary, as if they would rejoice to find delight in his life but feared for him, as well.

"I don't know these friends well," Robb said slowly. "I have given them too much, perhaps, of my trust." He glanced up at Leo, but his uncle said nothing—only tented his hands and held them to his lips, listening. "They are unusual people, Uncle. They fit into no social category I am aware of. They say they are American, and they—" His voice had dropped to a whisper. "They know things. Things they shouldn't know. And I don't know how—"

"How what?" his uncle prompted gently, after Robb had dwindled into silence. "You don't know how they know what they do? Or you don't know how you can go on befriending people who present you with such a mystery?"

Robb nodded painfully, a bitter admission. "Both. I've been dithering, too long. But—Uncle, I think—could they be spies?"

His uncle started. "Spies?" he asked, hissing, as if in pain. "Good God, Jonas, what makes you think so?"

It was uncomfortable, horribly so. But this was the professional part of their discussion. It was not personal, if it involved the empire. He had to get on with it, put on some professional distance.

"They are investigating a man who has become powerful over the last two years. You know him. Sir Jay Osborne." His uncle winced at the name. Robb said, "Yes. You have reservations about him yourself."

"Too influential," Leo said with some distaste. "Wielding that paper of his like the arbiter of our society and its political future. Of course I don't like him."

"It could be worse than that," Robb said, hesitant. "Sara. She's told me things."

"About Sir Jay?" His uncle asked, his eyes brightening.

Robb nodded. "Intimations. She has this idea . . . that he is somehow plotting to overthrow the crown."

Leo's eyebrows rose to nearly the top of his head. "You're joking," he said, an explosive sound with only a hint of hope in it. Then, delicately, he asked, "And this lady, Miss Grant. How, ah—?"

"Would she know? That's the problem, isn't it? I have no idea. Which is why I've come to you."

Leo nodded his head wisely. "I see. You do not like to question the lady's veracity. But she is, after all, a woman, and has no place in such business."

"Exactly," Robb said, stiff in his bones and his own skin. "And then there is her brother, who I would swear is a dangerous man but who I would also swear is of no threat to me. I know they have lied to me—not out of spite but because they cannot tell me the truth. But what could be so terrible that they could not tell me?"

The question fell hard in the paneled room. His uncle sat back, considering. "And these people, they are well placed in society? Well enough to do damage to Sir Jay or the crown themselves?"

Robb shrugged miserably. "I can't imagine how. They are newcomers. Rich, but that only goes so far. They have introductions, but most of the place they have in society right now they owe to me," he admitted, rueful—not missing the irony. He sighed heavily. "It could be nothing, Uncle. Perhaps I am just jealous of anything she's not telling me. Perhaps I want to know too much."

Leo shook his head. "You can never know too much about anyone." He smiled, wry but with a fire in his eyes, a kind of delight. "Gossip can be so enriching. Enlightening, too. I'd like to meet these friends of yours. It might be interesting to let them investigate Sir Jay more closely. Especially if we can watch."

"They'll be at the country party next weekend," Robb said. Fear and hope teetered precariously. He dampened both severely.

His uncle, surprised, said, "You *have* become close quickly." And, as Robb turned his head away, his uncle asked, "And your part of this misstep? You've crossed a line somewhere as well, beyond inviting them into society. That," he said, "you would have enjoyed—unleashing such unusual people into the staid ranks of your father's circle." He looked at Robb—watchful, suddenly, and terribly aware. "Where did you cross the line?"

Robb stood. He went to the large hearth, drawn suddenly to its warmth, though his own face was flushed and hot.

"Jonas?" his uncle asked gently.

Robb turned, fought not to stuff his hands in his pockets like a schoolboy who had stolen toffees. He said, "I asked her to marry me."

His uncle stood. "Did she accept?"

"No," Robb whispered. "But neither did she refuse. And it is early in our association. So perhaps," he shrugged, "there is still hope for me."

His uncle came out from behind the stately desk. He crossed the room to stand next to Robb at the fire. "No, there isn't," he said, quietly. "Let her go. She's only a dream that will give you grief."

Robb looked at his uncle, stunned. "What do you mean?" he asked. And then, when his uncle hesitated, Robb cried, "Why will no one tell me what I need to know?"

His uncle held up a hand and tried to smile; yet his hand trembled. "I know. I know. It must gall you terribly. You're an inspector. You should know everything."

"I'm a man, Uncle. I should know to protect my own heart."

This hit home squarely. His uncle straightened, closed his eyes. "Yes," he said heavily. "Indeed you should. Jonas, Her Majesty has expressed her wish for you to marry."

The words hit Robb just under the heart. "I see," he said, when he could speak at all.

His uncle nodded. Both of them stood in silence, absorbing the impact of it. The fire whispered in the hearth, nonsense words that held no comfort. Somewhere in the building, a grandfather clock tolled the hour: three bells, muffled by the walls.

Robb said, "I have proposed—"

"No," his uncle said, suddenly fierce. "She has not accepted, and now there is no time."

Robb looked up at his uncle, limbs cold. "Her Majesty—she has specified someone?"

His uncle smiled bitterly. "How well you know her. Yes, she has made her choice known. Not in so many words, of course."

"Who?" Robb asked, hoarse.

"Your cousin, Lillia Mersey."

"Lillia! But—she's like a sister to me."

"She is also the daughter of a duke, and you, the son of an earl. An earl who has few prospects of his other sons marrying."

"Damn it," Robb said, suddenly vicious.

Leo nodded, his hooded eyes heavy with pain. "Regal disappointment can be a sharp and dangerous thing. You must make a decision, Jonas, whether you will follow your heart or the crown."

"If I refuse?" Robb asked carefully.

His uncle shook his head. "You know the costs involved here, to you and Lillia both. Only you can weigh them." He paused, wanting to apologize but knowing it would only salt the wound.

Robb nodded, looking around the room without seeing it. "Then you may tell Her Majesty that I will certainly consider her suggestion."

His uncle smiled, a fleeting thing. "That will buy you time," he said, sage and just a little impious.

He turned. Their interview, with all of its wrinkles and folds, was over. Robb walked with him to the door.

"These friends of yours," Leo said. "You said they had introductions?"

Robb nodded. "Yes. They are supposed to be related to the Archduke Wilhelm of Bern. Cousin of the queen, isn't he?"

"A distant one," Leo said absently. Then he smiled, a visible putting away of all burdens. "I will look into it. And look forward, also, to meeting these friends at your father's house party."

Robb said, quietly, "You don't think they could be spies, do you? Does America do that to us?"

"Oh yes," his uncle told him, suddenly jaunty. "They spy on us all the time, and we on them. How do you think we stay friends?"

CHAPTER 30

October 16, 1888

David

"We could kill him," David said quietly. "Osborne. Make him disappear."

Sara glanced around the shop, even though she knew no one had heard. Around them, girls wearing feathered hats and beautifully tailored dresses sat beside chaperons and flirted discreetly with gentleman callers.

Sara put down her own cup, shaking her head. "No. Killing a man with that much influence would only make things worse. You saw how people hero-worship him—hang on his every word. There would be riots, David—riots worse than the one we saw."

"Damned if we do, damned if we don't," David said. The smoky incense of his coffee smelled of deep-tilled earth steaming under the sun. He breathed over the cup, taking it in deep. The day was warm for October, fragile as porcelain. It had rained for two days, clearing the air. Now the sun was out, daubing the sky overhead a pale Dresden blue. It was the first good day he'd seen since they'd come here.

Sara looked beyond him, thinking. A beautiful woman taking tea in a fine café: a Renoir setting, the salmon pink of her dress highlighting her golden skin. Face thoughtful, long neck balancing the mass of dark curls on her head and the pert orange hat that sailed above them. A picture of grace. Delicate, refined.

She cupped a china demitasse in her hands and said, "Do you know how the ancients used to eliminate an enemy?"

David smiled, the picture of delicacy shading to something more substantial. Dryly, he said, "I can imagine a few methods."

She put down the cup and looked at him, eyes keen. "Killing wasn't enough. They knew that. You have to erase his influence, all trace of him. Dismantle his temples, smash his statues, desecrate the tomb being built for his afterlife. Deface the standing stones that tell his story. Wipe his name from the records of the earth."

David raised an eyebrow. "Is that what we have to do to Avery, here?"

She shrugged, a picture of delicacy once again, but her eyes were grim. "It worked for history."

Sara
* Grant Townhouse * 1:36 PM

The ballroom was small and stacked with newspapers purchased from the Central News Agency's morgue. It had taken days to bring it all in, to organize. Dusty, dirty, Sara surveyed her small kingdom of newsprint and smiled, knowing she required permission from no one to read them.

Osborne owned all of these titles. He could have acquired just one or two and still been a voice of influence. Why would any man go to the expense of owning all of them?

She sat on a stack, thinking of the prostitute, Lottie, telling her about deaths that had never been recorded in Osborne's newspapers. *"Jack this, Jack that. But nothin' abaht anyfink else."* Was it true? Had Osborne deliberately focused on this one set of murders? Certainly the Ripper was a good story. In the right hands, it could become the symbol of everything wrong with the English class system. But to ignore all the other murders? No responsible journalist would do it. She couldn't conceive of any reason Osborne would.

And Mary Kelly saying, *"They ain't gonna pay for what they already know. Tom says the Boss tells 'em what they can and can't write. Frosts Tom that much sometimes. The Boss calls it 'editorial direction.' My sorry arse. In't nothing but one man tellin' us what he wants us to hear."*

Osborne. Advisor to the rich. Pied piper to the poor. Playing both communities against one another. If she knew why he was doing it, she might find out what he was planning to do.

To stop him, to ever go home, she had to know: Why wasn't he reporting all the deaths of Whitechapel?

She worked in the cold, not daring to use an open flame near the dry newsprint. The noon waxed over to the fullness of evening. A fine rain hissed outside. The sky darkened and evening crept along the windows, a voyeur layering kisses on the glass as she read.

Robb
* Huntingdon Street Men's Club * 7:56 PM

Robb moved wearily up the stairs to his room at the club. The attendant, Silas, met him at the top. "Will you be staying the night, sir?" he asked.

Robb nodded. "Bring a light dinner to my rooms, would you, Silas?"

He unlocked the door to his small apartment. Footsteps on the stairs made him hesitate, and turn. At the banister, the figure of a man, tall and slender, emerged from the shadows that always pooled there. *They need electric on that stoop*, Robb thought, startled to irritability by the unexpected movement. Then he straightened at the door.

Sir Jay Osborne melted out of the shadows, and nodded to him in passing. "Inspector," he murmured, smiling. He went three doors down, watching Robb, with that curve on his lips, as he unlocked his own door and went inside. The sound of the solid wood closing was brisk as any slap in the face.

"Might I get you a brandy before I bring up your meal, sir?" Silas asked behind him.

Robb shook his head. "No, thank you. Silas, how long has Osborne had rooms here?"

"Since last month, sir, though he rarely uses them. Perhaps it's the inclement weather tonight. Are you certain there's nothing more I can do for you, sir?"

Robb nodded. Silas moved down the hall to the stairs. Robb listened to the soft scuff of shoes on the runner until they faded, then went into his room and shut the door. All the familiarity of the room remained, but none of the comfort. In spite of the fire's warmth, he was cold with the awareness that Osborne, sleeping or awake, was just two walls away.

CHAPTER 31

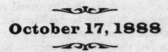

October 17, 1888

David
* Grant Townhouse * 11:15 AM

David came into the ballroom, settling on a stack of *Gazettes*. Motes of newsprint soot filtered the light from the tall ballroom windows. The air tasted of paper and dust.

"Having fun?" he asked.

"Not much," she admitted. "Take a look at this, will you?"

She handed him a set of newspapers—Osborne's version of the *Times*. Each had a different date. And each, in escalating positions of prominence, reported the vicious murders of women in the Whitechapel slums. The faces of each woman, photographed in death, were labeled with their names: Annie Millwood, Ada Wilson, Emma Smith, Martha Tabram, Mary Ann Nichols. The last, he noted, was dated on the day of the riot in the slums, the first day after he and Sara had arrived. Banner headlines emblazoned on the front cover:

WHITECHAPEL RIOTS OVER SIXTH RIPPER MURDER;
ANNIE CHAPMAN FOUND AT HANBURY STREET

David looked up. "The Ripper again. Sara, we don't have time for detours here."

"It's not a detour. David, nobody else in this time would have known these other women were the victims of Jack the Ripper. The first four were never associated with those killings. The newspapers on my PDA report their deaths, yes, but *don't* connect them. Their deaths are not even mentioned as the work of one man, much less Jack the Ripper. But the moment Osborne took over the *Times*, he reported every one, starting with Annie Millwood."

"I don't see Jack named in any of these reports," David said.

"If he doesn't remember his own name, he wouldn't have remembered Jack's," Sara said. "But he would have an instinct about these women—a pull, like he did with me. Jack, that name came out of a postcard, sent to the police by the killer early this month. Later scholars thought it had been written by a reporter at the *Times*."

"Even if he could intuit that their deaths were connected, why would Osborne report these other women in the news?" David asked.

Sara tapped a finger on her cheek slowly. "And why not report all the others?"

"What others?" David asked warily.

"The women in the slums knew of other killings," Sara told him, "murders that Osborne *hasn't* reported. Each women knew at least six or seven. Taken collectively, that could add up to dozens of dead women that Osborne has never reported in the news. But it can't be because he didn't know about them. It's one thing for the police precincts to be so out of touch with one another they don't realize the scope of what's happening. But with this many news outlets, Osborne has more men on the street than the police could put there. A lot more. And unlike the police, all of those men report to just one man—*Osborne*. So he knows, David. He *knows*. And yet he's done nothing, said nothing. Why?"

She straightened suddenly. "He's a creation. *Jack*. He's Osborne's creation. His claim to fame in this time. The ultimate scoop. Osborne is capitalizing—concentrating the focus on a handful of spectacular deaths to influence political and social outcomes."

"To what end?" David argued.

"Think of the first day we were here. The slums were a powder keg. Chapman's body was found at one end of the street and the police started rounding up women at the other end. That couldn't have been coincidence. And we know now that Osborne has more influence than just his editorials. *He* sparked the riot."

"If he wanted the slums to explode, why not report the other deaths, too? You'd think that whatever he was trying to achieve, if there are that many more women being killed, he'd use those to his advantage too."

"Exactly. Why would play up eight murders and hide dozens of others?" Her eyes widened. "He *will* use them. He's just waiting for the right time. We need to find out when, and how, he plans to do it. My God, David—he's using the news to start a revolution."

CHAPTER 32

October 18, 1888

Robb
* Dunwoody Park, Cotswolds * 4:30 PM

Fall was coming on, rolling against the earth as surely as a wall of fog. There was muscle in the chill of the day. The trees were dropping their brilliant leaves and the skies changed aspect with the wind. At times it was dazzling, the color etched with a clarity that sang in the blood; at others, it was a leaden gray balloon. Today, the sky over the dun fields was wildly, painfully blue.

Robb saw the carriage before he heard it. A skein of tension wormed along his neck, his heart racing, and for nothing. It was the wrong coach. Sir Jay Osborne stepped out. Robb's annoyance immediately discharged his disappointment and he noticed, with wry contentment, that Sir Jay's new coachmen were not nearly as well-matched a pair as David and George had been.

Robb watched as Bartley, his father's country house butler, took Osborne's coat and ushered him into the hall. Before Bartley could lead Osborne along to his rooms, Sir Jay caught sight of Robb, standing at the window.

"Waiting for anyone special?" Osborne asked, jovial.

Robb blinked at the outrageous familiarity, and Sir Jay smiled, shrugging apologetically—a gesture they both knew was so utterly insincere as to actually double the insult.

"Forgive me," Osborne said, watching him playfully, "but your father has already told me of your impending engagement. Congratulations."

"There is nothing to congratulate me for," Robb told him, offering only the blandest expression for Osborne to explore. "I have not yet announced my intentions."

"The queen herself has arranged your match." Osborne tilted his head to the side. "I would not think any man could refuse."

Robb said nothing, but kept his eyes steadily on Osborne. The constancy of it, and the silence, communicated more than words could between them. That look said, *You are the enemy.*

Osborne inclined his head and smiled, a gesture that accepted the fact and, at the same time, disregarded it as a threat. Maddeningly delighted. Osborne turned his back to Robb and followed Bartley upstairs to his rooms.

Outside, the clatter of hooves announced a new visitor. Robb went back to the window, but wearily. This time, he knew immediately who it was. Lillia. And her father. Gods.

"Jonas," Lord Mersey said, taking his hands, beaming. "How good it is to see you again."

"Of course," Robb said. "Father is in the library, Uncle, awaiting you—with brandy, I believe."

"Ah, excellent," Mersey said, and left them in the entry.

Robb was alone, finally, with Lillia, and the hall seemed suddenly too public a place, with nowhere to hide.

"Is it true?" she whispered, eyes wide. Outrage glimmered in her face—waiting for him, for his confirmation—to let it fully bloom. And yet she was not angry with him, he knew. She was as sure of his coercion as her own.

"Inasmuch as the queen has made her preferences known, yes." Lillia gave a fleeting smile. "Let's not think about it for now," he told her. "We have some time yet before we must make an announcement or hoist our sails against the crown."

"Only until Monday," Lillia said. Robb looked her, stunned. She nodded. "My father is planning on it, as a cap to the festivities."

Robb closed his eyes. She took his hand, and he looked down and realized she really was far lovelier than she knew. Had it not been for Sara, he might not have fought this so hard, might not have fought it at all.

"They can't *make* us marry," Lillia was telling him.

Robb smiled bitterly. "No. They can only press their displeasure until we break against it."

"I've never cared about society," she said fiercely. "I certainly will not let them force me into this."

"You've never been poor, either," Robb reminded her, grim,

"or a spinster shut away from the rest of the world to atone for your family's disappointment. As much as we've never honored the privileges of our fathers, we've never had to make our lives without them. I, at least, have a job—"

"I could work—"

"Doing what?" Robb asked, knowing a reality she had no way to grasp and suddenly, horribly, fearing for her. "Governess? Librarian? Who would hire a Duke's daughter? You certainly couldn't go into service. And though I know your father would see you were taken care of, at home, I cannot imagine living under his imperatives for the rest of your life."

Lillia looked down at their hands, clasped tight in mutual apprehension. "It's monstrous," she whispered.

"It is indeed," Robb said quietly. He put his arms around her, realizing how much more tenuous her position was than his, how brutal were the depredations of their society and its expectations: Holding her precious against them.

"What about you?" Lillia asked, muffled against his coat. "You love this woman, I'm told. How can you not marry her?"

"If she would have me, I would," he whispered.

Lillia pushed away from his chest. "She really did refuse you?"

"She didn't refuse me," Robb said, peevish. "She simply hasn't given me an answer yet."

Lillia smiled at his irritation. Then, out the window, he saw the outline of a light coach coming up the drive. "Yes, it's their carriage," she told him.

He threw her a fierce look. "You should not know me so damned well, cousin."

She laughed, and waited with him until Sara and David arrived at the house.

CHAPTER 33

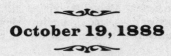

October 19, 1888

Sara
* Dunwoody Park * 7:45 PM

The formalities began Friday night with dinner and a light ball.
Standing at the top of the stairs, Sara watched a flickering
stream of people enter the hallway. Pearls and diamonds glittered fitfully, and top hats turned like fat periscopes, the sheen
of silk winking—ghostly silver fireflies.

"I thought Robb said this was an intimate weekend," David
growled in her ear.

"This is the Hunt Ball. It kicks off the festivities. Most of
these people will be gone by tonight."

"Yeah, well, stay close. Osborne's been trying to get me alone—to ask for your hand, I think."

"You're joking," Sara said, horrified.

"Two proposals in one Season. You're a popular girl with
these Victorian boys."

"The Season is over," Sara said sharply.

"Tell that to Osborne," David murmured, guiding her smoothly
down the stairs.

Osborne
* Dunwoody Park * 8:02 PM

Seating was never an open choice, but it was always an opportunity, and he had his connections. Made sure that David was
seated midway down the table. That Robb was safely ensconced
at the other end with Mersey's daughter.

And Sara was seated at his left, next to him.

Diamonds glittered in her hair under the candles and gaslight, set better than the velvet of a jeweler's case. Montcliffe, His Lordship, sat directly across. As he hoped, his immediate companions were awkward with one another.

"Lord Montcliffe," Sara said, hesitant. "How have you been?"

"Couldn't be better," Montcliffe replied stiffly. "Though my son has seen happier days, since you refused him."

Osborne glanced over to Sara. Few women had the grace to blush that well.

"I did not refuse him," she said quietly.

"What do you mean?" Montcliffe demanded, scandalized.

Sara said, "I gave him no answer at all."

Montcliffe relaxed, harrumphed. "Too late now, though, isn't it? The queen has made it clear the kind of match she wants him to make. He'll announce his engagement soon enough."

"His engagement?" Pale, her eyes dark against that honeyed skin, brilliantly staggered. Was that the glimmer of tears?

"To your niece, wasn't it?" Osborne asked, jollying the old man along. "Pity, had a bit of an eye on her myself."

"Yes," the earl said. He was fatuous now, scenting a kill. "Lillia Mersey. Sorry, chap. You'll have to make do with someone else."

"Oh, there's always someone," Osborne said softly, and glanced at Sara.

Montcliffe leaned back and nodded at Osborne, infinitely satisfied. "A young woman should always be married," he said softly.

"Hear, hear," Osborne murmured, raising his wine glass to his lips.

Watching her through pleasure-slitted eyes, he savored the high flush of her cheeks and the rosy glow at the top of her breasts.

"Are you cold, my dear?" he asked, laying his hand on hers.

Goose bumps exploded, spangling her arms. Osborne nodded to a servant. "See to the fire," he said, smiling. He slid his hand down to her wrist and held it possessively. "Quickly, the lady is cold."

David * Dunwoody Park * 9:12 PM

He found her sitting behind a banana plant in the foyer, drinking in the cold air each time the heavy door opened. "Learn anything?" he asked quietly.

"Only that Jonathan Avery is every bit as much as a shit now as he was when he could remember himself," she whispered.

David raised his eyebrows, scanning the people in the next room for reaction. There was none. The gentle babble of voices and the lilt of the chamber quartet in the corner had overshadowed her words, and only he had heard.

"Did you notice?" he asked. "Osborne. He's not wearing his ring."

"I did notice. Which means I could get it."

"You?"

"That thing isn't just a ring. Maybe it works like our transponders and unlocks the Portal by proximity alone, but maybe not. I may have to reprogram it. And once we get him to the Portal, we may not have time to do that."

"Then tell *me* how to do it," he said.

"There is no crash course in quantum programming," she scoffed.

"Do you have any idea what will happen if Osborne catches you in his bedroom?" David asked quietly.

She shot him a look of pure malice. "More than you know. But I have to do it. I'm the only one who knows the technology."

"It can't be you."

"It *has* to be me!" Sara said explosively.

The door opened. It was Robb. He looked significantly between Sara and David. "Anything wrong?" he asked warily.

David straightened. "No. Nothing. Nothing at all."

Robb hesitated. "David, Osborne has asked for you. Specifically asked for me to bring you to him. Do you know what this is about?"

"Nothing good, I'm sure," David told him.

"No," Robb said. "It seems that whatever reaction you wished to provoke with him, you have his full attention."

Robb bowed briefly as he left Sara in the library. On the way out, David glanced back at her with an unspoken, unmistakable order: *Stay out.*

Sara * 9:35 PM

She waited until David and Robb rounded the corner, their footsteps dying into the melee of noise where the rest of the crowd laughed and gossiped and showed themselves off. Then she approached the staircase, winding up to the top of the foyer.

Osborne • 9:38 PM

Osborne watched with amusement as Robb steered David Grant his way. It was almost like a dance, really. All the people between him and these men, each woman striving for a touch of grace, a bit of David's notice, the men stopping Robb for a word. The rhythm of it had a lilt of its own.

The majordomo, Harris, stopped at Osborne's elbow. "Sir," he said quietly, "the item you requested."

He slipped the ring box into Osborne's hand. Osborne opened the shining black box and smiled at the heavy gold thing inside. Why he was impelled to give her this, he didn't know. He would get her something better, later—something as delicate as she was, topped by a diamond large enough to tell the world that she was his.

But for now, this ring signified a moment between them. That evening in the conservatory, the first night they met. He had put it on her finger then and God, it had been delicious, that symbolic coupling. Tonight, he would do it again, and there would be nothing symbolic about it. He would slip into her as smoothly as she had his ring. He shivered with the pleasure of the thought, and snapped the lid shut.

"That's all," he said, waving Harris away and slipping the box into his pocket, warm with it and with his excitement. But Harris didn't go. Instead, he stared into the crowd. Irritated, Osborne turned coolly toward his servant. "Have you seen something among His Lordship's guests that displeases you, Harris?"

Harris blinked, flushing deeply. "I am sorry, sir. But that man," he said, and nodded discreetly at David. "He, he was—"

"Out with it," Osborne commanded, frowning.

"Well it can't be, sir, but I'd swear—that man, the one with Mr. Robb—worked only last month as your coachman."

Osborne snapped around, seeking David again in the crowd. "You're sure?" he asked, suddenly winded, as if he had climbed a great number of steps at high altitude.

"Well, sir, I do believe so," Harris said carefully. "The same man who vanished two days before you discovered your pack was gone."

Osborne waved Harris away. He could feel the furious splotches of red blooming on his cheeks, florets of rage. Robb was bringing David Grant ever closer, and suddenly, Osborne did not want to talk to him. Not tonight. Perhaps not ever. Making chitchat would be impossible now.

David Grant—of all people. *Knew* him. Knew the past he did not know himself. Knew the significance of the devices in the white bag, so powerful and yet so foreign to him.

A chill finger played along his belly, worming into his loins. It hurt. So cold inside, the core of him was freezing, beginning that teeth-rattling shiver. He needed to warm himself. Quite suddenly, he left the room, moving quickly through the kitchens, slipping past the green baize door.

Sara * 9:38 PM

Sara prowled quietly through Osborne's room at the Montcliffe country house, looking for the ring. It hadn't been in his closets, wasn't stashed in any of the drawers. The bright light of the gas sconce over his bed pooled around the pillows, around the squat marble-topped side table. The bedclothes were neatly made.

She pulled down the covers. The smooth sheets did not entirely disguise the smell of Osborne, the man: woody essence, like spice; and undertones of something bitter—musk and flatus, strangely acidic.

She felt under the pillows, under the mattress. Her fingers touched a thin nylon casing. She pulled it out.

It was a big knife. Attached to its casement were the straps of a nylon shoulder halter. Its tip was wicked, a vicious gleam, and the edges were sharp. It was military issue, she knew—as out of place in this time as she was herself.

She put it back in its place under his mattress. Then noticed, just under the bright, pooling light at his bed, that the marble-topped side table settled too deep into the pile of the carpet.

Sara knelt and opened the door. Inside the table sat a small safe. It wasn't locked. Within the safe, stacks of money sat in neatly banded rows. Sara slipped one stack quietly into her reticule.

When she stood, she saw it—it sat on his desk like a shadow, a simple book, loosely bound in leather. She opened it in the middle and recognized the flowing lines of script immediately.

Avery's handwriting. She had seen it in a dozen ways—on sticky notes, scratch pads.

His diary. Not every day was recorded. The earliest were unbound sheaves, stuffed at the back. They were not dated, and crackled with the years they'd spent tucked into the book, hidden and incoherent. Page upon page of writing, phrases blotched and scattered. It was hateful, violent stuff. Murderous. Reflecting a rage so great, it could not be communicated rationally.

She concentrated on the earliest entries, thumbing through the pages to sections with whole paragraphs she could read and make sense of:

> *Anarchy simmers in this cauldron of poverty—a lever to move the world. Agitation, revolution: the poor, cocked like a loaded pistol. . . .*
>
> *Purchased three more miserable rags today. These people will believe anything they are told. Especially the lower classes: If it comes from a printing press, it comes from God.*
>
> *Private docks off Surrey; shipments due tomorrow. Nearing 72 percent of stock; need only another 22 percent to move . . .*
>
> *Finally! Lord Remington has secured the nomination. Prince Albert endorsed it privately, of course. I am in. Salisbury is in check. His pawn to my queen. He hasn't a chance on this board . . .*
>
> *Delicious irony: That England will be overthrown by neither war nor crusade, but by an army of dead women suddenly revealed . . .*
>
> *A killer stalks them at every turn. Ah, but his name is Legion and I know every one. Oh, but there is a time for knowing . . .*
>
> *Another riot, this one in Whitechapel. Better than Bloody Sunday. A sergeant killed at the scene—be hangings over that . . .*

Like an illuminated text, illustrations danced in the margins. The face of a microchip, circled many times. Wavery, nightmarish etchings that looked like the Portal at full power-up. And a body on a gurney, slit open and flayed from sternum to pubis—

"Bastard," she hissed. She slammed the book shut, threw it back on the desk.

She couldn't take the diary. He would notice its theft.

She went to the door, hesitating at the threshold. Then she went back and tore out the most damning sheets, tucking the paper into her bodice, pushing it deep. It nestled just under her heart, flat against her stomach.

Osborne * 9:40 PM

Osborne crept up the servants' staircase to his room. On the way, a pretty young maid was descending, her arms loaded with towels. She was one of his own servants thank God.

Osborne discarded the towels without a word and took the girl's hand, leading her to his room. The girl didn't argue. They had learned not to.

He couldn't think. It was all chaos, a bedlam that narrowed everything to the most basic needs, childlike and yet voracious. He was cold. He needed warmth—that tight, warm place. His testicles were shrunk to the size of walnuts, and not crawled close to his body, seeking heat to relieve the chill.

As soon as he opened the door to his room, he began pulling off the maid's plain blue dress. A noise behind them startled the girl and she cried out. Osborne, hungry animal that he was, looked up beyond her shoulder.

Sara stood at the foot of his bed. Shimmering in indigo silk, all the diamonds glittering in her hair.

A slow smile crept hungrily to his lips. He pushed the maid away, not even looking to see if she went. Not taking his eyes off Sara.

"Oh, this is better," he breathed. "This is so much better."

David * 9:40 PM

At the end of their maddeningly slow circuit through the room, Robb had reached for a glass of champagne just as Osborne slipped away.

"Where's he going?" Robb had murmured. "If you wanted to make a connection with him, that was your chance."

David said, abruptly, "Where's Sara?" His eyes scanned the big room.

"I didn't see her come out of the library," Robb admitted. "She's not here, certainly."

"Damn it. She's gone to Osborne's room."

Robb spilled his champagne. "His *room*?"

But David was already moving. Swearing, he headed for the staircase, taking the stairs two at a time.

Sara * 9:42 PM

"It's not what you think," Sara said.

"Yes it is," he told her, approaching slowly, savoring the moment. "I knew it from the moment I saw you: You're just like the others. You all want it so bad it's killing you."

"That may be," Sara said sharply, "but some of us are more discriminating in our choice of partners."

Osborne stopped, breathing heavily, his face red, as if she'd slapped him. Then he grinned, a wide and wolfish thing. "But it's my bedroom you're in," he pointed out.

Sara watched warily. Osborne took another step.

"Stop," she told him. Amazingly, he did, but he was still smiling, enjoying the game.

"This is no time to play the fainting virgin, my dear," he rasped. "And you needn't worry. I'm more than happy to speak with your brother after. I'll make you an honest woman, I promise."

"Come one step closer," Sara said, "and I'll kill you."

Osborne recoiled. Something flared in his eyes, the look of a thwarted tomcat. He considered the distance between them.

"I can do it with a single blow," she told him. "You know I can, if you'll just think about it. Go ahead. Try to remember."

Osborne hesitated. The weight of her words sank deep. He stopped and stared at her—vacant, almost mesmerized. Then he swayed, like a cobra, metronoming a slow, patient rhythm. Smiling slowly.

"Avery—" Sara warned.

His eyes blanked immediately, his face went slack. He stopped swaying.

"What—? What did you say?"

His eyes cleared suddenly and seemed, just as abruptly, more Avery than Osborne—as she had known him years ago, at the start of the Project. It was a vulnerable thing: wide open and terrified. As if the man she knew were trapped inside someone else and neither of them knew it.

The door opened. David stepped into the room, and Robb followed shortly after.

For one deep-etched moment, silence was gravity itself.

Then David said, "This doesn't look good. I might have to marry you to this gentleman, Sara."

"Are you insane?" Robb said sharply.

But David held up his hand.

Sara said nothing. She knew what David was doing, and thanked God he had the presence of mind to do it. Her insides contracted as Robb slow straightened, as if expecting nothing less than their betrayal.

Osborne began laughing softly. "You see?" he asked Sara, hunching in on himself and smiling. "I always get what I want. I'm always first."

His eyes blinked, stuttered.

Sara looked soberly between the three men. David, so careful, so utterly dangerous. Robb, confused and watching—seeing too much and understanding none of it. And the other, his face guttering between personalities: Avery and Osborne and something darker, something devolving down to horror.

David, his eyes on Osborne, came to her side. "Sara," he said, "go downstairs. I'll have no talk. You and the gentleman are not even formally engaged."

Sara nodded, watching how closely David kept Osborne in his sights. She too moved slowly, passing Osborne. Heard him whisper in a different voice, his Avery voice, oddly anguished: "*Beloved—*"

Sara closed her eyes and stopped. That slight Southern twang. Right now, at this moment, he was the young genius she remembered. She might never get another chance to reach him again.

Breathless and sick, Sara turned.

The instant she saw his face, she realized how weary Avery had become here. The exhaustion of carrying so many unknown aspects of himself, of keeping them at bay, had to be overwhelming.

Careful now—ignoring David's frown and the sharp catch of Robb's breath—she drew close to Avery.

"Jon, do you remember?" she whispered.

Avery smiled. His tenderness was absolute. "You?" he said. "Always."

Sara touched his arm. "The Portal, Jon. What's wrong with it?"

Something stuttered in Avery's eyes—a quick flag of terror. David moved closer. But Avery only smiled. He took the shiny ring case out of his pocket, and opened it. Inside, the heavy ring gleamed yellow against its backdrop of jeweler's velvet.

Avery took the ring out and brought it close, bending his head curiously, as if he could read inscriptions on its face. "*He* wanted you to have this," Avery murmured. Anxiety hummed around him. He raised his head, lips trembling. "But I don't. If I give it to you, you'll leave me."

Even as he said it, he began to sob. A puppet controlled by forces greater than his own simple flesh, Avery slowly opened his hand.

He was morphing, she realized: a hiccupping loop of personalities, melting between one and the other so quickly, his basic self had simply fled from the chaos of it.

He reached for Sara.

She heard Robb move forward, to keep Osborne from coming too close; saw David put out a hand to stop him.

Within that fragmented second, Avery was gone, and the eyes she found in Osborne's face were strange—as foreign to either man as an alien soul crouched happily in its web.

The stranger held out his hand. Carefully, Sara put her hand in his.

Slowly, smiling with a vicious knowledge, the stranger inhabiting Osborne's eyes slid the golden ring onto her finger.

Sara closed her fist around the ring. And again, felt the slightest thrum of electronic energy.

"That's enough," Robb spat. He shook off David's hand and rounded on Sara. "It's bad enough just being here, God knows, but I will not consent to stealing jewelry, for Christ's sake."

"Robb," Sara gasped. But he snatched the ring from her hand and gave it back to Osborne.

Three different men looked out of the same pair of eyes in Osborne's face and agreed: Robb had to die.

Behind them, David took their arms. All three of them backed out of the room, and Sara wondered if facing Osborne again might ever be possible.

What stood there—what watched them leave like servants before the face of a slayer king—was not Osborne and was not Avery.

Just before she shut the door, he winked: flipped the ring, caught it squarely, and dropped it down one deep, slender pocket.

David · 10:12 PM

"I hope it was worth it," David said. "Getting caught in Osborne's room."

He stood at the window of their sitting room at Dunwoody. Outside, a bank of cream-colored clouds rolled across a blue-black sky of slate—eerie, enchanting, beautiful.

"It had to be done," Sara said, weary. "You read the pages. You know what he's planning to do. If we don't stop him, there's no point to having the key."

"I thought the key was hope," David said quietly.

Sara smiled. "It was your transponder I was referring to at the time. But I suppose it's all the same. Unless we dismantle Osborne's infrastructure here, we can't go back."

"That diary outlines one hell of an infrastructure, Sara. He's planning a major campaign. What if he *is* setting up a revolution? That's something bigger than we can stop."

"No one is so big they can't be brought down," Sara said, her face severe. "The bills I took from Osborne's safe are counterfeit. If Robb can get them to the proper authorities, he may be able to squelch whatever Osborne is planning." She approached the window. It was wide enough for both of them to stand in front of it. "Their economy is weakening. It wasn't strong to begin with, but the flood of paper money, with no bullion behind it—it could bring them down, David."

"Why would Osborne do that? Why ruin the economy of a country he's trying to take over?"

Staring out the window, her eyes tracked the clouds, seeing in them the shapes of animals, even faces. Quietly, she said, "Ride in on a white horse, be a hero. Buy up all the gold behind the pound note and, when it falls, cruise in with the remedy. It's been done before. George Soros bankrupted the Bank of England by flooding the English market with paper currency. That was in nineteen ninety-two."

"You think Avery remembered that?" David asked. "A man who can't even remember to take his antibiotics?"

"No. I think he flooded the market by accident when he created his own fortune, then saw the political opportunity after. The diary talks about shipments. What if those shipments were gold?"

"The government must have a way to track that kind of purchase."

"They do. As a man," she smiled, "you could probably find out. But if it *is* true—where would he put that much bullion? It's not like he could arrange an offshore set up."

"He wouldn't have to. He does have a bank account. At our bank, in fact, in London."

She turned to him—feeling, immediately, the cold of the glass near her arm, and the gleam in his eyes.

"You wouldn't," she said. Frowning, vehement. "David, you can't rob the Bank of London."

But David only smiled slowly, a world of experience in his eyes she knew nothing about.

CHAPTER 34

October 20, 1888

Robb
* Dunwoody Park * 8:32 AM

In the morning, Osborne remembered none of it. He was subdued and thoughtful at breakfast, but utterly at ease with them all. Courting Sara again, openly. Toadying up to David, jockeying for a moment alone. He was cool with Robb, but that was nothing new; it was an old contest between them now, vying for Sara's hand.

An hour later, Osborne rode to the hunt at Robb's father's side, laughing.

As if that horrible moment in his room simply hadn't happened.

In the field, David lined up his shot. They all waited for it: That heartbeat between sighting the target and pulling the trigger.

Waited.

Robb's father exchanged a look with Osborne. Mersey raised his eyebrows. They were a trio of cronies, on the verge of outright scorn.

The birds were small in the sky.

David fired. Both pheasants stuttered in their flight and fluttered slowly to the ground. After an astounded moment, Osborne led the others in enthusiastic applause.

"Bravo," Montcliffe said, sniffing. "Haven't seen a shot like that since, well—don't believe I ever have. Deucedly good with a gun, you are, Grant."

Yes, Robb thought. *Better than any man had any need to be.*

David nodded at Osborne, at the knife strapped to the man's belt. "Nice tack. Don't think I've seen one like that."

"Beautiful, isn't it?" Osborne said. He unsheathed the big

knife, letting the sun glint mirror-tattoo flashes off the surface. He handed it to David.

"Is that a production number?" David murmured. "Under the hilt. See? Right there. It says MANUFACTURED 2004."

Osborne took the knife back slowly. "The number on a limited run, perhaps. Really, I have no idea."

"Never looked, what?" Montcliffe said. "The devil's in the details, but damned if I care. Fine-looking thing either way. Wouldn't mind having its like myself. A good knife is almost as useful as a good whore—"

The three men laughed, riding ahead of David and Robb. As they passed out of earshot, Robb pushed David's mount to a slow canter, an aggressive move that culled them from the hunt. David clung to the saddle horn, but kept his gun well in hand.

"I won't ask where you learned to shoot like that," Robb said, disturbed and angry still. The emotion of the night had clung to him like sweat. "Or why you can shoot but can barely mount a horse, or dance, and have to watch to know which fork to use with every course."

"Good morning to you, too," David said. "I take it you slept well."

"I did not," Robb said hotly. "I barely slept at all, in fact. Kept thinking about last night. It's against the law, you know. To harry a man to his destruction, to take everything in his life apart. Even a man like Osborne. What she did to him—"

"Had to be done," David said.

"My God! The man is barely sane. You are toying with a lunatic. Nothing," Robb said, "*nothing* would justify what I saw last night."

"This might." David pulled a bundle of money from his vest pocket.

Robb just looked at it, aghast. "Money now? She's stealing *money*—"

David fanned the bills. "It's fake. Counterfeit. And it's how Osborne made his millions, which means he's floated enough paper currency to weaken your economy to a dangerous degree." He tossed the stack to Robb, who barely caught it. "Unless you find out what he's doing, collapse is inevitable."

Robb gave him a foul glance, then looked at the bills. They felt like they always did in his hand: dense paper and swirling textures, like the ridges of finger pads.

But every number was the same. Every date, every mark, even the treasurer's signatory—all the same.

Robb looked up, breakfast hard in his stomach. In the distance, Osborne stood easy in a shooter's stance, aiming at the sky.

David
* Dunwoody Park * 6:38 PM

David came into her room without knocking. The maid, who had been putting Sara's hair up for dinner, squeaked with scandalized outrage. Sara dismissed her quietly.

"You've found something?" she asked.

"The Ripper victims," he said. "Were there any details on the weapon used?" David asked.

"Only one," Sara said. "Martha Tabram. Killed by a knife so strange, authorities apparently couldn't describe it. Something between a dagger and a bayonet."

"Something like this?" David asked, and pulled his knife out of his boot.

"I saw a knife just like that under Osborne's mattress," Sara said.

"I saw it on his belt ten minutes ago." David handed it to her. "Standard military issue for Black Ops. Generals tend to give them to friends, as gifts. Especially friends who have a certain level of clearance. Like your buddy Avery."

Sara stared at the knife. It was six inches long and wide at the base, wickedly serrated along the tip. "Martha Tabram. Killed by a knife that hasn't been made yet. *Osborne's* knife." Sara looked up at David, stunned. "But *why*? Why would Osborne kill Martha Tabram—a woman who was already going to be killed by the Ripper?"

"Because he's not just intuiting these murders or even exploiting them," David said. "He's committing them. Orchestrating at the very least. Either way, he's directed his creation of 'Jack,' and not just through the power of the press. He's involved. Directly, Sara. Not just with reportage but with the murders themselves."

"No," Sara said, vehement, and sick. She shook her head. Pins the maid had placed so carefully scattered, leaving tendrils to drift, threads of dark smoke on her bare shoulders. "Simple physics. Jack killed those women before Avery was born."

"It has nothing to do with physics, Sara. If the knife used to kill these women didn't come from this time, then the man who killed them didn't either. That doesn't mean the original Jack doesn't exist. It just means," David said, lowering his voice, "that Osborne got to some of these women before the other guy did. Which may be why he doesn't want anyone to know about the other murders. At least not until he sets someone up to take the fall for him."

"You're wrong," Sara said.

"You mean you hope I'm wrong, because Osborne being Jack doesn't square with your theory of time."

"I hope you're wrong," Sara said soberly, "because if you're right, he could use that key at any time to jump beyond our reach. Or go back home—"

David nodded. "And leave us stranded here."

Sara
⋅ Dunwoody Park ⋅ 7:37 PM

Before they went in to dinner, Robb pointed out a lean gentleman, speaking in a huddle with Montcliffe and Mersey. Uncle Leo. Clearly, by the warmth in Robb's eyes, the uncle was more father to Robb than Montcliffe had ever been. No wonder Robb was the man he was. The old man, still slim, with a lush head of white hair, glanced at Sara briefly. His sharp golden eyes reminded her of an old but potent lion and foreshadowed what Robb would be like in another forty years.

"He's your source at Whitehall?" Sara asked. "The one you asked about the precinct report?"

"He is," Robb told her. "They are very close, HRH and my Uncle Leo."

"Indeed?"

The question came from behind them. Robb and Sara turned to see Osborne standing idly by the banister with a glass of brandy. He raised his eyebrows. "Please, do tell," he said.

"Inquiring minds want to know?" Sara asked. She thought of the knife. Of Martha Tabram's battered body. Suddenly, the delicious threads of scent from the kitchen—sizzled meat and sweet potatoes—made her stomach churn.

"I am merely an honest editor," Osborne told her, bowing slightly and smiling. "And a good story is always of interest."

"My uncle Leopold serves the queen as her chief advisor," Robb explained to Osborne. "He counsels her as to any detail concerning the state, however large or small. Even the activities of mere editors could hardly escape his notice."

"You make the poor man sound a bit like God," Osborne said.

"The editor or my uncle?" Robb asked coolly.

Osborne laughed. "You may take your pick, of course."

At dinner, the setting was compellingly intimate. Five of them at the opulent table were unmarried. The division between age and matrimony was painfully obvious. Sara was sharply aware of the tensions and expectations fluttering around the table. Those unspoken demands were like birds let loose—nervy and unsettled, launching in new directions with every skipped breath or quickened heartbeat.

Osborne reveled in it, his color high, eyes bright. Sitting next to her again, the heat of his body imposed on her naked arm; so close, his every breath and laugh was an invasion.

She was still staggered by it: Osborne, a murderer.

Robb sat across from her. No one could mistake that his attention wandered her way throughout the meal, though his cousin Lillia sat just next to him. Certainly Lord Montcliffe noticed. Every glance Robb gave her was recorded in the hiccup in his lordship's social rhythms. And so Sara braced herself when, at the end of the meal, Montcliffe targeted Robb specifically.

"I have taken the liberty of inviting our neighbors, the Bonhams, to luncheon with us tomorrow," Montcliffe pronounced. "They are newly wed, you know—an excellent example of that blessed state of matrimony I would like to see you soon embrace."

Robb closed his eyes. Sara saw the pain in his face and wondered why his father didn't, or if the old man simply didn't care. In that moment, she hated Montcliffe with a ferocity that surprised her, an anger that burned especially hot because it wasn't for herself but for Robb, pale and stiff at the table.

Montcliffe saw that heat, and said to her, "You disagree, Miss Grant?" Emphasis on the *Miss*.

Still smarting for Robb, Sara met Montcliffe's heavy-lidded gaze head on. "Are you asking my opinion on marriage in general or on the Bonhams' in specific?"

"Since you do not know the Bonhams, I cannot see anything but the former," Montcliffe said, not bothering to hide his peevishness. Apparently, he was not used to anyone countering his verbal attacks.

Robb had opened his eyes, watching her, warily but with interest. For his sake, Sara forgot herself, her distance, her directives. She canted her head and dimpled scathingly at his father. "Can't you? Without even meeting your neighbors, I could make certain assumptions about their marriage. The first being that she went to the highest bidder she could draw."

Gasps and the clatter of utensils sounded around the table. Uncle Leo's eyes sharpened and then a small, humorous smile touched his lips. She heard *"My God"* from one of the men and didn't bother to pinpoint its source.

"Second," she said, ignoring the cold stares around the table, "I can guess that she loved him no more than the average prostitute loves her next customer. And third, that she had little choice in making such a match. She would have to marry simply to have any choice at all. And even then, any legal freedoms she might possess would have been stripped the moment she said *I do*."

The women's eyes were already far beyond her. They looked to some unknown point in the distance, their concentration fierce. And the men: The men stared hard, as if they could erase her with their eyes.

"Are you actually likening marriage to prostitution?" Lord Mersey asked. His voice was grim, carrying the weight of his position in society and the outrage of her implication.

"Tell me the difference," Sara said quietly.

"God is the difference," Montcliffe exploded. "It is a union, sanctified by God and made holy by the church."

Sara nodded. "And broken time and again by men who see no dishonor in violating the promises they made in their marriage vows with mistresses and whores and God knows what else. Can you tell me one thing? Why is that the same men who would die before they'd go back on their word to another gentleman think absolutely nothing of breaking a vow made before God to a woman?"

None of them answered. She hadn't expected them to.

"Stop hiding. *Think.* If you took away a man's right to govern his life, to own property, to hold money, to participate in the government that rules his rights and then forced him, by law, to accommodate his 'patron' coitally without question or even recourse for whatever brutality might follow, what would you call it?"

Stunned silence. It was just too outrageous. And then, quietly, from across the table, Robb said, "Slavery."

The older men ruffled in their seats—except Leo, who closed his eyes and nodded painfully, imperceptibly.

"Good God," Mersey whispered.

"Stuff and nonsense," Montcliffe pronounced. "Radical idealistic poppycock, and dangerous as well, my girl," he said, pinpointing Sara in the gun sights of his gaze. "You have no right to upset everyone, saying such things."

"And yet you have no compunction whatsoever in making people *do* such things."

"Really, woman," Montcliffe huffed.

"She's right, you know," Leo said quietly. They all turned to stare at him, venerated as he was in his age and position. "All of it. We're terrible hypocrites and we like it that way. Admit it and let it go at that."

"Honestly, Leopold," Montcliffe scolded.

Leo only smiled gently. "The future is for them to change, William. Mind you, they'll have to live with those changes, for better and for worse. It's a little like marriage, isn't it?"

"Of course," Osborne said, soothing. "There are so many new ideas floating about these days." He patted her hand. "You do well to play devil's advocate for us, my dear. And we do well to listen, to choose which direction we want our society and, indeed, our country to go. Even if we choose against those ideas, in favor of what is more familiar and of greater value to us."

Their relief was amazing. His words were a salve on their outrage, flattered them with the idea that they were *avant garde* enough to consider the new and outrageous even as he validated their old beliefs.

"Bravo, Sir Osborne," Sara said tightly. "Just what I would have expected from our vanguard of the press."

Osborne, uncertain, said, "I am proud of the work we do."

"I am also proud of it," Sara told him, "especially giving the illiterate a chance to know the issues that surround them. Even if they can't do a thing about it yet, knowledge is a precious thing, is it not?"

Osborne met her eyes, and something behind them glittered dangerously. "Absolutely," he said. "All progress is based on knowledge." He went afield for support, casting Montcliffe in the net of his gaze. "Don't you think so, my lord? It may happen one day that the poor are given representation in making our laws—"

"God forbid," Mersey said, shaking his head.

"I agree," Osborne told him. "But if it does happen, educating them now will at least mitigate some of the disaster."

Sara nodded, probing again for that dangerous glimmer in his eyes. "Like the Ripper coverage. Do you think inciting violence is good for the common man, Sir Jay?"

Montcliffe drew breath but Leo's gaze shifted to Osborne. Inquiring. A servant of the government, the status quo: A litmus, was Leo. Watching not for himself or his family, but for his queen. Osborne knew it, too. He had stiffened to waxwork, eyes veiled.

"Surely it must be reported," Mersey said, coming to Osborne's defense. "Women and other unfortunates do not have to read the papers. Certainly no woman in my house does."

"Hear, hear," Montcliffe muttered loudly.

"And yet she's right," Leo said. "So much of this coverage is targeted at a population that has no power. They can do nothing about their vulnerability but become violently angry with the government. Anyone with any responsibility at all has to question the veracity of the press at some point, don't we? To dwell on these incidents without solving the problem serves no purpose but to foment upheaval. Violence has already occurred over it. Bloody Sunday, the Whitechapel riot. One does have to ask what's next."

Osborne waved his hand, dismissing it as a problem. "The news can only report what it sees. It does not create the problems it reports."

"Doesn't it?" Sara asked quietly. She turned to him. "You own every major news vehicle in the greater London area. There are different editors, yes, but they all report back to you. Which means you control what people think."

"*All* of them?" Leo asked, eyes sharpening.

"No one can control what people think," Osborne scoffed, half laughing, but also seething.

"If you control what they know, you control what they think," Sara said. "What you choose to tell them—or not—forms the basis for their opinions and decisions. From there, it's easy to use your readership to make things happen. You could influence voting, incite rebellion. Maybe even revolution."

Osborne was almost white. They all looked to him for explanation, Leo most keenly. It should have been nothing more than lively social interaction. But Osborne's reactions built up the undertow of something darker. Aware of this, suddenly, he narrowed his eyes and then smiled, tilting his head back lazily. "Hmmm. Possible. Or it could be that we simply have a deucedly inept police force."

A bubble of laughter burst at the table. Robb's father laughed loudest. "Now that's something you can address when you become a member of Parliament, eh, what, Osborne?" Montcliffe asked, jovial.

Osborne smiled, deprecating.

David raised an eyebrow. "That's a big step. Between owning all the papers in London and a high position in government, you'd have opinion in England pretty well sewn up, wouldn't you?"

Osborne's smile iced over, becoming brittle again. "I would, of course, step down from running the agency," he said graciously.

"But you would no doubt keep a controlling interest," Sara said stiffly. "From your position in Parliament."

"Of course," Osborne said, glancing at her. "No one in his right mind would give up such an interest. It's my legacy."

"Nor would anyone expect you to," Montcliffe assured him.

"Wouldn't they?" Robb asked. "Sara's right. He who controls the opinions of a people controls those people. How they think, how they vote, how they interact with one another and with their governments. Misinformation or even overt control over what people are told is far more dangerous than no information at all."

Leo looked to Osborne, his eyes lively. "Indeed, Sir Jay, the two would seem to be incompatible. So—which will you give up?" he asked politely.

Osborne said, "Since I have not yet been voted in, neither."

"And if you are?" Leo asked. "Which shall I tell Her Majesty you will focus your attentions on?"

"Parliament, of course," Osborne admitted reluctantly. "The papers all but run themselves. It is not necessary for me to be involved in their editorial content."

"Not directly," Sara murmured, and Osborne glanced at her in pained bewilderment, eyes asking *Why?* Why was she doing this to him?

The butler came in with dessert, and Montcliffe waved it away. "Thank you, Bartley, but I would prefer the smoking room and the company of men. I've had enough of liberal feminine opinion for the night, I think. Gentlemen?"

He looked around the table for takers. Immediately, most of the men stood and followed him out of the room. David trailed Osborne. Leo, smiling her way, winked and followed David just as closely.

Robb stood as well. "Sara, may I have a word?"

The older women glanced her way—small smiles, bitterly superior. Now she would see how a woman was schooled. And that, Sara knew, was all they had left to them. Imprisoned within the orbits of their small and guarded world, they would enforce strict submission to its rules—social laws they were not even permitted to make.

For Robb's sake, she had showed them something different. Too different. They could not comprehend its value. And worse, if they did, they could do nothing to grasp it in this time. Her cruelty was unintentional but crushing—showing the bird its cage. She was a scientist, and trained to know better.

Face burning, she went with Robb. Graciously, he led her outside.

"God, fresh air," he said, and smiled.

The night was cool. Against that sweet fall chill and the hot burn of her embarrassment, her body came painfully alive.

At the back of the house, a large greenhouse glimmered in the moonlight, hundreds of panes of glass set like jewels in a wrought iron structure. "It's beautiful," she told him. Shivering. The clouds moved like slow, great ships overhead.

"Come see it," Robb said. He led her inside. It was mostly empty now, ready for the plants that would thrive here in early spring. A tap dripped watery notes, like music. The place was warm with the latent heat of the glass, the earthy smell of soil.

There, she turned to him and said, "I am so sorry—"

He took hold of her arms gently. "You were magnificent. Don't apologize."

Sara nodded, pulling away—from the relief of his praise, from his warmth and the delicious sandalwood-and-gardenia smell of him. From the sudden, forceful shiver in her hips—infusing, enlightening every nerve; filaments burning, thrumming, breathless with it.

"You've met Lillia. You know what they want me to do," he said.

"You've been handed a command performance," she whispered.

Robb nodded. "Yes. If I have no other takers."

Sara looked up at him—dared it, though her breasts were painfully heavy, coming alive to him. "What I said in there, it's no better when it's done to a man."

Robb smiled. "No, it isn't, is it?" he murmured. Then frowned—aware, suddenly, of the heat in her. He touched her face, and a shiver claimed her.

He turned his back, looking out the windows to the roiling night sky, and said, "So much depends on the decision I make here. With Lillia. And me. I need to know—"

He turned when he heard the rustling of her gown, slipping down, coming to rest like a small sea at her ankles.

"Sara," he whispered.

Robb ' 10:22 PM

Prosaic country greenhouse turned to Eden. He and his Eve, lying along the old chaise put here for storage. Dusty and smelling of mold. No light but what the moon gave them, slow winks that revealed the rise her breasts, the curve of her hips.

It was heaven.

Her hair, her lips on his. He closed his eyes and slipped within the rhythms of her body, sailing out on a sea of sky and cloud, moving together again.

Sara ' 11:10 PM

He touched her face, her lips. Sure of her answer now. Kissing her naked shoulder. Beside her, he was saying, "I'll speak with David immediately. We could be wed here, in the village—"

Sara shivered. Pulled away. "Oh God," she said, shaking. Then stood, fumbling her arms through the sleeves of the gown. He helped her with it, fastening each button with care. When he was finished, she turned to look at him, into those burnished eyes, burning so bright, and shook her head, fierce with the pain of it.

"I can't. I've told you. I *can't*."

In Robb, life seemed to stop, his body turning slowly to stone. He dropped his hands and still she would not look at him. "I know you care for me," he said. "Good God, I know you *want* me—"

"You'd better get dressed," she whispered.

He stared at her. "You would make love to me. You would be here, with me, like this. But you would not be my wife?"

He stopped, unable to continue: at war with magnitudes of bewilderment.

She watched him absorb it, this new view of her—so illicit to his context, freighted with so many judgments. She saw it clearly, even then. He loved her, would forgive her and could not, in fact, bear to bring her to judgment.

He acknowledged that truth candidly, nodding, the defeat bleak in his face. He said, roughly, "My God, Sara, you could be *ruined*. If anyone knew, if they ever found out—"

She waited, shivering, the sweat on her skin cold. She didn't watch as he dressed. Her longing for his body, for the feel of his life within hers, still sang in her blood. Siren songs, impossibilities. Infinitely precious. She could not have him, but that did not stop the wanting, or the need.

Buttoned up, he faced her, his eyes grave. "If after all this you still will not have me, as a husband—I must know why."

"Robb—"

"I can live with your refusal," he told her, abrupt, severe; the sting of it growing into anger now. "But I cannot live with not knowing why, once and for all. Or at least without knowing why I cannot avoid this ridiculous engagement that neither I nor Lillia want when I love you and no one else."

Sara closed her eyes. God, it hurt. She would suffer for him and not blink an eye, but hurting him was so much worse, a grief that robbed breath from her body. Its clarity so sharp, it birthed a truth her body had known for weeks, blinding and clear and terrible: She loved him.

The thrill of it followed, just as suddenly, with the hot, bitter flush of grief. All of it together—so strong, it forced a gasp from her, like a shout—wondrous and bitter. Eyes wide, she put her hand to her lips to stifle it. If she let it fly, it would be the end of everything she knew.

"Sara?" he asked, suddenly concerned.

Her body burned with the birth and death of emotions running too fast to question or contain. The fear, finally, bursting from her. "I can't. I'm sorry. I'm so sorry."

She pushed past him and ran out of the greenhouse. Passing a growth of roses bruised brown by the coming frost, she ran until she came to the house and into the darkness of an unused room, empty and cold with the coming winter, where she could sit to weep alone for the both of them.

CHAPTER 35

❧✦❧

October 21, 1888

➵✦➵

Robb
⭑ Dunwoody Park ⭑ 9:02 AM

Robb beat everyone but his uncle to the table the next morning. The old man smiled up at him, refusing, as always, to allow Robb to wallow in anything but the most promising emotions.

"The pastry is excellent this morning," he told Robb dryly.

Robb shook his head. Sleep, impossible last night, had come only fitfully just hours before. He sat in the pale morning light, relishing the solitude, the shame and the grim, quiet thrill at his core. Whatever she said, she loved him; he knew that, if he knew nothing else.

"In answer to your inquiry," Leo said, "no, your friends do not appear to be spies for the American government. Though what they *are* remains a mystery—and a delightful one at that."

Robb looked at him ruefully. It did not feel delightful at the moment.

"Yes, she is beautiful," Leo murmured. "More than that, spirited and intelligent. Gracious when she wishes to be. And a tongue that could shred steel when she finds it necessary. A formidable opponent. I am grateful my sources in the American government have no knowledge of either one of them."

The implication settled heavily. If David and Sara were not who they said they were, who *were* they?

Robb put the stack of bills on the table. Leo raised an eyebrow.

"They're fake," Robb murmured. "According to the Grants, Osborne has manufactured millions of them. Sara says he launders all of this through new businesses she believes he has developed in the slums. There is no gold standard behind them. I'm sure you know what that means for England."

Leo grew paler with every word. Hands shaking, he picked up the stack. He riffled through it, checking at random, and put them down with a sigh. "How do they know?" he asked.

"Sara found those in Osborne's rooms."

Leo narrowed his eyes. "Did she now?"

"It wasn't like that. I was there, too."

"The entire time?"

"Uncle, it wasn't—"

"Could she have planted the money?" Leo asked, forcing Robb to look past the obvious, into unknown territories he didn't want to think of.

Robb blinked. He opened his mouth to answer. And then stopped, thinking. "I—I don't know. She was there first—"

"It's inconclusive, then," Leo said, bitterly disappointed.

"Perhaps, yes," Robb said. "But it's a lead. It may go nowhere, but it's worth looking into. What's strange, Uncle, is that Osborne—he doesn't even remember the incident."

"Osborne *caught* you there? My God, Jonas."

But Robb shook his head, holding the money out to the old man. "Use this. Find out what Osborne is doing. If Sara is right, if he's plotting revolution—"

The door opened. Leo and Robb both stood, automatically.

The girl in the doorway was still young enough for her voice to sound like small, silver bells. "You don't have to stand up for me."

Leo glanced at Robb, stashing the bills neatly in his coat pocket. He left silently. Robb sat back down. Amanda, Mersey's youngest, just nine years old, sat beside him.

"Amanda, you're up very early this morning," Robb said. His voice was still shaking. "Shouldn't you be in the nursery?"

"Nurse has an awful headache," she answered. "It's all those Lockhart children visiting us. She won't even notice I've gone."

"Nurse always has a headache around children. Your parents should get rid of the woman and get a proper governess. And yes, I do have to stand up for you."

Thinking: Sara's daughter would look like this. Their children would have been golden-skinned and dark-eyed, with these masses of rosewood hair.

"What's wrong?" Amanda asked.

Robb patted her head, the crown of it filling his palm. "Nothing, dear," he said. "Nothing at all."

The door opened again. For David. Lillia. And Sara.

Robb stood. Immediately, memory took hold. The smell of the greenhouse, of her; how the chill of the air had been satisfied by the warmth they had created between them. He was silent long enough for it to be awkward.

Then, "Aren't you going to introduce me?" Amanda whispered.

Robb inhaled, clearing his throat. "Of course. May I present my cousin, Amanda Mersey, Lord Mersey's youngest daughter. Amanda, please allow me to introduce you to our guests, Sara and David Grant."

Amanda looked over both the Grants appreciatively, and said, "Are you married, then?"

The others laughed, but inside Robb, something small shattered.

"No," David told Amanda. "Sara is my sister."

Amanda nodded slowly. Her eyes, suddenly solemn, never left his. She asked David, "May I dance with you, when I come out?"

"Of course," David told her. "By that time, I might have actually learned how."

Her eyes widened. "Oh. Do hurry, then, won't you?" she asked, breathless. "Papa would never let me marry anyone who couldn't dance."

Sara * 11:33 AM

On the way to the picnic, Sara had no choice but to sit with Osborne, who sat by himself in a small caleche and smiled as she realized she would be riding with him, alone.

The temptation to look out the window and ignore him was strong. The countryside was exquisite, canopies of trees overflowing with tinted leaves in a kaleidoscope of scarlet, orange and yellow. But she was not here for the ride—she had a job to do. So she met his eyes, assessing him coolly, as if he were not a man but a scientific riddle that needed to be solved.

His mocking smile faltered. He leaned back, assessing her too. "You were missed last night," he said slowly.

"My absence could not have been of consequence to anyone," she said.

"Oh, but the after-dinner conversation wasn't the same without you," he said. He leaned forward, suddenly grim. "Really, I barely salvaged your reputation. What *were* you thinking?"

"Not of you," she said tartly.

He barked a laugh, his eyes treacherous with humor and anger both. He leaned back against the plush leather seat. A smile played lazily on his face against the hazy backdrop of his eyes and whatever he saw in his mind behind them. "And yet, your brother has all but married us," he murmured.

"You remember that?" Sara asked coolly.

"Why wouldn't I?" he asked. The lazy smile deepening. But behind his eyes, Sara saw that he didn't remember everything. "You were in my rooms," Osborne said softly. "Your brother said—"

"I know what he said," Sara said. "The question is, did you know what he meant?"

The stippling of the leaves masked the stirring mass at Osborne's groin. He stretched his indolent, maddening smile. "I'm a man, my dear. Of course I know what he meant."

The coach rocked to a gentle stop where a hillock overlooked the estate. At the top, a small pond was surrounded by ancient trees still crowned with glorious heads of color. The others were exiting their coaches and carriages. David was already heading toward their coach, which was the last in the line.

The fact of her loathing, solid as the earth, bore down on Osborne's satisfaction. Softly she told him, "Hell will freeze over before you touch me."

Osborne's smile only broadened: tranquil, serene, convinced. "But Earth can be hell, my dear," he said cheerfully. "And it's nearly winter already. We shall see."

David opened the door and Osborne bounded up and out of the carriage, slapping David's shoulder. "Excellent job, Grant—almost like you've done it before, old man." Laughing, he strolled jauntily over to Montcliffe and his cronies.

Sara stared after him. "I hate that man," she said. "He was an amoral narcissist before his personalities fragmented. Now he's a psychopath. He remembers too much and knows too little. The damage that man has done, is capable of doing—"

"Could be time to cut our losses," David said. "At least when it comes to Osborne."

"Obviously we can't force him to go back," she reminded David.

"I wasn't thinking of the Portal," he told her, grim.

"The changes he's made," she murmured. Catastrophic changes, she knew. News monopolies swaying nations. Criminal gangs revitalizing the economy of the slums. The pound weakening toward collapse. Women dying to keep the engine of those changes alive. "We still don't know how he's going to do it, David. What catalyst he'll use to execute his plans."

"We won't learn it from him, Sara—"

A child's shrill scream cut him off. At the edge of the pond, a boy waved his arms and pointed to the water. A hint of blue cloth rippled like a small wave on the placid pond, a foot kicking feebly beneath it.

David was halfway there before Sara had even thought to move. The other guests turned, unbelieving—unwilling to believe—to the pond. Robb was already running.

Sara, too, ran for the water. At the edge, David was desperately working to pull up the blue cloth, yanking at something under the water. Robb splashed in with him and helped. With one great, final heave, they separated the cloth from what held it under the water—a tangle of thick branches that Robb immediately threw behind him, out of the way.

In his arms, David held the body of a child, legs and arms dangling limp. Robb took the body from him and looked at the face, pale blue and slack, and clutched the little body close. Suddenly he wailed, a keening cry beyond reason or pain.

Sara stopped at the water's edge. Amanda. Robb held Amanda in his arms and wept over her body.

David waded out of the water. He glanced at Sara, struggling with the defeat in his eyes. The older members of the party were just getting to the pond, the shock echoing from face to face, the mother screaming, falling against Lord Mersey, who stood, numb and uncomprehending, in front of Robb.

Leo, horrified, cried out and wept, smoothing wet hair out of the child's face; his hands shaking too hard, his touch too gentle on the delicate skin to make a difference—a man moving in the sudden thrall of a nightmare.

David swore viciously, suddenly, and tore the child out of Robb's arms.

"What are you doing?" Robb shouted, tears and spittle flying.

Without answering, David covered the girl's mouth with his own and breathed air from his lungs into hers.

"Stop him," Leo cried. "Good God—"

Robb grabbed at David.

But the girl twitched, shuddering heavily. Robb stepped back and David breathed into the child again. A flood of water poured from her mouth. David cleared the airway and breathed again.

This time, Amanda kicked and stretched convulsively, like an infant newly released from the womb. She cried out, a thin wail, and began to sob. Opening her eyes, she clung in her confusion first to David and then, blinking uncomprehendingly, reached for her mother. The woman took her in a fierce embrace, joined by Lord Mersey, who ran his hands over the child as if to ensure himself that she really was alive and unhurt.

Robb, taking in long, harsh gasps, stood a pace away from David and just looked at him. "How?" he asked, breathless. "I've never seen the like. How'd you do it?"

Amanda, snug within the circle of her parents' embrace, was slowly regaining her color. She was not yet a healthy pink, but her skin was no longer that horrible shade of blue. It was clear, from the awareness in her eyes, that she had suffered no damage.

David didn't answer. He kept his eyes on the child. He was pale himself, Sara saw: lips white, shaking with the aftermath of shock and the chill of the cool air against wet clothes.

Robb nodded and suddenly embraced him. David looked at him, startled. "Thank you," Robb whispered.

David nodded, looking away. "Better get her a blanket," he said unevenly, almost fierce. "She's cold."

"I'll do that," Robb told him, sprinting for the nearest carriage and the blankets stored under the inside seats.

Leo, staring at David with wide eyes, backed away from them. At the edge of the group of adults surrounding the resurrected child, he canted his head toward David soberly and then turned away from them, to his niece.

Alone now, on the green.

"David—" Sara began, looking carefully at him.

"Don't," he said, his breathing still labored. "Don't even start."

He turned his back to her and headed toward the carriage he'd come in, stripping the sopping brocade coat off his back and throwing it to the ground.

Robb · 1:25 PM

Weariness had settled into Robb's bones, and yet the amazement of Amanda, alive, still sang in his blood, buoyant and thrilling. Quietly he followed the corridor from his parents' rooms to the main stair. His uncle Leo stood there, unnoticed, watching Sara and David, who stood at the bottom of the stairs, in the entry hall.

"Fantastic, wasn't it?" Robb breathed. "Amazing."

"Yes," Leo whispered, nodding. "Absolutely amazing. And yet I don't think the lady is happy about what he did. Indeed, I don't think she's pleased with him at all."

"What do you mean? Of course Sara is grateful for what David did—"

"Then why isn't she speaking to him?" Leo asked quietly.

Robb opened his mouth to protest and then noticed: At the bottom of the stairs, David and Sara said nothing to one another—they simply stared, locked in a painful battle of wills. Robb watched as David turned away from Sara and walked into the library. She followed after him, still saying nothing—and yet there was a certain desperation in her face, as if, without saying a word, they had been quarreling bitterly.

"Keep your eyes open," Leo said.

"For what?" Robb asked, exasperated.

"Wilhelm does not know them." Leo nodded as Robb's eyes widened. "Exactly. Archduke Wilhelm of Bern, the very man who endorsed them in society with a letter of introduction, has never heard of them. The letter was forged." He watched the open doors of the library, pensive, his eyes too old for his face. "They seem good people, Jonas. God knows they have done us a great good today. But be careful, my boy."

Leo left without smiling, and Robb went down the stairs stealthily. He would listen and see. So intent as he went down the stairs (on the tight silence stretching out of the yawning mouth of the library), Robb did not see Osborne slip down the hall toward the balcony of the room's second tier, even as Robb himself silently approached the open doors below.

Sara ⋆ 1:32 PM

She followed David into the library. Inside, the vaulted ceiling rose two stories, with an ornate balcony on the second floor. Cupolas adorned the balcony, man-sized minarets complete with filigreed archways and doll-sized windows.

Standing at the fireplace, David finally looked up at her. Meeting the patient implacability in her eyes, he turned away again, staring into the laughing flames.

"You do realize you just changed history," she told him. Her voice, in the vaulted room, seemed especially small and ineffective.

"And you haven't?" he asked. "With Robb?"

For one second she wondered how he could know. Then realized he didn't—not about the greenhouse, at least. Though it felt like bile in her throat, she said, "We never had a choice about using these people. We have to work through them. Making a conscious choice to change history is not the same thing."

"He loves you," David said, vehement. "He's done what he's done here for you, put himself at risk for you."

"It's not the same," she said. Choking on it: on the look in Robb's eyes, making love to her. "This isn't about me," she whispered.

"It's about all of us," he told her, stonily.

"David, please. I know you're angry." She smothered the plea in her voice with studied firmness. "I know how helpless you feel. But David, that girl—"

"Amanda," he said.

"—Amanda, yes, David, I know her name. That girl was meant to die today."

Robb ⋆ 1:33 PM

Outside the library doors, about to enter, Robb froze at the words, his heart and all the heat in his body suddenly still and cold. Instinctively, he stepped into the shadows around the door.

David was laughing. Bitter, acidic, a sound like alum on the tongue. The words Robb heard were madness, but the emotions behind them were so strong, so utterly foreign, they charted the waters of an unimaginable sea. So Robb listened, and heard David, asking Sara: "So? And how much damage do you think she'll do? A little girl, not even ten yet?"

Sara saying, "That's not the point and you know it." Robb could hear her despair, her voice throaty with it.

He looked past the door to watch the way she held herself against that pain. *Why?* Why would she be angry with David for saving Amanda's life?

Suddenly, David lunged, turning so fast that Sara fell into the chair behind her. Robb clutched the edge of the door.

"Then what *is* the point, Sara?" David was asking. "We're changing history just by *being* here. You, me, Robb, and yes, now, Amanda. How do you clean that up? What do you want me to do—murder a child to correct a glitch in history? Poison Uncle Leo because he knows too damned much? Bury Robb in the backyard somewhere?"

"David!"

"You tell me, Sara. Just how far do we take this?"

My God, Robb thought. A new stillness came upon him. Silently, he left his station behind the library doors, and headed for the hunting room and the guns stored there.

David
* Dunwoody Park * 1:35 PM

He waited for Sara's answer. He knew that his face, inches from hers, showed lines etched by the impossible choices he'd made over the years.

A tear tracked its silent way down her cheek.

David stood. "Never mind," he said, weary.

But she reached out to him. And instead of pushing her away he hugged her fiercely and asked the thing he feared the most. "So what about us? What if we can't change what Avery's done here? We'll be here for good. You don't have to be a madman to change time, Sara. You just have to *be* here."

A sound caught them both off guard. David let Sara go and realized, too late, that anyone could have been listening at the door.

Robb came into the library, angry and grim. David let go of Sara, and went very still.

Wiping her cheeks with the back of her hand, Sara asked, "How is Amanda?"

But Robb didn't answer. Instead he looked between her and David coldly, an unnatural stiffness in his bearing. He held a hunting rifle, raising its long silvered muzzle. The bore, big as an eye, stared at David, unblinking.

"Jonas?" Sara whispered.

David moved his hand slowly around his back, where the slim silhouette of the Glock lay flat against his hip.

Robb said. "Don't move, David. Whatever you have there, just leave it alone."

David glanced at Sara. He could drop Robb before he could pull the trigger. Sara knew it too. She shook her head and David stilled even further.

"Don't do it, Jonas," she told Robb quietly. "We don't want you to get hurt."

Robb said, mockingly polite, "I *am* the one with the gun."

"David could still overpower you," Sara told him. "*Please.* Put it down."

In whatever way David's coiled readiness showed, Robb saw it. Slowly, he lowered the bore, but only a fraction, and he did not release the trigger. "In God's name, who are you people?" he whispered. David glanced at Sara but said nothing. "*Who?*" Robb demanded.

"Tell him, Sara," David said wearily, turning his back to them, facing the fireplace. Dismissing Robb and his gun.

"David—"

"He deserves to know." David looked over his shoulder, raising an eyebrow at her. "Don't you think?" All three knew exactly what he meant. As an Inspector, they could toy with him. But as a friend, as a man, Robb deserved to know everything.

To Robb, David said, "You can put the gun down."

Robb raised the bore slightly. It wavered, a minuscule shiver of doubt. "Tell me first."

David smiled. Then he lunged. So fast, neither Sara nor Robb saw how he did it. Just suddenly Robb staring at his empty hands and, David holding the rifle. Robb paled and stood to attention, waiting for a blow he knew he could not defend himself against.

"Amanda?" he asked stiffly. "Will you be killing her as well?"

"I'm not killing anyone," David said. He popped the cartridges out of the breech, and propped the gun against a fili-greed table at the door. There, he turned and told Sara, "Next time, send a machine to do this job. A man couldn't stand by and watch a child die—not in this century or any other."

He left Sara alone in the room with Robb, where the only the sounds he heard on his way out were the *tick-tick-tick* of the implacably advancing clock and the swift chuff of his shoes on the carpeted stairs, going up to his room.

Osborne
* Dunwoody Park * 1:36 PM

In the shadowed arches of the east-side minaret, the fear clamped through his jaws to spread its viselike fingers around his skull.

Nothing they said made sense. Everything they said made sense.

The thin whine of it, the thread of a tornado's finger.

Footsteps climbing the wide stairs: Grant coming this way.

Whimpering, whining, Osborne stole from the hollow safety of the miniature turret and hurried down the hall to his rooms.

Robb * 1:37 PM

In the library, Robb watched Sara warily. In his eyes, a thousand judgments were born and died, tiny galaxies of analysis he had no way to complete, even inaccurately.

"This century?" he finally asked, barely a whisper.

She looked away. "What do you want to know?" she whispered.

Robb laughed—a hard and wild thing. "What *don't* I want to know? Who you are, where you came from. If you'll be my wife." The start in her, such a guilty tremor. Before she could refuse him outright again, he swallowed and said, "Start with the basics, then. Where are you from?"

Sara hesitated, watching him carefully. "You do realize," she said, "you may not believe what I have to say about that, but you must believe what I've told you about everything else."

"Would you lie about one and not about the other?"

"I wouldn't lie about either of them. But you're not likely to believe anything I say if you think I'm insane, and if I were you, that's what I would think."

"I am more intrigued by the minute," Robb said, moving to stand, stiff and contained, across the rug from her; next to the fire and whatever little warmth still lived in the room. "Why wouldn't I believe you?"

So clear, those eyes. Like honey with sun behind it, thoughts ticking through them like ripples on the surface of a pond. Where to begin was obviously a problem.

He had sat with hundreds of liars. In his experience, they always searched for the one thing he would believe, relaying it with all the earnestness of evangelical faith. And there she was, looking for that one thing. Now, the earnestness would come. She would try to convince him of some wild lie, the stake in his heart that would end whatever love he felt for her.

Suddenly, he didn't want to hear it. "Sara, stop. Please. I've been patient enough. No more dancing around it. I once asked you to marry me. Twice. You have yet to give me a final answer." He held up his hand. "No, I know you won't, but before we go any further, I need to hear you say it."

She looked at him, eyes wide and round. "No, Jonas," she whispered. "I can't marry you."

Robb smiled and nodded, though his face felt hot and tight. He looked down at the blurring kaleidoscope of colors that was his father's Turkish carpet. Looked up to find tears on her cheek. He hadn't felt himself move, but he had taken her hand, and brushed her wet cheeks with his thumb. "There, you see? You can say it. Now tell me why."

"Oh God, Robb," she said. She tightened her fingers around his, and he breathed in deep.

"Tell me, Sara. Just tell me."

She nodded. "If I were free to stay here and marry you, I would. But I'm not."

Robb frowned. "If you were free? For God's sake, Sara. David is your brother, isn't he?"

"That's not the point—"

"Is he or isn't he?"

Her eyes were wide and swimming with verities he could not even guess at. But when she said it, when she finally whispered "No," that intolerable truth struck him with all the weight of the world he would not have. Her hand, warm and tight in his, felt like stone.

"That isn't the reason," she said. "We're not involved, not the way you're thinking. I'm in this time for a reason. I can only stay a short while—"

"*This* time?" he asked. Confusion a color whirling with the pain. Catching the reference at last. Well, they had said it often enough, hadn't they?

"Yes," she admitted. Confessing something mortifying in its madness and somehow almost trite. She watched it dawn on him slowly as she said, "I'm from the future."

Robb closed his eyes. He held her hand tightly for a moment, then let it go. Stood, looking blindly toward the window. Only half heard what she was saying now, listening as though it were music, beautiful and haunting but unreachable, so far away. Only the last phrase exploded into clarity, like the cork on a bottle, its Champagne-effervescence stinging into focus.

"David and I were sent here to find Avery, to bring him back to our century."

"David," Robb said, nodding his head. "Your century." An unholy anger was building in him, a blankness in his mind he could not understand. Was this really happening?

The sound of the words were brittle now. "Avery came here to change things. We have to stop him. From changing your world, from changing ours. That's why I'm here, Robb. We have to take him back. And with who he's become here, he won't want to go."

Robb let her go on, then finally he turned and said, very quietly, "If you don't wish to marry me, you do not have to make up ridiculous stories. I'm a grown man, and unlike some, I am perfectly capable of taking *no* for an answer."

A small cry escaped her. "That has *nothing* to do with it," she said. "I *warned* you."

"*Warned* me?"

"I told you, you *would not* believe me."

It was too much: Her resentment popped his protective bubble of cerebral distance and he strode over to her, his hands on the mantel of the fireplace, pinning her between them.

"It's too ridiculous to give credence to," he said. "Time travel does not exist, and neither does your bloody damned future."

"No, it doesn't," she said, pointed and stiff. "Yet."

He looked at her hard, but saw no prevarication in her face—only an absolute knowledge of something he did not understand. It stirred a shiver in his heart, a tiptoeing confusion of fear. He had seen too many lies to not know—she was telling the truth, or thought she was.

Sheer terror for the balance of her mind made him ask a question he would have sworn, seconds ago, he would refuse to entertain. Quietly, carefully, he asked, "And what time, exactly, are you from?"

"The twenty-first century," she whispered, her eyes not leaving his. "We left there on June fifth, two thousand seven."

The sound of the clock ticked over their heads, merciless and maddening.

All right," he said, letting her go. A cool numbness stole over him, blessed anesthesia against the horror of her belief. "We'll think of something. There are doctors for this sort of thing. We'll get through it, Sara. We'll get help—"

She swore savagely, a profanity so extreme it should have stunned him to his roots. It didn't. He was too numb. He watched, helplessly, as she picked up her reticule and pulled from it a silver disk no thicker than his finger.

"This is a data repository," she told him, holding the idiot thing out to him. Then, crazily, she spoke to it. "On."

The little box in the middle of the disc lit up, clear light filled with color. Surprised, Robb stepped away. The sight of it elicited in him something forgotten, even primordial—a fear so sudden and deeply out of place, it was almost religious. Awe, horror. A superstitious dread. Thomas the Doubter, touching the bloodied hands of Christ.

This, he would not touch.

"From this," she told him, "I can extract all the details of this time. Like this. *The Honourable Jonas Robb*," she said to the disk. Inside the glowing window, a phantom formed, grainy moving pictures of a much-older man. Even so, recognizably his own face.

"Jesus God, Sara—don't touch it. Put it down—"

She held the thing out to him again. Again, he stepped away from it. She put it, face up, on the chair.

"And this," she said, holding out a long silver case. "Avery used this to build the fortune he's amassed in your time. Enough to buy his media empire and all the gold he needs to drown England in paper currency."

It looked like nothing more than a sleek cigar case. "Oh for God's sake, Sara," Robb said. But his voice was weak, almost papery.

From the disk, a tiny voice droned on: *"Sixth Earl of Montcliffe, tenth in line for the throne. Married in 1889 to produce three heirs, Leopold, William and John—"*

Torn between the spiraling voices, hers and the device, the fixed orbit of his life went spinning madly, blown from its sturdy path by an awareness much larger than his own. She must have seen it. She went to his father's desk and tore a scrap of paper off the blotter, putting it into the mouth of the slim case she held.

Robb closed his eyes—suddenly he did not want to see—but the thing lit up, brilliant white against his eyelids, and it whirred, purring like a cat. His eyes snapped open.

From the other end, a hundred pounds sterling spit smoothly out of the machine. The air inside him shook, tiny tremors—voiding reason, shattering the fragile logic of common sense. She held the note out to him. He looked without touching it, knowing it would be inexplicably warm and horribly, utterly foreign. Deliberately, she slipped it into his hand and he dropped it, stepping away. "No."

"Take it," she told him. "It's the same as the bills I gave you. Use them to find out what Osborne's doing, buying his way to power so he can change your world."

"Sara, for God's sake, enough—"

"Jonas, the truth is right in front of you. *Look* at it," she said, pleading, "*see* it"—as, on the chair, the disk droned on, *"see also Lillia Mersey Robb."*

"Lillia—" Robb whispered, sick inside. No, no, no. He pushed it away with all the strength of oblivion, embracing ignorance with an abrupt and burning fervor.

Shouting, suddenly, *"How much more can you ask of me?"*

The shock of it: a vibration of the space and existence between them, the horrifying *twang* of that precious connection snapping—an unseen umbilicus that severed, suddenly, with a wicked, hollow sound. They looked at each other, stricken. Then he turned on his heel and headed silently for the door.

Robb ⋅ 2:02 PM

Robb left the house without taking his coat. He walked blindly, not even seeing where he was going. The blood of humiliation burned in his cheeks, his body, and with it, a terrifying, horrible fear. The air was bitter with a sudden fall storm, the light gray. Above him, clouds swarmed almost lazily, building some interior charge that leadened the air and made it thick.

Lightning so far into autumn was rare, and yet he thought for one wild beat of his heart, *Strike me. Knock me down.*

The sky darkened, as if intuiting his wish and weighing him. And yet, no lightning came. Even the sky found him lacking.

Finally, exhausted, he stopped at the top of a hillock and found himself staring blindly down on his father's property. He watched the rain sweep in from the south, a gray veil, moving slow. Long fields stretched out, fallow now: patch-works of muted color, buff stubbles of wheat, deep earth where the land had been turned and furrowed for the coming spring. Winter was approaching, a chill and subtle lamentation on the land. The house sat just beyond the river; the boiling water, quickened by the rain, moved sinuously under the gray clouds, a muscular current, dangerous. God alone knew what swam beneath its smooth, silvery surface.

Robb swept the rain from his face, keeping his eyes on the white glimmering silhouette of the house, all but obscured by mist as the rain came down. Took in the cleansing air, gulping its sharp, electric edge. Eventually, his heart rate slowed, and his breathing slowed with it.

He had fallen in love with a mad woman. With that understanding, everything he thought about her was nullified between them. Her interest in Osborne became an ugly thing. Osborne was a scoundrel and a cad, but nothing more.

She was mad, he had to admit: The woman he loved was mad. She had to be.

Could she manufacture a metal toy that spoke? That lit and shivered and produced pound notes as real any made at the Treasury?

A grain of fear rubbed the tender flesh of that hurting rage that let him be blind, chafed it like the hard surface of grit in an oyster bed and asked, simply, *How?*

No. He could not accept it. These things were not real. They didn't look real or feel real, and no place in his bones could recognize them as part of this world.

It was not true. It could not be. It was too horribly, pathetically ridiculous. He would have to watch them carefully, both of them. Because if she was mad, then what was David? (*A man who could breathe life into the dead.*) If not her brother, what? Dangerous, certainly. It breathed from his skin, an exhalation Robb could no longer ignore.

Thunder and the sound of footsteps came up behind him: Robb whirled, ready for David, for Osborne, for anyone. But it was only the groundsman, returning to the house after working on the land. The groundsman, amazed to find a son of the house standing half a mile from shelter, in the rain with no coat, stopped and gawked. "All right there, sir?" he asked, finding his voice.

Robb straightened. "Yes, thank you."

"You'll catch yer death, out here."

Robb laughed at the thought. He had been drenched once today already. If he hadn't already caught his death, it wouldn't come for him now. "I'm all right, Perkins. Truly. I will come down momentarily. You may go on ahead."

The servant looked doubtful, but nodded. Weren't all the gentry mad, and the nobility even madder? He went on his way into the darkness, shaking his head.

Leaving Robb alone. Empty, wrung out. His thoughts were crystalline, painfully sharp. Wiping the wet from his face once again, he began the long walk back to the house.

Robb · 2:36 PM

He came in through the kitchen, weary and cold. Someone in the room cleared his throat. Robb looked up to find his father sitting with a cup of tea at the kitchen table.

"Knew you'd come in this way," the old man said. "Oh don't go on about it, boy. She is a beautiful creature. Most exquisite. But not your kind. Marry Lillia. She's your cousin. You can't get any closer than that."

"Father, please. I can't. Don't ask it."

Montcliffe said, "She's left you, you know. Hightailed it back to London with that brother of hers, if he really is her brother. Can't dance, did you know? What kind of family teaches the women to dance and the men to shoot but not sit a damned horse?" He sniffed. "Doesn't look a thing like her, either. My God, Jonas, you're a lucky man. A woman with her ideas."

"Sara's ideas are her own, and I approve of them," Robb said tightly. Water dripped from his hair, a maddening reminder of the day, of the Library, and the irony of conclusions he couldn't even accept, much less approve of.

"No one else would bloody well approve," his father thundered. "That a woman who would give herself to a man the way she did to you, and still not marry him— Oh yes, you were noticed. There's no hiding anything from so damned many servants."

Robb closed his eyes. One quick quiver at the pit of his belly died under the immense, immediate weight of duty. He sat fighting against it, against the words. Eyes still closed against that bitter seasick pressure.

His father sat back. "Yes," he said softly. "You do understand. And if you don't, it is so easy to ruin a girl—"

Robb held up a hand. "All right," he said, the vicious closing of a door.

"And?" his father pressed. Robb said nothing, and Montcliffe, exasperated, said, "Oh take them both, Jonas. Give Lillia a place in society as your wife and take the Grant woman for a mistress. God knows she is good for little else now."

Robb opened his eyes and looked at his father. Knew his eyes spoke of patricide when the old man shut his mouth. "I will marry Lillia," Robb told him slowly. "But you will never say a word against Sara, not to any man. Do it and you'll never see me again."

His father leaned away from him. Reluctant, bitter, Montcliffe nodded and raised his tea to his lips. The eyes above his cup were old, and treacherous with the irony of incomplete victory.

CHAPTER 36

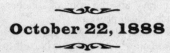

October 22, 1888

Robb
* Dunwoody Park * 10:32 AM

In the morning, he dressed as carefully as he ever had, immaculate in a gray morning suit, and went down late. They were all there, as knew they would be. Cold light filtered in through the breakfast room windows, rays of silver and broken dreams. He stood at the end of the table and tapped the rim of a glass quietly. The *ting* of it was small but so unexpected, he had their attention immediately.

"I have an announcement to make," he said. Letting the words fall like dropped stones. "I will be marrying Lillia Mersey next Monday at St. Peter's in London."

Lillia spun on her chair to stare at him, horrified.

He inclined his head with a bitter smile. "You are all invited to attend, of course."

Lillia scraped her chair harshly against the floor and fled the room. Uncle Leo closed his eyes and Osborne, sitting quietly at the end of the table, actually smiled.

Robb
* Oxford Train Station * 11:35 AM

Robb stood at the station platform, stiff in his formal clothes. A cold October wind pushed a swelter of desiccated leaves along the platform, rattling along the train windows, pelting against his legs—a startling fusillade of papery bullets. "The train? For God's sake, Lillia, let me get you a carriage."

She rounded on him. "How could you?" she asked, her voice low and savage.

"Your father sent me to bring you back to the house."

"My father has just sold me to your bed," she told him acidly. "If I'm old enough for that, I'm old enough to travel to London by myself, on the train. I do have a house key."

"That's hardly the point—"

"One *week*?" she spat, cornering him with a terrier's ferocity. "My God, Jonas, do you know what people will think?"

"You never cared what anyone thought before this," he said. Lips stiff, throat tight. "You can bloody well not care now."

Her eyes widened, another shock, as if he had slapped her right there, on the public platform in the middle of town. Anger quickly followed. Her face seemed to narrow, hawkish and on the attack. Before she could say anything, Robb took her shoulders, reaching for the old gentleness within himself and finding only a cold, haunted place, his hands shying from her warmth and the chaotic shivering of her bones.

"Lillia, please. I don't want to marry you and you don't want to marry me, but neither of us has any choice now. Let's just get it over with."

She broke away from him. "No, Jonas. This has nothing to do with me. It has to do with Sara. You love her and you're taking it out on me. It isn't fair. It *isn't*."

The train chuffed, sending a cloud of steam between them. He closed his eyes against the sudden heat of it, startling against the cold air; steeling himself against the shiver that started at the center of him and worked through the back of his neck where the steam breathed chill droplets along his hairline.

"Fair?" he echoed, barely aware that she had already left him, a welter of watercolor silk and clattering heels exploding staccato outbursts along the stone platform.

The stationmaster, watching her board, looked at him glumly. "Should be a lovely wedding, eh, guv?" he asked, and snapped his watch face shut.

ALIVE

&

BURIED

IN THE

GRAVEYARD

OF THE

PAST

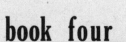

book four

CHAPTER 37

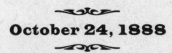

October 24, 1888

Robb
* PC Tompson's Home, Camden * 5:37 AM

PC Tompson didn't try to hide his surprise when Robb showed up at the bobby's home before sunrise. "Sir! It's good ta see yer again. Come back to work with us at Westminster, then, have yer?"

Robb shook his head. "I need a favor," he told Tompson, slipping into the house. It was quiet and cool, the chill only marginally muted by fading embers in the hearth.

Tompson led Robb to a small kitchen and sat him down at the table. Without preamble, Robb handed Tompson a slip of paper. "I need you to find out about three people. Here are their names. I need to know when they came to London, where they came from, and how they got here."

"I'll do what I can," Tompson told him honestly, looking at the names, "though I'll hav'ta hide it from Pershing."

"I know, and I appreciate it."

"This have to do with the case yer working down Whitechapel way, sir?"

"I don't know," Robb told him. "It could have direct bearing on it. Or it could have nothing to do with it at all." He hesitated, feeling the weight of too many empty years. "Either way, I need to know."

CHAPTER 38

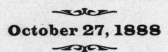

October 27, 1888

Sara
* Grant Townhouse * 7:06 AM

She couldn't eat. She looked out over the silver trays of food and thought of how much they wasted every day, of the children in the slums sifting through stinking middens for scraps. She couldn't get over the inequity, of knowing that even in her own time, in some places, poverty was every bit as bad as what she'd seen here.

David came in and sat down heavily at the table. Since the country house, he had barely spoken to her. At his elbow, the morning edition of the *Times* sat, freshly ironed. David glared at it. Abruptly, he asked, "Why is Avery still here? If time comes together on the other end and resets this whole deal to a completely different picture, why hasn't he disappeared by now?"

Sara put down her tea. "The equation could have a wide differential for the ratio. It could take a long time here for his changes to impact the future, and until that happened, we wouldn't notice any change."

"Four years is one hell of a long fuse, Sara."

She shrugged. "Doesn't matter. We still have to make them right. Stop Osborne's revolution, at least. It's the only thing that will reconstruct the timeline, get it as close to the original as possible."

"That's bullshit. Just with the changes Avery has already made—four years of them, for God's sake—why hasn't the picture already changed? Why haven't we disappeared if the future we were born into no longer exists?"

"We don't know what impact those changes will or won't

have on our time, David. Only large events might actually shift, not the lives of specific individuals."

"People live and die based on what's happening around them. Don't tell me the lives of individuals wouldn't change. The theory is wrong. Our best course of action is to get Avery back now, take us all out of the equation."

Sara leaned forward. "I understand your concern. But I'm not willing to risk the future with a hasty retreat."

He looked up at her sharply. "Sometimes, falling back is the best way to win."

"I prefer a strong defensive position myself," she said. "And that means taking Osborne apart here, piece by piece."

"Look, I'm as interested in taking Osborne apart as you are. But the longer we're here, the more changes we make ourselves."

"Nothing we've done yet even comes close to the changes Osborne has made, or what he's planning to do. Our impact has been minimal—"

"You sure of that?" David asked. His eyes narrowed, edginess a bee's nest scorching the air between them. "The Ripper hasn't killed this month," he said. "Yeah, I read the papers too. He may have started with sporadic murder, but beginning with Tabram, he'd worked up to killing cyclically, taking a victim every couple of weeks. According to our own history, he won't kill again until November. What do you think has stopped him for more than a month?"

Sara frowned. "Not every serial killer follows an exact pattern."

"This one was," David said. "Before he met you."

"I haven't met Jack," Sara scorned. Her impatience flooded its borders and she stood, her arms angrily crossed over her breasts. "I followed two of his historical victims and still have no idea who he is."

"What about the knife?" David asked.

"Inconclusive," she said.

"Out of all the women that have been killed since Avery came here," David said, "why would Osborne only report the Ripper's victims? How would he have known they were Jack's? How would he have even remembered them?"

"The same way he remembered me," Sara said. "No direct

recognition, but that same kind of fixation. He would have had that for each of these women."

"But when that happened between you and Osborne, he was *there*, Sara. He *saw* you. And the only way Osborne could have had the same experience with these women as he had with you—the only way he could have recognized them as Jack's victims—"

"He would have to have been there," Sara whispered.

"And now that Osborne has you to fixate on, Jack has stopped killing. That could be because there are no more Ripper victims for Osborne to recognize. But it could also mean that because he's so focused on you, Osborne has put Jack on the shelf—and that's why there are no Ripper victims recorded in history between the time Osborne met you and the last woman he decided to kill. If I'm remembering my history, that wasn't Catherine Eddowes. Who was she, Sara?"

"Mary Kelly," Sara whispered, and closed her eyes. "November eighth."

David stood. "Then it's an even bet that one of two things will happen. Either she'll be killed on that date because that's what happened before Avery came here. *Or*, somewhere between now and November eighth, you're going to do something to piss off Osborne so badly, he's going to start killing as Jack again."

"You don't *know* that," she cried.

David stepped close to her, his mouth set in harsh lines. "You don't know it either," he said. "No matter how great your theories are, you don't know a damned thing about time and how it works. Remember that."

Sara
✦ City of London Cemetery ✦ 10:22 AM

She stood in front of the grave without shivering. History, at least, was a tangible mystery, one where the answers could be found for those willing to look in odd places.

She hadn't found them going through the papers—all those women in the slums whose deaths she'd heard rumored. As a scientist observing the situation, she had wondered if even tough whores like Lottie Hanaman and Mary Kelly could fall prey to communal hysteria. It was not a given that so many more women had died than the authorities knew of; it was not a fact that human life could be so fleeting that even the news didn't seem to notice its passing.

But after a full mug of ale, Lottie Hanaman had given her six names, and Mary Kelly had given her four. Two living women—just two—who knew the names of ten dead. Each woman on the list had been murdered in Whitechapel in just the last three months, and Sara wondered how many others there were; how many others that different people knew of, and how many nobody knew about at all.

The small headstone in the East London Cemetery read: "Jane Hoscomb. Born July 29, 1866. Died January 12, 1888." She'd been twenty-two years old. Her grave was beautifully kept by the two children she had left behind, Charles and Peg.

Sara touched the words engraved into the stone. The letters were cool under her fingers, the edges deep and straight. And yet, according to her PDA, Hoscomb should not have died so young. Her death in the London Census was recorded as January 9, 1928.

Like the other five women whose graves she had visited, Jane Hoscomb should have been alive.

David
* Chart House Exchange
& Exchequer * 11:22 AM

"Investments like this are always a matter of public record, sir," said the clerk, who said his name was Eugene. "A volatile commodity, gold is. The movement of which is paramount to any country's stability. Obtaining bullion in large quantities would alarm the government, since, as you know, our paper currency is based on a gold standard. You're free to look those purchases up, as you please. But," he said, and hesitated.

"What?" David asked. He did his best to look earnest, and leaned forward, conspiratorially.

Eugene leaned in as well. "You must know that a paper trail will exist only for gold purchased legally. For those who wish to play Midas, there are other ways to buy. French pirates have been known to bring gold shipments up through Surrey, frigates filled with American bullion pillaged by Spanish ships. Highly irregular."

David nodded his thanks and sat down to scan through the transactions record. Row upon row showed Osborne buying bullion right up to the British-standard legal limit, ten percent per private individual. David took Osborne's diary pages out of his pocket. He sorted through the entries until he found it. *Private docks off Surrey; shipments due tomorrow. Nearing 72 percent of stock; need only another 22 percent to move . . .*

"Did you find everything you were looking for, sir?" Eugene asked, coming up behind him.

"I did. Maybe even a few of those irregular purchases you were telling me about."

"Irregular is a relative thing. As some might see it, stolen gold could be considered fair game."

"Fair?" David asked, raising his eyebrows.

"Well, sir," Eugene said, and smiled. "Your countrymen stole that gold from the Indians. Then the Spanish stole it from the Americans, and the English steal it from the Spaniards. And you can't really steal from thieves, now can you?"

"No," David murmured. "You really can't."

Sara
* Whitechapel Station * 12:36 PM

She had expected awkwardness, even anger, but not this coldness. "There are things you should know," she told Robb. Sitting in front of his desk, two feet of wood and a small geography of frigid terrains between them.

"It's a bit late for that, isn't it?" he asked.

"I wasn't talking about me. I've been researching other victims of the Ripper. Comparing those deaths with current news sources. Osborne hasn't reported them."

"We already know that Osborne plays the press as he pleases," Robb said. So formal, so distant. So cold.

She held to her patience, to what was important here. "Robb, even the police force hasn't connected these women to the Ripper. And yet there are obvious patterns in the victimology."

She handed him a copy of her notes. He glanced through what she'd written, and frowned. "Where did you get this information?" he asked, real starch in his voice.

"Since you already seem to know about them, where did you?" she asked pointedly.

"I work here at Whitechapel," he reminded her. "I am privy to the records of this station. You are not. So where—"

She held up her PDA. Robb sat back, took one breath of sheer annoyance.

"I've seen the graves," she said quietly. "And yet according to the London Census of 1889, these women should still be alive. They died because Jon Avery came here and became Osborne."

She stood up, held the PDA screen out to him. On the screen, the spidery handwriting of the census-taker was as clear as newspaper text.

She watched him look down, shaking his head, but she was determined that he would hear her. "Jane Holscomb," she said. "She died in Hackney last January. Stabbed six times in the heart. My records say she died in 1928, an old woman who had lived to see her great-grandchildren. Because of Osborne, she didn't live long enough to raise her kids to adulthood. Write it down. Keep her name in your memory. Because she's one of too damned many women who have died since Avery came here."

He raised his eyes to her. His face was white, his eyes narrow with anger. Sara pocketed the PDA and sat back down.

"The key," she said, "is the knife that killed Martha Tabram. It's unique, and there's only one type of knife that would be consistent to how it was described in the Ripper police reports."

"Reports you don't even have access to," he scorned.

"Robb, I *saw* the knife that could have done this. In Osborne's room, last weekend. David's knife is very much like it. It may even be the same. Standard military issue. Osborne, as Avery, had access to the same classified military weaponry. If that knife was used in these other murders—"

He sat up sharply, and frowned. "Are you—actually saying that Osborne is Jack the Ripper?"

"He's manipulating your system by way of murder," she told him. "The knife tells us that he's not just influencing others to kill but is participating in those killings himself. And the census proves these women were not meant to die."

"Oh, this is just insane," Robb said. A peevish lash of anger spasmed through his body. He stood, galvanized. "By your reasoning Jack could just as easily be David. He has the same knife. A knife you can't even compare to the wounds on any victim's body, I might add."

She sat in the face of his bitter disbelief, then said, "He'll get worse. Bolder. The mutilations will escalate. He's already posing the bodies, moving the legs just so. He's becoming ritualized, his method clarifying."

"What does any of it have to do with Osborne?"

"I told you," she said, suddenly fierce. "Because there are women who are dead right now who shouldn't be. Robb, why can't you see this?"

"*Why?*" he cried, throwing the word back at her. "How can you ask that? In order to believe you, I must pre-suppose the impossible. It's one damned fiction built on another. *That's* why."

She faced his anger quietly. "How many more women have to die before you'll do something about him?" she asked.

Robb straightened, stiffly polite. "I'm sorry, madam. Without legitimate proofs, I cannot even begin to investigate your allegations."

"Robb," she said, and began to stand.

"I will have to say good day, Miss Grant."

The finality in his words; the blank shell of his face.

She sat back down, legs suddenly weak. "My God," she whispered. "When you shut a door, you lock it behind you."

His eyes darkened to mud. It was all the answer she needed. Sara stood and left the chill little room, and did not look back when she snapped the door shut behind her.

Robb
* Whitechapel Station * 1:28 PM

Robb sat at his desk for half an hour, unmoving. Countering the sick shiver that wanted to grow, the ache at the core of him that would not ease.

When the world came back to him, the shabbiness of his office seemed unbearable. A copy of the *Times* lay on his desk, taunting him. Screaming the shame of the police for not finding the Ripper, morgue photographs of each dead woman's face and a full collection of letters from Saucy Jacky. Behind each word, he could hear Osborne, laughing.

Robb swore and shoved the paper aside.

A well-dressed clerk knocked at his open door tentatively. "Mr. Robb?"

His manners were as polished as his boots. Though young,

Robb guessed him to be of unusually good family. "Yes, I'm Robb," he said warily.

"Barnaby, sir," the clerk said, and smiled. It was the smile of near-equals. A very good family, then. "Your uncle Leopold sent me with some documents."

"Oh God. Yes, do come in," Robb said, and sighed. He was painfully aware that it was Sara who had sent him down this path to begin with, months ago.

Barnaby shut the door carefully, then sat at the front of Robb's battered desk. He sat back and looked at Robb for a long moment. Without his sober thoughtfulness, it would have been impertinence. Finally, he handed a thin dossier to Robb. "I won't say I'm not fascinated by it, in some awful way," he said.

Robb took the dossier warily. "What have you found?"

"The report gives details, of course," Barnaby said quietly. "But the conclusions are obvious—and alarming. The ramifications for the government, and for the police, are stunning."

Robb waited. Barnaby leaned toward him. "Over the last ten years," Barnaby said, "one hundred and sixty-four unfortunate women have been murdered in greater London and its environs. Of those, fifty-two have been accounted for—husbands, fathers, lovers, thieves. Deaths characteristic to the area."

Barnaby, to Robb's surprise, did not seem to judge the women any less for their misfortune. He hesitated, his young face grim. "The larger number, however," he said, "the remaining one hundred and twelve, are unaccounted for. It gets worse, sir. Are you sure you wish me to continue?"

"Please," Robb whispered.

"Of the deaths occurring over the last decade," Barnaby said, "only fourteen predate the last four years."

Robb snapped his head up, catching Barnaby's eyes—the fear in them matching the stunned and sudden silence in his own mind. "My God, are you sure?"

Barnaby nodded. "I'm afraid so, sir. I compiled the police reports myself." He paused. "Your uncle felt it wise to keep the original reports at Westminster, of course, but I've given you a breakdown of the details here. I hope it gives you what you need to catch this man, whoever the devil he is."

Shaking, Robb opened the file. Name upon name. He scanned through each one, reading the dates and locations of their deaths, their ages. Some were as young as fourteen. Robb made himself read to the end, eyes burning but dry.

At the end, three pages, in Barnaby's neat hand, codified a shorthand of more than one hundred deaths and a categorization of what was similar and what was not. Robb looked under the *W*s:

	METHOD	WOUNDS	ASSAILANT
WESTMINSTER			
I	CUT THROAT	BROKEN NECK	RIGHT HANDED
II	CUT THROAT	BREASTS	LEFT HANDED
WHITECHAPEL			
I	CUT THROAT	ABDOMEN	LEFT HANDED
II	STRANGLED	NONE	UNKNOWN
III	THROTTLED	NONE	UNKNOWN
IV	CUT THROAT	ABDOMEN	LEFT HANDED
V	THROTTLED	NONE	UNKNOWN
VI	CUT THROAT	NONE	RIGHT HANDED
VII	CUT THROAT	FACE, ABDOMEN	UNKNOWN
VIII	THROTTLED	NONE	UNKNOWN
IX	STRANGLED	NONE	UNKNOWN
X	GARROTED	NONE	UNKNOWN
XI	STABBED	LEGS, ABDOMEN	LEFT HANDED
XII	RAPED, BEATEN	VAGINAL TEARING	VARIOUS
XIII	STABBED	VARIOUS, HEART	VARIOUS—2 WEAPONS USED
XIV	STRANGLED	NONE	UNKNOWN

Whitechapel. Westminster. Deaths he'd seen himself, others he'd never heard of. He closed the report and set it back on his desk. It ruffled the pages of the *Times* as it settled, just beneath the shocking photographs of dead women lying in the Whitechapel morgue.

Robb glanced between them. Cold, suddenly. Realizing— Sara was right. Of all these murders, Osborne had reported only the Whitechapel killings. And yet he had men in the streets in every one of these places.

Why? Why would Osborne so viciously pursue the killings in

Whitechapel, but none of the killings of Lambeth or Southwark, Camden or Hackney or thirty other London precincts?

So many in such a short time. The numbers alone would have made a shocking, scandalous story—a story to topple governments.

At the back, a list of names indexed the dead. Robb read down to the "H" list.

Jane Holscomb.

Robb closed the report, the pages whispering shut.

Robb
* Whitehall * 2:45 PM

"You saw the report," his uncle said. Grim behind his desk, his body still. "We must keep it quiet at all costs. I know you want to tell your superiors in the force, but you can't. You can't let any of this out, ever."

Robb looked up at Leo, his eyes fierce beneath the dark dip of his hair. "And if someone else lets it out?"

Leo hesitated. "Revolution. But we won't let it come to that, will we?"

"No," Robb said grimly. "We won't. I need to know just one thing. I'd like you to send Barnaby to the London Library, to check on what our friend Osborne has printed about these deaths in the past."

Leo leaned back, his eyes keen. "Think that could be instructive, do you?" he asked.

"I do begin to think so," Robb murmured. He swore. "Damn it—I'm playing right into her hands again. No matter which way I turn, I'm right there, doing exactly what she wanted me to do from the start."

"Your mysterious American?" Leo asked. His gentleness, not surprising, was exactly the touch Robb needed.

"Yes," he said quietly. "I wouldn't have pursued this report myself. It was her idea. She said— Oh God, never mind. I can't even begin to tell you the insane things they've said about Osborne."

"Whatever they are," Leo said, his eyes solemn, "I would just as soon believe them. I would put nothing past Osborne, especially now."

Robb chuffed, a bitter laugh that did not meet his eyes. "You wouldn't believe this, trust me."

Leo stood and took the morning edition of *Punch* out of his desk. He threw it onto the surface. "I wouldn't have believed this, either," he said, "not even of Osborne. But I believe it now."

Robb read the headline:

SIR JAY NEXT PRIME MINISTER?

Slowly Robb raised his eyes, meeting his uncle's solemn gaze. A cold sweat broke out under his arms: Osborne as prime minister, a man who held sole possession of every credible news source governing the opinion of a nation.

"My God," he whispered, and his uncle nodded.

"You see the problem," Leo murmured.

CHAPTER 39

❧❧❧

October 28, 1888

❧❧❧

Osborne
* Huntingdon Street Men's Club * 7:10 PM

God, the things they had said. Osborne sat in his room at the club, curtains closed, the room silent but for the conspiratorial whispers of the fire and the slow, grinding tick of the clock on the wall.

In this century or any other. A shiver skittered deliciously through his bowels and danced on his arms. *We're changing history just by being here.*

He stood and hugged himself. A sharp elation surged through his body, radiating a sudden vitality, a warmth that raised the hair on his neck. So close to the heart of his dreams, and it wasn't frightening at all—wedding that sweating darkness to a delicious mystery. And that meddling damned policeman, asking, brokenhearted fool, "Who *are* you people?"

Who, indeed? Two rooms away, he heard a door shut and footsteps moving along the hall. Robb. Going down to dinner, or out. Smiling, Osborne left his room and, at Robb's door, tried the handle. It was not locked. Stealthily, he went inside.

Robb's room was dark. Osborne moved through it quietly, his eyes reflecting the low embers of the banked fire. Could you violate a man without his knowing it? Oh yes. Osborne traced his fingers along the spine of an old book, wandered past photographs and souvenirs from abroad.

He came to rest at Robb's desk. Under a ledger was an envelope, stamped with a palace seal. Smile predatory now, Osborne slid the envelope out from under the ledger and opened it.

His smile fled immediately, face filling with blood.

All of it. Documented here. Good God, where had Robb gotten it? How had he known? Who *else* knew?

Panic, pure and effervescent, weakened his knees. He smelled the pungent stink of his own sweat. *Think, damn it—think!*

Footsteps at the base of the stairway, stopping now. Murmur of voices. Robb's voice?

He could not just take the report. Not here, now—not with his own room paces away. It was part of Robb's work. The inspector would take it back to the station. And there—

Osborne slid the report back into the envelope, replaced it under the ledger. Quickly, he opened the door just enough to see that the hall outside was empty. He slid into the passage in time to see Robb clear the landing.

Seeing Osborne in the hall, between his room and the stairs, Robb stopped but said nothing. He was irritated, critical, mordant. Oh yes—he would marry in days. To a fine, lovely girl. But not Sara, and a good thing, too. Osborne would have had to kill the good inspector, had Sara Grant been his intended.

Smiling, Osborne moved aside, allowing Robb to open the door to his room. "How is our impending groom this afternoon, Inspector?" he asked quietly, eyes glittering with laughter.

"Piss off," Robb said flatly.

Osborne watched Robb enter his room and shut the door with a loud thump, and his smile widened. It was a lovely thing, the sound of another man's suffering; the smell and taste of it.

Lillia
* Grant Townhouse * 10:22 PM

She came looking for Sara, agitated, cheeks flushed with an unhealthy blotching of anxiety. Lillia had grown up in days— pushed to see the hypocrisy of her world without its illusions of comfort. The stamp of it was in her face.

"Sara isn't here," David told her, giving her room at the fireplace. "But if you're looking for anyone else to talk you out of getting married, I'd be happy to help."

She looked up at him, so beyond offense at the words, he wasn't sure she'd understood him. But if there was any pretense to cling to, it crumbled like a spit of island overwhelmed by the sea. "Oh, God," she sighed. "It's not that I don't love Jonas. I've always loved him. Just not like this."

Deliberately blunt, he said, "You mean, you don't want to have sex with him?"

She seized at the shock of it, furious. "Mr. Grant, *honestly*."

"Yes, honestly," he said quietly. "Are you being honest about how you feel? Even to yourself?"

She blinked, simply staring. And suddenly, miraculously, burst into tears.

He touched her arm, offering his. She didn't take it. She frowned at him fiercely. Snatching his offered handkerchief, she mopped at her face with an intense expression, one that painted a thin patina of dignity over repressed rage.

"Oh, God," she said again. Shaking now, she clutched the hanky without seeing it. "I wish I'd never heard Sara's outrageous opinions on marriage. This would be so easy to do, without knowing the truth."

David said, "You don't have to marry him if you don't want to."

Her eyes darkened. "Yes, I do. What else is there?"

"There's anything you want, if you're willing to work for it, risk for it."

"Spoken like a man," she scoffed. "If you had nothing—no money, no property, no skills—what would *you* do?"

He said, slowly, "Women can do anything, even here. You just have to tell the people who won't let you to go to hell."

"David!"

He shrugged. "There are always choices. Hard ones, maybe. With prices to be paid. But they are there."

She shook her head. "It's hopeless."

He took her face in his hands. Thought to talk sense, to make her hear. Instead, he kissed her. Meeting her mouth, tasting her tears. Feeling her surprise and the slow opening to a more profound revelation. She deepened into it with an unexpected heat.

He broke away and looked at her face. The anger was still there, but so was the revelation. And, finally, some thought behind the panic in her eyes.

David stepped away, standing at attention, hands behind his back. He gave her a solemn order. "Don't marry anyone you can't kiss like that. Whatever else you do, give yourself that much."

Watching him steadily, eyes wide and thoughtful, Lillia nodded. Tides of emotion burning her throat, she said, "I'd best go.
If anyone knew I was here, alone with you—"

"They'd what?" David chided softly. "Call off the wedding?"

She looked up, startled at the thought, ideas she didn't even
know she had swimming just below the surface.

It surprised them both when the door opened and Robb
came through, disheveled and sweating.

"Where's Sara?" Robb asked David.

"Jonas, for God's sake, that is so rude—" Lillia began.

"I need her. Need to talk to her," Robb interrupted hotly.
Then he frowned. "Lillia, go home. Please. I will explain to you
tomorrow."

"At our wedding?" she asked him pointedly, her anger curdling to concrete when she saw the surprise on his face. "You
forgot about it?" Tears flooded her eyes, sharpened by humiliation. "Are you planning to ask her one more time, Jonas?"

"Of course not," Robb snapped. "But I need—"

"What, Jonas?" Lillia asked. "To say good-bye? Or to make
love to her one last time, before you come to me?"

Robb stopped, stunned. "Who said it?" he asked, enraged.

"Your father, to mine," she cried, venomous. "Yes. He broke
your bargain. Will you break yours as well, then? Make me pay
for not being *her*?"

"You know I won't," Robb told her, equally angry.

"Hey," David said, coming between them. "You two are not
enemies. Don't let them do that to you."

They stepped apart, breathing heavily, and David took Lillia
aside.

"It's all right," he said, smoothing her hair, cupping her face.
Ignoring Robb's sudden frown. "Just remember what I said."

Lillia caught her breath. A tear fell, and she let it. She nodded
slowly and looked around the room. Seeing Robb. *Seeing* him.
She turned to David. "I will," she said. It was as if she'd finally
found the floor beneath her feet, and liked the feel of it under
her. She left quietly, without saying good-bye to either man.

David looked at Robb, who stood waiting, all confusion and
winded patience. "You really did forget?" David asked.

Robb ran his hands through his hair, grimacing. "God, yes."

"What do you need with Sara?"

Robb laughed, bitter hilarity stifled by apprehension. "I should have come yesterday. Wrestled with it instead. How's that for love?" He breathed deep. "I came to tell her," he said, "that she was right. About the killings, at least. That there were so many more than any our precincts, acting alone, had realized."

"She knows that," David said. "She also knows most of those deaths weren't supposed to happen—didn't happen until Avery came here and set up as Osborne. Now she's looking to prove that. By way of something you'll believe."

Robb barked a bitter laugh. "Ah yes, future-woman."

"She told you, then?"

"Yes," Robb whispered. "She told me."

"How much did you believe?"

Robb stared hard at him and David knew—not much.

And yet there was something there—hard facts glimmering in his peripheral vision that stung him into truculence. He shrugged. "Doesn't matter now, though, does it?" he asked bitterly. "I am, apparently, getting married in the morning."

Lillia
* Mersey House * 11:38 PM

Draped over a mounted form, her wedding dress stood guard over her virgin's bed, a ghostly portent in white lace.

Her mother, furious, entered the room. "Just what are you trying to do?" she demanded. "Calling at the Grants' house so late, and unattended—"

"Jonas was there," Lillia said wearily. Her mother stopped mid-tirade, her anger cooling, and Lillia did not admit to any other truth with her. It was a small treachery, but seemed somehow appropriate.

Sitting up in bed, Lillia cleared her throat. "Mother, what happens . . . after the wedding?" she asked. "That night, I mean."

Her mother raised her eyebrows, her face and neck flushing with embarrassment. She told Lillia, firmly, "It isn't necessary for a lady to know the—mechanics—of these things."

"Why?" Lillia asked. "Are you afraid that if I knew, I wouldn't do it?"

Her mother looked at her sharply, and Lillia knew, with a shrill stab of fear, that it was true. "It's something every woman faces," her mother told her. "Like your time of month, or birthing children. Unpleasant, but bearable."

"*How* unpleasant?" Lillia asked.

Her mother looked away and could not look at her—and that was more frightening than anything she had not yet said. But her mother did, finally, speak.

"No doubt it will hurt," she said quietly. "It always does, especially the first few times. And if he wants you . . . naked . . . the humiliation of it—"

"Naked?" Lillia breathed. She could not imagine what could transpire between a man and a woman that would require such a thing.

Her mother looked at her firmly, a dangerous steel in her eyes that broached no other possibilities. "You will become his wife tomorrow, Lillia. You will do as *he* wants, not as you want."

Her mother stood suddenly, and slowly, Lillia stood with her. "What if I won't do this?" she asked.

Her mother recoiled, aghast. "You *have* to do this. You have no choice."

Lillia closed her eyes as her mother left the room. Hearing the door close—a metallic snap as sharp as a crack of lightning—Lillia looked around the empty room and said, "But I do. Oh, yes, I do."

CHAPTER 40

October 29, 1888

Sara
* St. Peter's Cathedral * 10:02 AM

The day of the wedding howled with a wet wind that blew the first bite of winter against the stained glass windows, rattling the jeweled figures with its breath, probing cold fingers along the floor.

Few people spoke to them, but that didn't stop Sara and David from attending. Withering looks informed Sara that they should have known better. A society doyenne whispered into an old man's ear—Uncle Leo—nodding her head subtlely toward them. But instead of snubbing them, Leo left the doyenne's surprised clutch and made his graceful way over to her and David.

To her surprise, he smiled. "How are you holding up, my dear? Better than my poor nephew, I hope."

"How is he?" Sara asked.

Leo looked at her, solemn. "For a man who loves a mystery—a beautiful, unattainable mystery—he is doing surprisingly well. He is doing his duty. And that, at this time, is all anyone can ask of him."

Sara nodded, the movement jerky. She couldn't smile. Tears, ridiculously, welled up in her eyes. Leo kissed her hand. "Adieu," he whispered, and went up the aisle to take his seat just behind the queen.

Robb, resplendent in dove gray and the pale yellow sashing of his house, stood stiff and grim at the front of the chapel. He did not look toward David and Sara, though he could not have missed seeing them.

Sara listened, eyes closed, to the church sounds, hollow in the cavern of the cathedral. Discreet coughs were muffled in gloves. The rustle of silk skirts and low, murmuring voices surrounded them. Sara braced herself against the inevitable blast from the organ, which would be pitiless, amplified by the stone walls to an impact of sound and finality in her bones.

It never came. The long aisle, threaded with its red length of carpet, was empty. The appointed time wound down slowly and then passed. Lillia's family stood beside the queen and exchanged bewildered glances. Little Amanda stood among them, still pale in her pink silk, but alive.

Hurried whispers raced through the congregation. Leo stood to confer with Lord Mersey, then moved quietly to Robb's side, murmuring in his ear. He passed Robb a note. Robb read it, closed his eyes, and nodded bitterly.

When the queen stood to leave, Sara knew it was over. The monarch moved out of the cathedral with the slow grace of a barge. The moment she crossed the threshold, the gathering broke up, a bubble of murmured questions and painfully polite silences.

Sara looked for Robb, but the nave was empty. Only the shiver of flower petals marked his wake.

CHAPTER 41

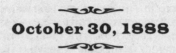

October 30, 1888

David
* Bank of London * 9:43 AM

"Thinking of gold," he said to Pinder. "Good investment, but can't imagine where I would store enough of it to make a difference. Not something you'd put in a cash box, eh?"

"Oh, no, sir," Pinder said, and smiled, that glorious avarice in his eyes again. "We have vaults for bulk storage."

"Really?" David asked, smiling slowly. "Show me."

In the basement, Pinder showed David the Victorian idea of bank vaulting. Concrete walls with wooden inner doors barred by locked iron gates. Proudly, Pinder introduced the doors of their best patrons as they passed. Salisbury, Stewart, Marchant.

Osborne.

David made note of the number.

Behind them, the muffled belch of a coal boiler thrummed the walls with a low vibration.

Pinder smiled. "Forced heat," he said, beaming.

"All the modern conveniences," David murmured.

"Oh yes," Pinder said. "Top grade."

Sara
* Grant Townhouse * 1:52 PM

In the *Times* she found a picture. A banner photograph in the society pages—Osborne and five other men were standing together, smiling. All of them were well dressed and impeccably groomed. The six of them gathered in front of a dark edifice, at the opening of a hospital.

BUILT IN 1785 IN WHITECHAPEL AS A TEACHING HOSPITAL, TODAY THE LONDON HOSPITAL BECOMES THE OSBORNE CHARITY FOUNDATION INFIRMARY, THE FIRST MAJOR MEDICAL FACILITY DEDICATED TO THE NEEDS OF THE POOR. IT WAS PURCHASED BY PHILANTHROPIC PUBLISHING MAGNATE JAY OSBORNE. THE HOSPITAL STAFF IS LED BY SENIOR DOCTORS OF GOOD REPUTATION. THE QUEEN HERSELF COMMENDED OSBORNE'S LEADERSHIP IN SERVING THE NEEDS OF SUCH A NEEDY POPULATION. TALK OF A KNIGHTHOOD ABOUNDS . . .

The article was dated March 10, 1887. Under the grainy photograph, the names of each man standing were carefully listed: MICHAEL OSTROG, GEORGE CHAPMAN, FRANCIS TUMBLETY, T. NEILL CREAM.

Sara read the names and felt a certain breathlessness hollow her stomach. Each of these men had been Ripper suspects. None of them had been men of means, nor had any real medical training. And yet here they were, standing with Osborne, proper Victorian gentlemen, physicians in a respected hospital.

What had they done for Osborne, to raise the quality of their lives so drastically?

Sara frowned, and reviewed her notes. Closed her eyes when she saw it.

It was the same hospital Emma Smith had died in, one year after this picture was taken.

David
⁺ Bank of London ⁺ 5:35 PM

Armed with his own vault key, he wasn't even noticed. *No one sees a servant,* he thought, *and no one questions a rich man with a key.*

At Osborne's vault, he pulled a slender pick from a key ring filled with them. Within minutes, he was inside, and surrounded by gold. "Jesus," David whispered. The vault was stacked to the ceiling.

He pulled a small camcorder out of his pocket, the one he'd found in Osborne's pack. Slowly, he recorded the size of the room and how the gold bars filled the place. Then he counted each row. The bars were arranged in pallets, stacked solidly on top of each other. He counted down, across, and over. Each pallet held 152 bars. There were thirty-six pallets in the room.

David picked up one bar and hefted it. It looked so light in its brilliance, but was so heavy—each single bar weighed twenty-seven pounds. Carefully, he slipped it into his briefcase. He left without saying a word to a soul, moving through the grand foyer, down the steps to the street. Passing bankers and bobbies alike without a flutter, his case heavy with that single bar of gold.

David
* Huntingdon Street Men's Club * 6:45 PM

Looking for Robb, he ascended the wide stairs quickly, quietly. He stopped halfway, suddenly wary. At the top, Osborne leaned against the newel post, smiling benignly.

"If you're looking for Robb, you won't find him here," Osborn beamed. "It could be a good while before he shows his face socially again. Imagine, being stood up at the altar, and with a queen watching, no less. Really, females are getting entirely out of line these days."

"Get used to it," David told him evenly.

Osborne's eyes darkened with an almost feral glee and a wide grin split his face. "Yes, we differ, don't we, on the subject of female subordination? Oh, come to my rooms, David," Osborne said, waving him up. Then he turned and sauntered down the hall, sure that David would follow. Carefully, David did, passing Robb's room on the way, quiet and empty and cold.

In his briefcase, the weight of the gold bar dragged at the earth, as if it were a living thing and carried a gravity all its own.

He entered Osborne's lair slowly. Osborne watched, amused, as he looked the room over. As if he found the interest at once vulgar and intensely funny.

David moved to the fireplace, turning his back on Osborne but keeping an eye on him in the mirror over the mantel. On the finely carved shelf, pictures of Osborne and Prince Eddie anchored a few scattered personal effects. On top of a silk scarf, mellow in the candlelight, sat a gold cuff link.

David froze. Recognizing, finally, the shape engraved like a wax seal in the gold.

The Portal. Avery. Of course. Now that he'd seen it, there

was no way not to. The cuff link was Avery's. The mate to the one he'd found in the alley, after he'd fought with—

"Beautiful, isn't it?" Osborne asked behind him.

The hair on David's neck stood up, as though Osborne had breathed on it deliberately. "Yes," David said, picking up the cufflink for a closer look. "I've only seen one other like it."

"Really?" Osborne asked, narrowing his eyes. The irises contracted, a tic of disturbing intensity, as he smiled. "Where?"

"In an alley," David said. He met Osborne's eyes directly. "I took it off a toff trying to throttle a young woman."

Osborne's eyes darkened, like smoke obscuring a window. "Did you really?" he asked, holding out his hand. Only a remnant of hilarity steamed through his smile now. David dropped the cuff link into his palm reluctantly. "One of my reporters found it by the body of a dead prostitute," Osborne told him, his smile sharklike. "Which means you may have fought with the Ripper himself, my good man."

"A frightening possibility," David agreed.

Osborne waved it away, as if the Ripper were merely the boogeyman, a parable to frighten poor girls away from prostitution. He leaned, smiling, against the mantel, cozy suddenly, even confidential. "By the way, David, I've been meaning to speak with you. Man to man."

"About?"

"Oh, you know." An odd vulnerability crept under the arrogance. "That lovely sister of yours. I would like to marry her, David. Do you think you could persuade her, old boy?" He laughed lightly, but his eyes were grim. "To forsake all others? To love only me?" He clutched the cuff link in his hand, and whispered, "Would you do that for me?"

David watched Osborne warily. "That would be her decision."

Osborne straightened, putting distance between them. And yet, he was still smiling, that humor in his eyes glittering now, and sharp. "You see. You're so very liberal. Like she is. Who are you really?"

"Osborne—"

"No, no. I mean it," Osborne protested. Dangerously jovial, his eyes predatory. "Any man of society would make that decision for a woman in his care. Or will you be content to let her refuse Robb's proposals for the rest of her life?"

Osborne's hand tightened around the cuff link. His eyes were shuttered wells of stagnant water, vile and malignant.

"I could give her your ring," David said slowly. "It might help her decide."

"This old thing?" Osborne asked, turning the fat gold ring around his finger playfully.

The voice was so coquettish, David glanced up quickly. Did Osborne even know he'd used Avery's slow Virginia drawl?

David gave Osborne a solemn bow—glad, for once, that he'd learned to do it well. "I'll take up your cause with my sister," he said, overly civil. "But I wouldn't expect anything. She's sworn herself off marriage. Won't play the wife to any man."

"She *says* this?" Osborne asked, playfully appalled. Closing in, as if scenting a kill. "And you *let* her. You see? You are ahead of your time, David. A dangerous thing. A dangerous thing, indeed."

David looked at Osborne's tightly clenched fist, where the cuff link must be biting into the flesh of his hand, leaving the shape of the Portal in his skin. He thought of the flowing cape in the alley with the young girl, and the knife that had skittered on the hard pavement, biting sparks in the darkness. Of the blood-red glints in the black of Osborne's carriage.

Beyond him, Osborne's cape hung on a broad coatrack, bat-like and menacing.

"You're a pretty dangerous man yourself, Osborne," David said quietly. He turned to leave, every instinct bristling.

"And do you still have it, David?" Osborne asked. He held up the cuff link, letting the fire gleam against the outline of the Portal and the shadow of red in his hand. "The mate to this one?"

David said nothing. He tilted his head in farewell and left Osborne alone, shutting the door quietly but securely behind him.

Osborne
* Huntingdon Street Men's Club * 7:12 PM

Osborne listened to David's footsteps recede until he could no longer hear them. "A very dangerous thing," he whispered, curling his fingers around the knot of gold, feeling its symbol mesh again with the grooves it had made in his flesh. Savoring the night in that dim alley; the girl's long hair, smooth skin. The quiver of a virgin.

And then there had been that fast hand in the dark, the sound of the cuff link skittering away from him. David Grant.

"How delightful," Osborne murmured darkly.

In the hearth, a cold wind shivered down the flue and the fire rippled violently, whispering in hungry tongues.

CHAPTER 42

❖⋙⟨⋘❖

October 31, 1888

❖⋙⟨⋘❖

Sara
* Osborne Charity Hospital * 11:10 AM

A dozen doors stretched in the long inside hall. Each door was fronted by frosted glass windows, the rooms behind them lit by gas sconces. The fitful yellow brilliance at each glass stitched Halloween faces on the gray marble floor.

She was ushered into Tumblety's office and told to wait. Pictures lined the bookcases: Tumblety as a young man in a fine moleskin coat; Tumblety in military uniform, complete with medals. So many certificates of achievement, it would have taken a single man several lifetimes to have acquired them all. Quickly, Sara bypassed the ornamentation. She went to Tumblety's desk and paged through his social diary. Appointments showed him gambling on September seventh in Liverpool, dining out with a friend on September twenty-ninth. Self-appointed alibis.

Chapman, Tumblety, Ostrog, and Cream. They had been Ripper suspects for more than a hundred years. Each man had been investigated for the crimes. None was ever charged. Any one of them could have been the original Ripper. But now, under Osborne's tutelage, what had the Ripper become? And which man was she looking for?

She went through the cupboards, finding personal effects, books, journals. A cabinet of drugs. A leather bag sat on the desk, filled with an odd assortment of tools, only two of which she recognized—a metal syringe in a hard leather case and two ivory-handled scalpels. In one deep drawer she found the jumble of a surgeon's kit: three brass-fitted tourniquets, one spool of wire, thread, two packets of needles, one tweezer forceps, a tapering cannula, two knives, a saw, a hammer, and a chisel.

Fighting the chill of thinking what each one could do to a human body.

She found what she was looking for in a wall beside the hearth, in a cabinet almost hidden by the paneling's design: row upon row of specimen jars. She picked one up and examined it closely. Inside was a floating object. A uterus. Pale pink, the blood was still threading from it. It was a torn globe of flesh, ragged at the upper end. There were at least forty of them in the cabinet.

The door opened. Sara straightened, turning to meet Francis Tumblety as he came in. He was a plain man, dressed in outrageously stylish clothing. Standing at the door, Tumblety curled his lip under the long whiskers of his handlebar mustache.

"You do many abortions, then?" Sara asked.

He stopped and stood very still, then smiled thinly. "That would be illegal. If you are pregnant and herbs cannot help you, you are doomed to motherhood."

"I have no need of your herbs," she told him.

Dark color filled the man's face. "Then why are you wasting my time?"

"I came to see a famous author."

He frowned. "I do not follow you."

"*The Kidnapping of Dr. Tumblety*," she quoted, watching him straighten slowly. "A textbook case of con artistry. Oh I'm sure you didn't mean to choose an alias so close to one of Lincoln's assassins, but the result was fairly amusing, you must admit."

"I was exonerated," Tumblety said, wary now.

"But never really forgiven," Sara said, stepping to the front of his desk. "Which is why you came to London in the first place. Tell me, Doctor, from what medical school did you actually graduate?"

"My credentials are openly displayed," he growled. "Don't tell me you didn't see them. I gave you plenty of time to snoop."

"Is that what took so long? You wanted me to peruse the fictions on your walls? And why would I think your medical diplomas were any more real than the medals you wore for military service you never did?"

Tumblety stood, coldly furious. "This interview is at an end, madam. Whatever plagues you, see someone else for it."

"Nothing plagues me," she said coldly. "It's what plagues the unfortunate women of the slums that concerns me. Poor women who can make no other living but prostitution. Not like your former wife. I've always wondered," she mused, as Tumblety's face darkened, "why she went back to practicing that particular art when she had a husband who could provide for her so well." She flicked a pointed gaze below his waistline. "You did," she asked, "provide for her. Didn't you?"

He shot out from behind the desk, his fist raised. Sara caught it and twisted his arm behind his back. Tumblety yelped at the pain of it, then whimpered as every joint, from shoulder to wrist, strained in their sockets.

"Where were you on the nights of September seventh and twenty-ninth?" Sara asked. Angry now—at Tumblety's arrogance, his hatred; at the sick collection in his office. "How many women have you killed, on and off your damned operating table? What does this hospital have to do with those deaths?"

He squirmed, trying to get out of her hold. Swore, bitter and violently. Sara ratcheted his arm to an unforgiving angle. Tumblety screamed, went down on his knees.

"Tell me," she said grimly, "about the women."

Tumblety, panting, sobbed and writhed and then cried, "It's a hospital. People die."

"And the other women?" she asked. "The ones who die in alleys and courtyards. Tell me what you have to do with that."

He swore at her in guttural grunts, an animal on his knees. Sara pulled his arm again and heard the crack, the wrench of the shoulder ball coming out of its socket.

Tumblety's face, as it turned to her, was blotched and mottled. One bloodshot eye marked her with its fury. Grating through his teeth, through the darkness of his ugly smile, he told her, "Ask Jack. He'll take care of you quick enough."

Sara wrenched his wrist to the left one final time and then let go. The snap of a greenstick fracture seemed thin, even in the close air of the office.

Tumblety fell to the floor, cradling his arm, sobbing. "God! Look at me—look at my arm. Oh God, *I can't move it.* I'm a physician. You hideous bitch. Do you have any idea what you've done—?"

Sara walked away as his voice rose to a thin reedy whine. She shut the door quietly behind her, raising her eyes to a ragged woman passing the office in the hall.

"Doctors," she murmured, shivering delicately.

The woman nodded, wide-eyed, and hurried toward the exit.

CHAPTER 43

Robb
* Whitechapel Station * 4:52 PM

He found her letter sitting on his office desk. The jolt of pain was surprising. He swore, astonished by the pain of it, by the lingering strength it had to hurt. He hadn't seen her for five days. He had thought of her every minute.

He let the letter sit for three hours, watching it between thoughts, between writing reports and studying them. Two hours before the pain subsided, when he finally opened it and read.

> *Robb, forgive me for writing, but you should know, I have seen them together: Osborne with Ostrog, Chapman, Tumblety, and Cream.*

"Sara, what are you doing?" he murmured. He almost stopped reading right there. Almost.

> *They are killers, Jonas. If you need evidence, go to the Osborne Charity Hospital. You will find samples of surgically removed uteri in Tumblety's office, in the closet behind his desk. I know you will not want to hear any of this, but I have been to his office—I have seen the jars. You should see them, too, before he destroys them. At least one was fresh, I'm certain.*

"Sweet Jesus, Sara," he whispered. He threw the letter on his desk. If what she said was in the least bit true, she had gone into a hospital staffed by murderers. Alone. *Gods—*

He drew in a breath deep enough to fill his lungs and, when

his pulse began to throb behind his eyes, let it out slowly, carefully. Fighting the sick pulse just under his breast, he went into Abberline's office.

Abberline smiled. "What is it, Robb?" he asked, and Robb wondered how he stayed so calm in the heart of so many horrors.

"I've received a letter from a source of mine," he said carefully, "who reports having visited the medical offices of one Francis Tumblety—"

"Tumblety," Abberline hissed. He had heard of Tumblety before, then.

"Yes. She, my source, has found some very disturbing evidence in Tumblety's office. She fears he may have something to do with our Whitechapel case."

"What did she find?" Abberline asked.

"Uteri," Robb said grimly. "Jars of them."

"He is a doctor," Abberline mused. "He has performed hysterectomies in years past. But as I remember, he was accused of doing abortions and warned off. Director of a hospital now, but not permitted to practice female surgeries."

"Osborne's hospital," Robb said grimly. "And the uteri—some were fresh."

"Well, well," Abberline murmured. "It does bear looking into, doesn't it?"

CHAPTER 44

⋘⋙

November 4, 1888
⋘⋙

Farley
* Whitechapel Station * 3:36 PM

Hidden in the stone crenellations of Whitechapel Station's imposing façade, Farley was a small man, dressed in the smock of the chimney sweep and blackened by soot. He opened Robb's office door and wasn't even noticed. But he went nowhere near Robb's chimney. Instead, he made for Robb's desk. Found what he was looking for in the file drawer and left without saying a word—into the hall, down the steps to the street.

All but invisible as London's lowest servant, Farley pottered along the lane and headed back to the Boss's offices at the agency, his deep pockets heavy with Robb's Ripper files.

Robb
* Montcliffe Townhouse * 4:38 PM

He spent Sunday holed up in his bedroom, in the deep leather chair by the hearth, soaking in the heat of the fire. Outside, a flurry of magenta leaves rolled across the lawn, and rain spit fitfully against the windows.

"Sir," Jasper said, handing him a silver tray, "this just came in the post for you."

Robb murmured his thanks. He looked eagerly to the tray for the cream vellum she used, but this letter was not from Sara. He opened the plain envelope and read the statement on the single piece of paper:

> *Robb, you were right about Tumblety. The coroner reports*
> *a match to the most recent specimen found in Tumblety's*

office to the Eddowes woman. He says he can identify it by the way it was torn out of her. Gruesome, but there it is: We have our Ripper! Congratulations. —Abberline

Robb smiled, the satisfaction reaching deep. It swept, like a clean wind, through his blood. He smiled slowly, savoring the taste of it. "Jasper, get my bag ready. I'm going back to the club."

CHAPTER 45

November 5, 1888

Sara
* Grant Townhouse * 10:35 AM

"Looks like you made them think," David said, and showed her the morning news.

Sara took the paper, frowning. Banner headlines reported the capture of the Ripper, Francis Tumblety. The police were celebratory, but the *Times* pled for caution:

> THOUGH THE POLICE BELIEVE THEY HAVE EVIDENCE IMPLI-
> CATING DR. TUMBLETY, THERE IS NOTHING IN TUMBLETY'S
> OFFICE, EXPERTS SAY, THAT ANY PHYSICIAN WOULD NOT
> HAVE. WITNESSES SAY HE WAS IN SURGERY OR IN THE PRES-
> ENCE OF HOSPITAL STAFF ON THE NIGHTS THE WOMEN OF
> WHITECHAPEL WERE ACTUALLY MURDERED. DR. T. NEILL
> CREAM STATED CATEGORICALLY THAT TUMBLETY WAS DIN-
> ING AT A LATE BANQUET AT CREAM'S HOME IN KENSINGTON
> THE NIGHT CATHERINE EDDOWES WAS KILLED. DR. GEORGE
> CHAPMAN ALSO INDICATED THAT DR. TUMBLETY WAS PER-
> FORMING EMERGENCY SURGERY THE NIGHT MARTHA TABRAM
> WAS MURDERED. "IT COULD NOT BE HIM," CHAPMAN SAID. "I
> ASSISTED WITH THAT SURGERY, AND IT WENT WELL INTO
> MORNING. AFTER THAT, I SAW THE MAN SAFELY TO HIS
> HOME IN CHELSEA."

"They're lying for each other," Sara whispered. "It's not just one of them. It's *all* of them. Osborne is directing all of them." She sat down by the fire, thinking. "Four years, all those women. Even for Osborne, hiding behind his respectability and his position, that would be too many, too great a risk. So he had accomplices. And since he controls the press here in London, he could hide news of the deaths—"

"Until he wanted them known," David said, finishing for her.

Sara nodded. "The perfect conditions for leading a coup, and who better for the people to turn to than the man who uncovered it all? Who just happens to be the same man leading the opposition party as a candidate for prime minister. Bastard," she whispered savagely.

Robb
* Huntingdon Street Men's Club * 12:26 PM

"Bastard," Robb hissed. He slammed the *Times* down on the breakfast table.

"Interesting news?" Osborne asked, and sat leisurely across from him.

Robb narrowed his eyes, heart beating too fast in his chest. "I wouldn't call it that," he said quietly. "A rape, perhaps. Of justice. And of the press. Sara's right, you know. You can make people think anything, if you're the only source they have."

"Sara," Osborne murmured, his eyes lowered lazily. "Now there's *interesting* for you. Did you know? Dr. Tumblety told me he'd been attacked—by a woman, of all things. Beautiful, tall. Broke his arm, apparently. Pulled the shoulder bone right out of its socket. Sound like someone we know?"

The temperature in Robb's blood cooled by degrees. "She's a woman," he said stiffly, knowing he was lying. But the taste of that lie was lighter in his mouth than revealing Sara to Osborne in any way. He shook his head, emphatic. "She couldn't do that to a man."

Osborne sipped his tea, green eyes artful over the cup. "Perhaps," he said, still smiling; it was a secret thing, hiding everything and nothing. "Or maybe our girl is a good deal more interesting than even we could have imagined. In fact, from what your father says, I may have to deny myself as a husband and simply keep the girl as mistress."

Robb stared back implacably, his face a mask, knowing the dangerous enormity of the rage that lived behind it. "My father?" he asked.

"Such a gossip," Osborne said, and barked a laugh. "Though I promise, really, old boy—knowing you've been there before me won't prevent my full enjoyment of the lady's pleasures."

His smile grew brittle, his eyes brilliant, and Robb knew with a breathtaking surety that his own face was not the only mask a dangerous rage lived behind.

Robb
• Whitechapel Station • 4:10 PM

On his desk, he had a stack of folders, each labeled with a name—the early deaths, women not considered victims of the Ripper. He was determined to find for himself the connection Sara had made between these deaths and Osborne.

He rifled through his file drawer again, looking for her notes. Found his Ripper file—but not the other folder beside it. Cold sweat broke out at the back of his neck, raising his hackles. He went through them again. It wasn't here. His outline of Leo's report was missing.

He was out of his office in three strides. "Who has been here?" he asked sharply. "In my office." His heart surely beating loud enough to bring the building down.

The sergeant noted the fear in Robb's face and said, "Just the sweep, sir. But that was Sunday, two days ago. Somefink wrong, sir?"

Robb
• Whitehall • 5:20 PM

"Someone's stolen the file," he told Leo.

His uncle paled, then sat carefully in his chair. "Good God," Leo said.

Behind them, the door opened without a knock, and Robb turned.

Barnaby stood in the doorway, the dust of ages lodged in his clothes and on his face. His cravat was missing, and his face, so fresh the last time Robb had seen him, seemed bruised.

Leo stood, alarmed. "Barnaby, what is it? Has there been a tragedy?"

Barnaby came into the room slowly. Robb shut the door behind him. The boy spoke, his voice husked and low. "I went to the library. Spent more than a week sorting through the last five years' worth of newspaper doggerel. I only meant to look through the last six months, but I kept going back," he whispered, "trying to find them."

Leo put a hand on Barnaby's arm. Gently, he steered the boy to a place by the fire. "What? Who couldn't you find?"

"The women!" Barnaby cried. "All the women who have been killed in the last four years in London. The ones in the file. I knew the precincts didn't communicate with one another, don't broadcast the news of death about. But sir, they've never even been reported in the papers. How could this happen—in *England*?"

"We will not let it stand," Leo told him. "Stay here. I'll have Roberts bring you tea."

Barnaby nodded, and Leo steered Robb to a far corner of the room.

"There's only one man who would profit from this," Robb said quietly.

"Osborne?" his uncle asked. For once, he looked his age; brown spots stood out on his skin, which hung like pale crepe over his cheeks and neck. "Do you think it's a lack of coordination? Could it be that simple?"

"No," Robb said, vehement. "Osborne knows. He has more men out there than we do, and they all report to him. He's keeping these murders quiet. There's only one reason he would do that. To use them—against us, against the police, against the government as it stands."

He looked away from his uncle's pale face, toward the fire that warmed the room but not the cold, sick tide spreading slowly through his gut. "A newsman who knows about the murders of one hundred and twelve women, murders not one commissioner on the entire police force is even aware of."

"When he lets this slip," Leo whispered, "there will be anarchy. Once it's out, there won't be any way to take it back. Or convince anyone it wasn't a deliberate conspiracy. As the man who uncovered this blasphemy, Osborne will be the man of the hour."

"And prime minister," Robb said grimly. "Now isn't that convenient?"

Robb
* Grant Townhouse * 8:25 PM

"What's happened?" David asked.

"My uncle," Robb said grimly. "He compiled a report detailing the murders of prostitutes, not just from Whitechapel or Westminster, but from all thirty-five precincts in the greater London area. What we found— It's inflammatory by itself, but the fact that Osborne owns the news and has reported none of these deaths is—well. If he knows, and he's not telling anyone; if he's waiting for the right moment: It's the death of this government."

Sara came into the room quietly. She wore a thick robe, and her hair was a tumbled mass around her face and shoulders. Her hands clutched the top of a velveteen chair. "How many?" she asked.

Robb hesitated, at war with the many aspects of her he knew, with all she'd told him and all he could and could not believe. Tumblety had been arrested, yes. But where she came from, what Osborne was supposed to be—

"How many women, Robb?" she asked again.

Finally, he whispered, "One hundred and twelve."

David handed Robb a bourbon. He drank the liquor in one quick toss. "The file was stolen," he said, "out of my office last weekend. I can't think of anyone but Osborne taking it, but for the life of me I can't imagine why—"

"Proof," Sara said. "He's always known about these deaths. They're his lever to move the world. But with this file, he has more than journalistic scandal. He has proof of a government-sponsored report documenting the deaths. A report the government hasn't released, has covered over. He would have done this anyway—used these deaths as a fulcrum—but with the report behind him, the impact is doubled."

"There's your context," David said. "But what's the trigger?"

"He's lobbying for votes to become prime minister," Robb said quietly. "The vote itself is scheduled for the ninth. That's three days. My God, I've got to find that file."

"We can help," Sara said.

"No," Robb cried. He gathered his coat, ran a hand through his hair. "Sara, this report wouldn't exist if you hadn't told me what to look for. If Osborne finds out you're involved, if there's any possibility of him being what you believe he is, I don't want you near him." Robb looked up, including David in his directive. "Either of you. Both of you, please, just—stay out of this."

Sara
⋆ Grant Townhouse ⋆ 8:59 PM

"He'll need help," she said, her eyes wide and sober. "He doesn't know who he's dealing with, how far Osborne will go."

The clock struck nine sharp notes and subsided, its mechanism quieting with a final click.

"You've given Osborne a paper trail," David said.

Sara nodded. "I did," she said, wonderingly. "Didn't mean to. I thought if I helped Robb with these cases, he would help us later. Establishing a contact in this world to work through. That's all. I never thought it would come to this."

"Time theory sounds more like chaos every minute," David murmured. He stood. "Whatever this file is, it gives a level of credibility to Osborne's plans he didn't have before. I'm betting he's got the report at his press offices. I have to get it back."

Sara stood. "I'm coming with you," she said.

"No you're not. Robb's right about one thing: If Osborne gets wind of your involvement, he'll kill you."

"I can take care of myself," she said, chin rising.

"Could you kill him?" David asked.

Startled into the truth, Sara said, "I don't know."

"That's your weakness. It's where he has the advantage. Osborne's a predator. You can smell it on him. He won't hesitate. He'll go for the kill. And until you're ready to do the same, stay away from him."

"Robb will go there," she said stubbornly. "You know that. It's the first place he'll look."

David shook his head. "He has to work through channels. I don't. I'll get there first."

David
⋆ Offices of the Central News Agency ⋆ 9:42 PM

The evening was moonless and cold. In camouflage, David scaled the walls of the Central News Agency. He stepped into the dark room, a shadow on the wall, a dark ghosting of movement.

At the layout table, he switched on his penlight. The words screamed out at him, a blow to the mind:

112 WOMEN KILLED IN LONDON: POLICE DO NOTHING

A brighter light went on in the room—the lamp on Osborne's desk. "Thought I 'eard someone sneakin' round yere," Farley said, his voice a grating sort of whisper. "Who'd a thought it would be the ol' coachman, though, eh?"

David shrugged. "Always did like to get my paper early."

He spun and crouched, pure instinct triggered by the sudden hiss of air, the breath of it passing his neck; the *thwock* and vibrating *tang* of a hefty knife sinking into the wood behind him. David kept moving, past the quivering blade and up over the desk where Farley sat, his face a white blur, the shocked *O* of his mouth. He landed on the smaller man, twisting him against the wall, pinning him with weight and the sharp edge of his own blade hard against Farley's neck.

"Where is it?" David asked.

But Farley matched his determination, sneering and saying nothing. Keeping Farley pinned, David worked a vial out of his thigh pocket and uncapped the top with his thumb. It fell with a plastic-tumbling skitter across the floor, and David held up the tip of the needle.

Farley's eyes darted to the needle, pure animal instinct against its strangeness. But the knife at his neck bit sharply, and before Farley could gain any purchase, David had administered the drug and let go of him.

The smaller man, furious now, grabbed at his carotid artery and the tiny puncture wound there. "What the 'ell yer done ter me?" he yelled, hoarse voice crackling. He sank slowly against the fireplace mantel and, by degrees, to the floor. "Whatcher done?" he mumbled again.

David grabbed his shirt, hauled him close. "How could Osborne know about those women? Was it the uncle's file? Did he get the file from Robb?"

"That old fing," Farley chided, sleepy now. "Naw, I got that one. Got it fer the Boss. Brung it 'ere, ter him."

"Where is it then?"

Farley nodded weakly toward Osborne's desk. David searched through it, found nothing, and heard Farley laughing behind him. He looked more carefully and found, almost immediately, the small catch beneath the largest drawer. David sprung it and the bottom of the drawer fell out. Inside, lying innocuously, was the file.

Farley, behind him, sniggered. "Won't do yer no good now. Be in tomorrow's papers, it will."

"Not if I burn down the building," David said mildly.

"You wouldna!" Farley cried. David looked back at him, and Farley growled a swear word.

"Why do you care?" David asked him.

"The Boss. Bring down the house, he will. Get a new gov'ment in, one what cares about the little people."

"And Osborne cares?" David scoffed softly. "That's why he had you steal a file that would cause riots in the slums and maybe even civil war? Plenty of people die in public conflicts. Especially people too damned poor to get out of the way."

Farley waved him away, disgusted. "He dint need that to know what he done," Farley muttered. He giggled again, an obscene titter. "But now we got proof, courtesy a' Whitehall. How the rozzers knew and dint do nuffink. Gonna show everyone, we will."

David paused. "So, Osborne really killed all those women?"

Robb
✦ Offices of the Central News Agency ✦ 9:49 PM

Outside, in the street, Robb directed a handful of men from Whitechapel Station to surround the building. He knew the risk he was taking. He had no official permission to enter Osborne's office, and no reason he could share with his superiors. He commanded a company of six men from the precinct, all volunteers.

If the file was in this building, he would find it and ask forgiveness later.

The Central News Agency stood silent and dark, the building's windows shivering the reflections of the gas street lamps. Then a stronger light from Osborne's office window flared and threw a brilliant glare against the glass. It quickly subsided to a dim glow that barely puddled at the sill.

Seeing it, Robb motioned to the six large men with him. "Let's go—slowly."

David * 9:50 PM

Farley was still laughing, a soundless chuff of breathlessness. Finally, he found his voice, stretched and strained and harsh. "Bin doin' it all along, all them four long years, dint he?" The sneer was back on his face, brutal with its own warped self-importance, slackening slowly under the drug. Pride wound down to drowsy boredom. "I picked the girls he were gonna kill," he whispered wearily. "I pick 'em for 'im still."

"Osborne did *all* the women?" David asked.

"We *all* did 'em," Farley murmured. "Perk o' the job. Nice li'l bonus. Me 'n Ostrog and Tumblety 'n all The Jay's boys." Farley's voice dwindled, and he looked with glazed eyes into the shadows.

David paused. "Then, Osborne *is* Jack the Ripper?"

Farley cackled, choking on it. "Course he is. We *all* are." Smiling weirdly, his head wobbling to look up at David, he began to laugh as the drug broke up in his system, sparking psychosis. Sudden energy flared in his eyes and the laugh became a shrieking bawl. Eyes bulging, neck straining, Farley snapped his teeth at David and screamed, "Idn't it grand? Idn't it *graaaand*—"

Robb * 9:51 PM

Step by careful step, they made their way into the printing bays of the building, past bewildered janitors and the dim snore of idle presses, and up the long stairs that led to Osborne's office. At the top, Robb saw the steady glow of golden light at the foot of the door. He listened, hearing nothing but low conversation. Two men, arguing.

He raised his hand to knock when one of the men inside the office shouted hysterically, "*Idn't it grand?*"

David * 9:52 PM

The door burst open. He looked up, and four men in blue uniforms yelled at him to stop. Running toward him, they pulled their heavy truncheons and descended on him.

Robb • 9:52 PM

Robb stepped in after his men, immediately noting the signs of struggle in the room: items from Sir Jay's desk scattered on the floor, the chair on its back. A man lay on the floor by the fireplace and a shadow hanging over him, black as pitch.

It all blurred when the shadow moved. Hands at the fallen man's throat, a glint of metal. It was harrowing, that shadow—a silhouette cutout from hell. His men stepped back from it, then surged forward again with terrible cries. Robb blinked, trying to focus. But that shadow seemed steeped right out of the black ash in the fire's grate and was impossible to see. His men reached it and were flung back, thrown about like rag dolls in an amazing, silent ballet of movement too fast and violent to see or understand.

Robb took his gun out of his pocket—his own gun, the one he'd carried since the night of the torso and his terrible fears for Sara. He pointed it at the whirling dervish of movement as the last constable fell, groaning, to the floor. Cocked back the hammer. "Stop," he said loudly. "I'm warning you, I will shoot."

Feeling a fool with his tiny gun against this force of air and earth, a dangerous djinn of vicious, spectral temperament. But it stopped when it saw him—didn't even try to resist as a small stream of bobbies poured behind Robb into the room and surrounded it, keeping a wary distance.

The djinn was played out. Compliance in his posture, he offered no resistance as Robb's men got up off the floor and came close enough to touch, to find him as real and solid as the earth—nothing but a man, after all. He held his hands out in front of his chest and Robb's men roughly took his wrists for the manacles.

Robb approached and saw why the man seemed such an otherworldly figure. The cloth he wore stretched tight against his skin; strangely nonreflective, as if it ate up the light. That same cloth was tight around his head, the skin behind it blackened around dark blue eyes.

Eyes he knew.

Robb hesitated, then tore the mask off. Recoiled immediately, as if the thing had bitten him. "David. Good Christ!"

Grant looked down at him, ironic, angry—still the pent djinn, a muscle ticking under one eye. Robb took one deep breath, then had to spin around to expel it. A sudden charge of energy blew through him. He walked like a caged tiger around the room, trying to dispel it.

Finally, he came back to face David Grant, who watched, unmoved and implacable, as he approached. "You look ridiculous," Robb spat, though this was not true. In truth, he looked dangerous. The one-piece garment framed a shocking physical power; it had no buttons, its closures. That awful black. It was as strange as the things Sara had shown him in his father's library, several lifetimes ago. "What are you doing here?" Robb asked, breathing heavily.

"Looking for your uncle's file," David told him.

"I told you to stay out of this. Told you both."

"Take a look at today's news," David told him, pointing down at a newspaper layout. Robb looked down at the front page, crumpled and torn and still screaming its wicked headlines from the floor. "The morning paper," David said quietly, "telling the world it's not just eight women who are dead, but one hundred and twelve. Accusing the government of a cover-up and the police of gross incompetence." He nodded at Uncle Leo's file, murmuring, "You might want to destroy that."

Robb knelt, picked up his uncle's file, and then riffled through the paper's front-page layout, reading swiftly. Then, hating himself, he slipped the layout into the fireplace. He found scattered lucifers on the floor and lit the whole pile. Fire licked eagerly at the dry paper and found it good. It caught quickly, a breath of brilliant light. Then it was gone.

"I have to take you in," he said to David, toneless and without looking at him.

Robb
* Outside the Central News Agency * 10:15 PM

They put him in a Black Maria. Robb locked the door himself, then sat on the box with the driver, slumped, pinching the bridge of his nose. Pinwheels of light split kaleidoscopic patterns behind his eyes, easing the dull, thudding pain in his head not at all.

"Hard night, sir?" the driver asked.

Robb nodded, leaning back against the hard wooden side of the wagon. Exhausted. How long had it been since he'd slept well? The wooden wheels grated over each cobble. Robb was jostled and swayed on the top of the box, and still slipped into a light doze. Images flickered, bright and dark, in the passing lamplight. Dancing with Sara, diamonds like stars in her hair. Amanda's blue face, the shuddering stretch as she came back to life. A whirling dervish in black; smoke in the shape of a man. Bloody torso with Sara's face—

The wagon stopped and Robb's eyes snapped open before he was fully awake. The barrage of images confused the reality of the tall gray façade in front of him. It made no sense: a medieval castle at night, stuttering torchlight in a cold drizzle.

"Coldbath Fields, sir," the driver told him.

Robb nodded, recognizing the prison and still unable to shake the disorientation that surrounded him, a fog of disquiet and fatigue. He stepped down, looking toward the entrance of the baths. It was a filthy place, gray as a storm at sea but not as clean. Misery was a grime that covered the weeping brick.

Robb turned his back to the Black Maria, giving the driver the key to the caged door at the back. He stood waiting, his blood stirring again to anger. To put David in this place, known for its brutal yard and sweating stone. It had come to this. That he had let it come to this—

The driver yelled and Robb swung around.

"Gone! He's gone, sir," the driver cried.

Robb ran to the back. The door hung open, neatly unlocked. The cage was empty. Robb scanned the streets but saw nothing. Inside, the metal cuffs his men had put on David lay on the floor. Like the door, they had been undone without force or violence, as though the man had simply had his own key.

"*Damn* it," Robb said. It was eaten up quickly by the smothering night, with only the driver there to agree.

CHAPTER 46

November 6, 1888

Robb
* Grant Townhouse * 3:46 AM

He woke her household out of their dreams, the uproar bringing the maids to tears. He hated it, but he stood with all the arrogant entitlement of his position against the silent, disapproving footman, George O'Connessey, who knew a roust when he saw one.

It had taken hours to clean up the mess at the Central News Agency. A strong force of men was still there, waiting to stop anyone who went into the building. And by itself, Robb knew, that kind of containment had all the potential for inciting a riot.

"Robb?"

He looked up to see her standing at the top of the stairs. Bewildered, still, with sleep. He met her in the shadows of the landing, mindful of his men searching the house. Beneath her open robe, it was clear she wore little to sleep in. The thin cotton shift barely covered her legs.

Breathless, Robb looked at the floor. "Where's David, Sara?" he asked, his voice shaking with both anger and desire and the amazing, lightninglike flint of their combination.

"I don't know," she said. He looked at her face. A wary pucker between her eyebrows spoke of exhaustion, confusion. Worry. "I haven't seen him since he left to find your uncle's report. He said he'd get there first," she whispered.

His eyes widened, anger rising, aftershocks of the night's upheavals. "Well, he certainly did. I arrested him tonight, at Osborne's offices. Clapped him into irons and a Black Maria. He escaped. As if it were nothing," he said, and tried to keep the truculence out of his voice. "But I will find him, Sara. All I have to do is follow Osborne."

"To all the places you know about," she murmured. "Osborne has other places, in the slums. David will find him first, Jonas."

"And do what with him, Sara?"

"Whatever he has to," she said, and sighed tiredly. "To put time back to the way it should be. So we won't both be stuck here forever."

It took the space of seconds to dawn on him. "You'd be here," he said. It was barely a breath, and harsh with his need. He drew her close enough to feel her heat under the thin cloth. "If you stayed here—"

It was a prayer to foreign gods. He realized she was crying, her lips against his—the taste of salt, never so sweet before this. And then the sound of his sergeant, miles away:

"Sir! We've found 'im! He's here! Runnin' out the back!"

Robb broke away, stung. The savor of her breath mingled with the electric scald of betrayal. He backed away, slowly, watching the confusion in her face, and the hope—not for him, not for them, but for David.

He turned at the top of the stairs and ran.

Sara
* Grant Townhouse * 3:58 AM

Sara ran to the window. There he was—David, pelting up the street, into the darkness of the trees surrounding the large roundabout where carriages turned gracefully in the neighborhood.

"Go, David," she whispered. Belly still singing with Robb's kiss, she urged the runner on to safety even as Robb himself leapt, almost cat-like, out the front door and after him.

She sat in the kitchen for more than an hour, waiting. Was not as surprised as she thought she'd be when the back door opened quietly and he crept in.

"David?" she asked.

He pulled the dark mask away from his face. George grinned. "Goodness no, miss, that weren't him. It were me."

Sara stood, took the black wool cap from George's hands. Stared at it, smiling. Then she remembered the wounded scald on Robb's face, realizing what he must have thought.

"Oh God, Jonas," she whispered.

Robb
* Osborne House * 5:10 AM

It was his final stop of a long and bitter morning. Thoroughly exhausted, Robb pounded on the front door with a ferocity that would bruise his hand for days.

The majordomo, disheveled, opened the door. "Really, sir," he snapped. "We receive *no one* at this hour."

"You do now," Robb said, and pushed his way in. The majordomo glanced at the two burly constables behind Robb and said nothing. "Go get him," Robb said.

"The master is still asleep," Harris protested.

"The master is within moments of being arrested," Robb said grimly. "Which he will be, immediately, if he doesn't explain himself. So you bring him to me now."

"It's all right, Harris," Osborne said. He stood at the top of the stairs, looking down on them all. Slowly, Osborne descended the steps.

Robb held out the Whitehall report. "Recognize this?" he asked. "You stole it from my office. Don't tell me you didn't take it. I found it this evening in *your* office."

Osborne looked at the report in Robb's hands. His hilarity, and its maddening smile, were finally gone. Wariness had replaced both. He said, carefully, "Or it was put there for you to find."

"And the layout for tomorrow's paper? Was that 'put' there as well?"

Osborne stiffened. "Be careful, Inspector. That layout is private property."

"Not anymore. It's been confiscated. As have your presses. You won't be printing a damned thing, Osborne—not anymore."

Osborne affected a pained look. "That decision is hardly one for a police inspector to make, no matter what his father's title is. Now, Mr. Robb, if you will excuse me, I have people to see, important people who will have me back in business before this evening. My man will see you out. He's very good at that."

"Which man?" Robb asked. "Your majordomo? Or that little chap called Farley?"

Osborne didn't move a muscle in his body, but in his eyes, a flash of hatred flared like a small star. "Really, Inspector," he said, voice tight and smooth, "I would so hate to give an earl's son the bum's rush."

Leopold
* Buckingham Palace * 9:32 AM

Victoria stood with her back to him, always a bad sign. Immediately she said, "We want you to let go of Sir Jay's presses, Leopold. He is our friend. A knight of the realm."

"What Osborne was going to print—Victoria, it's all your enemies need to destroy you."

She waved a hand, impatient. "Osborne would never harm us. You took away his favorite toy and now he's angry."

Leo went to the window, standing unbidden by her side, which he rarely did. Outside, the population of London was stirring. "Some toys are more dangerous than others," he said gently, and handed her Osborne's layout.

She glanced at it quickly. Like Jonas, she never could resist a mystery. She said nothing, but the sharp intake of her breath, and how quickly she looked away, told him everything.

Leo said, quietly, "Do you even know where this man comes from? Who he is?"

Still she said nothing. Stunned, but stubborn—she was a queen, after all. He didn't press her—knew his limits, and hers. He nodded. "Then I will do as you command, and release the presses. But I would like your permission to ensure that *this* headline, at least, will never see the light of day."

She looked at him, then. He saw the anger in her face. It was a small betrayal, Leo knew, among too many. She had liked Osborne—for his innovation, for his philanthropy. For his charm.

Eyes dry, she said, "Take it away, Leopold. Burn it, if you wish."

Leopold
* Offices of the Central News Agency * 11:32 AM

"Of course Her Majesty wishes to apologize for any undue liberties taken by the police," he said, sitting comfortably in the big leather chair in front of Osborne's desk.

"My presses are released, then?" Osborne growled.

"Of course," Leo smiled. "And you are free to print whatever you like."

Then he stood, and took a sheaf of paper out of his satchel. It was the layout Robb had appropriated. Barnaby, standing with him, lit a match and offered it up. Leo tipped the corner of the layout page into the flame. It began to burn, small flecks of ash taking flight.

Leo dropped the blazing thing on Osborne's desk and smiled. "Perhaps the next time you are in Whitehall, you should thank Her Majesty personally. I could, of course, set up an appointment for you. Say, next season sometime?"

The remnants of the layout glowed briefly and then, slowly, winked to ashes.

Osborne
* Offices of the Central News Agency * 11:52 AM

"Farley," Osborne cried. The rage in his throat was gravel, sharp and hard.

Farley came when called, a squat and squalid jack-in-the-box. He had spent the night in the hospital, raving. Whatever David Grant had given him, it had subsided only hours ago. For that, and for knowing what he knew, David Grant would have to die.

But not at his hand. Oh no. It was so much better to make Robb put the noose around Grant's neck.

Osborne reached into his pocket. He pulled out the golden cuff link, and smiled gently. "Farley, my boy," he said, "I do believe we've found our Ripper."

"I know what to do, Boss," Farley husked.

Osborne nodded. "Lead him to me slowly, would you?"

David * Burnbury's Dock Goods,
Whitechapel * 9:13 PM

Nestled in a corner of the attic eaves, lying flat against a wooden strut, David was a shadow in his matte-black *gi*. He watched Osborne as the man sat writing at a cherrywood desk.

Osborne was humming, happily weaving in and out of the words.

David recognized the song. It was a Beatles tune.

David slipped down to the floor. His movements were utterly silent, but still. Osborne looked up and smiled. He saw the black *gi*. His eyes sharpened, a dangerous glitter. Still smiling, Osborne continued to croon a fractured mélange of the chorus. "*Jackaroo, David, Ohhhh . . . nothin's gonna change my world . . .*"

Perfectly mimicking John Lennon's every inflection and nuance of timing. And then he said, "I'm so glad you came. We've been expecting you."

"You've got the words wrong," David told him. "It's Hindi. *Jai guru de va om.*"

"You know the tune, then? Can't place it myself. Woke up with it running through my head. *Jackaroo, David—*"

"Obsessing on this whole Jack thing, Osborne?" David asked.

Osborne laughed. "How have you been, old boy? You're tomorrow's news. Better than being yesterday's, isn't it?"

"How does it feel?" David asked, taking a step toward him. "To be the madman? To be the man you've sworn to catch? To slice into those women like they were nothing." Flexing his fists, his shoulders. "I bet you laugh while you do it."

Taking steps back against David's advance, Osborne's eyes grew somber, that pensive water-lily green. "I never laugh," he said.

He grabbed his walking stick and flicked his wrist. The covering shaft fell away, revealing a wickedly sharp point. Footsteps on the other side of the door surged over the staircase and into the room. David kicked the rapier into the air and tackled Osborne, who shrieked with acidic fury on the way down.

Scores of men flowed into the room. David sprang up, fighting his way through the first waves to be bowled over by the third.

He was beaten until he could no longer hold the darkness off, until it surrounded and engulfed him with the sound of endless waves lapping, and he felt the surge and tug of rope against his chest.

David
* Osborne's Carriage * 10:06 PM

Waking to a greater darkness than he'd left, David felt the bitter, sharp edge of the wind outside and the grinding bump of
wooden wheels on cobblestone. Osborne sat on a bench on the
other side. They were in Osborne's caleche. The top was up but
the frigid air stole in and bit the raw lacerations on David's face,
smarting like sea spray on the open wounds.

"Nice touch," David rasped. The ropes around his chest
made it difficult to breathe—or was that broken ribs?

Osborne grinned. "I have found, in my time as a criminal engineer, that it pays to have a loyal staff. Especially when one
might be expecting company."

"You expected me? That's flattering."

Osborne struck him with a closed first and then settled back,
smiling, as David rocked against the wall of the caleche, crack-
ing the back of his head and tasting blood.

"There are other ways," Osborne said. "I can still accomplish my goals, even with your meddling. They can't muzzle
every paper in the world, can they? Word will get out." Osborne
slid his hands into his gloves, a smooth and silent gesture, then
clenched and unclenched his fists to soften the wear of the
leather around his skin. The sound crackled between them. "I'm
thinking, oh, the death of a young society woman—rich, beautiful. That would do the trick. It doesn't *have* to be your lovely
sister, of course." He shrugged. "If she submits, becomes my
woman, I'll let her live." He flashed a boyish grin. "And if not—
Well, Inspector Robb may collect as many refusals as he likes,
but I will take only one."

The caleche rocked to a stop. Osborne bent to open the door
of the small carriage, then turned back and asked, "What does it
mean, by the way? *Jai*—"

"*Jai guru de va om,*" David said. "It's from an old Beatles
tune. You remember the Beatles, don't you, Osborne?"

He didn't remember. But it remembered him: Memory was
the shadow lurking in the darkness of his eyes. Osborne bared
his teeth in a wide, ferocious grin. He leaned toward David, his
nostrils flaring, as if sniffing the air and the smell of blood between them.

David stared back placidly. Then the bobbies were there,

hands reaching out, dragging him out of the carriage. Two broken ribs grated heavily against muscle and he yelled, powerless to stop the sound, the pain, or the darkness that gathered around the periphery of his sight line once again. The overriding thought like a record skipping in that netherworld between awareness and collapse keeping him barely on his feet. Osborne loose, Sara alone.

Sara—

CHAPTER 47

❧❧❧

November 7, 1888

❧❧❧

Robb
* Whitechapel Station * 9:22 AM

The newsboys shouted it on every other corner, and the shock recoiled through everyone hearing it. Men walking to work stopped to read. Even the society ladies, out to ride their horses up Rotten Row, whispered over it.

"Osborne catches Ripper in the act!" the newsies yelled. "Hands 'im o'er t' Scotland Yard!"

The sound of it detonated through Robb's exhaustion, a blow to every muscle. He stopped in front of a pile of papers newly opened on the corner. The newsboy said to him, "Ripper caught last night, guv. Find out who finally pinched him and put him into gaol."

Robb gave a penny to the boy and took a paper. He immediately recognized the photograph on the front cover: David, being led into Coldbath Fields. The photograph was blurred, and David's face turned away. Robb recognized him more by his bearing than by the caption printed under the picture in small print: DAVID GRANT LED AWAY. Emblazoned over that picture, the headline screamed *AMERICAN IS THE RIPPER!*

"My God!" Robb scanned the article quickly. Next to David's picture was an inset drawing: a golden cuff link with an odd horseshoe shape embossed upon it.

CAPTURED! THE RIPPER IS FINALLY IN POLICE CUSTODY, NO THANKS TO LONDON POLICE. HE WAS BROUGHT TO SCOT-LAND YARD BY SIR JAY OSBORNE HIMSELF—WITH IR-REFUTABLE PROOF. THIS CUFF LINK WAS KNOWN TO BE SEEN ON THE PERSON OF THE KILLER AT SOCIAL FUNCTIONS BY

ANY NUMBER OF HONEST HOSTS AND GUESTS. ITS MATE WAS
FOUND AT THE FEET OF HIS LATEST VICTIM, AN UNFORTU-
NATE WOMAN WHO WAS, ONCE AGAIN, BRUTALLY SAVAGED
AFTER SHE WAS KILLED—

Robb threw the paper in the gutter. Swearing—half begging
whatever gods sat at the seat of his soul, not even certain of what
endowment of theirs he was asking for—he began to run.

Robb · 9:35 AM

He stopped Thicke as the older man hurried past Abberline's
office. "What's happened?" he asked, breathless.

"Another one," Thicke said angrily. "Found in one o' them
back alleys over by the Yard. Blood on the pavers, all over the
walls. Like he were laughin' at us."

"Was there anything different about this one?" he asked.
Painfully aware of Sara's hypothesis, that the killer would grow
more ritualized, and bolder.

Thicke narrowed his eyes. "Yeah. How'd yer know?"

"Tell me," Robb said.

Thicke smiled bitterly and produced a large envelope from
his desk. He spilled its contents out: cheap rings, a paste necklace, and a man's cuff link.

"She were posed like a doll," Thicke said. "All this stuff set
out around 'er, like her body were an altar."

Robb nodded, and picked up the cuff link. "Strange. He's
never left anything of his behind before. Mind if I take this?" he
asked, curling his fist around the cuff link. "I've got someone
I'd like to try it on."

"Fine with me," Thicke said, and sniffed. "You go ahead and
find yer Cinderella, sir."

Robb
· Grant Townhouse · 10:13 AM

He came into the withdrawing room without the maid's escort.
"David?" he asked Sara. Fuming, emotion a bitter sting behind
his careful, professional mask. "If you're here to study our time,
why is he here?"

Sara was very still, sitting in the chaise. "You believe me, then?" she asked.

A long silence itched between them. Then he said, "I will withhold judgment for the moment. David?"

"David," she said slowly, "is with the military. Special forces. He was sent here to neutralize the threat Avery poses to your time."

"Neutralize?" Robb asked. "What does that mean, exactly?"

"It means, we hope, that we take him back to our own time."

"And if you can't?"

"If necessary, if we couldn't get him back," she admitted soberly, "David would have to kill him."

"Kill him," Robb said quietly.

"He's trained to it. He's covert operations. They go in without support, alone, into the most dangerous conditions—"

"Assassins," Robb hissed. His voice flat, shallow to his own ears: the shock of it.

Sara stood, suddenly furious. "I know for a fact that men like David can save thousands of innocent lives by taking the life of just one man bent on slaughter. Our time is very different from yours, Robb. Warfare is different. You have the Irish lobbing bombs that might kill one or two. We have our terrorists too—only they kill in the thousands, bombing buses and planes and schools, office buildings and bridges, theme parks and malls. Men like David prevent those attacks, killing one or a dozen paramilitary aggressors before they can kill hundreds or thousands of innocent people." She took a deep breath. "I can't fault him for that. Don't ask me to. Osborne as prime minister could imperil the world for generations to come. His life would be worth taking to prevent that. You know it."

Robb didn't ask what planes were, or theme parks or malls. They were incomprehensible—nonsense words. But they meant something to Sara. The verity of her knowledge was absolute, a sickening blow to his gut. He put it aside, along with the thought of murder on such a scale. Focused, instead, on the horror he could address here, now. "But he *is* trained to kill that way?" he asked. "To shoot a man in cold blood. To strangle him, or cut his throat. Or even—just maybe—a woman's."

"Oh God," Sara breathed. She met his eyes sharply. "You don't believe that David is the Ripper. You *can't* believe it. The Ripper had been killing for years before we came here—"

"And yet he ran. From my arrest. An innocent man doesn't run, Sara."

"He does if he has more important things to do than rot in an English prison cell," she said severely.

Robb turned, saying nothing. Left her there. Going up the stairs to find the truth and knowing that what he might find—what he had to find—might be the end of them all.

Robb
* David's Closet * 10:32 AM

He made a thorough search of David's room, sifting through drawers and finding a startling spareness, the spartan accumulation of clothing and effects that indicated a short stay in this place, with no intentions to make it any kind of home.

He found nothing more than that. Fingered through David's sparse collection of cuff links and cravats and noticed that the man's taste was as lean as his closet. He favored silver, with no jewels.

Robb sat back and thought. If he had just killed a woman, had arranged his cuff link like an obscene offering at her feet, what would he do with its mate? What did a man do when he lost a cuff link? Certainly, one didn't wear mismatched cuffs—

Robb searched through the pockets of every set of trousers in the closet, and then every jacket.

He felt it before he saw it. A molten lump of a thing. Held it in the pocket, not wanting to see. Then he pulled it out and looked. Like an Etruscan earring, it was roughly formed around the edges, as though someone had taken a wax seal and pressed it into gold to form it. In the center sat that elongated horseshoe shape.

Robb closed his hand around it again. Surprised by the pain of finding it.

He left the house as quietly as he imagined David could, telling no one, the beating of his heart growing horribly in his head—the pressure of pain and a sudden fury that threatened to tear him apart.

Robb
⋆ Coldbath Fields ⋆ 12:16 PM

When he got there, the sergeant said, "Wait, sir," and held out a package to Robb. "One o' the bobbies detailed to Osborne's office found this. Said you'd want to see it. Figure it came from, you know—'*im*.'"

Robb opened the package and found in it two knives. The first, he recognized. Standard fishmonger's, used around the docks in knife fights and robberies; sharp and efficient. Farley's, he guessed. He'd seen it lodged in the wall by the layout desk.

But the second knife—it was hideously serrated at the tip, with a scalpel-sharp edge. The hilt was made of some unearthly material, light in his hand, the real weight of the thing reflected in its mirrorlike surface.

Kin to the strange cuff link that sat in his pocket.

Something in Robb snapped. He could hear it break, like a small bone that had once held everything in place. It rang in his head and continued to ring, and Robb held it at that tight place hard, heading toward David's cell—holding it as one fixed high note, feeling it burn through his body all the way through the door, leaving little left of him but a roaring trail of ash.

Robb ⋆ 12:25 PM

He walked into the cell and stood, saying nothing. David met his eyes, and was suddenly, dangerously still.

"What do you think you know?" he asked carefully.

Robb drew the strange knife out of his inside pocket, shaking the tip end at David. "This was found at Osborne's office. Is it yours?"

David nodded. Robb closed his eyes. He put the knife on the table and held out the cuff link. "And I found this," he said, "in your pocket. And the other," pulling out the link, "on a dead woman in Scotland Yard. Throat slashed, legs splayed, her breasts and private parts cut out of her."

He looked sick, stomach churning. Then he lunged, pushing David against the wall, holding on to his shirt. "They were cut right out of her, David. Did you do this? How *could* you do this?"

David didn't move—just looked at him steadily. "You know I didn't."

Robb snorted, then stepped away, not looking at him. "I don't know anything of the sort."

"Then why do you have your back to me?" David asked. "With an unsheathed knife within reach?"

Robb turned back quickly, scowling. "All I know," he husked, "is this. You knocked four of my men flat while caught trespassing. You brought down a man in the dark and you damned well looked like you were about to kill him. Given how we found this man Farley, I'm almost relieved you didn't get to Osborne alone."

"Only almost?" David asked, raising an eyebrow.

"It isn't funny," Robb cried. "What better way is there to get away with murder than to steal away to the future when you're done killing here?"

Sara
* Whitechapel Station * 12:26 PM

The moment she'd introduced herself, Abberline had ushered her personally into his office at Whitechapel Station.

She was an enigma to him, she knew. Abberline's bleached blue eyes were as affable and kind as any grandfather's. And yet behind them, a shrewd intelligence was taking her measure.

Dressed for the slums, she looked like a citizen of Whitechapel and spoke like an American heiress. Part of her cringed at exposing so much. But this was November seventh. Mary Kelly would die in two days, and if Osborne had been her killer, she had to stop it.

There was no time to play Victorian anymore.

"Your brother, you say, is missing?" Abberline asked politely.

"Yes," she said firmly. "I haven't seen him since last night."

Abberline raised his eyebrows. He told her, gently, "A gentleman is hardly 'missing' if he's gone for just one night, miss."

"My brother," Sara said, holding tight to her patience, "keeps in close contact with me for very good reasons. I have learned something today of vital interest to our business here. I must find him."

"Why would you come here, then?" Abberline asked. "If

you'll pardon me for saying so, you don't sound as if you or your brother would have any legitimate business in this part of the city. Surely you should be inquiring at Westminster or Kensington stations?"

"Inspector Robb is a friend of mine." Impatience painted a grim asperity into her words. "*He* could help me find my brother, if *you* could find Mr. Robb any better than *I* could."

Abberline nodded, his eyes not leaving hers—the unspoken obvious in his somber gaze telling her that perhaps Robb could not be located because, at this moment, he did not want to be found. "A worried man, is our Robb," Abberline murmured. "A great deal on his mind."

Sara met Abberline's continuing gaze without flinching, and Abberline cleared his throat. "I can't tell you where Inspector Robb is at the moment. Quite possibly, he is busy interrogating your brother as we speak."

"*Interrogating* him? He's been arrested?"

"He has," Abberline told her, lighting his pipe; the pungent scents of vanilla, tobacco, and bitter stink drifted between them.

"Why was he arrested?" Sara asked.

Abberline smiled. "You should discuss this with Robb, really. Last night, it seems, your brother was caught in the offices of the Central News Agency. Sir Jay's offices. Wouldn't know anything about it, would you, miss?" His eyes gleamed at her from under white brows and a wreath of smoke. Then, languid but still watching her keenly, he murmured, "Then this morning, he was brought to gaol by Sir Jay himself. Tried to get into yet another one of the man's properties. Seems to have a bit of an obsession there, eh, miss?"

Sara stared back at him, implacable as stonework. "Then if you have him, he shouldn't be hard to find."

"No, not a bit," Abberline admitted. "But don't worry, miss. I'm sure Inspector Robb will have no problems at all."

Sara stood. Anxiety wailed through her bones. What had Robb done, after he'd left her this morning? "I have to speak with him," she said.

"Your brother, miss, or Inspector Robb?" Abberline inquired.

"Both, if possible," Sara said stiffly.

"It isn't possible," Abberline said. "For your brother's protection, he's been moved several times."

"His *protection*?" Sara asked. Her knees weakened with the implications of it. She sat back down slowly as she watched Abberline's face, as a heavy sadness leached through the canny intelligence.

He didn't want to tell her. Hesitated, then said, as gently as he could, "Your brother was named as the Ripper this morning."

"The Ripper?" Sara cried. Her anxiety exploded. "*Where* do you people get this ridiculous idea?"

Wordless, Abberline slid the *Times* across his desk. On the cover, Sara saw the blurred photo of David being led into prison, and the artifact found at the latest murder.

A simple drawing of a cuff link.

Sara sat very still. "Oh God," she whispered.

Abberline nodded. "You see the problem, miss."

"You actually believe this? Just because it's in the newspaper?" Her anger was returning, magnifying exponentially as she sat in this grim office, imagining David in prison. Fiercely, she asked, "Are even the police taking orders from Osborne these days?"

"I wish I could say they weren't," Abberline said softly. "Certainly if you have any information that would aid your brother's cause, we would be happy to hear it." Almost wistful, he smiled and said, "I would try Inspector Robb at his club."

He stood. "Your brother, I'm afraid, will be transferred to the Old Bailey at some point tomorrow evening. I wish I could tell you more, miss, I do—but for his safety, I cannot divulge any more to you than that. His situation is precarious. The last thing any of us wants is another riot and a lynch mob."

Sara met Abberline's eyes. Saw the fear there, the threat of the world as it should be turned upside down by hysteria. "I see," she whispered. "I do."

Knowing, with a sudden surety, that no theory or formula could account for the variables of human behavior and the infinite paths that falling dominoes could take.

Sara
* Ten Bells Pub * 1:32 PM

She went into the slums alone, searching for proof—for even one thing Robb could believe. She knew at least two women who had known Osborne here. She couldn't locate Lottie, but found Mary Kelly at the Ten Bells, nursing cloudy dregs of ale. Sara slipped in beside her. "Buy yer a pint?" she asked, and nodded at the bartender.

The man pushed a new ale over to Kelly. Kelly took it and sighed, receiving it like a baby put into her hands. She looked up. It took a moment for her eyes to focus, longer for her to remember Sara's face. "Hey," she said, smiling. "You're back."

Sara hesitated. "I heard about Liz and Kate. I'm sorry."

The mug slipped from Kelly's fingers, falling back to the bar with a bloodless thump; it landed solidly on its wide bottom, sloshing the dark ale on her hands. "Don't want ter talk about that," Kelly said, shivering.

Sara put her arm around the other woman, who glared at her for bringing the subject up but also began to weep. The anger, mingled with tears, made her fierce and somehow lost. "They killed Kate, when she wore my hat—" She buttoned up; started to cry again.

Sara patted her hand. "No, Mary, the Ripper killed Kate."

Kelly shrugged miserably. "Naw, that's just what the rozzers think. Jack never did nobody twice in one night. It were the Frenchies, and they're lookin' for me. I gotta get outta yere."

"You do, Mary, you really do," Sara said. Knowing, now, that Osborne was almost certain to remember, in his warped way, the gruesome death of Mary Kelly on November ninth.

"Who're you to say what I do?" Mary snapped perversely. Holding hard to her hot temper, as if it could buoy her up from a slow slide into despair. The skin around her eyes was a glaring pink, speaking of illness and drink and failing spirit.

"I know what it's like to be hunted," Sara said. "I've got a man looking for me, too. Sir Jay Osborne. Remember when you said Tom Bulling worked for him? If you can tell me about Osborne—something I can use against him—I might be good enough to spare you a bob or two and we can both make ourselves scarce."

"Yeah?" Kelly said, speculative. "Where'd you get that kinda doff?"

Sara put two gold coins down on the bar.

Kelly hesitated, thinking—staring at the money, her vision turned inward. She seemed to like what she saw there. A sudden, certain hope kindled in her eyes. She put the tankard down.

"All right, then. This is secret. But I know it for a fact, cause I worked for him myself. Sir Jay's only been high and mighty for the last couple of years. Afore that, he was The Jay." She sat back and looked at Sara triumphantly.

Sara said, "The Jay? Who's that?"

"Yer don't know nothing, do you?" Kelly scorned. "Biggest hooligan in the slums, he was. Organized rackets from here to Highgate. Whorehouses, bribery, gambling—you name it. Ah hell, I worked in one of his houses, too, before I went as a lady to France." She giggled. "Even had The Jay hisself. Not much of a lover but he's got the biggest donger—"

Kelly cawed with laughter when Sara ducked her head, face red.

"How long ago?" Sara asked as Kelly's laughter wound down.

"What do you mean?" Kelly asked, hiccupping. "What's it matter? He was big, I tell you—and not just that way." She got pensive, suddenly. "Then he came into money. Lots of it, God only knows how. And he was gone. Just like that."

"I mean, when did he come into the slums? I heard he just appeared here, came overnight. But I don't know when." She clutched Kelly's arm. "Think, Mary—it's important."

"Eh?" Kelly asked. Laughter on top of the drink had left her pleasantly wrung out and dreamy. "Yeah, you're right, you know. He did kinda just pop in round yere, didn't he? Funny thing. Got here about the same time as me, back in eighty-four. I was living in a convent then, doing domestic. Can you imagine? A year later I was workin' at the tobacconist's shop. He came in there one day, bold as you please, already richer than a king for these parts. Had Emma with him then; Emma Smith, as was. Liked me so much, he came back later without her. And then, after, he set me up in one of his houses."

"You knew Emma Smith?" Sara asked.

"Oh yeah, me and Emma were of a sort." A smile widened Kelly's mouth, appallingly delighted. "Found The Jay in an alley, she did—pukin' and mewlin' like a kid, sick as hell and not even knowin' his own name. Can you imagine? I remember because she'd found him in June, same month I'd come to the convent. Yeah, June. God, what was I thinking, leaving the country when it was June, and so beautiful?"

Sara touched Kelly's arm, reluctant to disturb the woman's

memories of that early summer four years ago and the beauty of the countryside she had traded for the slums. "June, in eighty-four," she reminded her. "Do you know where she found him, Mary?"

Mary smiled, focusing. "Oh yeah, and it wasn't far from where I walked every day. Coulda found him myself, if I'd been luckier. Knew the name of the alley, even—Osborn Street. Oh, that's funny, isn't it? And now he's Sir Jay Osborne, and you know how he come by his name." Kelly sighed, her eyes hazy. "He still comes back sometimes."

"He what?" Sara asked, breathless.

"Sure, he has places around yere. Still runs the gangs and all. Sad about Emma, though. Thought she could get him back. Threatened him, stupid cow. She got beat that same night, an' died in Osborne's hospital. Idn't that somethin'?"

Sara slipped another coin into Kelly's hand. Though the rest of Kelly's body had relaxed, her hand automatically closed over it. She hadn't even looked to see how much it was—a golden guinea.

"Get yourself some food and a place to sleep tonight," Sara whispered, hugging her.

"Got a place," Kelly murmured, smiling. "Little place of my own."

Sara, remembering the photos of the little room in Miller's Court—blood coating the walls—shivered and left the pub.

Robb
* Coldbath Fields * 1:46 PM

"Now you believe in time travel?" David asked. He chuffed ironically. Then he asked, nonsensically, "Has she refused him yet?"

"*What?*"

"Has Sara refused to marry Osborne?"

"I didn't know he'd asked," Robb said. "You know she will. She hates the man."

"Then he'll kill her. Because she refused him."

Robb flinched, then let his breath out in one sharp exhalation. "Bollocks. A man doesn't kill a woman for refusing him. *Believe* me."

David stood, and Robb backed away a step. "I don't have my

tools," David said quietly, "and I can't escape without them. Which means I can't protect Sara. So listen very carefully: Osborne is out there. He can get to her at any time. You know who we think he is. Sooner or later, he'll have her. One way or the other."

Robb narrowed his eyes, his belly tightening in fear. He looked at David, at the bruises and cuts on his face and the way he held himself, still and hunched, protecting his ribs. Osborne had done that, he and his men.

"Osborne," Robb swore, the bitterness of it as sharp as bile in his throat. He walked to the other end of the cell. Scrubbed his unshaven face. "It's hopeless, you know," he said, and sniffed. "The papers all say it's you. You're right about that, at least. Osborne can say whatever he likes and get away with it. I'll be surprised if you get a jury before you're hung."

"And you?" David asked. "Do you believe everything you read in the papers?"

Robb knocked at the thick wooden door. When it opened, he said, bitterly, "I don't know what to think anymore."

"Have you showed that cufflink to Sara?" David asked him.

"Sara? God, no. Why would I do that?"

David said, "Show her, Robb. *Trust* her."

Robb stared. "*Trust?*" he cried.

Outside the baths, for the first time since the killings, he found a quiet alley and vomited it all up—all that he hadn't eaten in days, all the lies and threats and the horror, that sickening, vile horror.

Sara
⋆ Huntingdon Street Men's Club ⋆ 3:32 PM

No kid gloves, now. No concessions to the time beyond what was required. Feathers in the hat perched high on her head, the requisite upper-class dress. Nothing more.

Men coming through the foyer of the club stared as they passed. "Really, miss," the manager said. "Women are not allowed. You *must* leave."

"I know he won't want to see me," she said. "But I won't leave until he does, and you may tell him that if you wish."

"I have no intention of telling any gentleman here to appear simply because a woman wishes to speak with him."

A surge of rage overflowed the banks of her reserve and

flooded her body with the devastating force of her full will. The manager watched it build, his eyes widening. It was obviously something he'd never seen before. She hissed, "*Get him. Or I will go up those stairs and drag him out myself.*"

The manager backed up, horrified. He stumbled away from her, and up the stairs.

"Really, my dear, if you make too many enemies, even a man of my stature could hardly afford to keep you."

Sara turned. Osborne stood grimly at the dining room's entrance. The almost giddy reversals of the week had crystallized, distilling to something grim and dangerous.

"Stuff it," she said—as sharp and plainly as she would to any man of her own time, any pretense of centuries between them falling instantly away.

A spasm of rage burst through Osborne. He grabbed her, crowding her into the shadows of the coatrack. Shoved the thick ring into her face.

"Take it," he growled. He towered over her, bending her back. His face, inches from hers, was mottled by fury. "Take it and be my woman. *Now.* Or die. Because, by Christ, it's all the same to me."

Sara swatted the ring away. She heard it fall on the mellow wooden floorboards, bouncing a small infinity of echoes as it spun away. Knowing he wouldn't crawl on the floor for it; was so enraged he wouldn't even track where it fell. But she would— and would make him angry enough to forget it altogether, for the moment.

"I make my own decisions," she told him fiercely. "If you don't like that fact, that's your problem."

"It's everyone's problem," he hissed. "Mine, your brother's, even the good Inspector Robb's. You've made it impossible for every man who loves you—"

She shoved him back into the flickering light of the hall, a vicious heave that infuriated but stopped him from coming close again in so public a place. "*You,*" she said bitterly. "You wouldn't know love if it crawled up your ass and died there."

The glare of his eyes. Far more than thwarted, now. Grief tossed on an ocean of rage. Murderous.

"Sara?"

A barely whispered word. She turned. Robb had come quietly down the stairs, watching them.

"I need to speak with you," she said. She stepped away from Osborne. Robb looked between the two of them, then away from both, and nodded.

Osborne straightened his coat and smoothed his hair. "Ladies have been put into asylums for less than your behavior here tonight," he said without looking at her. His voice was low, the words stiff. "Be careful, my dear. Be very careful, indeed."

Slowly, he walked up the elegant wooden stairs to his room, not even looking at Robb as he passed him on the landing.

Robb came down the stairs quietly, watching her. She turned her back, searching the hall for that glimmer of gold that Osborne had, for the moment, forgotten and abandoned.

"What are you doing?" Robb asked hopelessly.

"What I have to," she said.

"And you have no better answer than that?"

She stood, and her eyes blazed into his. "Don't ask for any better answer. You don't deserve one. All the answers you ever needed were right in front of you."

She crouched by the door and plucked up the ugly ring. Then she slipped outside and waited for Robb to follow. It was cold under the porte cochere, but after the heat of her own fury, the November air cooled the hectic patches of red on her cheeks to pale blotches of white.

Robb came out slowly. "Then why did you come?" he asked, looking out over the gray skies as they darkened into evening.

Her teeth began to chatter as the tide of adrenaline washed away. She was left with exhaustion and a weight of hopeless, hollow composure. Pulling her coat closer, she said, "You arrested David. You came into my home and used whatever you found there to put him away."

"Osborne brought him to the prison," Robb said sharply. "But what I found in David's closet—"

Sara held up Osborne's ring. Its face shined dull in the dim light, but even he could see it: the crude shape of a horseshoe, twin to the image imprinted on the killer's cuff link.

"My God," Robb said. He took the ring, inspecting it closely.

"You recognize it, then," Sara said grimly. "The cuff link you found on that woman's body wasn't David's. It's Osborne's—Avery's. My father had them made for every man on the Project team, two years before David had even heard of the Portal. *That*, of course, is one of those impossibilities I can't prove," she said bitterly.

"How did you know about this—the cuff link?" Robb asked.

"Osborne's newspaper," she said. "The same way everyone else 'knows' about it."

He glanced at the club's upper floors, sighting the dark window of Osborne's room, then looked back down at her. "You could have saved us all a lot of grief by pointing this out to me before," he said severely.

"You could have saved yourself the trouble if you'd told me about it earlier this morning," she snapped.

"Ah, *God*." Robb palmed the ring viciously. She saw it dawn, then, the sudden self-reproach in his face. "How could I have missed it? I saw you take this damned thing from him in my own house. I gave it back to him myself. I've talked to the man a dozen times and I never even *looked* at it."

"Context is everything," Sara said tiredly. She took the ring back from him, sliding it down on her thumb.

Robb looked soberly at the ring on her finger, and she knew he was thinking of the night in Osborne's rooms. A part of Osborne had seemed to see the ungainly thing as a private promise of commitment, a hideous sort of engagement ring. She saw the brief, jealous heat that spangled through him, making him hesitate.

"And now?" he asked quietly. "Why do you need the ring now? Not just to show me it matches the cuff link, surely."

"I'd tell you," she said woodenly, "but that is apparently more impossibility than you can accept."

"Sara—"

She held up her hand, watching him severely. "Listen to me, Robb, because it's all the proof you need to destroy him."

"Proof? The ring is proof enough."

"And you can't have it," she said, turning on him savagely. "I need it to get home. So listen. The Yellow Jackets—Osborne runs them. He has for years. That's how he's laundering his counterfeit bills. I talked to a source in the slums last night—"

"You went into the slums, alone?" Robb asked.

Sara shrugged, her eyes cool, feeling bruised. "I had to find something you could use. My source, she's known Osborne as

'The Jay' for four years. A lot of people have. Certainly that's something you can prove—something that doesn't depend on accepting the impossible."

"Jesus, Sara," Robb said. The weariness of it threatened to overwhelm, a dark tide he was obviously tired of fighting against. "First Osborne is Jack the Ripper and now he's the boss of a criminal gang. You can't give me the one thing I need to prove David is innocent and Osborne is not. And yet I don't have to accept the impossible to believe you?"

"Sir Jay is a criminal kingpin," she said coldly. "That is a verifiable fact. If you use it with any intelligence at all, it should lead you directly to any other crimes he has committed in the slums."

"My God, Sara, *please*—" Robb whispered tiredly.

But she was already gone, walking away, the feathers of her hat straining against the wind like muted flags of surrender.

Sara
* Whitehall * 4:25 PM

"My God," Leo said. "No, let her in, Barnaby. It's all right. Please, my dear, do sit down."

She didn't. Kept standing. "David is not the Ripper," she said.

Leo grimaced. "None of us believes Osborne's crucifixion of your brother in the press, but Osborne is determined to see him swing for these crimes. David is in gaol even now. It's the crime of the century. He will be tried in court, and there is nothing any of us can do about it. Really, my dear," he asked gently, distressed, "why are you here?"

She said nothing, but opened her satchel and brought out from its depths a startling flash of gold. She put it on his desk. The sound of it was solid, signifying its tremendous weight.

Leo frowned. "What has this to do with Osborne?" he asked.

"David traced Osborne's investments over the last two years," Sara said. "Osborne purchased bullion up to the legal limit openly. But then he went afield, buying from pirates. According to his diary, he needed only a little more to accomplish his goal."

"Which was?" Leo said gently. Not believing—not yet.

Eyes hard, she pulled the camcorder out of her pocket.

Watched his face as she flipped the ON button and the mechanics inside began to whir. Then she pressed PLAY.

On the small screen, Osborne's vault exploded into light and color. Leo gasped and stood, backing away from it. But as the screen displayed row after row of gold bars, his brow beetled slowly, and Leo leaned in to look.

The digital recording of David's voice took a count of each pallet. When he tallied up the final numbers, Leo shivered. Tentative, he reached out to touch the side of the screen, then shied away from its warmth.

"Where—where did you get this?"

"You'll have to ask Robb some day," Sara said grimly. "Right now, you have bigger problems. There's enough bullion in that vault to buy up an entire market of paper currency. Maybe even the national treasury. Trace it. See for yourself. Osborne is determined to bring down your government. You can't let happen."

"I don't understand," he cried.

Sara put the gold bar in his hand. He clutched it, feeling the startling heft—the weight of an empire's economy.

"When paper money becomes useless," she said, "who happens to come along with all the gold backing England needs to save its economy?"

Leo's eyes widened. "Osborne," he hissed.

Robb
* Whitechapel Station * 4:30 PM

"Osborne?" Abberline asked, astounded. "My God, Robb. Are you certain, man?"

He had told Abberline everything. Sketched a verbal picture of his uncle's report. Then he'd shown Abberline the paper where the cuff link was drawn, the crude horseshoe outline so unique.

"I am," Robb said calmly. "Any one thing I could dismiss as coincidence. But taken together, the pieces simply fit too well to ignore."

Abberline sat down. "Good Christ," he said, hollow and amazed. "The only thing worse would be to accuse the Prince."

"I am aware of that, sir," Robb said soberly.

Abberline touched the newspaper, finger hovering over the

drawing of the cuff link. "And you believe this design is the same on both the cuff link and Osborne's ring?" he asked. His eyes, so sharp and blue, were troubled by the implications, by the weight of all Robb had told him.

"I don't have to believe it," Robb said grimly. "I've seen the ring itself on the man's hand a dozen times. The likeness is the same, exactly. I only feel like a fool for not realizing the connection earlier."

"Why would Osborne *do* such a thing?" Abberline asked— distress, confusion, even outrage on his face. "Why would he plant a cuff link that looked like his own ring?"

"Arrogance, I would guess," Robb said. "Osborne uses the news like a weapon, aiming it so precisely, no one would think to look at the man behind the trigger. I certainly didn't," he admitted.

Abberline looked up at Robb, a spark of his old shrewdness showing in his eyes. "Your source again?"

Robb shifted uncomfortably. "Yes. She's known Osborne for years. Knew him better than any of the rest of us. I should have believed her from the beginning."

"None of us would have believed it," Abberline said. "I still don't. Can't wrap my mind around it. One of England's most prominent men, Jack the Ripper? Who *would* have given it credit?"

Robb nodded in agreement but said nothing, and Abberline had sighed. "This can't get out," he said, running his hands through his silvering hair. "Anyone else lets this slip, and there will be anarchy. Once it's out, there won't be any way to take it back—"

"Or to convince anyone it wasn't a deliberate conspiracy," Robb said, nodding.

"If it does," Abberline said, his blue eyes hard, "it had damned well better come from us, or the government. You can see that, can't you?"

"Absolutely, sir," Robb said quietly.

Big Ben sounded in the distance, a single note on the half hour. In the silence after, the Marley clock on Abberline's desk ticked its rush of seconds onward. Robb simply sat, perfectly still, while Abberline absorbed the enormity of the evidence.

After long minutes, Abberline stirred. He grimaced, the conclusion Robb knew he would come to a bitter, painful thing to accept. "Better it doesn't come from the police, then, son," Abberline said, gruff. "Better it never even goes to trial. You'll use your resources, won't you? In Whitehall?"

Robb nodded. Knowing how hard it would be for a man like Abberline to have asked—to have given away the prize for the good of the nation. Admiring him, respecting him more than ever, Robb said, "I will sir. With my compliments."

CHAPTER 48

~~~

November 8, 1888

~~~

Robb
* Huntingdon Street Men's Club * 10:25 AM

A tentative knock brought him awake, bobbing up, like a cork, from the strange dreams he'd fallen into. Outside, the club's assistant looked up at him, worried.

"Forgive me, sir," he whispered. "Your man from the, ah, station is downstairs again. I do hope the news isn't serious."

Robb looked at the face of the clock down the hall. God, but he had overslept. He pushed past the astonished assistant and went quickly downstairs.

In the foyer, PC Tompson looked up, startled.

"What is it?" Robb asked disoriented. "Has there been another murder in Westminster?"

"No, sir," Tompson said, and Robb found he could breathe again. Remembering, finally, what he had asked Tompson to do.

"I'm sorry," Robb told him. "It's been a long while since I slept well."

"Aye, sir. Sorry to have wakened yer, but I had a bit of time, so I came to tell yer what I've found on—you know."

Robb nodded, his heart beat slowing again. He'd spent the night and early morning with his uncle, at Whitehall. Leo would need no further proof, of course—and Osborne would never go to trial for his crimes. But Robb would not insult Tompson by turning the man away without hearing his report. "Of course," he said. "Let's go to the smoking room. Send us in some hot tea and sandwiches, Mason?"

The assistant nodded, and left them in the comfortable room where fat cushions breathed the mellow ghosts of leather and the pungent afterbite of cigars. Robb collapsed into a deep chair while Tompson looked around the room, his eyes round, and sat gingerly on the edge of a peacock tapestry couch.

Robb rubbed his eyes. He expected to learn nothing that was pertinent to his case, and was exhausted beyond remembering. "What have you heard?" he asked.

"Strange tales, sir," Tompson intoned, affecting a dire quality halfway between scared sobriety and high-Irish mummery. "Not sure if I believe any of it, meself," he scoffed, as Mason brought in their meal. Tompson sipped his tea, enjoying its warmth and the puzzle that Robb had set before him. "These Grants," he said, "first showed up in the slums on September eighth in the wee hours."

Robb nodded. "That agrees with what she's told me."

"I'd be willin' to bet the rest of it don't," Tompson said, quirking a smile. "After I talked to the proprietor, this codger comes up to me and says they came outta nowhere. Yeah," Tompson said, nodding, as Robb raised his eyebrows. "Tells me, 'big flash of light, guv, and—wham!—there she was, plain as day.' First the girl and then, not three minutes later, the man." Tompson sighed, shaking his head. "Or so he says, sir. But how can yer take that serious, eh?"

Robb sat silent, the hair dancing at the back of his neck. "A big flash of light," he murmured. He looked up at Tompson. "Did you believe him?"

Tompson, uncomfortable, said, "*Gorn*, sir. An old sailor like that, drunk as hell these last twenty year at least. Seen a ball of lightning, nothin' more. But that's not the strangest thing. The strangest thing is that it happened before. Years before. In the same place. I'm beginnin' to think that alley is accursed, sir."

A certain breathlessness came upon Robb, as if he'd stepped into a void. "What do you mean, Tompson?"

"Chatted up a woman who'd lived in Whitechapel fer years. Says she were comin' back from the fact'ry late and passed that same damned alley when there were this big flash a' light. Scared her that bad. Thought it were an explosion, she did. But it only lasted a second."

"And?" Robb asked.

Tompson sighed. "And then there were nothing but a man standin there, lookin' like Christ on the cross, she says—arms flung wide and screamin at the top o' his lungs."

"Did she know who this man was?" Robb asked. Urgency

racing, making his heart a small, fine engine straining against a half-known fear.

Tompson smiled, the catbird in victory. "Aye, sir, and tha's the queerest thing of all. She seen 'im again, years after— His portrait in the *Comix*, right there on the masthead."

"Sir Jay Osborne," Robb said. The shock of it vibrated along his skin, sharp little bells zinging through his blood. He stood, pacing restlessly through the room. "When was this? When Osborne appeared?"

"June 1884. More'n four years ago," Tompson told him. "Any o' this help you in yer investigation, sir?" he asked, doubtful.

Four years. All the dead women. Proof of the impossible. Robb hesitated. "I've had other corroboration," he admitted. "As far as Osborne is concerned, at least. But yes, it helps—to verify other things. Things I would have sworn were just not possible. It's good work, Tompson. I owe you a debt."

"You think somethin' will come of it?"

That specter of brilliant light, reported now by three different sources, haunted Robb. "I don't know," he said. Then he grinned, a tired flag of humor. "But I think I can tell you who *won't* be prime minister this year."

Sara
⋆ Grant Townhouse ⋆ 12:22 PM

She curled in the big poufy chaise, knowing she wouldn't see this house again. In her hands, she held Osborne's ring. It was an ugly thing. Touching the hairline seal, her fingers met nothing but smooth metal. There was no catch, no trigger for opening the face.

Sara frowned, then aligned that golden face with her wrist. Inside the ring, a mechanism shivered. The top popped open, revealing a tiny lit keypad. She drew a breath of surprise.

Her hands began to shake when she realized it, remembering the night Osborne had fallen into the Portal. He had gone through without warning. He'd had no need to open the ring, to take any overt action to unlock the Portal's power.

Which meant it had been open that night, unlocked by simple proximity to the ring. And like a door, once the Portal was unlocked, any of them could go through it. As long as the ring was in proximity to the Portal, it would open.

But that alone would not help them. With Osborne's transporter chip programmed as it was, he would return here within hours. Allowing him to return to this time again was not an option.

George came up behind her. "Can I get you some tea, miss?" he asked.

"You're very quiet when you do that," Sara told him. "One day, you might see something you shouldn't."

"Seen plenty in my time," George scoffed. He glanced at the ring, and blinked. "Never seen that, though."

Sara pulled a hairpin out of her hair and touched the START key. A hologram sprang up to hover over the keypad, its transparent colors brilliant and clear.

"It's not just a lock," Sara whispered. A certain hope, fragile as glass, sketched a riot of possibilities. "This ring," she said. "It's Avery's console for programming his transponder. With this, he could travel anywhere. Reroute his destination wherever he was starting from."

"I'll get the tea," George whispered.

Osborne • Victoria Tower, Parliament Building, London • 3:55 PM

He walked up the cold stone steps knowing that this moment would mark the day of his creation. The wind blustered and howled around him, gray clouds filled with storms. But the portico protected him. That entrance was shaped like a wishbone, a graceful arc of polished stone. Osborne relished the image of it snapping in two.

The high wooden doors reached well above his head. He put his hand on the oversized door handle, enjoying the feel of it in his grip. He depressed the hock and felt it give, but only slightly. He pressed again, and again. Each time hearing the dull clank of the tongue striking the interior lock, a grinding staccato ricochet under the stone portico.

"Don't bother to fight it."

Osborne whirled. "You did this," he whispered.

Leopold canted his head. "Most people are not locked out of social circles quite so literally. But you're not 'most people.' We thought it best to make it permanent."

"I'll have you," Osborne whispered. "You and your nephew. I'll ruin your whole damned family."

Leo said, quietly, "I don't think you grasp the gravity of the situation, Osborne." He stepped forward, hands clasped behind his back. Three strong young men stood behind him, grim and watching. "Your chance for a position in Parliament," Leo said, "is not the only thing that has been revoked. Your assets have been frozen. Your possessions have been seized. You are a banished man. And the only thing that keeps me from lining you up against a wall to be shot is to deny you the one thing you may have left: the crown of martyr."

"What are you talking about?" Osborne cried.

"Did you think no one would find out?" Leo bellowed. "The gold, and the counterfeit bills? The dead women all over London? You did your damnedest to destroy this government."

He came nose to nose with Osborne, breathing heavily.

"But you will find, sir, what our enemies have always discovered," Leo said quietly. "That when you attack Britain, Britain will always prevail."

Robb
⁺ Coldbath Fields Storage Room ⁺ 4:32 PM

Finished with his duty to crown and country, he came to this place to seek relief from own demons—the last of which he hoped to exorcise here.

Robb faced David's bag under the full light of three lanterns, each of which fought to illuminate the room against the oppressive dark of the storm clouds outside. The bag was not large, but it struck Robb with fear, and he didn't know why.

Like David's black garment, it had no apparent latches or buckles. Robb fumbled with it until a flap gave with a soft chuffing sound, discovering bristly patches of material. He fingered the material and recoiled. One side was like matted dog hair; but the other was stubbly and foreign, like nothing he'd ever touched. Not metal, not glass, not wood.

And if not that, then what?

He pulled items out of the bag slowly. A kit with tiny syringes and scalpels no longer than his thumb. A set of lock picks with the words UNIVERSAL KEY stamped in the hilt. A glistening white rope that looked wet but was dry and slick to the touch.

He lifted an oracular device, a weirdly stretched glass at the front of a helmet. Instinctively, Robb put it over his head. Suction pulled the thing tight, and red light exploded. He closed his eyes against the light and tugged on the helmet but could not dislodge it. Breathing heavily, fumbling, he touched a button on its side. The suction released with a soft sighing sound. Robb tore it off his head and looked at it, warily. The red light was gone. Grimacing, he put it back into the bag with no idea of what it was or did.

He touched the sleek gray curves of a gun that was nothing like the bulky pistols he knew. Its surface was cool on his fingers. Not metal. Not glass. Like something—

—*not made in this world.*

Robb sat on the table slowly and took one deep, long breath after another. The clock above the hearth ticked, an inescapable progression into the coming night. Then he noticed it. Tucked in the front pocket was a letter, a small parchment envelope he recognized from the precinct stationery. The handwriting on the envelope was Abberline's. Robb opened it, and looked inside.

There, an object the size and shape of an almond sat snug in the envelope's corner. Robb slid it into his hand, surprised at its warmth, at how smooth it was. He took out the one-page note and read.

Found this in Osborne's office, where Grant came in through the window. No one else could make sense of it, and few men want to touch it. Superstitious nonsense, but I know you will be thorough. —Abberline

Robb looked closely at the object in his hand. The base was metal, the rest encased in a clear substance, like glass but not at all fragile. Inside were intricate workings too tiny to see clearly. Robb rummaged in a desk, picking up a large round magnifying glass. He held it over the lozenge, standing under the light of the room's strongest gas lamp.

The glass exaggerated the lozenge's interior by several degrees, and Robb could see it clearly: a flat green rectangle with thin gold segments running in patterns, and a glowing green orb, brilliantly lit—no bigger than a mustard seed. That light pulsed softly in his hand, a rhythm he could, if he stood still enough, actually feel in his blood.

Robb thought of David imprisoned in Coldbath Fields. How he had said, *"I don't have my tools, and I can't escape without them."* And Sara, saying, *he has more important things to do than rot in an English prison cell.*

David didn't need British law. The entire force could not protect him from the noose and the damage Osborne had already done against him. He had already been pilloried in the press. Now, no court in England would find him innocent.

The only thing David needed was the chance to get home.

Robb repacked David's bag but for the last small item, which he slipped into his trouser pocket. He meshed the thistly and furry sides of material to close the bag, then shouldered it. If David couldn't get back to it, Robb wouldn't leave it for anyone else to find. His instinct told him that much. But knowing its bizarre contents, he found it impossible not to twitch when the strange fabric of the bag bumped against his back.

As he left the building, he tucked the lozenge in his breast pocket and could swear that the pulse of it and his heart began, at once, to keep time together.

Sara
* Grant Townhouse * 5:52 PM

No amount of exploration would start the program. The hologram simply blinked at her, one maddening word hovering like a magician's trick in the air: ACTIVATE?

She sat for a moment, stymied. The ideas that had revolved so fast around the possibilities of the ring stalled to sour frustration. Activate *what*? The word itself indicated an interface with something else, a reaction between the ring's program and—

Sara lifted her hand, touched the outline of the transponder buried in her flesh. Slowly, she pointed the ring at her wrist. A list of destination codes promptly popped up, watery images jittering in the air. She breathed in a heady smile, then realized that hundreds of destination codes were listed. She had no idea which was the code for home.

Carefully, she selected the INFO button, then aligned the ring with her wrist again. A quick *ping* indicated interaction between the chip and the ring. Her origination code came into view, instantly identified by the program. But the return-destination code programmed into her transponder matched none of the codes listed in the rings' data bank. Clearly Avery had had no intention of ever going home.

The hologram blinked over her wrist. APPLY? Using the hair-pin stylus, she selected YES. Immediately, her code was added to the destinations listed, selected now as the default. Then another line appeared: PASS / TRANS.

Avery had a password.

Frustration bit deep. Sara closed her fist over the ring, feeling the halves of it come together slowly like a magnet.

Robb
* Tower of London * 8:35 PM

"My authority should be enough," he told the gaoler, adamant, insisting. "This man is innocent. We have the names of other suspects and are investigating them even as we speak."

"Can't 'elp yer there, Inspector," the gaoler said. "I wouldna even be takin' him out now but fer the crowds. We're transfer-rin' him to a cell in the Old Bailey, fer his trial in th' morning. They bin movin' him around like the pebble under a chestnut, so afraid, they are, of riots an' such. He's bin to the Fields an' Newgate an' all the way to The Clink out in Southwark afore they brung him 'ere."

"Which is why it took me so long to find him. Please, I've been all over London."

The gaoler shook his head with a terrible slowness. "Yer idn't got a pardon, and yer idn't his solicitor. I can't do a fing, not fer yer nor that poor bastard bound fer the Bailey. I yeard mor'n a thousand gentlemen have paid to see 'im hang, an' he ain't even been tried yet. Strewth, I'll count meself damned lucky to get yer boy to the Bailey w'out he gets torn apart."

"At least let me speak to him," Robb pled.

"Why'j er want ter do that, sir?" the gaoler asked, aghast.

Outside the drafty stone hall, a downpour misted the streets and erased visibility. The sound of the droplets hitting the cobbles was almost deafening. "He's my fiancée's brother," Robb lied.

The gaoler looked at Robb, staggered. "Christ," he said. But as David was brought into the entry, the gaoler stepped well aside to let them talk. Beyond the hall, the Black Maria that would take David to the Old Bailey darkened the yard, dun horses huddling miserably in the rain.

"David, I'm sorry," Robb said, and spread his hands help-lessly. "We'll find proof, I'm certain, that you're innocent. Don't worry, chap." He stuffed his hands in his trouser pockets, then brightened. "Osborne is gone, at least. He's a banished man, a threat to no one. Last I'd heard, he's vanished into the slums."

David nodded. He was sweating, which surprised Robb. Somewhere along the line, he had come to see David as invincible.

Robb shook his hand carefully. "Good luck with the trial," he whispered.

David met Robb's eyes. He nodded, somber. Then held his arms out in front of him, allowing the gaoler to shackle his wrists, hands clenched, understandably, into fists.

Robb ‣ 8:42 PM

Standing under the stone arch leading into the Yard, hair plas-tered to his forehead, he squinted to see beyond the gray curtain of rain. Distant shapes moved, black smudges on the cobbles as David stepped up the stairs to the Black Maria.

The driver clambered up onto the seat and snapped his whip. The horses, heads low, started forward slowly.

The sound of Big Ben began to toll the hour. Robb strained to see through the rain, a veil between one world and the next. He saw:

The door of the Maria swinging wildly. The cage empty. And David, pelting across the Yard.

Cries of alarm went up. "He's runnin'! God's Blood, get a gun, *quick!*"

Robb laughed openly now, with the rain pelting his face. Yelling, "Go, David—*go!*" Knowing, with an incredible cer-tainty of joy; turning to the gaping gaoler, and telling him: "They'll never catch him now."

Robb
‣ Grant Townhouse ‣ 11:02 PM

Still infused with it, Robb was grinning like an idiot, the blood singing through his body, as he opened the door to the Grants' townhouse. David stood in the foyer, loading his gun. Robb handed David the black bag and clapped him on the back.

"You did it!" Robb cried, euphoric. "You got that bloody damned universal key. I thought, when I passed it to you, there was no way the gaoler wouldn't glance over right then and give the whole damned game away—" He paused. Registering the other bag sitting at David's feet, a white bag, with an open grin of metal at its head. "What are you doing? Where's Sara? Does she know you're safe?"

"Sara's gone to the slums," David said, grim.

"What?" The euphoria thawed quickly, leaving Robb numb, almost tingling. "But—*why?*"

"Because that's where Osborne has gone," David said. He slammed a rectangular cartridge into his gun and swept back the hock, then slipped the gun into his waistband. "His world is over." He looked at Robb levelly. "You do know what that means, don't you? We've done our jobs. It's time for us to go."

"Take me with you," Robb said, straightening. "To the slums. I could help."

"Robb—"

"I love her, David. Please."

David raised an eyebrow, then handed him a round black object not much bigger than a button. "Put it in your ear," he said, fitting his own snugly into his ear canal.

Robb hesitated. The orb was spongy, but hard underneath. *Down the rabbit hole*, he thought. Tentative, he stuck it in his ear and tapped it into place.

A crackle of sound startled him. And a voice. Her voice:

"Robb?"

Robb · 11:33 PM

Robb sat in the cab, holding himself still, afraid the earpiece would fall out. He concentrated hard, but the sound in his head was dizzying, disorienting.

"Mary Kelly was killed at Miller's Court," Sara was saying. "Historically, she's the last Ripper murder. If Osborne is the Ripper, he'll be there. It's our one chance of catching him, David. If we miss him, he'll disappear for good."

"Sara, where are you?" Robb cried. Surprised when she could hear him, and answer back.

"I'm at the Ten Bells, Jonas. Looking for Mary Kelly. I need to warn her not to go anywhere near Miller's Court."

"You can't stop her murder," David reminded her.

"If it's not Osborne who comes for her, you're right. But if it is—" A burst of static, and Sara said, tentative, "If it is, I can't sacrifice anyone else to theory."

"Listen, Sara, Osborne knows you were at the Charity Hospital," Robb said to her, shouting; his own voice, in his ear, told him it was unnecessary, and he tried to speak normally. "He's told David he'd kill you for refusing him, if you did. You did, didn't you? At the club."

Another burst of static made him wince. But she said, "I did." Then, "We always knew it could come to this."

"But in the slums, Sara—he has all the advantages. Hello? Sara?"

He looked at David, helpless. David tapped his ear, then said, to Robb, "Interference. We'll get her back in the slums. The signal may be patchy—all those walls, the rain, the electricity in the clouds." He squinted up at the pitch-slate sky as he said it, then put a hand on Robb's shoulder. "It's okay, Robb. The closer we get, the more likely we are to hear her."

Sara
* Miller's Court * 11:34 PM

So dark outside. The clouds overhead were black, and the gas lamps spat under drizzle, fitful orbs blinking their orange eyes like owls in the murk.

She hadn't found Kelly at the Bells. Now she stood outside Kelly's corner room. The windows were pitifully thin, and warped. Sara peered inside.

Mary Kelly wasn't there.

"Great," Sara whispered.

She turned toward the Bells. From one shadowy corner, she heard a woman call to her, quiet and severe: "What the 'ell yer doin' on these streets, girl?"

Robb
* Whitechapel * 11:42 PM

David handed him a boxy-looking thing. It was a gun of sorts, its sharp nose sticking bluntly out of an awkward, rectangular body. Robb grasped the handle but not the trigger.

"Safety's off," David said. "Don't point that at anyone you don't want to kill."

Robb didn't ask what a safety was. Instead, he asked, "Who's Mary Kelly?"

David glanced at him sharply. "Mary Kelly," he said, "is the Ripper's last victim."

"You mean Sara's walking right into a murder?" Robb asked, breathless as he tried to keep up with David. "Is she insane?"

"No, she's not insane," David told him. "She's a lure. She's using herself as bait, to get Osborne—Avery—into the Portal."

"The Portal? What the hell *is* this Portal?"

David stopped. Miller's Court was just ahead. "A very small place. We have to get Avery into it, to get him back home."

"And the problem with that is?" Robb asked, knowing there were complications to everything.

"The problem is, Mary Kelly was never really identified. Her face was all but obliterated. So she could have been anyone." David looked at Robb. "You understand?"

Sara
* Miller's Court * 11:42 PM

Lottie came out of the shadows at the corner, crushing her cigarette with her heel. "Dint I tell yer this weren't no place for a pretty fing like yer t'be?"

"Lottie. Christ," Sara said. "You scared me."

"Yer should be scart, yer stupid bint," another woman said. She came out of the shadows, looking both ways down the street, furtive but defiant. "Out on these streets at a time like this."

"Then what are you doing here?" Sara asked. Because it was evident: They were not looking for customers.

"Patrollin'," Lottie said, and sniffed. "If 'n the men won't do it, we damned well will."

As she spoke, other women slid out of the shadows. More than a dozen. Some of them were armed pathetically, with hoes and brooms; others had small kitchen knives.

Lottie looked at her small army proudly. "Since we bin yere, Jack idn't struck once. More'n month gone. We ain't gonna let it happen again. We're sicka dyin' out yere."

Sara said, slowly, "What are you willing to do to stop it?"

Robb
* Miller's Court * 11:48 PM

There was no one at Miller's Court, at the back of 26 Dorset Street. "You sure this is where Kelly lives?" Robb asked.

David opened the door. The room was empty. He said, "There's no more time for this. I'm going to the Portal. If Sara has managed to find Avery, she'll be there—could be there with him now. You check the flat at Crossingham's. If she's not there, look down at the Ten Bells. If she's not at either place, come back here to Miller's Court and wait." Robb opened his mouth to protest. David held up his hand. "This is where Jack killed his final victim. In that back room there. Your first duty is to catch the Ripper and keep him from killing Mary Kelly. And if by some crazy chance Sara *was* his victim, you'll be able to stop him—and save her life."

"And you?" Robb asked, suddenly breathless. Would it really be Osborne's face, smiling back at him? Or Tumblety's or even that dog-boy Farley's? "Where will you be? If Osborne *is* the Ripper, you won't be here to get him where he needs to be. I'll have to lead him to you."

"Dartmore Court," David said. "You know the street? The Portal is in that courtyard, two-thirds along the way." He looked at Robb keenly. "*Don't* let him corner you there. He may not look it but he's a damned dangerous man."

Robb smiled, the grin of a regiment regular about to play a rough game of rugby. "I won't worry, old man. You'll be there."

David chuffed. "Be careful. If you get him in the courtyard and a blue light appears, don't hesitate. Shove him into the damned thing as hard as you can."

Robb sobered. "All right," he said. His mouth was suddenly dry, and his heart beat painfully fast.

Sara
* Miller's Court * 11:58 PM

"She's going to be killed here," Sara told Lottie. "Number twenty-six."

"I knows Mary," one woman piped up. "Christ—"

"How do yer know this?" Lottie asked Sara, grim; a hardscrabble truculence was in her face, born of struggle and bitter realities.

"When Jack strikes, there's always a big black carriage that comes here, isn't there? Mahogany, dark with reddish tints to it."

"Tha's The Jay's carriage," Lottie scoffed. "He comes yere often enough. Don't mean it's Jack."

"Look," Sara told her. "The Jay *is* Jack. You want proof, go to the hospital. That big charity hospital of Osborne's. See for yourself. They have specimen jars filled with body parts. *Women's* parts. I've seen them. And tonight—Jack will kill Mary Kelly. Right here."

"You can't know that," Lottie whispered.

"Lottie, please: Just remember what I've told you about this man. Your menfolk don't know what he is. And the women find out too late—"

"Too late for what, my dear?"

They all turned at the sound of that golden voice: Sir Jay Osborne, blooming out of the night.

Robb * Crossingham's Common Lodgings, Room Six * 11:59 PM

Robb went to Crossingham's alone, aware of the edginess in the streets. His feet echoed on the cobbles, up the wooden stairs. Every minute seemed to have a sound of its own, ticking slowly through the night.

Once inside Sara's small room, he wondered how anyone could have lived there at all. A clean chamber pot sat in the corner. It hadn't been used for some time, and was clean. It could barely compete with other stenches in the air, but his imagination provided it for him: missing notes in a symphony of smells.

"Christ," he growled.

Where *was* she?

"Be at the Bells," he prayed aloud, morbidly aware that she would hear him only as a ghost, and already dead.

In answer to his appeal, the bud came to life in his ear. Sara was speaking on the other end, to someone Robb couldn't see. Then he heard it: Osborne's voice; an echo, a breathless whisper from a conch shell.

CHAPTER 49

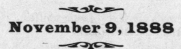

November 9, 1888

Sara
* Miller's Court * 12:03 AM

Mary Kelly had her arm entwined in Osborne's. Sara glanced at Lottie and saw the understanding come alive in her harsh face, along with blunt determination. She nodded once to Sara and walked away slowly, her eyes on Osborne. Her little gang went with her, holding their weapons close to their skirts.

"Pity they're gone," Osborne said. He chuckled richly, opening his arms to the night. "I could have used an audience."

"For what you do," Sara said, "you'd think Saucy Jacky would want to be alone."

In reply, Osborne, smiling, drew Kelly's hand slowly to his mouth. Kelly smiled at him, playing coquette. Then he bit her palm—sinking his teeth deep into the meat of it. Kelly shrieked and Osborne slapped her without blinking, a blow so hard the girl fell reeling to the ground.

Robb
* Crossingham's Common Lodgings * 12:07 AM

He heard the shriek, a woman's scream: Not outside the walls but in his head.

"Sara!" he cried.

He pelted for the Ten Bells and realizing, even as he did it, he had no idea where she actually was.

David
* Dartmore Court * 12:08 AM

"Sara, where are you?" he asked.

Her voice was a steady whisper, "Miller's Court. We're at Miller's Court."

Sara
* Miller's Court * 12:09 AM

Mary hit the side of the building. A window broke, a small, star-like gap blossoming at the corner. Osborne looked at Sara strangely, oblivious to Mary, who fell in a heap on the cobbles. "Of course we're at Miller's Court," he said. "You knew I had to come, didn't you?"

"I did," Sara told him. "But did you know why?"

He dismissed Sara with a wave of his hand, and stood over Mary Kelly. "Open your legs," he said to her softly. "Let's see what you have on, under all those rags."

Mary, crying, whispered, "Please, Jay, no." Osborne kicked her head; it whipped against the wall and Kelly cried out, stunned and numb. He straddled her, throwing her skirts up over her head. Looked in triumph at what he saw, surveying a landscape at once expected and despised: Mary Kelly's bare body.

"Please, Jay," Mary was crying, muffled under her skirts. "We had some times, dint we? I'll do yer square—"

"You'll do me fine," Osborne murmured, and slowly spread Mary's legs, admiring the view. "But I'll do you better."

"I won't let you kill her," Sara told him.

"Really my dear," he murmured, sotto voce. "I don't see how you could stop me."

He dipped a hand under his coat and brought out the long, thick knife Sara had seen in his room. Its tip gleamed wickedly in the guttering gaslight.

Mary glimpsed it, peering over her skirts. Eyes wide, she caught her sobbing breath and screamed.

David
* Commercial Street * 12:10 AM

He heard the scream, but couldn't identify the voice.

Shouting as he ran, "Converge on Miller's Court. Robb, do you acknowledge? Converge on Miller's Court."

Sara
* Miller's Court * 12:10 AM

"Shhhh," Osborne told Mary Kelly. With one hand, he put a finger to her lips. With the other, he clutched the knife, and raised it.

He had forgotten about Sara. Standing behind him, she leveled a quick, vicious kick at his kidneys.

Mouth exploding in a silent scream, Osborne doubled up, helpless, and fell away from Mary Kelly. Kelly thrashed and kicked away from him, and Sara helped the other woman to her feet. "Get to the Yellow Jackets," she told Mary. "Tell them who the Ripper really is."

"What abaht you?" Kelly asked, panting.

Osborne rocked on the cobbles, gaining his breath. He still had the knife. "You little bitch," he breathed.

David * 12:11 AM

"Report," he ordered. "Sara!"

Not far from Miller's Court, David had slowed as he heard Osborne's grunt and the sound of scuffle. Heard Sara say, "Osborne. He's winded, but that won't last long."

"Kill him," David said. "Do it, Sara. Now."

"Not yet. I can do this. I can get him there."

"Sara, goddammit—"

Hearing Robb: "I'm almost there, David. Sara, for God's sake, stay where you are."

Sara
* Miller's Court * 12:12 AM

The mirror-sharp blade drew reflections from the shadows, black ghosts moving in the steel.

"Who in the world are you talking to?" Osborne asked her,

panting. He was standing now, but still bent. His left hand was pressed to his kidney, and his right held the knife.

"Go on, Mary," Sara whispered. Mary Kelly backed away slowly.

Sara put herself between Kelly and Osborne. When Kelly began to run, Osborne didn't try to follow her. He stood, instead, contemplating Sara. Smiling, knife hand on his hip. Winded but enjoying the moment. Just watching her.

Sara pulled the bud out of her ear. She opened her hand, showing it to him. From it, voices continued to cry out: David, and Robb.

Osborne looked at it warily, and at her. As if she'd somehow captured souls within this tight black orb.

"It's not magic," she said. "It's yours. I got it from your bag. The one you brought with you, when you came here."

His eyes glazed when he saw it, but in the stuttering gaslight, she missed the ferocity behind them. He lunged. So quick, she saw a black blur, and the wicked gleam of the knife, coming at her heart.

David * 12:16 AM

He heard the clatter of the earbud hitting the ground and, over that, Osborne's roar—a fury let loose between the walls of Miller's Court, and the grinding brittle snap of the bud being crushed.

"Sara! Robb, I've lost her. Sara's down. Repeat: Sara is down."

Robb
* Miller's Court * 12:16 AM

He heard the sounds of their altercation in two places at once: first in his head as they scuffled over the earbud on the street, and then echoed in the air, inside the dark archway leading into Miller's Court.

Robb heard a slam, a grunt, a man's enraged bellow. And then he saw Sara, running east.

Robb began to follow her, then saw the man emerge from the archway. Winded, limping, holding his bloodied nose with one hand and in the other, the wickedly gleaming knife.

"Osborne!" Robb shouted, unable to keep the rage from his voice. He pointed the boxy gun David had given him, sighting Osborne's heart in the notch. "Leave her alone!"

Osborne looked his way and his smiled widened. Oddly, he began to laugh. Brought the knife up to throw it, taking a bead on Sara's back as she ran.

Robb pulled the trigger.

The gun exploded in his hands, kicking violently. Bullets clattered and popped on the brick façade of Miller's Court and the buildings around it. Instinctively, Robb clutched the gun to keep hold of it, pulling the trigger, still, as hundreds of rounds spewed from the muzzle. His arm jerked helplessly, jolting his body up and back.

Osborne dipped his hand to the street and whipped it around, hurling a solid chunk of brick at Robb as he struggled with the gun. Robb ducked, but not fast enough. The brick hit him just above the temple, glancing against bone and reeling him up against the wall and onto the hard cobbled road, falling heavily onto the searing-hot gun on the pavement.

Lottie
* Whitechapel * 12:26 AM

The little band of women grew between Miller's Court and Whitechapel Road. They found Mary Kelly sitting at the corner on Goulston Street, crying and terrified. Lottie bandaged her bleeding head with a torn strip of skirt.

"It was The Jay," Kelly stuttered, shivering. "He had a knife. Was gonna shove it right inta me, the b-bastard."

"An' yer sure it were The Jay did this?"

"You saw him!" Kelly cried. "He was right there with me."

"So he were," Lottie said grimly. "So he were."

Sara
* Whitechapel Mews * 12:29 AM

Puddles splashed around her hightop boots and the maddening clack of her heels echoed off the cobbled stone like a signal, telling him exactly where she was.

She ducked through alleys and middens, circling north toward Dartmore Court. The gaslight crazed each time the wind blew, a stuttering syncopation of shadow and light. Sharp tines of rusted metal caught at her skirt. She pulled and heard the material shred; pulled again and still, could not get free. Heard the calm footsteps approaching and tore at the snagged skirt. It gave with a loud belch and she overbalanced into a pile of garbage. A dozen rats sprang out of it, screeching. Sara bounced up and whirled for the end of the alley, pelting hard.

It was a blind, the sheer drop of brick wall in front of her. Too close to stop, nowhere to go, she hit the brick with her hands and whirled to meet her stalker, straining to see through the shifting light and billows of fog—

—to glimpse only shapes, the outline of a man. That featureless golem cut out of ice, both darker and brighter than the fog.

She remembered the eyeless face of her dreams and didn't wait to see it—turned and clambered up a rickety pile of broken wooden boxes and liquor barrels standing on end. It gave her just enough height to grab the lip of the brick wall and pull herself over.

As she fell, headfirst, toward the other side, she felt the whisper of fingers lovingly brush her heel.

Lottie
* Whitechapel Road * 12:37 AM

The Yellow Jackets stopped them, of course, at the wide stone steps of the hospital. Her sometime man, John Mallory, stood hard before her.

"Yer daft," John scoffed. "The Jay idn't Jack, no'mor'n I am."

"Then let me see fer meself. Let me through, John. Just me. If I find anyfink, I'll bring it to yer."

He moved aside, frowning. "Ah, go ahead, but yer won't find a damned fing." And, as she slipped through the big front doors, he barked, "Not you bints. Just 'er."

Sara * 12:38 AM

She came out onto a highly populated thoroughfare, walking along the sidewalk behind clumps of factory women, shifts just letting out. She stayed just far enough behind not to be noticed, glancing at each street sign they passed, catching her breath and her bearings.

She saw the Ten Bells less than a block away and knew she was close. Her torturous path through the mews had brought her almost full circle. She saw no sight of Osborne—had gotten ahead of him. Relief throbbed through her belly and made her sick, the acids churning in her empty stomach.

He would follow her to the Portal. From there, she would find a way to get him into it, even if she had to throw him head-long into the light. But she had to get there first. She had to be there before him. The ungainly ring sat on her thumb, throbbing quietly.

Stopping at the corner across the block from the Ten Bells, she leaned against a cool brick wall and breathed, slow and deep, until the queasiness eased and the shaking passed. Then she pushed off the wall, heading into the streets. The Black and Tan would be the next corner down, and behind that, she'd find the Portal. Her lungs still ached. She wiped the grime from her cheeks and was surprised to find tears wetting her fingers.

"Damn it, David," she whispered. She felt for the earbud and remembered it wasn't there. She'd dropped it on the cobbles at Miller's Court, when Osborne had lunged for her heart. Instead of running, she'd stepped so close he couldn't drive the blade down. He'd slashed at her back; she'd broken his nose.

She considered them even, for the moment.

Then, half a block to the Black and Tan, her nightmare ma-terialized out of the ever-present mist: black silk hat and flutter-ing cape, spread like a wingspan around the tall, thin body. Coming her way. Blocking her path to the Black and Tan and the vital alley behind it.

Sara took in a shuddering breath and began, slowly, veering to the left. As she did, Osborne matched her trajectory, zeroing in on her path. There was no alley or opening between this block and the next and Sara, sliding along the busy sidewalk, suddenly disappeared into the open door of a meat-pie shop.

"Yere!"

Sara heard the owner's yelp of surprise but didn't stop for it. She pelted through the shop and burst out the back door. Heard it bang behind her and dodged through a complicated mews, calculating distance and direction to the alley on Vere Street.

Lottie
* Osborne Charity Hospital * 12:52 AM

She crept inside, ignoring the nurses who told her to wait. Ghosted along the mostly silent halls of the hospital and wondered why the hell it was so quiet, with so many sick outside, and why most of those who were ill didn't come to this place.

Quietly, she slipped along to one of the surgeries. Inside, it was dark, the only light a sludge from the glass in the door. She bumped into a gurney and whirled. There were three bodies in the room—fresh, by the smell of them. Lying on the metal slabs. They had been flayed opened like the pages of a book: skin pulled away to show things underneath she never knew existed.

"Jesus," she whispered, holding her stomach.

Not one of the bodies, she noticed, was male.

Shaking, she turned to a locked cabinet. Picked it with her hatpin and thanked God she'd worked as a petty thief a few times in her life.

She almost screamed when she saw them. When the gaslight flared and the jars with all their horrors jumped into being under its illumination, and a man's rummy voice said, "Welcome, my dear."

Sara • 12:53 AM

She skidded to a stop when she heard the fluttering of his cape. He rounded the corner just as she would have gotten there. Had she kept running, she would have plowed into his arms.

He saw her, three feet away, and smiled. Sara backpedaled, darted for the only turn in the passage she hadn't taken before. She ran through a series of twists, skirts hiked to her thighs, heels pounding hollow on the pavement.

She stopped, bent to catch her breath. He would be coming soon. With his knowledge of the place, she would never be able to shake him. But if she could outrun him, just enough to get him to the courtyard—

She was in a small mews, kept a wooden fence behind her. She saw in front of her two arches. She had come here through one, but had no idea where the other went—or what might come at her out of it. Her breath, pulled into her lungs, whistled high and harsh. She clutched her throat, as if that could stop the pain of the heat searing inside.

"I know where you're going, Sara," he whispered behind her. Sara whirled, facing the fence. Between the cracked spaces of the slats, she saw only the outlines of where his body blocked the smoky light. "I don't know how I know or why. I don't even know why I can't let you get there. But I do know." His voice whispered from the wood: "The shimmering place."

Keeping an eye on the two arches to either side of her—the only way in or out—Sara said, "I know why." There was a hiss of breath on the other side, and a scraping sound. The knife was slowly scoring shallow grooves on his side of the fence. Breathless, she lowered her voice and said, "You feel you should know me and you do. You feel you are out of place in this time, and you are."

"I was born for this world," Osborne told her.

"That may be," Sara said, "but you weren't born *in* it."

The knife stopped moving. He whispered, "Tell me."

"You are Jonathan Alexander Avery," Sara told him, ignoring the shiver that wormed its way through her guts. "You were born—somewhere around 1960."

Osborne laughed, a rich chuckle. The path of the knife started up again, its scraping slow against the wall like a caress. "You don't know the exact date?"

"I didn't know you half so well as you wanted me to," she said sharply.

Sudden coldness on the other side, the stuttering scrape of the knife as it bit deeply once and was silent. "Go on," Osborne intoned. His voice was frighteningly flat.

"You're a scientist," she said, peering down the brick archway she hadn't come in through; it curved too sharply to see where it led or what was on the other side. "Quantum dynamics, quantum physics. You've won the most prestigious awards in the world for your work."

Silence. Sara backed against the other side of the wall and tried to watch both entrances at once. "Then why am I here, do you suppose?" he asked idly, as if they were discussing the weather and were bored with it.

"Because we developed the ability to travel through time," Sara whispered. Remembering Robb's reaction and not at all sure how Osborne would respond. "You developed it. It was your brainchild. You came through the Portal—"

"And?" he asked. Now he was interested.

"And something happened," Sara said. "An accident."

"It was no accident!" he cried, suddenly vicious.

Sara paused. "Jon, how much do you remember?" She barely

raised her voice to ask. Waiting for the answer, she heard only the sharpening wind breathing through the eaves.

The knife slammed into the fence between them. The tip of it thrust through shattered wood. She could hear the metal quiver as it shuddered with the impact. Got ready to run but had no idea which arch he would come through. Her back tingling, Sara tried to find a place in the blind where she could keep an eye on Osborne and the dark, forbidding arches.

She heard Osborne groaning, still on the other side of the fence, leaning against the wood.

"Jon," she whispered. "Someone went into the Portal with you." A hiss from him, like a pain suddenly remembered and the surprise of it startled. "Someone went into the Portal with you and she shouldn't have—"

A shriek came from the other side of the fence: "*She!*"

There were depths of hatred in that one word. The knife snapped—a crack like the earth breaking.

Osborne dropped down in front of her.

Lottie
* Osborne Charity Hospital * 12:54 AM

Lottie grabbed a specimen jar and ran for it. The door was small, the man blocking it big. Good-looking gent, so somber, she felt like a right fool: He were a doctor, fer god's sake, and a toff; her superior in every way—

But when he smiled, she knew it was not gaol he intended for her. She knew how to run when she had to. Knew how to dodge the big hands coming for her.

She made it out to the big hall. There, three other men were waiting. The big one behind caught her up, wrapping his arms around her waist and lifting her.

She screamed like she'd never done before.

The outside doors opened. John Mallory stuck his head in, saw her struggling. He stepped in with a crowd of men. Lottie threw the specimen jar toward them. It exploded in a shower of glass and formaldehyde. The uterus slid with a hideous whisper along the floor, coming to rest at John's feet.

John looked at it, then looked up in astonishment at the men holding Lottie.

"Bastards," he breathed.

Sara · 1:12 AM

"A *woman*!" Osborne hissed, rising slowly from the crouch he'd landed in. His voice was guttural, manic—the knife in his right hand, its broken edge ragged and slick.

Sara didn't move, stayed still. The opportunity to escape him would present itself, but not with the knife so close. She took in breath to speak, and he shoved the jagged shaft of the knife against her ribs.

Sara gasped. She heard the material of her dress give and felt the sudden biting cold of the shard under her left breast, not far from her heart.

Osborne brought his face close to hers—sniffing, nostrils flaring. His eyes were cold. Then he asked, "Was it you?"

She wanted to shake her head but didn't dare move. "No," she whispered.

He pulled the knife away from her skin and then slowly pushed the sharp edge along her blouse, watching the material part—revealing the bell of breast. He cocked the blade in his hand like a paintbrush, stepping back to appreciate his work.

"Then who was it?"

Sara caught her breath, still feeling the ghost of the steel edge at her breast. She whispered the name: "*Joan.*"

Osborne spasmed; his face convulsing—as if jolted with of a burst of electricity or perhaps just the high voltage of memory. He closed his eyes tight and shifted the knife in his hand. Shaking, shaking—raising it to strike.

She saw he was vulnerable. "What's the code, Jon?" she asked. "You hold the password," Sara told him suddenly. The knife winked over her head, hesitating, reflections of the moon's cool face skittering along its shaft. "You built in a Cipher. That was very clever. What's the secret word, Jon?"

In Osborne's eyes, the stranger guttered—a flame in the wind, suddenly uncertain. Like the moon sailing beyond the clouds, for one breathless moment, Jon Avery slid out from under Osborne's grasp.

"The secret is *you*," he said, smiling beatifically.

Sara frowned. "Me?" she whispered. The big gold ring sat like a frog on her thumb, hidden by her torn sleeve.

Avery grinned widely. He still had the knife, and with it lightly traced elegant filigrees on her shoulder before bending down to kiss it. Sara moved away from the cold touch of his lips, and he shoved the broken nose of the knife next to her arm, burying its head in the wood, pinning her in place. "Such beautiful skin," he murmured against her shoulder. No slow Virginia drawl now: Osborne's melodic English-gentry burr whispered along her flesh. "You've always had—"

She stilled her revulsion—crushed it—and bent to whisper in his ear. "Every woman you've killed since then has been Joan."

He growled, nipped at her skin. When she dodged, he slapped her—a large, arcing blow. She let him do it, knowing the force of it would propel her away from him, from the knife. She stumbled back, farther than the blow really took her.

Osborne pulled his arm back to hit her again.

Sara surged forward and punched him in the armpit.

He screamed, dropped the knife. Tried to burrow his way against her to keep her from leaving. She jabbed his instep with the sharp heel of her boot. He howled again, doubled over, and she slammed her knee into his face.

He pitched back and she didn't look to see where or how he landed—just ran. Took the other archway into sanity and the Ten Bells to her left down the street, the Black and Tan just two doors down.

Above the roofline, toward the west, the sky began to glow. It was too early for sunrise—Sara knew the Osborne Charity Hospital was on fire. Distantly, she wondered if they would rebuild.

She ran across the cobbles into the dark oblong between the pub and the hostelier and along the murky path to the blind court on Vere Street. Then headlong into the darkness of Dartmore Court, and into utter blindness.

Sara
* Dartmore Court * 1:22 AM

She heard the subtlest sound of movement to her right and struck out, flat hand hitting a solid wall of chest.

"Ow. Damn it, Sara!"

A light went on in her face—not the blue light of the Portal but the cold, brilliant lance of the future. David's penlight.

"David!" She felt for him next to her, then suddenly, unexpectedly, wrapped her arms around his chest and pulled him close. "Where the hell have you been?" she demanded.

He held her tightly. "You missed me," he accused. Then took in her torn clothing and her face, scuffed and filthy with mud. "Looks like you took care of yourself."

"Avery—" she told him, pulling David farther into Dartmore Court. As she approached, the light of the Portal began to shimmer in the darkness around them—a miraculous circle of blue, its shape a curtain of electric air in the court. "Avery's coming. Where's Robb?"

"Miller's Court, waiting for Jack the Ripper to show."

"He won't," Sara said, breathless. "Was that an Uzi I heard?"

David nodded, smiling crookedly. With her presence, the Portal thrummed deeply, the unearthly blue intensifying. Whatever locking mechanism had dampened its full power before was now released. She realized she had never seen the Portal working normally from this side before; hadn't known what it should look like. Would never forget this intensity of color again, a blue that made the summer sky seem pale.

Sara looked down at the ring. "Proximity," she said. "It's unlocked, for all of us now." She pulled the ring off of her thumb and opened its face. "But Avery's destination code has to be reset. There's a password that enables the ring to transmit the origin destination code to his transponder."

"What's the password?" David asked, frowning.

Sara glanced at him. "I got to Avery. Just a few seconds, but— He said I was the secret, the solution to the password."

"He's full of shit," David muttered.

"No," Sara said. "He made it a point to know everything about me. That's all I'd ever let him have, and he knew it. He could have pulled my personal data at any time. I think the password is one of those numbers."

Quickly, she keyed in the numeric values for her birthday. There was no change in the Portal, no sound from the ring.

"Try something else," David said, watching the courtyard's entrance. The dark beyond the Portal's light seemed absolute.

Sara keyed in her social security number. Again, nothing.

"Rearrange the order of your birth date," David said.

"There's about a hundred different variables for that," she shot back, but poised the hairpin to try it. Then she looked at her

wrist, where her transponder slept under tendon and tissue.
"Each transponder is unique," she murmured.

"Coded to your DNA," David said. He smiled. "Just like
knowing a girl's locker combination."

Quickly, Sara keyed in her personal code, the identity se-
quence that belonged only to her. The ring chimed its flat note.
Sara popped the hatch, and the hologram sprang up, inquiring,
CHANGE DES-CODE? YES/NO.

Sara touched YES on the keypad.

"Now what?" David asked.

"Now we wait for Osborne. The ring will reprogram his
transponder as soon as he gets close to it."

Osborne's shadow darkened the arch of the court.

"Speak of the devil," David said grimly, and stood between
Osborne and Sara.

But Osborne had stopped, watching the undulant shiver of
the Portal at the further side of the court. The light traced lines
of wonder on his face and he watched it, walking slowly into the
courtyard. He turned to David and Sara, who were dim blue
ghosts in that light. His eyes shifted, the expression of awe curdling to mock urbanity.

"David," he grated, the cutting politeness so at odds with the
blood on his face. "Why is it that whenever I wish to be alone
with the lady, I always find you in the way?"

Somewhere between the mews and Vere Street, Osborne had
found a gun, a little one-shot pistol. He came farther down the
court, holding it on David.

Sara and David both backed toward the Portal. It hummed
softly, energized by Sara's transponder.

"Stop," Osborne told them.

"What if we won't?" David asked.

Osborne smiled angelically. "I only have the one bullet. If I
kill you, that leaves her alone."

"She can take care of herself," David said. "Looks like she
took care of you pretty well."

"Not exactly the behavior of a lady," Avery agreed, and
grinned widely—the smile of a sick coyote.

David stepped slowly toward the other side of the courtyard,
motioning for Sara to move closer to the Portal, putting just
enough distance between them. Osborne had to keep moving

the gun to cover them both. Frustrated, he centered the barrel on David but kept his eyes on Sara, his other hand rubbing his armpit. "Stop it. Both of you. Just stop it."

"Come with us, Jonathan," she said. "You don't belong here."

"Stop calling me that," he shrilled at her, furious and indignant but also afraid. He swung the gun around to her.

David slowly drew his hand behind his back, circling around. Osborne's head snapped back to him and David allowed the nose of the man's gun to follow, drawing the line of fire.

Osborne took a bead directly over David's heart. "I don't know what you're doing, David, but I don't like it."

David brought his own gun out from behind his back, careful not to point it yet at Osborne. Let him get a good look at it. Even in the dim light, it looked absurd, fitted with a wildly fluorescent purple pompom at the end of the muzzle.

Osborne laughed. And then, as a part of him recognized the dart element, that laughter faltered. "I am not going to duel with you, David," he said, suddenly sobered.

"One shot, Avery," David said. "You get one shot. Take it, or I take mine."

"I don't want to kill you," Osborne said, suddenly peevish. "You're my Ripper. I have uses for you. I could make you famous. Everyone wants to be famous."

David smiled slowly. "I have news for you, Osborne. I'm not the Ripper. And I'm not *her* brother."

Osborne looked suddenly at Sara, then at David. Shock showed in every line of his body. An ugly ripple moved along his face. Swearing, he swung the gun in a slow and deliberate arc for Sara, the promise of her death in his eyes, in every inch the barrel moved.

"Sara," David said quietly, and fired.

Sara dropped to the cobbles at the foot of the Portal, but Osborne's gun did not fire. The only crack she heard was the sound of the single-shot clattering to the stones. David's dart had buried its head in Osborne's neck. Clutching at it, Osborne fell slowly to the ground, first to his knees and then, with a bewildered whimper, to his back.

David approached Osborne warily, evaluating his condition. He stashed the gun in his waistband, then bent and pulled Osborne off the pavement. He waited until the older man could begin to stand on his own, panting and sick from the drug. Then he turned them both toward the Portal.

Avery began to wail. Sara, watching at the Portal's entry, knew all the other personas had fled: With no strength and no bullies to drive him, the innocent Avery faced this end alone.

"No—I don't want to. Please, not that. Not through there." He took David's lapels, as if to tell him a terrible secret. Brought his ear down to his lips and whispered, with all the conspiratorial trust of a toddler: "It's death."

Sara reached out her hand and touched his wrist. Heard the faintest note from the ring, accepting transmission of the destination code she had programmed. Avery looked down at the sound of it. "See?" she told him gently. "We have the ring, Jon. The door is unlocked. Your destination is set. You're not going to die."

Avery looked at the light and shook his head. "No, no—you don't know where it goes."

"It goes home," Sara said. "You'll be OK." She laid a comforting hand on his arm. "Go, Jonathan. We'll be right behind you."

Shaking, Avery let David usher him into the Portal. As the light took him, Avery turned and looked back at them, fearful, needing human contact. He reached out—

And was gone. Taken by the light.

David
* Dartmore Court * 1:37 AM

Sara sighed, her shoulders relaxing.

"You're next," David told her.

"What about you?" she asked.

"I don't know. But you have to report, now. You can't let Avery arrive back home alone."

"I can't just leave you here, either. Robb has your transponder."

"So that's where it is. Don't worry. I can find him."

"*Then* you'll come back," she said. She looked keenly at him. "David, you *will* come back, right?"

He shrugged, uncomfortable suddenly. "If I exist to come back to, I'll be back," he told her.

"Why wouldn't you exist?"

David sighed. "George is my great-great grandfather. He

died in the slums when he was sixty-five. Destitute." He smiled crookedly. "But not anymore. I gave him our money."

Sara stared at him. "Take it back," she whispered.

"Too late," he murmured. He wiped a smudge of dirt from her cheek. "But it's okay."

"It's *not* okay."

Reluctant, doubtful, she slowly handed him the ring. It dropped into his palm heavily. He closed his hand around it.

"I'll *be* there," he told her. "Go on, Sara. Go."

Her eyes, anguished, tracked his face, and then caught sight of something beyond it. She gasped, and David took that moment of lapsed attention to push her firmly into the shimmering light.

"David!"

She had time to scream, to reach out, before it took her. As she left, a bit of the radiance in the courtyard went with her.

David turned to see what she had seen, before he'd sent her home. The slums were not usually this quiet, even early in the pale hours, but now, on this night, the courtyard was a bubble of silence and dimming blue.

Robb stood at the mouth of the courtyard, staring. Over his head, the shabby brilliance of gaslight shone, dithering a ring of shadows around him.

David nodded to him. "I wondered if you'd make it."

Robb came, hesitant, into the court. He had the black bag in his hands. Moving forward, he couldn't take his eyes off the dimming light of the Portal.

"She's gone," David told him.

"I know," Robb whispered. He reached into his vest pocket and pulled out the oblong lozenge—dropping it into David's hand.

David curled his fist around his transponder. "Be needing that."

He pulled the black bag off Robb's shoulder and rummaged through it, while Robb simply stood and stared at the whispering blue light of the Portal. It was still open, responding to David's transponder.

"Here," David told him, putting a large vial of yellow pills into his hand. "He needs to swallow one of these with water once a day for at least three months."

"Who?" Robb asked, staring dumbly at the pills.

"Your brother. William. The one with consumption."

Robb looked up, suddenly keen. "Will it help?"

David shrugged. "I hope so." He squeezed Robb's shoulder. "It can't hurt," he said, and turned to go.

"Wait." Robb pulled a glittering object from his waistcoat pocket. "Give her this. For me—please."

David took it, brought it into the light.

It had probably been in the family for generations. A wedding ring. Old-fashioned: Two circlets of diamonds wrapped around a center stone. It looked like the petals of a flower.

David caught Robb's eyes, inquiring. Then, with a nod, he slipped the ring into his pocket. And stepped into the shimmering light.

It took less than a moment—a heartbeat between this time and the next—before he disappeared.

Robb
⋆ Dartmore Court ⋆ 1:56 AM

Robb stayed in the court until the last vestiges of light had faded, miraculous, blue and vibrant, an ache in the heart of memory—the soul recalling a time when angels walked the earth and men could still laugh and talk with God.

Clutching the vial of pills in the darkness. Knowing he had loved something precious, something singular.

Something that could not be returned to him.

The grit of the cobbles echoed through his shinbones as he turned away from the place. Heading toward home, and suddenly he was an old man: an ancient who has lived the last fifty years of his life in one night, and has seen a glimpse into the bluest shades of eternity.

"Sara, forgive me," he thought, and realized he'd spoken only after the dank air of the slums swallowed up the words, like a prayer in the heat of a shimmering votive.

He tasted the tears before he felt them, salted and sharp and aching, the pale blue waters of a warm and foreign sea.

Sara
⋆ Coral Mountain Facility ⋆ 2:02 AM

At the gantry, Sara waited, counting the seconds as they turned into minutes. "Come on, David," she whispered. "Come back home."

Within minutes, the Portal began to buzz. She stood away, wincing against the weight of the brilliant energy it radiated around itself. Stumbling on a step she hadn't seen and righting herself in time to look up, to watch the Portal unwrap its sweet blue light like an orchid opening out, petals peeling back to reveal the stamen inside: plumb length, tall and solid—

David.

CHAPTER 50

❧❧❧

November 9, 2007

❧❧❧

Sara
* Coral Mountain Facility * 6:26 AM

Her father told them Avery had never made it back.

Wrapped in a warm blanket, the feel of familiar clothing against her skin, Sara blinked slowly, remembering the impossible innocence of Avery's eyes, clean at those last helpless moments.

David sat beside her. Breakfast was spread on the table before them. The patio view overlooked a wild spread of the Black Hills, with no further concession to civilization in sight. "Why not?" he asked. "We got him into the Portal. Sara programmed his return codes herself."

Proctor Grant grimaced, a genuine sorrow deepening the lines of his face. "We don't know. He never came out on this end."

"No," Sara said, cold and stunned. She was shivering, her jaw beginning to tremble with the shock of it. "We saw him go through—"

"But we didn't see where he went," David said.

"If he went anywhere at all," her father said, his face grim.

"Eternity on hold," David murmured. Sara looked stricken. "Don't let it haunt you," David said. "He would have murdered you without thinking twice."

"He was that far gone?" asked Proctor Grant, surprised.

Sara smiled up at him wearily. "He was Jack the Ripper."

"Jack the—" Grant looked between them. "That can't be. It's a scientific impossibility. Everyone knows Francis Tumblety and Michael Ostrog were the Jacks."

Sara and David exchanged a look. "Yes it is impossible," she said. "And yet it happened. A lot of things happened that we didn't expect."

A sudden yawn claimed her, stretching and shuddering through her body. It dismissed their breakfast meeting, she and David plodding to different quarters deep inside the bunker to sleep.

But sleep was not the usual easy slide it had always been for her. Beyond exhaustion, her muscles ached, and she was feverish with fatigue. Still, Sara sat on her bed and clutched the printout she'd had Lyn Bouley make for her.

Robb.

So handsome as he aged, still slim in his elegant coat and dark boots. The familiarity of his face, the intensity of his expression: the reality of him reached beyond the grainy stamp of ink and held her breathless before she read, in the text, the briefest description of his life.

She dwelt on the highlights, absurdly proud of his accomplishments. Appointed to commissioner at a young age, serving with honors. Responsible for bringing precincts together to track the migration of criminal activities throughout England and then through connected parts of Europe—an early version of Interpol. Author of the Women & Children's Protection Act, passed by Parliament in 1902. Credited with solving the worst crime in London's history: the doctors of Osborne Charity Hospital had all been charged with the Ripper's crimes and hanged in London, December 18, 1888.

No children. No wife. In all this long life punctuated by intrigues and accomplishments, inexplicable mysteries, unexpected sweetness and a few genuine horrors, historians would record that he had never married. Sara knew them to be wrong: He had married her, in the sweet darkness of a country house conservatory, in those sliding breathless moments between them.

The tears came then, without warning, without sound or heat. She let them fall, but the terrible bubble inside (that choked emotional magma seething along her throat) held tight to his memory and would not release. As if by holding that pain, her heart could still hold on to him. Demanding, insisting that she hold to it.

Because just hours ago, he had been vibrantly alive; the warmth of his skin: that miraculous throb in her body at his touch, and the tenderness between them.

The absurd joy of his smile.

His eyes.

And dear God, she had stepped out of the Portal knowing (*knowing*) that within the span of those heartbeats (no matter that she could still smell the scent of him on her skin, and feel his breathing warmth), he had lived, aged—and died.

David
⋆ Coral Mountain Quarters ⋆ 8:04 AM

He knocked on the door a good three minutes before she opened it, wrapped in a blanket, hair ruffled, eyes red.

"Couldn't sleep," he said. "You?"

"No," she whispered.

He nodded. Tilted her chin to see the reddened eyes, sorrow burrowing in the tenderness under her skin.

He pulled a ring out of his pocket. "He asked me to give you this," David said quietly.

Sara stared at the ring before she touched it, breaking down, finally; and finally, beginning to cry.

David gathered her close. "I know," he murmured. "I know."

When the storm of it began to diminish, he carried her back to her bed, sliding her into the cool sheets, tucking the blankets up under her chin. He turned the lamplight down to a glimmer of warmth. He stood to leave and she caught his sleeve, her other hand still clutching Robb's ring. "Don't go," she whispered: A child's plea against nightmares.

"I won't," he said, and sat down to watch her fall slowly into a doze, her muscles releasing bit by bit. He kissed her cheek where the warm susurration of her breath was childlike, and finally deepening into sleep. "Don't dream," he whispered.

As an American born in Germany, Virginia Baker grew up steeped in ancient cities, caught up in the history breathing from their stones. She has a BS in Near Eastern Studies and an MA in English Literature. She runs her own business, writes award-winning stories, and operates a rescue sanctuary for parrots. Today, she lives in Utah with a flock of large birds and the cats who fear them. Her greatest achievement so far has been her daughter, Sara, who was born in Vladivostok, Russia.